07- 14- 18

Ground Truth

by

Rob Sangster

IMAJINN

ImaJinn Books

This is a work of fiction. Names, characters, places and incidents are either the products of the author's imagination or are used fictitiously. Any resemblance to actual persons (living or dead), events or locations is entirely coincidental.

IMAJINN

ImaJinn Books
PO BOX 300921
Memphis, TN 38130
Print ISBN: 978-1-61026-096-1

ImaJinn Books is an Imprint of BelleBooks, Inc.

ImaJinn Books was founded by Linda Kichline.

We at ImaJinn Books enjoy hearing from readers. Visit our websites
ImaJinnBooks.com
BelleBooks.com
BellBridgeBooks.com.

*10 9 8 7 6 5 4 3 2

Cover design: Debra Dixon
Interior design: Hank Smith
Photo/Art credits:
Mexican street (manipulated) © Rfoxphoto | Dreamstime.com

:Ltgb:01:

Dedication

My warmest thanks to Lisa C. Turner, best-selling author and my loving inspiration. She made *Ground Truth* possible.

Chapter 1

May 30
5:30 p.m.

A SQUALL SWEPT across San Francisco Bay, pummeling a dozen sailboats racing for the Commodore's Cup in the chaotic water.

Jack Strider, stuck in second place, wrestled the tiller, keeping Simba on the fastest heading she could handle without capsizing. Already heeled hard over to port, a strong gust could drive her sails into a wave and rip her rigging apart. Several skippers had dropped their mainsails all the way down. He could do that too—and lose the race. No way he'd play it safe. Feet braced to keep from being washed overboard, he kept a wary eye on a stretch of nearly submerged rocks to his left. His course was dangerous, but still the best way to pass Mistral, the red-hulled sloop just ahead.

Mistral's captain glanced back and edged his boat to the left in front of Simba. He waved for Jack to fall back.

Jack quickly calculated distance and wind speed. He still had room to squeeze between the red-hulled boat and the rocks, but only if Mistral didn't continue to crowd in front of him. Knuckling a blast of salt spray out of his eyes, Jack pointed to the closing gap, signaling his intention to sail through.

Judge H. Peckford Strider, Jack's father, gave Jack a scornful smile as he eased Mistral's tiller more, cutting off Jack's route and moving so far left he was close to driving both boats into the rocks.

Damn him. Trying to win a trophy had never made Peck act like this before. Had he gone nuts?

At the last second, Jack steered sharply to starboard, *Simba's* bow passing inches behind *Mistral's* stern. The instant he was clear, he cut back to port, passing close to *Mistral's* right side. *Simba's* big sails blocked the wind and left *Mistral's* sails flapping uselessly.

As he shot past *Mistral* toward the finish line Jack couldn't hear Peck over the wind, but saw him shouting angrily.

He'd gambled that Peck was so intent on winning that he'd misread Jack's strategy until it was too late. And he had. The bang from the starter's gun signaled Jack that he had crossed the finish line and won the Commodore's Cup.

Fifteen minutes later, Jack had secured *Simba's* lines to cleats on the pier and climbed back aboard to make her shipshape for foul weather. While he was fastening the sail cover, *Mistral* pulled slowly into her space at the far end of the pier. After making her lines fast, his father sat hunched over in the cockpit with his cell phone to his ear, ignoring Jack.

Jack was locking the cabin hatch when Peck strode past *Simba,* cap pulled low, still not looking his way. *No congratulations, not even "kiss my ass."* The silent treatment was out of character, but it was for the best, because right now he was primed to tell his father exactly what he thought of his race tactics.

As Jack walked toward the clubhouse, he stopped and turned to admire his boat, a 29-foot Dragon racing sloop with mahogany planks and teak decking. She was a thoroughbred. Together they'd won the Commodore's Cup and beaten his father. *Damned good job.*

IN THE CLUBHOUSE, he changed into dry clothes and walked into the Schooner Room where skippers and crews gathered after races. Aromas of fried onions and sizzling burgers filled the room. It was a comfortable place with a long redwood bar, cedar paneling, and barrel armchairs around the tables. Photographs hung on the walls of mustachioed schooner captains, all long dead, and tall ships in exotic ports. There were a few blue-blazer types in the crowd, but some of the other men could have stepped out of the old photos.

He was greeted by cheers and applause.

From the far end of the bar, Ronnie Patterson called, "You've got guts, Jack. Nasty trick Peck pulled, trying to drive you into the rocks. What got into him today?"

He raised his glass to Patterson. "No big deal." *Maybe not, but his triumph felt tarnished by Peck's behavior.*

He'd known many of the guys in the room since he'd been a kid in Learn-to-Sail classes. Later, he'd given summer sailing lessons to pay for his own sailing gear, a rebellion against his father's attempts to use money to control him.

As he built his skills, some of the old salts had invited him to crew for them, teaching him how to read the wind, trim sails, and win on race days. A few of them had become like surrogate fathers, accepting him for who he was. *Which was more than his own father had ever done.* No matter how little they might have in common outside these walls, here they were family.

"Hey, Jack," the bartender said, "where's your old man? Pissed off because you stuck it to him?"

"He took off up the pier while I was still aboard *Simba*. Now, how about Dark 'n' Stormys all around—on me." It was a tradition for the winner to buy a round, and a little rum would change the subject.

As usual, the guys debated race tactics—which ones worked and which failed miserably. Tonight they were topping one another with stories of how badly the squall had knocked them around and what they'd done to survive. And every time the talk circled back to Peck and the rocks, Jack got more slaps on the shoulder. The ones that meant the most came from the old salts who had been his mentors. Drinks were disappearing faster than normal.

When his cell phone rang, he pulled it out and checked caller ID. It was Peck's latest lady friend, a relentless shark in pursuit of his father. Provocative in uninspired ways, she was determined to seduce Peck into marrying her and made it clear she didn't intend to let Jack interfere. At this moment she was possibly the last person on earth he wanted to talk with but, since she almost never called him, instinct told him to answer.

"Yes, Anita?" Terse but not rude.

"I'm at your father's house. He got home a little while ago, headed straight for his study and slammed the door. Something's terribly wrong. You have to help me."

Wheedling and high drama were Anita's favorite modes of speech. This time she'd chosen the latter, the one Jack found most jarring.

"Forget it, Anita. He's just angry that I beat him for the Commodore's Cup."

"That's not it. I know he flares up then gets over it, so I knocked on the door and said, 'What's the matter, sweetie?' He jerked it open, gave me a nasty look, and said, 'The biggest shit of all time is about to hit the fan. Get your ass out of my house and don't come back.' Then he locked the door. He's never talked to me like that before."

Jack knew all about his father's flare-ups. He'd been on the receiving end too often.

"Look, I'm tied up at the club. I'll stop by in a couple of hours."

"No, come *now*. I knocked on his door two more times, but there was no answer." Her voice rose almost to a shriek. "He could have had a heart attack or something."

Damn it. Maybe something really was wrong. "Okay, I'm on my way." He clicked off and called out to the room, "Have to take care of something, guys. Shouldn't be long."

"Get back in time to pick up your trophy," Patterson said.

Yeah, right. He'd wanted to win the race, but he didn't give a damn about the two-foot tall silver cup donated by a former Commodore whose name was inscribed on it three times: H. Peckford Strider.

In the parking lot, he stuffed his long legs into his black BMW convertible. Halyards still clattered against masts, but the fierce wind had slacked off. As he sped down Beach Road toward his father's house the sky ahead looked menacing.

Jack had been in the mood to get a little buzzed and talk about sailing. If this was just about losing the race, his father deserved a swift kick in the ass.

He dug out his phone, hit speed dial, and called the private number that rang only in Peck's office. One ring. Three. Five. Seven. Was Peck playing him again, smirking as he listened to the phone ring? Or was he lying on his back, red faced and gasping for breath?

Chapter 2

May 30
7:00 p.m.

AT THE END OF the long driveway, he pulled up in front of Peck's house, a Craftsman redwood rustic place at water's edge. As soon as he got out of the car, Anita, wearing tight jeans and a form-fitting cashmere top, ran along the flagstone walkway and threw her arms around him.

"Hey, take it easy." He held her shoulders at arm's length. "Let's find out what Peck's up to."

He tossed his jacket on a chair inside the door and walked from the entrance hall into the great room. After Jack's mother died, Peck bought this place to suit his new life: gourmet kitchen, hot tub and sauna, wine cellar and floor-to-ceiling west-facing glass to take in the spectacular view of Sausalito and Mount Tamalpais. Jack hadn't grown up here and had never related to it. All he wanted now was to get this over with.

He turned right and walked down the corridor past the game room to Peck's study at the end of the hall, Anita sniffling close behind him.

He knocked on the door. Nothing. He knocked again, harder, and tried the handle. Locked.

"Damn it, Peck," he called, "I didn't leave the club and drive over here to be jerked around." The answer was more silence. Worried now, he went back to the game room for the set of house keys Peck kept taped to the bottom of the billiard table. When the lock clicked, he swung the door open and walked in.

Peck, still wearing his sailing gear, sat behind his antique walnut partners' desk. His puffy cheeks and full lips made him look self-indulgent and dissolute, very unlike his formal portrait at the far end of the room in which he wore a judge's robe.

He didn't turn his head as Jack approached. He simply shifted his gaze like an owl, his face fixed in a stern expression, head tilted just a few degrees back from vertical. *Jane's Fighting Ships,* the massive book Peck often read as a kind of diversion, lay open on the desk in front of him. Next to it was a bottle of Glen Breton Rare Canadian single malt whiskey and an almost empty glass. *Odd.* Not like his father to drink whiskey early in the evening.

He also didn't look sick, and his bad temper had to be about more than losing the race. That wouldn't have caused him to order Anita out of the house. He walked to the desk.

"You're just in time," Peck said in a flat tone.

Before Jack could ask what the hell he was talking about, Peck raised a remote control and pointed it at a television monitor across the room. The sound came on, screen filled with the heavy-jowled face of the KNBC NewsCenter 5 anchorman.

". . . and that's the uplifting story of how one Menlo Park mother got her child the care he desperately needed."

The anchorman's tone dropped into his trademark melancholy growl. "Now we have a tragedy to report. KNBC has learned that Customs and Immigration officials boarded *Pacific Dawn,* a cargo ship tied up at Pier 7, and discovered a horrifying scene. The bodies of six women were shackled together in a locked container against the bulkhead of *Pacific Dawn's* engine room where temperatures are reported to exceed 120 degrees. Likely causes of death were dehydration and heat stroke."

Peck usually offered a string of critical comments during the news, but never for a listener's benefit. That was Peck. He was the star of Peck's World in which everyone else was a bit player. This time he was silent, watching the screen as if hypnotized.

"KNBC NewsCenter 5 investigative reporter Mary Kim has learned that *Pacific Dawn* was chartered by a trading company based in Panama City. District Attorney Rick Calder said his office is in the process of tracing ownership of the vessel. More at eleven."

Peck clicked the TV into silence, finished the whiskey in his glass, and took in a deep breath, as if appraising the alcohol's bouquet.

"That's terrible," Anita said softly from beside Jack.

It was, but why had Peck wanted to watch it? Jack asked, "What did you mean when you said we were 'just in time?'"

"Forget that. Just get out, both of you."

"No, I want to stay with you," Anita cried.

Peck looked at her with no empathy in his expression. "Touching thought my dear, but you're already a dead woman."

That sounded like he was pronouncing sentence on a convicted defendant.

Anita gasped and covered her mouth with her hand.

Peck paid no attention to her. Instead he shifted his gaze to Jack. "Your life is about to change more than you can imagine, and there's nothing you can do to prevent that . . . not that I give a damn." His tone was cold. "But I'll tell you this," he said with more energy, "those bastards on Wall Street have it right. Buy on the rumor, sell on the news. Well, you just heard the news."

From behind *Jane's Fighting Ships,* Peck raised the silver Smith & Wesson .45 that he always kept in the second drawer of his desk. "To fend off pirates from Sausalito," he'd once told Jack.

Index finger curled around the trigger, Peck swung the muzzle toward Anita. She screamed and turned away, bending over at the waist. "No! No! No!"

Jack hurled himself across the desk to knock the gun from his father's hand.

Chapter 3

May 30
7:30 p.m.

THE MAN HAD talked his way through hundreds of high society gatherings like this one, but even the incredible view from the penthouse did nothing to relieve his mid-evening boredom. Brain cruising on autopilot, he offered periodic nods and random "hmmms" as three men and a woman debated conflicting ways to reduce suffering caused by drought in the Sahel. He knew they were putting on a performance and didn't give a damn about the ugly reality. As his mind wandered, his attention was caught by the comments of a man standing behind him to his left.

"I'll spend thirty million for a short term fix," the man said, "and then get run out of town on a rail."

Interested, he half-turned to glance at the speaker. The voice belonged to a bulky, middle-aged man named Bronkowski, who looked as if he might be wearing football shoulder pads inside his suit coat.

"Oh, be serious," said a woman with the super-buff figure of an exercise addict. "Why would anyone run you out of town?"

"When our shareholders watch that thirty million knock down the price of their stock and realize we'll have to spend much more in the future, they'll blame me," Bronkowski said, "and start heating the tar."

"Can't all the states get together and—"

"About the time hell freezes over. Those assholes in Washington have avoided dealing with this for fifty years."

He knew what Bronkowski did for a living, so he understood exactly what the man was talking about. With an abrupt apology, he walked outside to the wrought iron railing on the terrace to think. A fireworks show was going off in the distance. Smoke trails arched into the sky, spreading apart and bursting into red, green and white blossoms, followed seconds later by a string of staccato pops.

He tried to think about the conversation he'd overheard because it concerned a problem he'd thought about many times. Failure to solve it could throw the American economy into serious recession. God knows, there had been some crackpot schemes proposed. Whoever provided a real solution would be paid any price he demanded. He could be—he *should* be—that person. He had a gift for seeing what others could not and the guts to take advantage of it.

His efforts to sort through the elements of the problem kept being interrupted by bursts of laughter from the guests. Seeing a nearby door, he escaped from the terrace into the host's darkened study and settled into a high-back chair.

After a few minutes, the outline and then the details of the solution coalesced with the clarity of an equation drawn on a blackboard. It was incredibly simple.

But despite his desire for total secrecy, he would require help. That's when the second "ah ha!" hit. The missing piece of his mosaic had a name and needed only to be fitted into place.

There was just one problem. She hated him.

Chapter 4

May 30
7:45 p.m.

IN THE SPLIT second before Jack could reach him, Peck swung the barrel of the Smith & Wesson .45 away from Anita, stuck the muzzle in his own mouth, and squeezed the trigger. The sound of the blast filled the room. Shock filled Peck's eyes as the back of his skull exploded.

His chair crashed backward. Peck sprawled awkwardly, eyes staring vacantly toward the wicker ceiling fan. A dark stain spread from beneath his head. In the bookcase, which stood a few feet behind the desk, a gluey mess of tissue and blood had splattered the rows of beige and red Pacific Reporter 3rd Series law casebooks.

Jack's ears rang. Gasping for breath, he struggled to his feet from where he lay across the broad desk. Peck had been too fast.

This was impossible, incomprehensible. Peck had been such a powerful force, he couldn't have done this to himself, couldn't be dead. Jack's impulse was to pull the chair upright and restore his father to his authoritative place. Instead, he backed away.

Behind him, Anita screamed and screamed while beating his back with her fists. "You bastard," she sobbed. "You could have stopped him."

He turned to comfort her, but her eyes were wide with shock. She backed out the door, ran down the hall and up the stairs. A moment later, a door slammed.

Was she right? Could he have stopped Peck?

He dropped into the leather chair near the door of the study, sweat cold on his face. His hands trembled. His body was reacting while his mind remained in shock—disconnected, unable to take action. But beneath his horror at Peck's gruesome act there was an odd detachment, and for a moment he experienced more relief than grief. The son-of-a-bitch was gone. The pressure was off.

Peck had long ago made himself impossible to love. The wedge between them probably started when Jack was five, the day his father said, "Time to stop that 'Dad' crap. Call me Peck." Being a father was only a role he played in public, and even then, only when it suited him. It was something he did because part of his own reputation depended on how well his protégé performed. Peck needed Jack the same way a grand master chess player needs a pawn to move around the board.

Peck had named his only son John Jay Strider and insisted that everyone call him John Jay because he was related to the famous jurist through his mother's lineage. Peck reminded him from time to time that John Jay had been president of the Continental Congress, author of some of the Federalist Papers, and first Chief Justice of the U.S. Supreme Court.

When he was eight, he had rebelled at the affectation and would answer only to "Jack."

A few weeks before she died, his mother told him bluntly that he should stop teaching at Stanford Law. "You've locked yourself in an ivory tower, focused on that damned 'Supreme Court track.'"

She was referring to the fact that Peck had tried to plan every step of Jack's life to put him in position to be appointed to the Supreme Court of the United States. He called it "keeping on the Supreme Court track." Whatever Jack did was met with Peck's stern admonition to do better. Jack's instinct had been to push back against his father's heavy hand but, truth was, striving for excellence suited him fine. In his first year at the university he'd also realized that a career in law sounded good too.

As a Stanford Law student, he graduated first in his class. As a professor of law, he projected an easygoing but confident image, published articles in major legal journals, and was called a rising star on the law school faculty. At the same time, he'd been developing the skills and temperament needed to make a contribution on the Court if he got the opportunity.

Now, with one squeeze of a trigger, Peck had set in motion an irreversible chain of events that could not end well. Jack pulled himself together and dialed 911.

Chapter 5

June 2
2:30 p.m.

JACK WALKED through the unimpressive front door of the San Francisco Hall of Justice and checked the directory for District Attorney Rick Calder's office number.

He'd been awake half the night trying to figure out why Peck killed himself. Had he been severely depressed? No signs. Could someone be blackmailing him? No, he'd have fought back.

Peck had been such a prominent judge that the same question probably troubled the District Attorney and was the reason Calder had summoned him to come in this afternoon. Maybe Calder thought Jack, as Peck's son, knew something that would help solve the puzzle. If that was it, he was in for a disappointment.

An assistant showed him into Rick Calder's corner office. It was orderly, the walls filled with seascapes in cheap frames and photographs of people who could only be his wife and children.

Calder, middle-aged, well-tanned, wearing a starched white shirt, didn't rise from the chair behind his desk. He looked up and poked horn-rimmed glasses into place. "Thanks for coming in, Mr. Strider." He gestured to the chair across the desk from him.

"No problem," Jack said as he sat.

"This is about your father's death, of course. I knew him, but we didn't run in the same circles." Calder slid a file folder aside and put one hand on top of the other. "I have a few questions for you. In the statement you made last night you said that just before the incident you, your father, and Ms. Anita Hudson were watching a KNBC News show that pertained to a vessel known as *Pacific Dawn*, correct?"

"Yes."

"And you recall that six people were found dead aboard that vessel, correct?"

"Yes."

"And as soon as that report ended, the judge killed himself?"

"That's right." Jack crossed his arms. "Is this going somewhere?"

Calder ignored his question. "After those bodies were discovered, I ordered my people to find out who owns *Pacific Dawn*."

"According to the news report, it's some company in Panama City."

Calder shook his head. "The KNBC reporter only got as far as that company. My men dug deeper and learned it was a front. They had to pierce two more corporate shells before we identified the real owner." He stopped, interlaced his fingers, and looked straight at Jack.

"That owner is—" He paused. Jack recognized the sleazy courtroom trick. Calder had set up his little dramatic moment to watch how Jack would react. "—the Honorable H. Peckford Strider."

The accusation hit Jack like a rock between the eyes. In a blink, Calder had switched from ally to adversary. He froze his features, giving Calder nothing. "That can't be true."

"It's true, all right, and someone in this office—and I'll find and fire the bastard—tipped off Judge Strider that we knew who the real owner was and that the story about the deaths would break on the KNBC seven o'clock news." Calder leaned forward. "The fact that the judge watched the show tends to confirm I'm right."

His implication was clear. Peck had killed himself because he was about to be busted for some connection with those deaths. But there must be a mistake. Even if Peck had owned that ship, he couldn't possibly be responsible for the deaths.

"Maybe—"

Calder cut him off and changed the subject. "I made certain the ME and the forensics lab took a hard look at whether the cause of Peck Strider's death was suicide or whether it could have been murder. I also ordered an autopsy."

"Oh, for God's sake! Of course it was suicide. I saw him pull the trigger. So did his friend, Anita Hudson. Or maybe you think one of us shot him." He let his face show his scorn.

"We consider all possibilities, Mr. Strider. I don't have the autopsy report back yet, but the ME concluded yesterday that it was suicide. Right after that, I got a warrant to search your father's house."

Jack's knowledge of constitutional law kicked in. "Wait a damn minute. Since you knew it was suicide, you knew his home wasn't a crime scene. You had no grounds for a search warrant."

"Not for your father's death, but *Pacific Dawn* was definitely a crime scene. Linking your father to that ship was all it took to get the search warrant and put our team in his house. They brought back a load of files and documents and have been reviewing them. We now know that back when Judge Strider was practicing law, he had a client named Esposito who owned *Pacific Dawn.* When the client died, your father was the executor for his estate. Instead of selling the vessel, he kept it and took over Esposito's business of transporting illegal aliens into the U.S." He thumbed through a stack of papers in front of him and glanced at one. "My men found bank statements showing it was a very profitable business. We're following the money trail to see who else is involved." Calder leaned back with a triumphant look. "Any questions?"

Jack's throat tightened. *Illegal aliens?* Calder had to be wrong. Peck cared about money, but he cared far more about his image. He'd never cross the line into illegality, never risk a discovery that would ruin him. He bristled at the smug look on Calder's face.

"Your charges don't deserve any questions. Your men have made a bad mistake, but that doesn't matter, because you can't prosecute a dead man. So this is over."

"Not even close," Calder said. "Those young women were cooked to death in that container. I'm going to find every damned person responsible. We're going to uncover a lot more before this is over. However, I'm not going to release any of this to the media until my Investigative Bureau has finished digging. In the meantime, I want you to agree to a private burial for your father. No visitation. No crowd. No media. I'm not going to allow speeches praising Judge Strider as a paragon of virtue, then have all this leak out to the media. That would make me, and the Mayor, look like idiots. That's not going to happen."

Jack was tempted to tell Calder to go to hell, but the last things he wanted were speeches and crowds.

"Agreed." He stood.

Calder didn't move. "I'm not finished. Tell me about all bank accounts and safe deposit boxes to which both you and your father had access."

"I haven't had a joint bank account with my father since I was thirteen, and never a joint safe deposit box."

"But he could have set up such a joint account or box without your knowing about it, correct?"

"Theoretically, but he didn't." *He was certain of that. Peck had been obsessed with the Supreme Court track. No way he'd leave a trail that could implicate his protégé.* "Leak anything like that to the media, and I'll haul you into court."

"I'll keep that in mind," Calder said, but his thin smile communicated that he'd go for the front page whenever he felt like it. "I can't prosecute Judge Strider, but I intend to find something that implicates you. When I do, I'll go for an indictment the same day. Make no mistake. I will get you." He stood. "Now we're finished . . . for today."

"Calder, you slandered my father even though you can't prosecute him. Now you're threatening me. I think you have some sort of vendetta going, and you're way out of bounds. Give me an excuse, and I'll be coming after *you*. Any questions?" He clenched his fists, hoping Calder wanted to make a move.

Chapter 6

June 2
5 p.m.

THE FORMER Stanford Law School building had been converted into a warren of small rooms for study and research. As Jack walked inside, he encountered four of his students lugging book bags and daypacks. As soon as they saw him, conversation stopped.

"Professor Strider," said a dark-haired young woman, "we're really sorry about your loss." She looked at her friends. "Listen, we're heading for beer at The Oasis. Want to come?"

It was the kind of invitation he accepted from time to time, mostly because he liked fielding the thorny legal questions they cooked up to try to stump him. He sharpened their wits and made them laugh when they got stressed out. Because he was so accessible, they thought they had him pegged, but none of them knew what he really wanted in life or how badly he wanted it. They saw only what he wanted them to see.

"Thanks . . . another time." He turned right and climbed the wide, worn stairs.

His destination was a spacious second-floor office with a sweeping view of the palm-lined drive that connected Palo Alto with the Stanford campus. After Samuel Butler announced years ago that the law school would be moving to new quarters near the center of campus, he'd retired as dean of the school, taken emeritus status, and claimed possession of his cherished office in the old building.

Once in a while during the eight years he'd taught at Stanford Law, Jack had asked Butler to be his sounding board concerning some issue or another. But this time it was Butler who'd left a message inviting him to come to his office. Since the topic was likely to be Peck's death, he wasn't looking forward to the meeting.

Through the opaque glass in the door, Jack heard the erratic tapping of the manual Olivetti on which Butler wrote a stream of essays for legal journals. Jack rapped and opened the door.

Butler sat at his roll top desk, spidery hands scrabbling around among handwritten notes and heaps of legal references.

"Good afternoon, Sam."

"And to you, Jack. I'm looking for one last citation for a law review piece I'm writing."

The man's eyesight was dim and his voice a scratchy remnant of the smooth baritone that had held the attention of justices of the Supreme Court on several occasions, but he still loved to shower legal insights on an unruly public.

"No hurry." Jack let his gaze wander around the room, especially to the paintings that took up most of two walls. Butler loved Paul Gauguin's work and had admired the artist's courage in tossing aside a career in a London bank to seek happiness in the South Pacific.

Butler had started with prints, slowly replacing them with expertly painted reproductions. To Jack's eye, they looked like originals even though he knew there was no chance of that, not on a professor's salary. Butler did consulting work for a couple of foreign governments and played the market. That would provide enough money for the reproductions.

A painting of two women carrying mangos radiated quality. Since he hadn't seen it before, it must be a recently acquired reproduction.

Butler stood up, buttoned his vest, returned the knot in his tie to its proper place and reached out to shake hands. "My condolences, Jack. I saw the article in the Sunday *Chronicle* yesterday. Very complimentary about Peck's career." Butler eased into the venerable leather chair that had supported him through more than forty years of scholarship. "Take that chair across from me. Comfortable? Now, would you like to tell me what happened?"

Hell no, he didn't want to talk about it. After two days, he was no closer to processing what had happened in his father's study, but Butler deserved some response.

"It started at the yacht club when I got a call from Peck's lady friend." He filled in the details about watching the report on the seven o'clock news and his father's cryptic comments. "Suddenly, Peck—" He swallowed hard as the horrendous scene washed over him. "—pulled a gun, put the muzzle into his mouth, looked straight at me, and squeezed the trigger."

Butler frowned. "That was cruel."

Jack shrugged. "Typical Peck. He had a plan, and my showing up didn't change it at all."

"What happened . . . afterwards?"

"Anita started screaming that I could have gotten the gun away from him."

"Could you have?"

"He was too fast." He'd thought through those moments often. It was the truth.

"This is a hard time for you," Butler said.

"It'll get worse. There's about to be some very bad publicity about Peck. Not about how he died, but how he lived. He wasn't the man we thought he was."

"True for many of us, Jack." Butler nodded solemnly.

"Maybe, but because Peck was such a prominent alum of this law school, and a big donor, it could make the school look bad."

Butler's eyebrows lifted. "What haven't you told me?" he asked, his tone sharp.

Jack took a deep breath. The conversation was about to get heavy. "Earlier this afternoon, I met with District Attorney Rick Calder in his office."

Butler closed his eyes as he listened to the revelations at that meeting, including Peck's ownership of *Pacific Dawn* and his importation of illegal aliens. When Jack finished, Butler exhaled with a puff, as if he'd been holding his breath. He looked over the tops of his glasses.

"That's very bad, indeed. And Calder thinks you may be involved?"

"He was damned insulting. He thinks I was making money from what Peck was doing. His people are hunting for bank accounts and safe deposit boxes, trying to connect me to Peck's business. He said he'd indict me if he got evidence."

"Calder has a lot of power, and DAs often indict people as a fishing expedition, especially if they get a political lift from it."

"I told him if he even hints publicly that I was involved, I'd sue him."

"You'd be right to do so. I just regret that your father won't get a traditional burial service. And, unfortunately, some people will gossip."

"I don't give a damn if they gossip, but—" He stopped, surprised. How could Butler know about the restriction Calder had imposed on Peck's burial?

As if reading his mind, Butler cleared his throat and said, "When I heard on the news about the deaths on *Pacific Dawn*, I didn't think much about it. Then the next morning, I learned about Peck's suicide and read a follow-up story about the ship. I had an odd intuition there might be a connection."

"Why would you think that?"

"At a Friday night happy hour at the yacht club last summer, Peck was tipsy and smoking hot about an insurance company that had refused to pay for damage to a cargo ship he owned. We had two rums worth of discussion about legal remedies, but when I asked him how he came to own a cargo ship, he changed the subject. That left me wondering. Anyway, this morning, out of curiosity I phoned someone who could answer my questions." Butler looked down at his interlaced fingers, then up at him.

"I've known Rick Calder for years."

Butler, his mentor, his friend, had sandbagged him. What a bastard. "So you already knew everything I just told you?"

"I wanted to hear it from you," he said in a voice that held no hint of apology. "However, my conversation with Calder isn't why I asked you to come here. Dean Thomson is nearly hysterical about this scandal tying dead illegal aliens to a very prominent alum whose son is on the faculty. He kept shouting about 'human trafficking.' He's afraid the notoriety will kill fundraising, grants, even recruiting. Never underestimate how fear can motivate a gutless administrator. And, I'm sorry to say, I have some more bad news for you."

Jack stared at him, his stomach knotting. His father was newly dead and disgraced. The DA was investigating him. What was left?

Butler continued. "Dean Thompson has rescinded your pending appointment to the chairmanship of your department."

Anger surged through Jack. He jumped to his feet, but got control of himself before blurting, "That's bull. There was nothing 'pending' about that appointment. It was locked in before any of this happened. Thompson made an offer, and I accepted. He can't rescind it now."

"Technically," he said, looking Jack in the eyes, "he can. The contract hasn't been approved by the Board."

"I won't let him get away with this. Let's go see him. Both of us. Right now." He could reason with Thompson, he assured himself, get him to back down.

"There's no point." Butler said softly, corners of his mouth turned down. "He sees you as being a threat to his job someday. Fact is, he really wants to fire you, but doesn't dare go that far. All I could get from him was to let me tell you his decision myself."

So Thompson's insecurities were behind his decision to yank the Chairmanship away. Well, he was in for a fight. "I have tenure. I'll get an injunction."

"You don't have to worry about that at this point. Thompson can't fire you unless Calder proves you were involved in that nasty business. What he can and will do is assign you to teach civil procedure to first year students until you run screaming down Palm Drive. He'll make sure you get no promotions, no grants, no perks. You're the most gifted professor on the faculty, but let's face reality . . . your career here is over."

Butler pinched his glasses off, cleaned the lenses with a special cloth he pulled from his jacket pocket, and took his time restoring the glasses to his nose. "Jack, this is a sea change in your life. I recommend you get out of academia. Get into the arena. Go into private practice."

What in the hell was going on? Suicide, scandal, loss of the promotion—and now it sounded like Butler was conning him into accepting being kicked out the door.

"Not a chance. If I'd wanted to go into private practice, I would have done it years ago." He didn't add that building a national reputation as a law professor was a better step on the path to the Supreme Court.

Butler leaned toward Jack. "I understand," he said, nodding his head, "but that was then. Now, some experience in the rough-and-tumble side of the profession will make you a better lawyer—and I can help you. Sinclair & Simms is the hottest law firm in California. Several offices overseas. Big money. Justin Sinclair and I are longtime friends. We actually served together in the, uh, intelligence business inside the old Soviet Union."

"Intelligence? Soviet Union? You never told me about that." Somehow, given the way Butler was behaving, he wasn't completely surprised.

Butler waved the subject away. "Long time ago. What matters now is your career. Justin Sinclair doesn't worry about fundraising, grants, or any of that crap. In you, he'd get a potential leader for his firm. You'd join at partner level, of course, but to move up you'll have to climb over the bodies of some very tough people. As it happens, I spoke with Justin an hour ago. He'll make you an offer you can't refuse. So, shall we give him a call?"

Butler was rushing ahead like an express train. To slow it down, Jack said, "The Chairman of the Board of the Sierra Club has been after me for a couple of years to be its general counsel. That might be a better fit."

Butler shook his head. "A terrible mistake. It's a dead end job, no upside. Remember, the government will confiscate every penny of Peck's estate, so you need a good income. And if Calder can find anything to tie you to *Pacific Dawn,* no matter how flimsy, he'll go public, and all your options will go up in smoke. The Sierra Club can't protect you, but maybe Justin Sinclair can."

Was Butler implying that Sinclair had some leverage he would use on Calder? Well, that didn't matter because Calder could never get him on substance. There wasn't any. But Calder might concoct something that would look suspicious. Jack had to make a decision before that happened.

"Sam, there's something else that will affect my decision, something I've discussed only with Peck. My goal is to be appointed to the U.S. Supreme Court."

Until a few minutes ago, he would have added that an aide to the governor had called him recently. One of the justices on the California Supreme Court would probably resign within a couple of years for health reasons. The aide had asked whether Jack might be interested in being appointed to the vacancy. Not a firm offer, but a strong feeler. Now, because of mixed messages from Butler, he held that information back.

Butler looked pensive for a few moments. "You were Editor-in-Chief of law review and clerked for a respected judge. And Stanford has been like a freeway leading to the Supreme Court for past and present justices. Yes, you had a good shot, but now . . ." His slow head shake said it all.

A slight movement in the corner of the room caught Jack's attention. It was the pendulum of a stately Benjamin clock. He felt it measuring and discarding seconds of his life, one after another.

"Jack, you're like a son to me," Butler said, breaking into his thoughts, "so I'll give you some advice. Bury your father. Chart a new course."

Given his experience with Peck, the phrase "you're like a son to me" didn't sound appealing. But that didn't matter. He had a decision to make. "I'll call you in a few days and let you know what I'm thinking."

"In a few days you'll be lucky to find a job with an insurance company in Omaha. Call me by nine o'clock tonight, or I can't help you."

The sound of the pendulum ticking seemed louder, filling the room.

JACK PARKED HIS BMW in the driveway of his two-story, gray shingle home in Atherton. Once inside, his muscles relaxed a little. He clicked on a Dave Brubeck jazz CD and dropped into his big chair in front of the fireplace. The books—in shelves and in toppled piles around him—and the memorabilia on the walls always relaxed him. After a few minutes, he pulled on track shorts and a Stanford Crew T-shirt. As he tied the lace on his running shoe, it snapped. It was that kind of day. He found a new lace, not a match, and tried to slow down the clamor in his brain.

As he ran along the shaded streets and settled into a familiar routine, he thought about teaching. He'd spent eight years making the law comprehensible, even intriguing, to bright-eyed students. In an instant, that was over. He'd taken so much for granted, assuming that hard work would carry him to his goal. He'd never lost at anything. Now, in one day, he'd lost everything, but he'd be damned if he'd feel sorry for himself. He'd suck it up and start over.

He had a life-changing decision to make. Butler's ultimatum rang in his ears: "Call me by nine o'clock tonight, or I can't help you."

If he accepted the offer from the Sierra Club, he'd be working in the public interest. On the other hand, Sinclair & Simms meant so much money he'd have to guard against becoming addicted to it. Success at S & S also meant the Supreme Court track might come back to life.

Most lawyers would say he'd be nuts to turn down a partnership at S & S. If the dead could give their opinions, Peck would steer him to S & S for sure. Well, Sam Butler had advised him to bury his father, and that's what he intended to do. He didn't care what Peck would advise. This decision was his alone.

Before their conversation today, he'd trusted Butler completely. But Butler had telephoned Calder, and, in his zeal to protect the school, the old man had probably told Thompson what he'd learned. That had set off the firestorm that cost Jack his job, maybe his future. Butler might be trying to compensate by lining him up with Sinclair.

Jack liked to analyze all variables, options, and consequences before making a decision. No time for that tonight. He had to make a decision now.

He turned for home.

Chapter 7

June 3
10:30 am

HEIDI KLEIN'S stomach tightened the second her assistant identified the caller. She detested the man, but didn't have the will to decline the call. Not from *him*. She waved at the masseur to leave her office and clutched the front of her silk kimono over her breasts as if, somehow, the caller could see her. She picked up the receiver.

"This is Dr. Klein," she said.

"So it's 'Dr. Klein' now? Well, you'll always be Heidi to me. I remember—"

"There's nothing to remember," she said sharply. "I'm surprised to hear from you." Her tone was less respectful than during the years she'd worked for him. She slipped into the soft leather Knoll chair behind her desk.

"I'll get to the point," he said, with no effort to be cordial. "I'm about to give you the best proposition you'll ever get."

"I've had a few, and you'd rank at the bottom."

"Please don't interrupt, Heidi."

His power trips had always infuriated her, but she no longer had to put up with them. "Fine. I'll just hang up if I get bored."

A moment passed without reply. He was deciding whether to challenge her. If he didn't, it meant he needed her for some reason.

He let it slide. "There's a situation that's costing companies all across the country hundreds of millions of dollars and will eventually screw up the whole damned economy. I know exactly what to do about it. That's why I'm calling you."

He either didn't realize how much she loathed him, or he was so arrogant he didn't care.

"My solution is incredibly simple," he said when she didn't respond.

"Then maybe you can simply explain the problem."

"Hazardous waste."

What a letdown. "You want me to help you collect trash?"

"Not trash, for God's sake. I'm talking about materials that have to be transported by rail, truck, or barge to treatment facilities. Then it's sent somewhere remote for permanent storage. Most of it is chemical and biological, and stuff like cadmium, lead, mercury, and dioxin, that you definitely don't want to migrate into water supplies and kill people."

"Are you including nuclear waste?"

"Some of it is, but nothing you have to worry about."

"Well, it's all outside my area of expertise. You're calling the wrong person."

"Just hear me out."

She didn't have to hear him out. In their past, he'd suckered her into his schemes, even seduced and used her emotionally. That was over. "Why should I?"

"Because I'm asking. Please."

That was better. "Go ahead."

"The volume of hazardous waste is skyrocketing, but most treatment facilities are mom-and-pop operations. Storage sites are filling up, so they charge whatever they want. Research labs, hospitals, and scrap yards can't get hazardous waste off-site fast enough, so they started dumping it illegally. Sooner or later they poison a neighborhood. Do you remember Love Canal, near Niagara Falls?"

"Not the details, but I remember it was a public health emergency."

"Hooker Chemical buried 21,000 tons of toxic chemicals and then sold the property. Many years later, a neighborhood was built on top of the dump site. After that, homeowners began noticing high rates of epilepsy, retardation, birth defects, and more. We can help prevent that sort of thing.

"Here's my point," he hurried on, as if he sensed she was ready to hang up. "Every state refuses to be a dumping ground for the rest of the country. To make it worse, Homeland Security now requires companies to spend millions to make chemical, biological and nuclear waste secure from terrorists—which they can't do. Businesses are going to be forced to shut down, and that includes some very large public utilities. Together, we can fix all that."

The man had an ego the size of Alaska, but this sounded too big, even for him. Still, it might be worth playing along.

"What about regulations?"

"They're usually ignored. Once in a while some hero snitches, and a company pays a few fines."

"Does anyone inspect those places?"

"The inspectors are low-paid grunts eager to get off the property as fast as they can. They leave owners to operate on the honor system. You can guess how that works out."

Where was this conversation going? She wanted him to get to the point so she could tell him no, hang up and get back to her massage.

"Bottom line, what do you want from me?"

"My new way of disposing of hazardous waste is today's equivalent of inventing the microchip, worth hundreds of millions of dollars, maybe billions. And you can be part of it," he said magnanimously.

"If you're going to suggest that my company starts treating hazardous waste, that's not going to happen."

"You're way off the mark. I can solve this hazardous waste crisis, at least for those lucky enough to sign up as my clients. And I can make a place for you. In fact, my dear Heidi, I'd take it very badly if we don't go forward with this together."

"That sounded like a threat. Do it again and I'll hang up."

"Ah, you're so feisty now. I rather preferred the relationship we had in the old days, but I suppose things change. All right, here's the plan. I'll arrange for a continuing flow of hazardous waste to be shipped to your site."

"I just told you—"

"Listen to me. You'll only be a middleman, transferring incoming material into trucks to be dispatched to their final destination. Each round trip will take two or three days."

"They could reach any of 20 states in that time. Where would they be going?"

"That's not something you need to know, my dear."

She clamped down on her emotions. *Jerk.* "Hold on, my assistant needs me," she said, and left him listening to elevator music.

She wanted a moment to think. Something about his plan wasn't logical. Bringing the two of them in as middlemen in an existing system would have to cost the clients more, unless . . . she got it! He wasn't going to use any of the existing hazardous waste storage sites. He planned to dispose of tons of lethal waste somewhere beyond the reach of regulations.

Because of far lower costs, he could undercut the legitimate market. That's why his plan required shipping to a location as remote as hers. Using her company as a drop-off would prevent clients from tracking where their waste wound up. She had to admire him. As always, he was far out in front of the pack.

It had to be illegal as hell, but if she confronted him with that it might be a deal breaker. Anyway, in her line of work she'd learned not to be squeamish about the letter of the law. No, she wouldn't raise the illegality of his proposal, but it would definitely raise her price.

She clicked back on the line. "I'm here. Look, my company would have to buy or lease trucks, then hire drivers and laborers. I'd have to build a cover story and produce a reasonable flow of revenue for the company.

So exactly what are you offering?"

"I'll be paying you directly and in cash. You make whatever deal you want with your company or none at all."

She ran her tongue along her upper lip. Tax-free income would enable her to leave the company before one of its covert operations landed her in jail. But making a deal with the devil also meant a high risk of being incinerated.

"That's fine, but the risks are high, so I have two conditions. First, make me a dollar offer, and I'll accept or reject it. No second chance. Next, give me all the details of how your plan works."

"The deal is fifty thousand dollars for every truck that leaves your site fully loaded for the destination I set. Expect a minimum of one million dollars a month. Your second request is out of the question." Before she could object, he said, "Now I have two requirements of my own. This agreement will be verbal only, and we deal solely with each other."

The amount of money took her breath away. At those numbers, she didn't care where he disposed of the stuff or how much he raked off for himself. She didn't answer right away even though she knew he'd just bought her.

Finally, she announced, "You have a deal, partner."

"We're in business together, not partners. By the way, people who think they're indispensable are always wrong, and it costs them. Don't make that mistake. I'll call you in a few days with a timetable and the specs for the trucks." He broke the connection.

From the yellow pad, she tore off two pages of notes she'd made during the conversation and slipped them into the bottom drawer. She reached across her desk and picked up an eight-inch tall pyramid-shaped wedge of black basalt she'd found while kayaking through the Grand Canyon. Holding an object over two billion years old had always calmed her. This time, however, it couldn't offset the wave of anxiety that swept over her.

Chapter 8

June 3
10:50 a.m.

OUTSIDE HEIDI'S office window, a Land Rover with a swivel-mounted M-60 cannon rolled along an asphalt strip that wound like a black anaconda across the wasteland.

She remembered the afternoon several years ago when two men had come to her former office. Before they'd sat down at her conference table, the older man, who'd introduced himself as Callahan, started the kind of full body scan she endured often. When his gaze dropped from her green eyes and curly auburn hair to linger on her chest she said, "What else may I do for you gentlemen?"

"Dr. Klein," the other man, named Lee, had said, "we represent the Board of Directors of a certain company whose CEO skied off a cliff. Dead at the bottom. We're here to offer you a job as our new CEO. We'll double your present salary to start, and if you've met our objectives at the end of the first year, you can expect further increases."

Guessing it had been a trap set up by her boss, wanting to see if she'd bite, she'd decided that if a few blunt questions didn't expose the hoax, she'd show them the door.

"Why me? And what's the name of your company?"

"We know you've been very successful managing top secret projects," Lee had said. "But despite that, you're underpaid, excluded from the inner circle, and your boss doesn't give you credit for your good work. Do we have that about right?"

They damn sure had. "You forgot to mention what your company does."

"You're familiar with 'gray companies' that do billions of dollars of business with the government," Callahan had told her, "the kind of business that never becomes public."

"I also know," she'd replied, "that gray companies operate at the edge of the law, sometimes over the edge. I'm not interested in prison."

"As our CEO, we'll see to it that you are untouchable."

"Think about our offer in principle," Callahan had said. "I'll call you at four on Friday. If you're interested, we'll fly you out for a look at our headquarters. If you decide not to come on board, this conversation never happened. By the way, our deceased CEO never used his real name when he traveled, including ski trips."

He'd been clever. He'd anticipated she'd research accidental deaths at ski resorts to find out whether their story was true.

The big money, a new challenge, and getting credit for her work had been powerful incentives. But it would be a one-way trip. The ego of her present boss would never let him take her back.

A week later she'd boarded the company's Gulfstream G450 with its luxurious stateroom, exercise bike wired to the Internet, and burled maple everywhere. After three hours flying west, they'd passed above brown mountains where horizontal yellow bands rose and fell like waves. The Gulfstream had dropped altitude fast and landed like a whisper on a private airstrip in the high desert. A man wearing a camouflage uniform loaded her suitcase into a Lexus SUV left running so the air-conditioning could combat the fierce heat.

On the other side of a rock-strewn ridge stood a very unimpressive cluster of office buildings, a dozen warehouses, and a line of eighteen-wheel trailer trucks.

It turned out that the reality was quite different. The five adobe-style office buildings, designed to blend into the landscape, were state-of-the-art inside. Top-secret assignments took place underground in a fortified, four-level complex whose boundaries extended far beyond the offices on the surface. Yellow sulfur lights hung from gooseneck poles. An electrified razor-wire fence, twice the height of a man, guarded the company's 18,000 acres.

The environment was foreign to her, but the salary had been too good to pass up.

NOW, HAVING MASTERED the job of ruling her desert kingdom, she was bored. Socially, she felt locked up in a high-tech nunnery. Her senses were starved. She was long overdue for some excitement. Suddenly, this unexpected telephone call had dropped a combination of both a golden goose—and a lifeline—in her lap. She couldn't resist the money or the risk, but had a lurking feeling she was going to regret it.

Chapter 9

June 4
9:45 a.m.

AT NINE FORTY-FIVE Sunday morning, San Francisco's city center was eerily empty. Instead of sidewalks crowded with well-dressed businessmen and women, the few people in sight looked like tourists wandering in search of a Starbucks-and-New-York-Times fix.

Jack turned off Fremont into the underground parking garage at 333 Market Street. He easily located the prime parking spaces bearing signs with "Sinclair & Simms, LLC" in gold letters.

"May I help you, sir?" The guard at the Shorenstein Security desk in the wall-to-wall marble lobby asked softly. The words were civil, but came across as a challenge.

"Jack Strider. Here to see Mr. Sinclair. Sinclair & Simms."

The guard nodded toward the bank of elevators. "Number three is waiting for you."

As soon as he stepped in, the door closed, and the car began to rise. When the door slid open on the 54th floor, he was inside the S & S office. It was even grander than he'd expected: a foyer the size of a tennis court, polished black marble, antique Persian rugs, and acres of etched glass. The leather smelled like its color—butterscotch. The paintings were worthy of hanging in the de Young Museum in Golden Gate Park.

This firm was a newcomer by San Francisco standards, so this display was to persuade prospective clients that the firm had been in business since the Gold Rush.

He glanced at his watch. It read ten a.m. exactly.

From a broad hallway to Jack's left, Justin Sinclair strode into sight wearing gray trousers, a white turtleneck, and a Whitbread International Race windbreaker. His bright blue eyes, deep set beneath shaggy brows, white hair worn in a ruff like a male lion, and craggy features gave him a remarkable resemblance to the late Charlton Heston. He'd been quoted as saying the comparison should run in the other direction. He had to be about 6'4" because they stood eye to eye.

"Good to meet you, Jack." As his right hand stretched forward to shake, his left hand gripped Jack's right wrist, a smooth move Jack associated with many politicians. "Sam told me all about you."

Jack heard the slight emphasis on the word "all."

"Good to meet you too, sir."

"Thanks for coming in on a Sunday morning. I'd be playing golf, but I have to prepare for an important negotiation first thing tomorrow. That's life in the private sector. Not like the university."

Sinclair led him down a corridor whose carpet was so thick it felt like a wrestling mat underfoot. Photographs of a pantheon of business tycoons, politicians and dictators lined the walls. Justin Sinclair was in every one.

"We call this a 'love me' wall, Jack. We like reminders of the old days." He dismissed it with a backhanded wave.

They turned into an immense corner office. Straight ahead, a commanding view across San Francisco Bay seemed to stretch north to the wine country and east to the Sierra Nevada Mountains.

Every vertical surface that was not floor-to-ceiling glass was covered with plaques, images, and mementoes. A series of photos mounted in a row showed Justin Sinclair in the Oval Office being smiled at by three successive presidents. In others, he was delivering an address to the UN General Assembly and relaxing in the late Chief Justice Renquist's private office. Jack noticed that the photos were at least ten years old, some much older. It looked as if Sinclair's life in the spotlight had stopped when his term as Secretary of State ended.

Some men covered walls with the heads of beasts they'd killed. Sinclair's trophies were the heads of fellow humans. Jack suddenly understood that he was standing *inside* a trophy case. Prospective clients ushered into this sanctum couldn't miss Sinclair's message that he was a man of power and influence.

At Sinclair's gesture, they settled into a pair of overstuffed chairs, but instead of talking business, Sinclair began to reminisce, pointing out items around the room that represented high points in his career. "I've had a lot of good fortune in my life, but the crown jewel was my term at State. We were handed a God-awful mess. Pulling America back together wasn't easy. I can't count how many problems we took care of that would have scared the hell out of the public if we'd ever let them break the surface."

"The old Soviet Union was still quite a threat then," Jack said.

"A walk in the park compared to the Middle East. If I hadn't held the Israelis back, they'd have bombed Syria, Iran, and Saudi Arabia, and that would have dragged us into a war for sure. We stopped that, and the public never knew. Think about that goddamned Kissinger stealing the Nobel Peace Prize in '73 without even getting a damned peace. They gave it to him because he talked as if he were Moses and knew things nobody else could understand. Everybody knows I *earned* the Nobel I never got." He leaned over and jammed his cigar into the ashtray so hard the wrapper burst.

Obviously, Kissinger's ghostly presence had shattered Sinclair's amiable mood, because he abruptly shifted his attention to the point of the meeting.

"Look here, Jack, I understand you've left Stanford Law and want a job here. Do I have that right?"

"Your firm has a fine reputation and—"

"Yes, yes, we both know that. You're here because Sam Butler asked me to talk with you. Thing is, I'm not a sentimental man. We don't have a bunch of school kids here who think the professor is the source of all knowledge. We swim with sharks, and I'm a hell of a lot tougher to work for than some bureaucratic Dean. Frankly, I don't know whether you can cut it. Plus you're carrying a lot of baggage. I know you understand my position."

Although Jack retained his outward expression of calm, he was confused. What was going on? Butler had told him an offer was a sure thing, that Sinclair & Simms would feel lucky to get him. Now it sounded as if Sinclair was leading up to a brush-off.

"But," Sinclair went on, "I need to fill a gap in our international corporate division. In other words, you've got the job."

That was more like it. "What kind of gap are you looking to fill?"

"Two of your specialties, environmental law and water law. When the *New York Times* rants about companies polluting the planet, they're often talking about our clients. So we can use your strong reputation for environmental, shall we say, sensitivity. You'll be front and center whenever one of our clients gets hauled up before the Environmental Protection Agency, state attorneys general, that sort of thing."

That was a slow pitch over the center of the plate, even though his way of dealing with clients' environmental violations might not be what Sinclair was used to. "I can handle—"

"In the area of water law," Sinclair interrupted, "I see an increasing load of major conflicts coming up. I want to be ready."

"Exactly right. Before long, water will be the hottest commodity in the world. The first water wars have already started between nations, cities and states, farmers and manufacturers, and the rest, over who owns water rights. Everyone will be suing everyone for destroying water resources."

"Exactly. My goal is to be ready to represent our clients. *Damn!*" He pointed at the Bay. "Look at that schooner out near Alcatraz, flying like a bat out of hell." He looked back at Jack. "Where was I? Oh yes, so that's what you can expect. On the big ones, you'll report directly to me. Understood?"

"Yes, of course."

He hadn't known what to expect from Sinclair, but he certainly wasn't getting much respect. Still, he reminded himself, signing on with Sinclair & Simms was the best move he had right now. The California Supreme Court would still be an option when the vacancy came up.

"That's it then. I'll put the word out that I'm your godfather, and I'll do whatever I can to help you succeed. One warning, and hear me well on this. If something comes up later that makes you a liability to the firm, I'll have to cut you loose. It's just business. *Capisce?*"

Oh, yeah, he got the message. "Nothing else will come up, Mr. Secretary."

"I wish I were still 'Mr. Secretary.'" He looked out the window. "Those were good days. People don't talk about patriotism anymore, not fashionable I guess. But I'm the biggest flag-waving patriot you'll ever meet. I've always done what's best for my country."

Sinclair picked up an envelope and handed it to him. "This contains the terms of your employment. Your salary is triple what it was at the law school. You come in as a partner, but on probation until I see how you do."

They shook hands, ending the meeting. Jack walked down the long hall alone.

Probation? Sinclair had treated him like he'd just passed the Bar exam yesterday. Instead of a leisurely conversation with the famous politician and superstar lawyer, he'd gotten a monologue and disrespectful dismissal. He should have tossed the envelope on the desk and salvaged his pride. But Sinclair was a big name, and S & S was the only ticket he had to the big show. Somehow, he'd make it pay off. He'd be damned if he'd let Peck destroy his Supreme Court dream.

Number three elevator waited, door open.

BACK ON THE Stanford campus, Jack walked into Dean Thompson's office and dropped his letter of resignation on the desk. He didn't sit, and Thompson didn't stand. Thompson scanned the letter and looked up. He had to be worried that Jack was going to tear into him. As soon as he sensed that wasn't Jack's intention, he relaxed. If he was embarrassed by having denied Jack the chairmanship of the department, he concealed it behind a grave look on his smooth, round face. He thanked Jack for his service to the law school and started a blatantly insincere attempt to get him to reconsider leaving. He stopped in mid-sentence when he saw the dark expression on Jack's face.

The meeting lasted less than three minutes, and even that was too long for Jack.

When he left his office for the last time at the end of the week, the halls were empty. Everyone was in the city or the wine country or at the beach.

Without a single person to say 'good-bye' to, he left the only professional home he'd ever known. He didn't feel as if a new dawn was breaking. He felt more like there were black clouds overhead, that a thunder and lightning storm was about to cut loose.

Chapter 10

June 12
10:00 a.m.

IT WAS JACK'S sixth day at Sinclair & Simms. He was working in an office full of expensive furniture and no personality, like a place kept for lawyers visiting from out-of-town. He'd hung the obligatory diplomas and certificates and added his three-foot-square Cibachrome print of *Simba*, but had done nothing more to make this place his own.

Peck had committed suicide less than two weeks ago, and thoughts about that traumatic experience sometimes prevented Jack from keeping his head in the game. When that happened, he shook his head and concentrated on the work in front of him. At the moment, he was drafting a licensing agreement for NorCal Power to import tidal turbine technology from a firm in Holland when the phone rang.

"It's District Attorney Calder, sir," his temporary secretary said.

"Please put him on."

"Good morning, Mr. Strider. I'd like you to meet me at the Park Pacifica Riding Academy in Hillsborough at five o'clock today. It's important."

"Of course, but why at a riding academy?"

"I bought a show horse for my daughter, and I've never seen her ride him. She's training this afternoon, so I can kill two birds with one shot. See you there."

During the next six hours, Jack thought about the upcoming meeting. Calder's staff must have gone through all of Peck's files by now, so Calder would be ready to back off. The price Jack had paid for Peck's crimes had been heavy, but at least it wouldn't get worse.

During the drive down the peninsula to Hillsborough the air began to smell fresher, the sky looked bluer.

He was a few minutes early, so he sat in the top row of bleachers looking down at the sawdust and dirt ring where six teenage girls were being instructed by a young man in a black turtleneck. Hooves thudded rhythmically as horses circled the ring. The musky smell of sweat was laced with the sharp tang of urine.

He spotted Calder entering the far end of the arena and saw him catch the eye of a girl with long black braids, wearing a red T-shirt. She smiled, and then her attention went back to her instructor.

Calder climbed the bleacher steps to where Jack waited.

"Mr. Strider," he said brusquely and sat down. "I've had my best men investigating the circumstances of H. Peckford Strider's death. Now I'm going to tell you what we've learned, part of it anyway. *Pacific Dawn* started its final voyage from the port of Salina Cruz, Mexico, a refinery town south of Acapulco. It was loaded with tin, zinc, and sugar. Even though your father owned that ship, we still can't prove he was criminally responsible for the deaths on board. In fact, he had structured his whole importing business to avoid personal liability for anything. So the million dollar question is why would he kill himself?"

"I've asked myself that a hundred times," Jack confessed. "The only answer I've come up with is that he was a respected judge about to be tainted by a tragic event. He'd have been humiliated. Maybe that was more than he could take."

"You're wrong. *Pacific Dawn* had made many trips carrying human cargo, so I decided to find out what had happened to all the people who had reached San Francisco alive. The ship's crew couldn't, or wouldn't, tell us anything except that vehicles showed up to take the human cargo away. So I started over, looking at everything we had. I found out that my investigator who examined your father's home computer had been blocked by password protection. I brought in our IT specialist to break through the password. That gave us access to almost all of the folders, and we found nothing useful in any of them. According to the IT guy, your father must have had a professional encrypt the remaining three folders. It took quite a while for my man to decipher the encryption, but he finally cracked it." Calder paused and studied the girls cantering around the perimeter of the ring, and then looked back, eyes full of contempt. "That's how I found out why your father pulled the trigger."

The sounds of the arena vanished from Jack's consciousness. Calder's tone warned him to brace himself.

"It's all there," Calder said. "Peck Strider bought girls in Mexico and brought them to San Francisco, Sacramento and San Jose. They were kept in secret dormitories with handlers who raped them repeatedly to break them down, to control them. Then they were delivered to johns and special parties. They were little girls, mostly under fourteen. The computer memory held photographs of them having sex with—well, it was revolting." Calder's eyes glittered with hostility.

"Shut up!" *Not my father.* Jack slammed his fist on the bench. Kids in the arena looked up at him, startled. He glared at Calder, willing him to back down.

Calder was unfazed. "That computer was a cesspool, including an e-mail your father sent to a man in Salina Cruz. Your father threatened to stop buying from the man if he kept sending girls who had contracted HIV. That means those girls have been spreading the virus all over the Bay Area. Maybe some of the judge's buddies at the yacht club who sent gin and tonics over to his table got HIV from his little girls."

"I don't believe you. My father would never have been involved in any of that." He didn't believe Calder because he *couldn't*.

"You will. In my office I told you we had an autopsy performed on your father, but I hadn't received the results at that time. When I got them they showed that he had HIV. He knew that if he were jailed he'd be given a physical that would reveal HIV. So in addition to human trafficking, the world, including other inmates, would know he'd been having sex with girls under 14 years old. *That's* why he killed himself."

Calder's words entered Jack's ears, but his brain couldn't make sense of them. Then he remembered Peck saying to Anita, 'I'm afraid you're already a dead woman.' That meant . . . Dear God, it couldn't be! Peck had known he was HIV positive, and he'd had sex with Anita anyway. Anita had schemed to make a killing by marrying Peck. Instead, he had doomed her.

"Normally," Calder said, "I wouldn't reveal this much about an ongoing investigation. In this case I want you to know I intend to prove you made blood money out of this. I will never drop this investigation."

Calder stopped and looked at his wristwatch. Then he said, "Right about now, vice squads are raiding those dormitories to rescue what's left of the . . . girls." His voice choked off for several seconds. "This will be on every front page and on every television news program in California tomorrow. I want everyone who might be infected to get the warning." He stared at Jack with what felt like X-ray vision, then stood. "Does it sound like I'm taking this personally? I damn sure am. See my daughter down there? She's the same age as those poor girls who—"

He was so furious he couldn't finish. He started down the stairs, then turned back to face Jack. "When my family emigrated from Mexico, my father changed my name from Ricardo Calderon Ramirez to Rick Calder. Bastards like your father have exploited my people for decades. It's payback time."

Calder's animosity was like a heat wave. Peck had done the crime but, if Calder got his way, Jack would do the time.

Chapter 11

June 13
8:30 a.m.

SITTING IN HIS office at S & S with the door closed, Jack was still rocked by the filthy scenario involving his father that Calder had dumped on him, the same father who had always berated him, had never found him good enough.

He'd read the article in the morning *Chronicle*, so he wasn't surprised when the call came summoning him to Sinclair's office. He walked slowly down the corridor. When he arrived, Mrs. Pounders nodded curtly, and he entered.

Sinclair, seated behind his desk, looked up, eyes narrow over his glasses. "Hell of a thing. Couldn't be more damaging." He held up the front section of the *Chronicle* between two fingers, as if he'd just pulled it from the garbage bin. He didn't invite Jack to sit.

"This is the worst thing I've ever gone through," Jack said.

"I meant for the firm. I had a call today from a guy I haven't heard from since the Berlin Wall came down. And from a French son-of-a-bitch I knew in . . . well, doesn't matter. Just a shame that my firm's name was mentioned so prominently. I'll make Rick Calder wish he hadn't dragged me into this."

"The fallout will be bad for a few days, but then—"

"You have no idea how bad," Sinclair interrupted, angry. "It's *my* name on the door." He slammed his hand on his desk.

Sinclair's office door opened. Stan Simms stood framed in the doorway, filling it side-to-side. He shook his head, giving Jack a menacing look. "For Christ's sake, why is Strider still here? I said—"

"Hold on, Stan. I'm just finishing a discussion with him. I'll bring you up to date in a few minutes. Getting excited is bad for your—" He gestured at Simms' huge body. "—everything."

"I'm not kidding about this," Simms shot back and closed the door behind him loudly enough to register his disapproval.

When he looked back, Sinclair's face showed his exasperation. "That's a sample of what I've been getting this morning, Jack. Your presence in the firm is killing me."

"That article is about Peck, not me. And you knew about his problems when you hired me."

"Just a damn minute," Sinclair snarled. "I knew nothing about the scandal delivered to my breakfast table this morning—child whores, HIV, and all the rest. Simms has called a meeting of the senior members of the firm to move that we fire you. He thinks he can scare up enough votes from old farts worried about protecting their fat bonuses."

Suddenly the walls were closing in. He'd walked away from Stanford Law. Now Simms was trying to get him fired. This time he'd fight. If he didn't, everything he'd worked so damned hard for would go up in smoke.

"I can tell from your face," Sinclair said, "that you're thinking about going to war with us over this. Not only would that be a bad mistake, but it won't be necessary. I'm the managing partner, and I won't be stampeded by Stan Simms or anyone else. But I have to give Stan something, so I've come up with a solution that will satisfy everyone."

Jack doubted that any solution that worked for him would be acceptable to Stan Simms. He waited for Sinclair to continue.

"One of our overseas offices might be the place for you. I thought maybe the Paris office."

Sinclair's hard eyes warned him that nothing was open for debate. If he didn't accept, Sinclair was ready for an execution. Besides, Paris wasn't exactly a hardship post.

"That might be best all around," Jack agreed.

"Good, good. I was sure you'd see it my way. As I said, I had the Paris branch in mind, but then I had a better idea. When I bought a law firm in Buenos Aires a few years ago, I got its field office in Mexico City as part of the deal. I've steered a lot of clients to them, Americans doing business in Mexico, but I don't trust the managing partner. That's where I'm sending you."

The corner of Sinclair's mouth lifted slightly, and Jack mentally cursed him. Sinclair had trapped him, dangling Paris to get his agreement, and then switching to Mexico City.

"So it's settled. Now here's the situation. One of our biggest clients, Palmer Industries, has its main hazardous waste treatment plant in Juarez, Mexico. Right now they could be headed for big trouble. A Mexican government agency is hell-bent on putting them out of business, locking the doors. That makes me so mad I'd like to go down there and kick some ass." He shook his right fist. "Then, after I saw the morning paper I realized that you're the right man to protect that plant, to stop the bureaucrats cold. Your 'brand' as an environmentalist has taken a hit around here, but should still be okay down there."

"Sounds like you're sending me into exile," Jack stated tightly.

"Not at all. Your environmental credentials are money in the bank for that client." Sinclair stood. "I'll send the files to your office and set up a meeting right away with Arthur Palmer. Oh, and I'll tell him to bring his brother Edward."

"How soon will I be transferred to Mexico City?"

"Immediately. You'll be working out of that office, but it won't exactly be a transfer. You'll be on assignment to pull Palmer Industries out of the ditch. You'll report only to me."

Another crossroads. Maybe it really was time to walk away.

Before he could open his mouth, Sinclair said, "Jack, your future is in your own hands. Pull off a big win for Palmer Industries, and I'll stash you in the Mexico City office for a year or so until the climate is less toxic around here. Then I'll bring you back. I could even make you head of a new department dealing with water and environmental issues. But I want to be clear about one thing. If you blow this, we go our separate ways."

He came from behind his desk and put a hand on Jack's shoulder. "Remember, you owe me a big one."

For what, being manipulated like a puck in a pinball machine? On the other hand, despite all the heat, instead of firing him outright Sinclair had found him a safe haven.

"All right, we're done here. Mrs. Pounders will send you the details."

As Jack reached the door, Sinclair called after him. "By the way, you know the judicial appointment that twit in the governor's office talked to you about? Well, that's off the table now. Tough break." Sinclair turned away and reached for the phone.

How in God's name had Sinclair known about that?

Chapter 12

June 16
3:00 p.m.

JACK HAD FOUND plenty of work to do during the couple of days after his meeting with Sinclair, but he now had only one client who mattered, Palmer Industries. Until he could meet the Palmer brothers, he felt like he was treading water. Finally, the call had come to join Sinclair in his office.

Minutes after Jack seated himself in Sinclair's office, Mrs. Pounders entered and announced quietly, "Sir, Mr. Arthur Palmer and Mr. Edward Palmer have arrived."

She was a buxom lady wearing a gray tailored blouse. Silver hair in a tight bun, Mrs. Pounders had the air of a woman who never used her first name. She looked only at Sinclair and paid no more attention to Jack than she would to a floor lamp.

Sinclair, from behind his desk, glanced at her over the top of his half-glasses. "Invite the gentlemen to join us."

Arthur Palmer walked in first, keen eyes scanning the room like a hawk alert to the possibility of a pigeon within reach. An expensive black suit failed to disguise his lanky frame. He nodded at Sinclair, squinted at Jack without a greeting, and strode directly to the great expanse of window-wall. "Storm coming," he said sourly.

Edward came in smiling broadly, suit coat open, revealing a bulging belly. The crown of his head looked more than bald. It looked polished.

Sinclair stood and gestured toward Arthur. "Jack Strider, meet Arthur Palmer, head of Palmer Industries. His brother Edward here is Chief Financial Officer."

Edward stepped up to pump Jack's hand.

"Strider," Arthur grunted and walked over to a long bookcase. When he pulled on the spine of a volume in a row of Pacific Law Reporters, a chest-high three-foot long section of false casebook covers swung out, revealing a well-stocked bar. "I need a damn drink," he announced. Choosing Glenlivet, he poured a tall glass half-full, tossed in three ice cubes, looked at the glass, and fished one out.

Jack had inferred from reading the files that Arthur Palmer provided the high-octane energy that powered the corporate motor. Edward was the cautious mechanic who kept the motor tuned. Their need for legal counsel over the years had been similar to that of most major corporations except in one important way. The company had been cited repeatedly for violations of federal and state environmental protection laws and had paid hundreds of thousands of dollars in legal fees to defeat enforcement. They were environmental barbarians he'd rather see prosecuted.

But the cold reality was that to keep his Supreme Court dream alive, he needed the job at S & S, and that meant working with Arthur Palmer, even if the man had a personality like a T-Rex. Jack would give Palmer Industries the best defense he could, as long as he could change the company in the process. It was the only way to get his career back on track.

Was he rationalizing? Selling out? Doing something he'd regret? No, he had the tools to turn this into a win-win.

Mrs. Pounders returned, setting a sterling tea service on an oval table and adding two ginger cookies beside each teacup. She backed away, closing the door with no audible click.

"Come over here, gentlemen. We'll sit around this old table of mine." Sinclair gestured with a casual courtliness that made Jack think of President Kennedy inviting guests to be seated in the Oval Office. As they settled in Chippendale chairs, Edward's chair creaked in protest. "Don't worry, Edward, that chair has supported you for years. It won't let you down now, and neither will I."

"I need all the support I can get." Edward's smile showed he took no offense at the joke at his expense. "Our problems in Mexico have pegged my blood pressure in the red zone."

"As I told you on the phone, I've assigned Jack to deal with those problems."

Arthur's mouth looked like he'd bitten an unripe persimmon. "Hold on, Justin, this guy Strider isn't even on your letterhead. I don't need some goddamn amateur giving me advice."

Sinclair chuckled. "Always ready to give a man the benefit of the doubt, eh, Arthur? As for Jack being an amateur, in one sense you're right. As a Stanford undergraduate, Jack rowed single shell in the Olympics. A damned good amateur I'd say."

"I don't care if he paddled around the goddamn planet," Arthur said. "The Mexican government didn't challenge us to a canoe race. They're trying to shut down our goddamn plant."

Sinclair was unperturbed. "As I was about to say, Jack clerked for Chief Judge Warner on the Eighth Circuit, then taught international business law, riparian rights—that means water law, in case you don't know—and environmental policy. Youngest person to win a Distinguished Professor award."

That almost persuaded Jack that Sinclair respected him, but not quite.

Arthur took a drink and banged his glass down hard on the table. "All very nice, but his father was a . . . well, we all read the paper. It would look like hell for someone named Strider to represent Palmer Industries."

Sinclair's glance at Jack conveyed the message that Arthur's reaction was exactly what he'd predicted. Peck was a millstone around Jack's neck, and a negative for the firm. Then Sinclair surprised him.

"Forget what his father did," Sinclair said. "Jack will be working in Mexico, far away from the *San Francisco Chronicle*. And let's not be hypocritical, Arthur, there're no saints in this room."

"All right, damn it, I'll go along . . . for now." Arthur took a long swallow of Glenlivet. "Strider, guys like you always do their homework, so you know we moved our plant to Mexico because the union went on strike at our main operation in Concord. That piled up tons of carcinogenic and toxic waste we treat for manufacturing plants from Boston to San Diego. We were looking at a dozen lawsuits, maybe even—" Arthur practically spat the word. "—bankruptcy."

"Even Justin," Edward said, "couldn't come up with any more legal rabbits to pull out of his hat."

Arthur continued. "At the last minute, Tom Montana, one of our VPs, convinced us to move our operations to Juarez, Mexico. His plan saved the company and tripled the profits of our best year."

Jack remembered a memo written by the S & S lawyer handling Palmer Industries prior to the move. It outlined the strict Mexican environmental protection laws governing the handling of hazardous waste. A handwritten note attached to the file copy said that the decision to move to Mexico had been made with Justin Sinclair's full support.

"So that's how we wound up being a—what the hell is that word, Edward?"

"*Maquiladora.* It's time for you to remember it."

"You know what that word means, Strider?" Arthur challenged.

What a condescending bastard. "It originally referred to plants along the U.S.-Mexico border that assembled products for companies based in other countries. Now it includes operations like yours that provide mostly services." He couldn't resist adding, "By the way, most people call them *maquilas.*"

Arthur shrugged that off. "Anyway, Montana located an 800-acre site on the outskirts of Juarez, across the Rio Grande from El Paso. We bought the site from PEMEX, the giant Mexican oil company, along with a dozen warehouses and the tanks they used to store oil. Montana greased the deal through the bureaucrats, all the way to the top." He took another drink. "Then we invested millions in equipping the plant to treat the most toxic waste known to man. Montana even got a special water line run from the city to the plant site. That's why I take good care of Montana. I reward people who get things done no matter what it takes. That's also why four hundred union pricks who used to work for us are now playing pinochle all day out in Concord." He lifted his glass in a mocking toast.

Four hundred fired. Wonder if the people who pushed passage of NAFTA saw that coming?

"For quite a while, things were fine," Edward said. "Suddenly we're being hassled, just like with the unions, except this time we're buried in citations."

"What we have is a sweet deal we're damn sure going to protect," Arthur broke in. "Profits are piling up faster than we can get to the bank. And that, dear brother, is what it's all about."

Edward struggled to his feet. Light from the chandelier outlined tension lines around his eyes. "We make money, sure, but Montana swore we'd have no problems in Mexico. Now the government is trying to shut us down. How much money will we make if that happens?"

"Calm down, Edward," Sinclair cut in. "I think it's time to get some input from the front lines. I'll tell Mrs. Pounders to set up Montana for a video conference on that monitor in the corner."

Within three minutes, Jack was looking at Tom Montana on a 30-inch screen. The man was leaning back in a leather chair, one elbow hooked over its back. He had the air of a minor movie star—deep set eyes, thick eyebrows, sleek black hair swept back without a part. His unlined face gave no clue to his age.

He'd obviously adapted to his Mexican environment. He wore a *guayabera* shirt designed not to be tucked in, white with yellow stallions embroidered on it, and unbuttoned half way down his bare chest.

Without a greeting, Arthur took control. "For God's sake, tell Edward there is nothing to worry about down there."

"Just a few bureaucratic flunkies jerking us around," Montana said. "I've told you that the people at the top know the Mexican economy lives or dies on the money *maquilas* bring in. I'll take care of this."

"You always say that," Edward said. "But when I ask you questions, you give me the shortest answer you can get away with." He grumbled under his breath, "I want our company back."

"Relax," Arthur said. "Tom keeps me posted on everything."

Edward's round face flushed. "That's what I'm saying. You've cut me out of the loop."

"I'm sure there's no conspiracy here." Sinclair projected his calm voice between them. "Tom, Jack Strider is here with us. He's familiar with Palmer Industries' business, and he'll be in our Mexico City office to work with me on this problem. Jack, do you have any questions for Tom?"

Out of the corner of his eye, Jack caught Sinclair watching him with an appraising look, waiting to see how he'd deal with the situation.

"Good afternoon, Tom. Do you know what provoked the government into going after the company?"

"No mystery there. Either some sleazy competitor made ridiculous charges, or it's a bureaucrat looking for a payoff."

"Listen, Justin—" Arthur looked disgusted. "—this is wasting my time. It's Montana's job to keep the plant operating. He's doing that and has my full support, whatever it takes. I don't need Strider's help."

"And I don't want any outsiders down here," Montana added. "We take care of our own problems."

"Whether you want his help or not," Sinclair said, "you *need* it."

"I may be able to turn this into a win for Palmer Industries," Jack said. "If it's harassment, I can try to stop it. If the problem is more than that, a rational compromise with regulatory authorities usually works out better than defending against injunctions and lawsuits. A cost benefit analysis could show that in the long term—"

"Long term, my ass," Arthur growled.

"All right, gentlemen," Sinclair broke in, "let's wrap this up. Arthur, you pay me to protect you. That's what I'm doing. Tom, Jack will give you a call in a few days to get whatever he needs." Before Montana could respond, Sinclair touched a button. The monitor went black.

"I'll tell you again," Edward glared at his brother, "we made a big mistake caving in to that sweetheart bonus deal he demanded."

"He doesn't have a chance in hell of meeting the terms we set. He'll never collect one dime of that bonus," Arthur said. "We outsmarted him."

"But if he does meet the terms, we have to pay him millions."

"Edward," Arthur said, "I'm fed up with you looking at a peach and calling it a damned lemon. Leave it alone."

"Montana's a loose cannon. We can go to jail for condoning what he's doing."

"You can't condone what you don't know about, so butt out."

"But we *do* know about it. When we first went into business down there, the border guards stopped our trucks and buried us in paperwork and fines. Suddenly, the problems stopped. There's only one way Montana could have pulled that off. By ignoring it, we sent him a message. This time it's not some penny ante border guards. He'll try to bribe the federal government."

Sinclair held up his hand to stop the bickering, then took off his glasses and slowly polished each lens with a handkerchief, a telltale sign he was losing patience. "Then it's settled," he said. "Worst case, we go to court or a Hearing and kick their ass. If everything else fails, there are still a few heavyweights in Washington willing to do a favor for an old man. In the meantime, Jack goes to Mexico City. His pro-environment reputation is exactly what you need right now."

Arthur said, nodding at Jack, "Is he one of those goddamn environmental nuts?"

"Of course not."

"All right, goddamn it, but on one condition." Arthur shook his finger at Jack. "Leave Montana alone. Period. And remember that the client is always right." He stood and headed for the door, followed by Sinclair. Edward hurried to catch up.

Jack sat in silence, waiting for Sinclair to return. The meeting had been a disaster. Sinclair was a master at creating an illusion, so maybe he had a strategy he'd chosen not to reveal to the Palmers. If he didn't have something clever up his sleeve, Jack's job prospects would swirl down the toilet bowl.

Sinclair walked back in. "Arthur's a hothead, so stay in bounds."

"I'll keep that in mind. Sounds as if Montana is effectively running the company."

"I'm sure he keeps Arthur informed, at least about anything he wants to hear."

"Then Edward was right. They've cut him out."

"Edward would raise hell if he had proof that Montana is, shall we say, cutting corners. Arthur's the realist. He understands that people who do business in Mexico get crap on their boots."

"If Montana tries to bribe his way out of this, Arthur may get crap on more than his boots. I mean fines, being shut down, even prison."

"We'll keep that from happening."

"But if they're doing serious harm, we have a duty to advise them to stop."

"Arthur's not paying us to lecture him on morality."

"The stuff Palmer Industries processes is deadly. We're obligated to—"

"We're obligated only to advise the client when asked."

Jack sucked in a breath. *Dead end. Time to change the subject.*

"Edward distrusted Montana even before these citations. Do you know why?"

"That bonus deal rankles him so he watches the financial statements like a hawk. Profits are so much higher than projected that he believes

Montana must be cutting expenses way below budget."

"If that's what the government citations are about, then we—"

"That's enough. You're not this firm's chaplain." He moved behind his desk, ending the meeting.

JACK WALKED SLOWLY down the corridor from Sinclair's office. This time, the politicians' Wall of Fame barely registered on him.

When he reached his office, he dropped into his chair. He was in a field full of land mines and needed some kind of edge—and fast. He'd talk with one of the other lawyers who had dealt with Palmer. The lawyer whose name showed up most often in the files had left the firm, but there were others. One was Debra Vanderberg. He'd seen her name in the Palmer files, handling some zoning matter. She'd been a student in two of his classes, riparian rights and, his toughest one, advanced international economics. He'd found her insightful and accurate. And very attractive, but hadn't been willing to cross the barrier between professor and student. When he'd seen her in the S & S hall a few days earlier, he'd wanted to stop, but was so pressed by preparing for Mexico he only waved. Thinking about her made him smile.

The career reversal between them now was dramatic. His career had the upward momentum of a soggy sparkler, while she was referred to as the firm's wonder child. Still, she was the perfect person to talk with about Palmer.

He tapped Debra's number into the interoffice phone.

The line was busy.

Another bad omen.

Chapter 13

June 16
7:00 p.m.

"I'M SORRY SIR, we're fully booked tonight," said the woman who answered the phone at Boulevard restaurant. "Would you like to make a dinner reservation for next Thursday?"

Not wanting to look for someplace else, Jack tested the firm's clout. "I'm a partner at Sinclair & Simms. Would you mind checking again?"

Without missing a beat, she replied, "Actually, if seven o'clock is okay we have a very nice corner table. And your name, sir?"

"Jack Strider. Dinner for two. Thanks."

He'd finally gotten through to Debra and, on the spur of the moment, decided to invite her to dinner. He needed to get out of the office.

When he and Debra entered the restaurant, the hostess called him by name twice as she led them to the big money table. The sommelier arrived and handed him the wine list in a black Moroccan leather folder, as if entrusting an heirloom. Jack made his selection without a glance at the right hand column.

Debra had seemed a little distant in the car, responding rather than initiating conversation. Still, as he looked at her across the table he was glad he'd kept calling until he reached her. Not only was she a brilliant lawyer, but she was familiar with the Palmer files, a good sounding board for his predicament. With her fine features, dark eyes, long silky black hair and tall, athletic figure, she was also the most beautiful woman in the room.

As soon as the ritual of sampling the white Bordeaux was finished, Jack raised his glass.

"Thanks for joining me on such short notice."

"My pleasure, but I'm puzzled. Except for a fly-by the other afternoon, I haven't seen you since law school. So this must be a business meeting—but Boulevard is not exactly a conference room. So what's up?"

"It *is* business, but I'd like to hold off on that and talk about something more pleasant first. Like about your personal background."

That was clumsy. He'd just asked the equivalent of what her zodiac sign was.

"You mean my family?"

He nodded.

She sipped her wine and gave him an amused expression. "Okay. My mother was Balinese, a painter. Father, an anesthesiologist. He's Dutch, the reason I'm tall. We lived in Amsterdam until he brought the family to San Francisco. Mother wanted me to be a dancer, but at sixteen I switched from ballet lessons to tai chi and karate. That about sums up my childhood."

"How did you wind up in law school?"

"In Holland, the law is almost sacred. In the U.S.—oh, don't get me started. Anyway, in high school I wrote a paper called 'Balancing the Scales of Justice.' I thought being a lawyer would help me do that. So that was my first step toward Stanford Law."

"Is your dream coming true at S & S?"

Her quick frown said she didn't like his comment, but she blew it off. "Of course not. This isn't a lifetime gig. After graduation, despite my scholarships, I owed $70,000 in loans. S & S offered me a lot of money, so I'm using this firm to get what I need. Sort of like you. There must be some reason you chose this sausage factory."

"Sore subject right now," he said.

The bantering expression left her face. Her dark eyes looked steadily at him. "Fair enough, but can we talk about the gorilla in the room?" She sipped her Bordeaux without breaking eye contact. "You lost your father a couple of weeks ago. Now there's all that awful stuff about him in the *Chronicle*. Are you okay?"

His defenses rose like a shield. "Our relationship was complex, but, yeah, the way he died will be raw for me for a long time. And stories in the paper pretty much knocked the wind out of me. At least my friends on the faculty have been very supportive."

He wouldn't tell her about the call from the wife of a man who was infected with HIV by a girl Peck had smuggled in. Or the message left by Anita asking questions he could never answer.

"Of course your colleagues are supportive," she said. "They know who you really are. But there is one guy who isn't a fan. My secretary overheard Stan Simms in the elevator talking to another senior partner. It seems Simms has a real hard on, his words, about getting you out of the firm. He said the bad publicity about your father makes the firm look sleazy. Simms is a real bastard."

Fortunately, Simms' opinion of him was irrelevant. But if he didn't hit a home run in Mexico City, he could be out of the fast track law business for good. "Sinclair hired me, so I don't have to worry about Simms."

"Good. Now satisfy my curiosity about something else. I heard you spent half the afternoon with guys who make their living sending poison and jobs to Mexico. That surprised me. At Stanford, you had a reputation as an environmental white knight. Has something changed?"

"No, but it's true that Sinclair and I met with the Palmers."

"That must have been fun."

"Let's just say I didn't see eye to eye with Arthur Palmer. By the end of the meeting, I sort of had my tail caught in a ringer."

"I love a good tail-in-a-ringer story."

"This stays between the two of us."

"Done."

Since she'd already made clear how she felt about Palmer Industries, he told her about the toxic waste violations, Arthur Palmer's orders to keep away from Montana, and Sinclair's *laissez faire* attitude.

"I said we have a duty to advise the client not to break the law, especially when what they're doing may wind up poisoning some unknown number of people."

"What did our fearless leader say?"

"He pushed back, told me to leave it alone."

"We never know what to expect from him, except that he loves dealmaking and feeding his ego. Oh, and he detests one of his predecessors, Henry Kissinger. It's about the Nobel Prize."

"The morning I met him he seemed upset that Kissinger had won."

"More than upset, but let's go back to your situation. Here's a hypothetical. If your client told you he planned to murder the mayor, would you intervene?"

"What city?" He smiled. "Just kidding."

"If you're right about Palmer poisoning people, it sounds damn serious."

A server arrived to refill the wine glasses and recommend the Lobster Martinique. He then contemplated the ceiling as he awaited their decisions.

After they ordered, Jack said, "Of course, it's serious, but Arthur Palmer is only worried that the Mexican government may shut down his plant."

"Let me guess. Sinclair wants to use your pro-environment track record to improve the odds for Palmer, and to hell with your principles."

"That's about it."

"Even if you agreed, how much can you do from here?"

"Actually, I'll be on site in Mexico City."

"Wow! The office scuttlebutt let me down. We wondered where Sinclair intended to fit you into the firm. In fact, I thought we might be working together. How soon will you be back?"

"Could be a while." She didn't need to know he was being exiled, that his future was opaque.

A team of servers swooped in, laid out their dinners, and withdrew.

"Okay," she said. "While I'm digesting that bit of news, let's go back to a lawyer's duty in this situation."

Over Lobster Martinique, they talked about legal ethics, finding themselves in complete agreement. Their intense conversation about the law was a reminder of what a fine mind she had. She blew past irrelevant arguments, made sense of apparently contradictory points of view, and, damn it, she was so drop dead gorgeous he found it hard to concentrate.

"I don't see how you're going to defend what the Palmers are doing in Juarez."

"For one thing, I don't know yet what they're actually doing. Second, if they're guilty, I'll use pressure from the Mexican government to make them stop."

"Why not get Sinclair to have someone else in the firm handle it? He has plenty of guns on staff who wouldn't blink at helping a client serve poison cocktails to the neighbors." She gazed at him over the rim of her glass.

He tried to imagine how she must have seen him in law school—always in control of himself and the classroom, reasonable, analytical, easygoing, and sometimes humorous. And he'd said all the right things about protecting the environment. Now she might see him as selling out, letting Sinclair use him to bail out a ruthless client. He didn't like that.

"Look, you admit to using S & S to get what you need. The fact is, my father's acid rain burned me badly. Cut my options. So I *have* to represent Palmer, and I intend to succeed in Mexico."

She blinked several times, absorbing his serious tone. "And if you don't?"

He wasn't going there. "I will. And I've promised myself to pull it off without getting a scratch on my ethics."

She swirled the contents of her wineglass and turned away. "I made a promise to myself too. Not to bring up a certain topic tonight. But I just can't let it go."

She wasn't looking at him. A bad sign.

"It's something you did to me, and I've never gotten over it." She drained the wine, took a deep breath, then reached under her seat and came up with her purse.

"No, I've changed my mind again. I don't want to talk about it. Thanks for dinner. I'll catch a cab."

Before he could say a word, she was gone.

He had to wonder, was a day coming when things didn't get worse?

Chapter 14

June 17
2:00 p.m.

"FERNANDO! THE binoculars. Quick." Heidi Klein jumped up from the chaise longue and pointed to Banderas Bay and the Pacific Ocean. "They're back. This time they're hunting."

A pod of killer whales cruised by, working together to corral a colony of seals. This must be the same pod she'd seen playing a few hours earlier—spyhopping and flipper-slapping. They were amusing then. Now their 30-foot torpedo shapes with erect six-foot dorsal fins looked ominous as they moved in for a meal of seal.

Fernando rushed to her side with the binoculars. She caught his sideways glance and remembered she was topless. Well, what the hell. She could do whatever she wanted here. When she lost the pod in the sunlight glinting off the blue water, she eased back onto the chaise lounge.

Fernando set a fresh piña colada on the small table next to her and backed away. As she reached for the drink, her gaze stopped again on the copy of *Architectural Digest* lying on the table. There it was, Ranchero Casacaditas, her dream house pictured on the glossy cover. Arches, deeply inset windows, vaulted ceilings, gourmet kitchen, gym, open-air spa, and a thirty-meter infinity pool that seemed to flow over the edge of the cliff into the Pacific. A hedonist's paradise. She looked back over her shoulder at the actual house in the photographs. It might soon be hers, including the Wellington jet boat at the wharf. Renting the estate for five days had been one of her best decisions.

The French owners were asking five million U.S. Only the guarantee of the income from her new venture would make purchasing this paradise possible.

She reached for the cell phone and called the warehouse foreman she'd hired to supervise her new business. Pleased by the information he gave her, her next call was to the Christie's International real estate agent who represented the sellers of Ranchero Casacaditas. After some serious negotiating on her part, the owners accepted her offer so long as she made a down payment of $300,000 before close of business and put $500,000, all of it nonrefundable, in escrow within seven days. She arranged that all paperwork would show Heureux Ltd, a Bahamian corporation, as the buyer. One more call and the $300,000 was wired to the Christie's International account. She had done it.

She sent Fernando for the $300 bottle of Dom Perignon '90 she'd bought to celebrate the deal. After he removed the cork, she gave him a nod of dismissal, and he returned to the house—*her* house. She watched the mist of bubbles against the darker ocean backdrop, closed her eyes and took a long sip. Then she impulsively drained the flute. *There's fifty bucks down my throat.* She drank again, this time to her courage at committing to $800,000 out-of-pocket. She needed to make her next call before she lost her edge.

She entered her business associate's private cell phone number. No answer. Then she remembered there was a code. Call three times. Three different numbers of rings. By the time she called and disconnected three times she was thoroughly annoyed. When he finally answered, she ignored his greeting.

"How about coming up with a code that doesn't waste half the afternoon before you pick up? Besides, you must have caller ID, so you know it's me."

"Caller ID only tells me a call is coming from a certain phone. The code tells me whether it's you who is calling. It's a small price for what you're getting out of this." Having brushed off her complaint, he went on. "I take it the trucks have arrived."

"I just talked with my supervisor. The first three are there, stored in our Number 4 cargo building."

The delay was long enough that she wondered whether he'd heard her. Then he said in a tight voice, "They're transferring the loads on those trucks without you?"

"Calm down. I ordered my people never to touch those trucks without me present. I'll be back there in three hours." She would never tell him about buying the estate. The less he knew about her private life, the better. "Now, what about the cargo manifests?"

"The cargo containers are locked. Each incoming driver will hand you a sealed envelope with the manifest inside. Give them to your lead driver for the convoy. He must not open the package unless required to do so en route."

He's keeping the contents secret from me. She could make an issue of it, but if this deal blew up now, the purchase of Ranchero Casacaditas, and her $300,000 down payment, went with it. It didn't matter anyway, because he could fake the manifests, knowing she was unlikely to open the hazardous waste containers to check. She let it go.

"Why would anyone require the driver to open the manifest en route?" she asked.

"Your drivers will cross the U.S. border into Mexico. There's a remote possibility they'll have to hand over the cargo manifest."

Mexico? That knocked her off stride. Then the implications began to sink in. "My drivers aren't licensed for Mexico. My trucks aren't insured there."

"I'll send you instructions on how to handle the insurance, and your men will drive only to a location outside Ciudad Juarez, just a few miles across the border. They'll be wined and dined for a night and then make the turnaround trip the next afternoon. Very simple."

It wasn't simple at all. Red flags whipped in her mind. If the trucks were offloading in Juarez they could return right away. So why the overnight layover? It had to mean the trucks were continuing on to somewhere else with different drivers.

"Where does the cargo go when it leaves Juarez?"

"You don't need to know."

Then she saw what he'd done. The clever bastard had set up a double disconnect. The drivers who brought hazardous waste from around the country would assume her company was its final destination. They would unload and then head back to where they'd come from. The original shippers wouldn't know their cargo would then be loaded into her trucks and sent to another destination. First disconnect. Once her drivers got off in Juarez and holed up in some cathouse, neither they nor she would know the final destination. Second disconnect. Only he knew the whole route.

She chuckled. There was so much money in this deal for her that she didn't care what he did with the stuff so long as it didn't burn her.

"You're right. I don't need to know. Let's go back to crossing the border. We're shipping hazardous waste into a foreign country. Won't my trucks get hung up by Customs or security?"

"Legally, they can't touch them. I can explain, but I doubt you really care about the details."

He was such a condescending skunk. He used to pull her forward when they shook hands to throw her off balance, and then step inside her personal space to intimidate her. Well, his little tricks no longer worked.

"I *do* care. Spell it out."

"A California company wanted to open a hazardous waste treatment and disposal site in central Mexico. Local government hacks refused permission, so a World Bank court ordered Mexico to pay seventeen million for lost profits. They said NAFTA and WTO regulations trump local and national laws."

"I can't believe Congress agreed to that kind of 'super law.'"

"That provision slipped through because NAFTA legislation was complicated, and many big-business lobbyists pushed their own pieces of it. When they catch onto the implications of these rulings for America, you'll see a backlash even from the free-trade-at-any-cost crowd. The rulings mean Mexico can't use some crackpot local environmental laws to stop our shipments. And something else. I'm happy to dump this crap in Mexico. They've been whining for decades about the bad things Uncle Sam has done to them. Hell, they wouldn't even have a damned economy if the U.S. didn't keep propping up their sorry peso. They owe us."

"Right. I'll just have my drivers carry a copy of the World Bank court transcript."

"Kill the sarcasm. Tomorrow I'll tell you what border crossing they'll use—and I mean *only* that one. The guards will be expecting them and wave them through."

"You mean you're going to—"

"I mean what I said."

"But the border got much tighter after 9/11."

"Still no problem. These trucks are going *into* Mexico. The so-called tightening, which is a joke anyway, focuses on traffic coming *out* of Mexico into the U.S. Also, our cargo won't attract suspicion because we're hiding it in plain sight. Your trucks will be marked with the "Danger" logo, and the manifests clearly state that the cargo is hazardous. Guards will stay as far away as they can."

He had an answer for everything, as he always had. In this case, that was reassuring.

"Got it. As soon as I'm back, we'll switch the containers to our trucks. That just leaves one little detail. Your payment to me."

Some detail. That was the money she was counting on to fund the $500,000 due to the escrow in seven days.

"It always gets down to money. Well, I'm not paying you for the first load. I've had a lot of front-end expenses and, to be candid, this is a test to be sure you can handle your part."

"A test? Screw you! I run an international company just fine, so I can certainly handle this pissant business. And you need me to make this work." The son-of-a-bitch was trying to run over her again. She resented that almost as much as him withholding the money.

"You want to pull out now?" His voice was steely cold. "Just say so, and I'll have those trucks out of there before you're back."

She'd made the classic blunder, spending the money before it was in the bank. The $300,000 she'd already paid would be lost if she couldn't come up with the next $500,000. Now she'd have to get a bridge loan to do that. And she could never handle the mortgage payments without this deal.

She could hardly make herself say the words: "I'm in."

And, she said to herself, *I have a long memory.* That made her feel a little better until she remembered, *so does he.*

Chapter 15

June 20
9:15 a.m.

JACK'S TAXI RIDE to SFO was uneventful except for the uncomfortable feeling of being ridden out of town on a rail. He checked in at a computer terminal and passed through security.

"Hey, *compadre,* did you think I'd let you go without saying *adios?*"

The question came from a woman wearing a gray business suit. Her black hair flowed from beneath a floppy red sombrero with yellow fringe around its perimeter that concealed her face. But he recognized Debra's voice, and his sour mood evaporated.

"You're on this flight?" He couldn't believe it.

"No such luck," Debra said.

"Then how did you get all the way to this gate?"

"The Airport Authority is one of my clients. I have more than enough pull to get a gate pass." She gave him a firm handshake, then laughed. "Oh, what the hell."

She dropped the sombrero on the floor, wrapped her arms around him, stretched up on her toes and kissed him soundly.

Wow! That caught him by surprise. He was eager to continue, but she stepped back, head cocked a little.

"I came bearing an apology," she said. "At dinner, I let some of my old stuff about you jump up and bite me. I shouldn't have walked out. I'm sorry about that."

He was still off balance, so all he could manage was, "What 'old stuff' are you talking about?"

She smiled, shook her head. "We don't have time to go into that now. Listen, while you're exploring Aztec ruins and drinking margaritas, think of me working my tail off in the salt mine."

She scooped up the sombrero, walked briskly away, and waved without looking back.

As the 747 lifted heavily into a slow southbound arc a short time later, he looked through the window into the night sky. The morning after Debra walked out on him at Boulevard, he'd gone to her office to find out why.

Her assistant said she'd just left for a trial in Miami. Not wanting to deal with it by phone, his question had remained unanswered.   It still was, but the effort she'd made to meet him at SFO lifted his spirits. And made him sorry he was leaving.

He signaled to the flight attendant. "Scotch, single malt please." He slipped out his MP3 player and listened to the melodious voice of the teacher refreshing his rusty Spanish.

3:15 p.m.

A mid-afternoon haze shrouded Mexico City—a bad omen for getting a fresh start. After his luggage was X-rayed to check for guns, he quickly wheeled it through immigration, customs and security. Unlike their American counterparts, Mexican officials seemed only mildly interested in what entered their country.

He had less than an hour before his four o'clock meeting with Fidelio Ramos, managing partner of the local S & S office. Given the traffic, he had to go straight to the meeting. Confronted by a dozen shouting taxi drivers, he chose a man wearing a San Francisco Giants cap. The moment the driver spotted a tiny opening in traffic, he swung his old Buick Century full speed into the six-lane destruction derby. Looking out the cab window, Jack already missed the steep hills and sea breezes of San Francisco.

When the taxi jolted to a stop, double-parked at a busy corner in the central business district, a chorus of horns blared from behind. Jack stepped onto a sidewalk crowded with well-dressed men and women trying to maneuver around beggars and street musicians.

Three young girls closed around him holding up watercolors for sale. Their shirts were worn; their bare feet black with street grime. He'd read there were thousands like them around the city trying to earn a few pesos on the streets.

"*Señor Americano.*" The youngest held a painting high over her head. "*Compra de mí.* Buy from me."

About a foot square, the painting was a Spanish galleon drawn with the sparse lines of Picasso. The price on the small tag was cheap, but he didn't want a painting at any price. He pulled out his wallet, took out thirty pesos, less than three dollars, and replaced the wallet. Keeping his luggage in front of him so it wouldn't disappear, he handed her the money as a gift. She threw her arms around his waist and the others crowded in, laughing and clapping.

He grabbed his bags and set off toward the skyscraper in mid-block. It was show time.

On the thirty-eighth floor, the elevator door opened into the firm's private reception area. Beyond a discreet fountain in the center of the room, the receptionist sat inside a semicircular counter of clear glass. Behind her, spotlights focused on two-foot-tall words in raised brass letters. "SINCLAIR & SIMMS."

Designers had spent a fortune to recreate the affluence of the home office, but the result had neither the elegance of San Francisco nor the soul of Mexico.

"Good morning, I'm Jack Strider. *Señor* Ramos is expecting me." He reached to get a business card from his wallet. It wasn't there. He checked all his pockets. His wallet was gone.

The young woman watched impassively and then called Ramos. A portly man with a Pancho Villa mustache immediately strode into the reception area.

"*Buenos días, Señor* Strider. A pleasure to meet you." Ramos took Jack's hand in both of his. "Join me in my office for coffee."

"Thank you, but I have a problem. My wallet is missing. I had it five minutes ago when I paid the taxi driver. And then I gave some money to a little girl selling a painting on the street."

"Were there several kids, and did they crowd around you?" Ramos asked.

The receptionist covered her giggles with her fingers.

"I guess they did."

"Then you've just been introduced to street crime in Mexico City. Soon as they saw where you keep your wallet, one slipped in and—" He shrugged. "—you know the rest."

"I'll go back down there right now." Then his brain caught up with his anger. "But I have no proof, and the wallet is probably already blocks away. Damn it, that wallet has my ID, credit cards, money—"

"My secretary will handle cancellation and replacements, including IDs, and I'll send you ten thousand pesos. So, shall we have that coffee now?"

No point in staying angry; time to get down to business, Jack told himself.

After coffee was served, Ramos said, "We're a young office, but we have some of the best lawyers in the city, twenty-six altogether."

"Having Justin Sinclair at the top of the letterhead must help with recruiting."

"Yes, everyone knows the firm is very successful in the U.S. But—" Ramos paused, as if choosing his words carefully. "—some older lawyers won't join us because they disagree with certain of his actions when he was Secretary of State. I certainly understand their feelings."

"Certain actions?"

"It was a long time ago, not worth going into. Naturally, I meant no criticism of Mr. Sinclair."

"Naturally."

Ramos changed the subject. "I've been told you'll be working on the legal affairs of one American client doing business in Mexico. I regret Mr. Sinclair wasn't confident that one of my lawyers could do the job, but—" He shrugged. "—that's the way it is with foreign ownership."

Ramos had just taken two quick shots at Sinclair. So there was resentment on this end of the equation, distrust on the other.

Ramos leaned forward and spoke more softly. "I'm afraid I have something unpleasant to tell you." His eyes suddenly became hard. "One of your San Francisco partners told one of our lawyers about your father and the young girls he stole from Mexico."

Ouch. Simms had sent his vendetta south. Jack felt his face flush, but that was the only reaction he was going to let Ramos see.

"What my father did was reprehensible, but I knew nothing about it. Maybe while I'm in Mexico I can do something to—"

"Maybe, maybe not." Ramos's tone was hostile.

So much for the new beginning. Was this place going to be a another snakepit?

Chapter 16

June 25
9:30 p.m.

THE TROUBLED EYES and turned down mouth reflected in the bar mirror beside Jack's table looked like they belonged to a stranger. But it was his own face, reflecting his aggravation after days of trying to pin down the lawyers from the Office of the Attorney General for Protection of the Environment—known as PROFEPA—to a meeting time.

After each frustrating day of reviewing paperwork and generally spinning his wheels, he started the evening at Café la Selva, sitting alone among hip artist types who either had no worries or, if they did, blew them off after sundown. The server set down a generous shot of Zacapa Centenario, a rum aged for 23 years in oak barrels. After four days of experimentation, he could taste the vanilla, cloves and cinnamon, and appreciate the aromas of the different brands.

As soon as the rum had begun to take effect, he walked down Calle Michoacan to Fonda Garufo, an Argentine steakhouse where he ordered dinner for a little ballast. The sidewalk tables were fenced in, and an armed guard stood at one end to protect patrons from thieves looking for prey. Toward the end of his meal, he noticed that his taste buds were no longer aware of the spices on the Redfish Veracruzano.

After watching the parade of streetwalkers for a while, he moved on to Bar Nuevo Leon where foreign correspondents gathered to mix alcohol with gossip, sharing stories about exotic places.

He sipped his Drambuie slowly, stretching out the night, delaying his return to his penthouse condo in La Condesa Colonia that S & S had provided for him.

How had he wound up in Mexico, his bright future jerked away? Was representing Palmer Industries the first step on the slippery slope to becoming the kind of lawyer he detested? Maybe Peck had started going bad just like this, sacrificing his principles to pursue a goal he considered worth it. Everyone chases something, not watching their footing, not noticing what they step in—or on. Would that happen to him?

Before he could come up with any answers to his questions, a very tan *gringo* walked in, tilting slightly off center, a few sheets to the wind. He scanned the room, obviously looking for someone. Spotting a free chair at Jack's table, he came over.

"Hey, mate, mind if I fill this chair for a couple of minutes until my friend shows up?"

Jack nodded that it was okay. He wasn't in the mood for bar chat, but the newcomer was. In a syrupy Louisiana drawl he talked about a favorite restaurant and Mexican women.

"I'm a freelance pilot based in the Copper Canyon. Lots of action up that way." He tossed a card on the table that read, "Gano LeMoyne" and bore a photograph of a P-51 Mustang fighter.

"That your plane?" Jack asked, to be polite.

"Just for air shows. I have another one for deliveries. If the money's right, I'll deliver anything, absolutely, positively anywhere."

After a few minutes of conversation, Gano saw his friend arrive, shook hands with Jack, and walked away.

Jack was relieved not to have any more company. He had to figure out an ethical way to stay in the law business and get back on track for the Supreme Court of the United States, or SCOTUS as most lawyers called it. If he couldn't do that, he'd say "to hell with you" to Sinclair and go sailing in the Caribbean, which would be a one-way trip for his career. If he pissed off the elders of the law tribes, they'd never let him back in.

Impulsively, he left Bar Nueva Leon and walked back to his La Condesa neighborhood, inhabited by rich pseudo-hippies and home of the local bureau of the *New York Times*. He'd heard it called the Greenwich Village of Mexico City. When he reached the entrance to the condo he still felt restless, so he kept walking until he was in a low-income *colonia* where he stopped at a tiny open-air restaurant under a grove of dusty elm trees. As he sat enjoying a Bohemia beer, a wiry man wearing a pair of sunglasses walked slowly up to his rickety table.

"Pardon me, *señor.* You are American?"

"Yes. California."

"I lived in California for many years," the man said in heavily accented English. "I picked grapes near Fresno. Maybe we could talk for a minute? I hear so little English in this *colonia.*" He pulled off the dark glasses.

"Please sit. Have a beer?" Jack turned to wave for service.

"No, *señor.* No beer. Thank you." He sat tentatively in the other chair. His khakis were bleached white. The red and green stripes on his shirt were faded. His eyes were deep set, cheekbones sharp. Hard to tell if it was Indian blood or . . . hunger.

"My name's Jack Strider." He stretched his hand across the table.

"I am Luis-Felipe Ibanez. In California they called me Lou." The way he said "Lou" made it clear how he felt about the Anglo nickname.

After listening to some of Luis-Felipe's experiences in the semidesert of southern California, Jack asked, "These people," he gestured at the men and boys standing in groups near the side of the road or idly kicking a scuffed soccer ball among themselves, "how do they earn a living, pay for food and a place to stay?"

"No real jobs around here. Some have never had a job. Others get paid, not much, for breaking their backs for a few days. Some have sisters who go to the border to work in *maquilas* and send money home. But now some women forget their families and save up to get into the U.S. Then their families go hungry, maybe nothing but beans and some corn."

What a contrast with the States with its safety net of homeless shelters, public housing, food banks, Medicaid, welfare, and the rest.

Luis-Felipe went on. "Some turn bad. That one," he said, barely nodding toward a hawk-faced man in a flashy L.A. Lakers warm-up jacket, "comes here to hire mules. They make a delivery for him, they get five dollars. They get caught, they go to jail. He doesn't even bail them out."

Jack knew there were plenty of that type in many low-income neighborhoods in the States, vultures who preyed on despair and addiction. He stared hard at the L.A. Laker fan as if that would let him know how he felt.

"I have no right," Luis-Felipe said quietly, "and it shames me, but I have a favor to ask."

"Of course. What is it?"

"Water. One liter to take with me? Where I live, we have none."

"Good Lord!" Jack shook his head in disbelief.

Luis-Felipe stood. "I have offended you. I'm sorry."

"No. No. I'll get plenty of water." He waved toward the bartender and placed the order.

When the plastic bottles of water arrived at the table, Luis-Felipe examined the neck of each.

"What's the matter?"

"Sometimes this man sells water that came out of the tap, not pure. It makes everyone sick. These are all right because he knows I will check the seal. Now *Señor* Jack, you must leave here. The later it gets, the more dangerous it is, especially for outsiders. *Con muchas gracias.*" He touched his heart with his right fist, picked up the bottles with wrinkled hands and walked across the road with dignity.

Luis-Felipe hadn't wanted conversation. It had been about water from the start. Jack realized the man had no choice.

He watched Luis-Felipe disappear into a cluster of one-story, mud-brick dwellings. Thinking about the man's dignity, Jack was ashamed that he'd just blown enough money on liquor in one night to pay for water for a large family for weeks.

When he looked back, he saw the hawk-faced man in the L.A. Lakers jacket staring at him with a scowl.

Chapter 17

June 26
1:30 p.m.

THE ROCKY START with Ramos at the S & S office had made Jack decide to do as much of his work as he could in the study of the condo. Reviewing the dozens of files he'd asked Tom Montana to send from the Palmer plant in Juarez had been a colossal waste of time. What he needed was solid information he could use to form a framework for a defense against PROFEPA and a basis for negotiations. What Montana had sent were boxes of files that included many duplicates and no index. He had no way to tell if they were even authentic and, of course, Montana hadn't sent any he didn't want Jack to see. It was a fiasco.

Montana claimed the existing violations were trivial. "They wrote up one of the restrooms," he'd said. "A white glove inspection in a toxic waste treatment plant? They just want to nail us."

Jack wasn't convinced. In their video conference, Montana had blamed the investigation on a jealous competitor or bribe-seeking bureaucrats. Now he admitted violations and brushed them off. But would the government really try to shut down such a big player in Juarez for penny ante stuff?

Evaluating the list of infractions alleged by PROFEPA was slow going because they were in technical Spanish. One infraction stood out: an allegation that the plant didn't possess some of the equipment needed to treat certain types of waste it accepted. *How would Montana explain that away?* Tucked away at the end of the list was a time bomb. PROFEPA retained the right to amend the list, even at the Hearing. The PROFEPA lawyers were probably holding back some of their ammunition. Smart move. With what Montana had sent him, he couldn't construct a defense.

His research had shown that the lead PROFEPA lawyer, Roberto Alvarez Nunez, had finished in the top ten percent of his law class at *Escuela Libre de Derecho*, a school known for intellectual students who excelled in oral argument. After graduation he joined PROFEPA, where he'd been ever since.

His associate, Linda Santiago, had a magna cum laude B.Sc. in microbiology from UCLA, and had earned honors in law school. After three years with the highly-regarded firm of Marquez, Alonso & Correa, she'd opted for public service with PROFEPA. She was also chairperson for the Mexico City Sierra Club.

Neither seemed likely to take a bribe or be conned by an angry competitor of Palmer's. Nor would they be pushovers in a Hearing. They could turn out to be Palmer Industries' worst nightmare.

JACK STOOD ON his condo balcony, looking down at Avenida Argentina. "I finally got the PROFEPA lawyers to agree to meet with me, but not until the first of next week," he reported to Justin Sinclair on the phone.

"They're jerking us around," Sinclair roared. "I won't stand for it."

"They're jerking us around because we have no leverage." He spoke in a calm, measured voice, suppressing his desire to tell Sinclair to get a grip on himself. Sinclair's posturing must have worked somewhere, maybe when he testified before Congress, but it would get them in trouble when dealing with low-level bureaucrats in Mexico. Sinclair was letting his determination to protect Palmer Industries cloud his judgment.

"Listen carefully, Jack. There are about ten days until the Hearing. Don't let them get a temporary injunction to shut down the plant between now and then. This is why you're there, for Christ's sake."

He held his tongue again. "Look, they didn't want to meet, but I got that done. Then I got them to agree not to move against the plant before meeting with me. That took another twenty minutes. If I had either a cooperative client or some facts on my side this might be a little easier."

"Well, that's something. Just so you'll know, I'm working the political angle, but it's very risky. That's why I want you to show the PROFEPA lawyers that Palmer is ready to fight them in court. They'll cave. They're flunkies with no personal stake in this. Make sure that Hearing never happens. And remember, if paying a fine will end this, agree to it."

"What's the upper limit?"

"One million."

"Pesos? That's more than eighty thousand dollars."

"One million *U.S.* dollars," Sinclair said. "If that plant is shut down, the company will be in breach of dozens of contracts, liable for huge damages and penalties. Get them to name their price. We'll pay it." He paused, then spoke in a more conciliatory tone. "Jack, your future is on the line. Be someone I can count on."

Sinclair hung up before Jack could answer.

Jack stared across the avenue at Parque Mexico. *Why was Palmer willing to pay a million bucks to make this go away? He had a strong feeling that if he ever found out, the answer wouldn't make him happy.*

Chapter 18

June 30
2:30 p.m.

THE PROFEPA conference table consisted of two large panes of scratched glass resting loosely in a black metal frame. It looked as if it had served for decades somewhere else until, nearing the end of its useful life, it filtered down to the lowest rung in the bureaucratic ladder—PROFEPA. In contrast, the art on the walls was inspired: hand-woven wall tapestries whose abstract designs brought forests, meadows, and mountain peaks into the room.

He took a seat, pulled his notes from his briefcase and gave them a quick review. He didn't have facts on his side, and he sure as hell couldn't count on getting sympathy for his client. He had to rely on common sense and goodwill to end this conflict short of legal warfare. The PROFEPA lawyers would be reasonable, as would he. He *could* make a deal.

A neat stack of files across the table caught his attention. The label on the top file read "PROFEPA v. Palmer Industries, Injunction, Abstract and Brief." He smiled to himself at the old ploy of "accidentally" leaving in plain sight what appeared to be documents ready to file with a court. The idea was to intimidate the opponent. *Nice try, guys.*

At that moment, the two government lawyers walked in. After completing introductions and receiving coffee from the receptionist, Alvarez asked him politely how he liked Mexico City.

When the chitchat continued past the usual time given to pleasantries, Jack understood that they were waiting for him to take the lead. Either it was a trap or they were so confident that the meeting was meaningless to them.

When Alvarez finished a story about jailing the owner of an auto repair shop caught dumping dead batteries into a lake, Jack said, "Sounds like he deserved punishment, but let's talk about someone who doesn't. That's my client, Palmer Industries. Speaking hypothetically, if Palmer stipulated to certain infractions, you'd be willing to give them time to correct the problems, isn't that right?"

The two lawyers looked at him without expression, waiting for him to go on. He didn't like going ahead without feedback, but they gave him no choice.

"In addition, my clients might be willing to pay a reasonable fine if you will assure them that PROFEPA won't seek an injunction against the company." He smiled and stacked the papers in front of him. "Both sides get what they want."

"And what amount of fine would your client consider reasonable?" Alvarez asked.

"I think they might consider anything up to a half-million U.S. dollars."

Alvarez looked at Linda Santiago and nodded his head slightly. "A half million is fifteen times my salary for a year. Would they be paying that to us in cash?"

Good God! Had Alvarez misunderstood? Did he think he was being offered a bribe? But wait a minute. Maybe Alvarez was testing him to see if he'd bite, offer to make the payment personal. If he did, they'd have the *federales* on site in ten minutes.

"Any fine would be paid by the company as directed by the head of the governmental entity," he said stiffly. In his gut, he knew he was doing the exact opposite of what Montana would have done had he been in Jack's place.

Linda Santiago cleared her throat. "Mr. Strider, Mexico has excellent environmental protection laws, most based on Articles 25, 27, 73 and 115 of our Constitution. PROFEPA monitors complaints, investigates violations, enforces regulations, prosecutes, and assesses penalties. We can also refer charges to the Federal Attorney General requesting criminal sanctions."

"Yes, I've read—"

"But that's only theory," she interrupted smoothly. "In reality, we don't have the money to enforce the law against most violators. Besides that, sometimes we're ordered back into our cages no matter how strong a case we have. But," she smiled slightly, "the Palmer case is different."

"Why is it different?"

"We haven't been called off, and we're going to get our injunction. Our agents will put seals on the equipment and install surveillance cameras in all major spaces. We're going to put Palmer Industries out of business for good."

Alvarez leaned forward. "And put your clients in prison."

Whoa. They're after blood. All he could do was act as if he hadn't heard what they'd just said.

"Okay, just lay out for me what Palmer Industries needs to do, or stop doing, and I'll make it happen."

"Don't bother, Mr. Strider." Alvarez shook his head. "If they've been poisoning the water supply of Juarez and El Paso, the damage could be catastrophic. It's too late to un-ring that bell."

Jack stared at the man, bewildered. *Poisoning the water supply? Was that a scare tactic?* "I've seen no evidence about any threat to the water supply. But here's a fact. My client provides hundreds of jobs. Juarez needs those jobs."

"Palmer Industries didn't come to Mexico to help out Juarez," Alvarez said. "It came because it can get away with paying absurdly low wages."

Police sirens, one after another, passed by outside the windows. Jack looked at Santiago. "You and I have something in common. We're both active in the Sierra Club. We both work to protect our environment. Let's work together to resolve this."

"If Sierra Club membership was really a big deal for you, you wouldn't be defending environmental thugs," Alvarez said flatly. "And, by the way, we did some research on you. Your involvement in that scandal where Mexican girls were forced into prostitution doesn't do much for your reputation with us."

"I was *not* involved in any scandal. It was my—" He choked back his anger and shifted his approach. "Regardless of what you think of me, you can't justify a vendetta against my client simply because the company's based in another country."

"Vendetta?" Alvarez repeated loudly. *"Maquilas* like your client are coddled. They do whatever they want to the Mexican people. I'll tell you the truth about *maquilas."*

"Roberto," Santiago intervened, "let it go. It won't make any difference."

Alvarez stood. "No, I want him to hear this." He gripped the edge of the table with both hands and leaned toward Jack. "Most border towns are in a desert with barely enough water to get by. Then the *maquilas* came and started sucking up all the water they wanted. The law says they have to treat it before sending it back into the water supply but many won't do it. Some *colonias* have no water at all. Municipal water treatment systems barely function. *Gringos* make fortunes while our people die of thirst. I'll tell you this." He stood straight, and his chin rose. "You stole our gold and land in the past. But today you won't steal our water without a fight."

Santiago spoke up. *"Maquilas* provide jobs, sure, but do you know who they hire? Women between the ages of sixteen and twenty-five from rural villages because they've been brought up not to complain. These young women are far from home, unprotected, barely surviving. The pregnancy rate is sky high, and there's almost no medical care. When a worker drops out, they replace her in an hour."

"To keep those miserable jobs," Alvarez said as he sat down, "hundreds of thousands have to live in huts with no insulation, no electricity to run even a small fridge or a fan, no running water and no sewer. And the jobs have no security. When an economic slowdown hit the U.S., 80,000 workers in Ciudad Juarez were fired. Not one day's notice. No severance pay. Not even bus fare back to their villages. And if a *maquila* can increase profits by moving to China or Malaysia, it's gone overnight, leaving nothing but empty buildings. Now, maybe you understand more about why we're going to take down Palmer Industries."

He certainly did. In different circumstances, he might have been on their side. Their anti-*maquila* sentiment was a wild card he hadn't counted on. He let seconds pass in silence so some of the intensity could dissipate. Finally he said, "I understand, so let's talk about what Palmer Industries can do to be a better citizen of Juarez."

"Palmer Industries is *not* a citizen of Juarez," Santiago said. "The owners live in San Francisco. Even the manager crosses the border into Mexico each morning, then goes back to El Paso at night. By the way, it's obvious you don't *know* Tomás Montana."

"So," Alvarez added, "no settlement."

The two PROFEPA lawyers shook hands with him coldly and walked out.

Jack stayed behind for a moment to compose himself. He'd just run into a brick wall where a brick wall wasn't an option.

4:30 p.m.

"ROBERTO ALVAREZ hates *maquilas* and sees a chance to knock down a big one," Jack said into the phone. "He smells Palmer blood in the water."

He pictured Sinclair in his shrine room, leaning back, ankles crossed on the desk, leafing through *Foreign Affairs* while he manipulated as much of the world as he could reach.

"Oh, Christ! I told you to make a deal and end this thing. I shouldn't have to do everything myself."

It's what you haven't done that's part of the problem, Jack thought. Aloud, he said, "If you don't like my work, I won't send you a bill."

"Don't be a smart ass."

"Look, Alvarez isn't bluffing. He's ready to go for an immediate injunction."

Sinclair was silent for a moment. "We just took over handling this. The judge has to grant us time to prepare."

Jack knew he had to at least sound patient. "If the judge delays the Hearing, Alvarez will move for a temporary injunction to shut down operations. Palmer Industries doesn't have clean hands, so it will probably be granted."

"How much do they have on Palmer anyway?"

"A lot of petty stuff, and they can probably prove it all. But there has to be more to this. Since Alvarez is being so hard-nosed, I think he has something else, something big. He'll amend his complaint to make it more damning."

"Do I have to send a skywriter down there to get my message across? We're not handing this over to some damn penny-ante judge we don't know, hoping he rules in our favor."

"Then send someone to Juarez to find the facts and build a defense. That's not me. Arthur Palmer made that clear."

Silence on the line stretched out. Finally, Sinclair said, "I'll tell Arthur he's looking at padlocked doors unless you go to the plant and get everything you need to put together a defense. It has to be you, because I don't trust anyone from the Mexico City office. Catch a plane to Juarez tomorrow. You'll be back in Mexico City in a couple of days." He hung up.

Jack stood holding the phone, listening to the dial tone. His back was against the wall. Alvarez couldn't be bluffed into folding his hand, and he wouldn't settle. Nor would he let the plant stay open based on Palmer's promise to clean up its act. And Montana would need the best criminal lawyer in Mexico if he tried to bribe Alvarez.

Nice irony. Arthur Palmer had thrown his American workers out on the street. Now he was determined to keep the plant open and that meant saving the jobs of his Mexican workers. If Palmer and Montana couldn't prove that Palmer Industries' operations were lawful, or nearly so, Jack would be out of a job.

Chapter 19

July 1
6 p.m.

THE BAGGAGE screener in the Mexico City airport used his hand like the scoop of a backhoe to paw through Jack's bag.

Jack watched closely to make sure the guard had no chance to plant something, like a few rocks of crack cocaine, and then loudly call a colleague to witness what he'd "discovered." After that, they would muscle him into a small room and demand payment of a hefty "fine." They knew that most travelers, terrified of being locked up in a Mexican jail, would pay and keep quiet. He'd seen the same scam worked in other countries. When the guard saw Jack watching, he scowled and slammed the bag closed with a grunt.

Jack headed for the gate and his flight to Juarez.

When they landed in Juarez, he joined other passengers leaving the restricted area. Having seen Montana on the video conference should have been sufficient to spot him, but it wasn't. Then a man holding a sign that read "Sr. J. STRIDER" approached and smiled. *"Buenas tardes, señor.* I am Antonio. *Señor* Montana sent me." As they reached an Oldsmobile double-parked at the curb, Antonio slipped several bills to the cop who stood next to the car, pretending it didn't exist.

"Antonio, how long will it take to get to the Hotel Rialto?"

"But, *señor*, I'm taking you to the Palmer Industries plant."

"I'd rather go to the hotel first, check in and rent a car."

"I was told to go straight to the plant. Your rental car is already there, and *Señor* Montana is waiting for you." Reflected in the rearview mirror, Antonio's eyes were wide. He looked like a man caught in the middle.

"No problem."

One thing he'd learned about Mexico: nothing went as expected.

In Spanish and English, the sign at the airport exit read: "Juarez: Fastest Growing City in the Americas." That was news to Jack, especially since he knew its homicide rate was the highest in the Americas. Drug cartel members gunned each other down day and night, pausing only to turn their weapons on police and soldiers.

As they entered Juarez, traffic became dense and signs of "growth" were everywhere: junked cars, abandoned mechanical parts, and litter blowing along the curbs. A web of overhead electric wires formed a canopy above the urban jungle. Dilapidated buses rattled along, passengers leaping on or off at will. In the absence of traffic lights, *topes*—steep concrete speed bumps known as "sleeping policemen"—punished speeders. Indifferent to them, Antonio made the heavy car swerve like a tango dancer to avoid axle-bending potholes. But as Jack was driven across the dusty, low-rise city, he was jolted emotionally more than physically.

"Antonio, how many people live in Juarez?"

"My cousin says maybe two million. The mayor, he says one million, but he doesn't count the people in the *colonias* who came for jobs. He pretends they aren't here."

Glancing to his right, there was El Paso no more than a half-mile away, separated from Juarez by the sludgy seep of the Rio Grande river. A concrete canal enclosed by barbed wire ran down the center of the ruined river. On the Juarez side, clusters of cement block and tarpaper shacks near the riverbank reminded him of the worst he'd seen in Cairo and Lima. On the U.S. side, in El Paso, glass and steel high-rise buildings were labeled Wells Fargo and JPMorgan Chase in garish neon. At the base of a mesa, giant sprinklers ensured the health of a lush green golf course.

Antonio noticed Jack looking across the border. "We have a saying, *Señor* Strider. 'Alas, poor Mexico. So far from God, so close to the United States.'"

Out the window, he saw a woman crouched beside a ditch bordering the road. She was washing an infant in its murky, scummy water. For a second her large dark eyes fixed on him. It was like a lightning strike, zapping his emotions.

At that moment, an amplified voice blaring from across the river caught his attention. "What's that sound?"

"The race announcer at Sunland Park Racetrack and Casino. Many slot machines. Free tequila for gamblers. Mariachi music all day. Every night, somebody who used to be famous sings or tells jokes."

Fifteen minutes later, Antonio turned into Palmer Industries. Despite passing through an impressive gate, the sight ahead didn't look like anyone's paradise. In fact, the noxious atmosphere and July heat created a miasma of latent hostility. This was going to be a tough gig.

Directly ahead was a long one-story brick building. To the right of a door a sign read "Administration." Behind that building, Jack saw rows of warehouse-like structures. Farther away, a smoke stack belching yellow-white smoke. Two men in camouflage uniforms watched as he got out of the car. After Antonio waved, they turned away.

"*Señor* Montana's office is inside. Your car is over there." Antonio pointed to a gold Lincoln Town Car. It might as well have had a sign on it that said "gringo tourist." *Was that Montana's idea of a joke?* The only other car in the staff parking lot was a black Hummer with dark tinted windows and oversized tires that raised it high above the gravel. He checked his watch. Seven p.m.

There was no receptionist at the desk inside the Administration building, but a man in workman's coveralls quickly stepped forward.

"*Buenas tardes, señor. Me llamo Manuel.*" He led Jack back outside the Administration building and behind it to a warehouse he opened with a key. It was dark inside until Manuel flipped four switches. Banks of lights far overhead came on with a series of "whumps." The great cavern seemed to be a storage depot for forklifts, backhoes, and other heavy equipment. All were covered with dirt and grime; workhorses, not show horses.

"Pardon me," Jack said in Spanish. "I'm here to see *Señor* Montana. Are you taking me to him?"

"*Señor* Montana, *si,*" Manuel said, gesturing back to the Administration building. Then he continued gently guiding Jack from one vast building to the next, most of them full of equipment evidently designed to treat various kinds of hazardous waste. A network of metal catwalks far overhead provided access to control valves and distant vents. The pipes, spheres, and hissing chambers looked like a giant's chemistry set. The stink in the different buildings ranged from stinging chlorine to overpowering rotten eggs.

He hated wasting time like this when he and Montana should be talking about PROFEPA lawyers who wouldn't settle for anything less than the corporate death penalty. Coming up with a plausible defense was going to be like climbing Mt. Everest.

When Manuel unlocked the entrance to the next warehouse, Jack saw a beam of light streaming through a doorway in the wall to his left. A sign near the office door read *Director de Planta.* A silhouetted man stood yelling at someone just inside the office. It was a young woman at a desk, sobbing, face in her hands. When Manuel turned on the big overhead lights, the man swung to face them.

"*Vayanse, bastardos,*" the thickset man shouted, moving fast across the empty floor toward them. Jack didn't need a translator to know that "*bastardos*" wasn't a friendly greeting.

"*Si, Señor Guzman, vamanos horita,*" Manuel said and jerked Jack by his sleeve back toward the door.

"*Alto!*" The man demanded, moving in.

Manuel backed away from Jack.

"Eres un gringo," Guzman said and switched to English. "Off limits. Get out."

Behind him, Manuel whined something that included Montana's name over and over. That must have gotten through to Guzman. He stopped moving in on Jack, dropped his fists, and growled, "Don't come back," then stalked toward his office.

It happened so fast Jack didn't have a clear image of Guzman except that he had a bulldog face and moved like a seasoned street fighter.

Manuel tugged him outside and pointed toward the Admin building across the gravel yard. *"Señor* Montana."

Inside, he took Jack down a dimly lit hall into an anteroom to Montana's office, pointed to the door and fled, apparently shaken by the encounter with Guzman. From inside the office, Jack heard a loud voice talking in bursts, clearly on the phone.

Taking a moment to calm down, he realized he'd learned something from the tour. There were places Montana didn't want him to go, things he didn't want him to see. Well he would, by God, see them. He knocked firmly on the office door.

After a delay came a curt command. "Enter."

Thomas Montana, leaning back in his chair, tooled boots propped on his desk, gestured for Jack to sit. He continued talking on the phone, making no eye contact.

What a snake. Can't be bothered to meet me at the airport, sends me on a snipe hunt through the plant, and leaves me hanging while he chats on the phone. Annoying, but not surprising. Okay, Montana was showing him how he wanted to play, and that's the way it would be.

On the wall behind Montana's desk hung a photograph signed by the famous photographer Alberto Korba of what looked like a revolutionary battle. Along the wall to Montana's right was a shelf of very old sculptures in the Inca style. Resting on the corner of Montana's desk stood a foot-tall bronze cock with feathers and spurs flaring. They showed a side of Montana he hadn't expected.

"Go screw yourself," Montana shouted and slammed down the receiver.

He looked at Jack and asked in a completely tranquil voice, "You were checking out my art. Some good shit here, but you should see what I have in El Paso. Crates of it. I'm like a black hole for art. Costs a fortune, but I can't get enough." His tone was so self-satisfied that it said he didn't give a damn whether or not Jack liked his art. "So now you've seen the set up I have here. Twice as much space under roof as we had in California, and I've cut labor costs seventy percent." He waved the stump of his cigar. "Sweet deal, no?"

"Guess so. I couldn't tell exactly what I was seeing as we walked around, and there were some buildings Manuel wouldn't take me into." He watched to see if Montana's face gave away anything. No change. "And your Plant Manager seemed pretty upset when we ran into him."

"Guzman? Manuel took you into Shipping & Receiving?" Montana's face went dark, and the corners of his mouth turned down. "Anyway . . . that tour is all we can do for you here."

"Meaning?"

"That there's no point in hanging around. We're not set up for a research project. Besides, you already have most of our records. Anything else you want, I can get to you in Mexico City on twelve hours notice. Believe me, you have my one hundred percent support for what you're doing."

Montana did his best to make his smile look genuine while, at the same time, giving Jack the bum's rush.

"I need more than just records. I have to know about anything that could give Palmer trouble in court. Surprises kill a defense. And I need your responses to each PROFEPA charge. You and I will be spending several hours together."

Montana lighted the cigar and blew a coil of smoke across the desk. "I've got meetings in Mexico City in the morning, the kind I can't miss." He shrugged.

"Listen," Jack said, trying to rein in his anger, "I have a job to do. You shouldn't—"

"I run this place." Montana's eyes narrowed. "No one tells me what I shouldn't do. But, hey, let's not have a misunderstanding here." As if shooting a free throw, he arched an empty beer bottle into a wastebasket. "How about a Tecate? Better than that horse piss you call beer in the States."

Jack hesitated. He'd like the smooth honey of single malt on his tongue, but not a beer with Montana. "No thanks."

"Suit yourself." He pulled another Tecate from a built-in refrigerator behind his desk, opened it, and poured half of it down his throat.

Jack's bullshit meter was sounding loudly. *This guy's an asshole, but there's something else going on here.* Montana had tried to rush him back to Mexico City. But he knew Jack had been assigned to defend the plant, so what was motivating him?

"Tom," he said calmly. "By the way, do you prefer 'Tom' or 'Thomas'?"

"In Mexico, friends call me *Tomás.* You can call me Tom."

Oh, nice touch. "What you sent me in Mexico City wasn't enough. Since then, I've reviewed the actual PROFEPA charges. Now I know what I need to see, including the equipment. Just point me to a desk and ask your assistant to give me the documents I need. I should be out of here in a couple of days."

"Strider, I don't need you showing up with some bullshit San Francisco attitude . . . but I'll leave a note telling Ana-Maria Archuletta what to give you in the morning. She's in charge of our filing, knows where everything is. Just do what you've been told, and don't be snooping around my plant." He fired the empty Tecate at the wastebasket. It shattered against the wall. He wrenched the cap off another.

"I'll be here in the morning, Tom, but since we're both here right now, let's take ten minutes to go over some questions." Once they got going, he'd pin Montana down for a lot more than ten minutes.

"No way. I'm eating at the Mayor's house tonight. In fact, I'm out of here right now." He came to his feet and headed out of the room, flicking off the office light, leaving Jack in the dark.

He gritted his teeth. *Calm down. Ignore his little games. Get the job done.*

In the parking lot, Montana pointed in the direction of the city lights of El Paso. "Don't confuse that beat-to-hell river over there with your San Francisco Bay. This is a different ballpark. *My* ballpark. *Comprende?*"

"Here's some breaking news for you, *Tom.* Palmer Industries *isn't* your ballpark. It's a corporation whose owners live in San Francisco. They sent me to do a job, and that's exactly what I'm going to do." He let that sink in. *"Comprende?"*

Montana moved closer. "Stick your nose where it doesn't belong, and you'll answer to me." He smiled an empty smile and spread his arms wide, palms up. "Hey, we're on the same team, *amigo.*" He climbed into the Hummer and leaned out the window. "This is a tough city, so watch your back. *Buena suerte.*" He gunned the engine and pulled out of the lot at high speed, leaving a cloud of swirling dust.

Buena suerte, my ass. We'll see who needs good luck the most.

JACK PULLED OFF Paseo Triumfo de la Republica into the drive of the pink and beige Hotel Rialto. Next to the main entrance a sign bolted to the cut stone read, ***"Five Star ***** Finest Hotel in Juarez."*** He noticed that the guest parking lot had a gatehouse and a guard with a very ugly automatic shotgun on a sling. Wonder what the second finest hotel is like? That guard might need a machine gun.

At the front desk, he said to the clerk, "Good evening. I have a reservation. Name's Strider."

After asking twice for the spelling of his name, the clerk frowned and announced that no such reservation existed.

"Any good room is fine."

"I'm very sorry, *señor*. The hotel is full, well almost full."

"What do you mean, almost?"

"The only room we have left is the *El Presidente* Suite, but it's our most expensive suite. Would you like that one, *señor?*" The clerk's smug smile confirmed that his squeeze play worked on Americans more often than not.

He was being hustled, but getting angry wouldn't help, and he wasn't in the mood to search for another hotel.

"That will be fine. You said you can't find my reservation, but the company that booked it for me has it, so that's the rate I'll pay for the suite. Correct?"

The clerk's smug look vanished, replaced by an obsequious smile. Without missing a beat, he said, "Of course, sir."

A mosaic path of colored stones in an Aztec pattern led through an impeccable garden and alongside a swimming pool shaped like a dolphin. Midway down, the bellman swept open the door of the *El Presidente* Suite. On an oval table in the center of the room stood a bottle of Porfidio tequila with a ribbon around its neck: "Compliments from the Management. We are here to serve you."

He'd had his fill of Juarez hospitality. Guzman, Montana, now this. What the hell was coming up tomorrow?

Chapter 20

July 2
8:00 a.m.

JACK STRODE INTO the Admin Building at Palmer Industries at eight a.m. As he neared Montana's office, a strikingly beautiful woman called to him.

"Good morning. I am Ana-Maria Archuletta. May I take you to your . . . office?"

Her smile improved his state of mind considerably, but that lasted only until she showed him to a small cubicle where the sun blazed in through a propped-open window. Just outside, eighteen-wheelers rolled past through waves of exhaust. His nostrils burned.

"This is where *Señor* Montana said for me to take you," Ana-Maria told him in clear, schoolbook English. "I reminded him the air-conditioning is broken but—I'm sorry. If I can help you, please ask." She left, obviously embarrassed.

He could insist on a better workspace, even commandeer one, but that would put Ana-Maria in a bind. Montana had sent him a message. He'd find a way to return the favor.

She'd stacked the metal desk high with neatly-labeled folders full of files, graphs, schedules and receipts. Now it was up to him to evaluate their credibility. If Montana had laid down a smoke screen, he had to penetrate it.

Four hours later he leaned back from his laptop and rubbed his eyes. No smoking gun, nothing that proved Palmer Industries had dealt with hazardous waste illegally.

He stood and looked out the window, idly watching a truck marked Brown & Root Chemical leaving the yard.

The records Montana had sent to him in Mexico City were useless. The ones in front of him now were organized and seemingly comprehensive, but were they authentic? He'd come to Juarez to find a way to defend Palmer Industries. If these records were valid, they could help him keep the plant open. Even if there were minor violations, he'd convince Arthur it was in his best interests to clean them up.

But Roberto Alvarez had acted as though he were holding aces. So if these records were bogus, Alvarez probably had a trap ready to discredit the records and the lawyer who put them forward.

He looked at the situation in another way. The Palmer plant is a big business. To run it, Montana had to keep real books to monitor costs, pay bills, detect theft, whatever. If these records were fake, he had to have a real set, probably locked up somewhere. He'd hide them from his own lawyer because they'd convict him.

He'd taught his law students that a client who lies to his lawyer is like a hand grenade with the pin out. He thinks he can game the system, including his own lawyer. Once in a while he gets away with it. More often, the lie blows up the case and takes the lawyer with it. Now, here he was with a client who might be lying through his smile.

Next step? Find out if there was another set of records stashed away somewhere. If so, and they were incriminating, that would be a turning point. He wouldn't walk away and pretend he'd seen nothing. Instead, he'd dump copies of the relevant parts in Sinclair's lap so he could deal with his client.

He remembered Ana-Maria saying, "If I can help you, please ask." If there were skeletons, Ana-Maria would know in which closet. But why would she reveal anything about Palmer if it could sink the company?

The stakes were so high that if he had to "use" her, that's the way it would be. He needed to get her alone.

Chapter 21

July 2
1:00 p.m.

JACK TWISTED THE cork out of a bottle of white wine and filled two glasses. This was his chance to persuade Ana-Maria to reveal Montana's secrets. "I wanted to take you to a nice restaurant."

She sat in a folding chair next to the desk in his cubicle. After a moment she said, "In a restaurant, many eyes would see us together. Someone would tell someone. Anyway, look at this feast you brought from Café Carmella." She gestured at the half dozen containers on the desk. "*Señor* Montana has never even offered me a beer." She cocked her head. "May I ask you a question?"

"Of course."

"Some people say you are spy for the San Francisco home office, others say maybe for *Señor* Montana. Which is it, *Señor* Strider?"

That hit home. He felt exactly like a spy. "I'm a lawyer from San Francisco, and I'm here to help solve a problem for Palmer Industries."

She looked pensive. Maybe she believed him. Maybe not.

"Tell me about San Francisco."

"It's on a peninsula almost surrounded by water, the Pacific Ocean to the west, the Bay to the east."

"Juarez is in a desert," she said, "and the water in the Rio Grande would eat the soles off your shoes. Where I came from, the mountain streams are sweet and full."

For a moment, her large dark eyes seemed focused on a distant place. Her shiny brown hair, cut short, showed off her graceful neck.

"Years ago, the Bay was so polluted the government started enforcing laws against dumping anything toxic into the water. Now the Bay is clean. I read somewhere that some *maquilas* dump chemicals and other toxic garbage into ponds or even on the ground."

"Some of them don't care what damage they do. My cousin works in a factory where they use much, much water to make blue jeans look worn out. The factory is so hot that one girl used the wash water to soak her headband so she could suck on it. She started throwing up. The floor manager took her away. My cousin never saw her again."

"Didn't the other workers complain?"

"Most workers are girls who left a husband and children in a village to come to the borderland to earn a living. If they say anything, they get fired. So they are silent."

"I understand," was all he could say. But what he thought about were the rich businessmen and power-hungry legislators that make rules that benefit themselves, indifferent to how they affect millions of ordinary people they will never see. He was disgusted.

"But you *don't* understand," she replied. "You see only what you see as you drive from your fancy hotel to this plant. You don't see real life in Juarez. At your home, you're surrounded by water. In Juarez, we sometimes don't have enough water to cook our meals or wash our bodies, even to drink. It's getting worse."

"What's the government doing about that?"

"The President in Mexico City pays no attention to us. In Chihuahua, the state governor says it would cost ten billion pesos to bring water from beyond the mountains, and they don't even have enough money to fix the traffic lights. The Mayor claims the problem was made up by American consultants. Others say, 'The water still comes out of the wells, more salty, but still coming.' Everybody tells us 'No problem, don't worry about it.'"

"We should worry a lot more about it," Jack told her. "The number of places around the world that are beginning to run out of water is growing so quickly that I taught my students about it."

She nodded, but didn't speak, so he said, "I'm sorry, but right now I need your help with something that's happening in this plant. The records on this desk aren't the real records for the company. I need you to tell me what's really going on."

He was pessimistic as he waited for her response. Montana signs her paycheck, so she'd probably report these questions to him. So what? He wasn't going to win a popularity contest with Montana anyway.

She crossed her arms. Her face closed. "I have nothing to say, *Señor* Strider." She looked at her wristwatch, then down at the table.

"Ana-Maria, if PROFEPA closes this plant, all of you will lose your jobs. If you know anything that can help prevent that, you should tell me. I want to help."

She eyed him suspiciously. "Then why did *Señor* Montana tell me not to do anything for you except what he said?"

"Maybe because he's doing something he doesn't want me to know about. If he's dumping hazardous waste illegally, he's poisoning the water supply. You need to help me stop that."

She looked at him as if trying to read his mind. "Why would you care what happens to people here? You don't know us."

This was his chance to get her on his side. "Then take me into the city. Show me what I should see. Help me understand."

"I'm sorry," she said softly, "but I don't trust you."

"I'll give you one thousand pesos to drive around with me for a couple of hours. Just drive, nothing else." It sounded crass, but he didn't know what else to do. If she thought Montana was guilty of something, she might want to keep it concealed. Or she might want to help the *gringo* fix the problem. If she thought Montana was clean, she'd walk away.

She stood. "I'll tell my best friend Juanita I'm going with you. At five o'clock, I'll be walking somewhere past the first bus stop down the road to the right. Pick me up there."

"I will."

"*Señor* Strider. I promise nothing."

Shortly after five, Ana-Maria settled into the Town Car without a word, so he kept driving, waiting for directions. After a couple of miles, she told him to turn off onto a two-lane road so full of craters it looked as if it had been bombed. When the road led through the city dump, he powered the windows up to reduce the odor and the din from heavy machinery compacting mountains of debris. They rounded a gravel bank, and straight ahead was a sprawling landscape of human habitation that almost looked like a continuation of the dump.

"Anapra," Ana-Maria said as if it were a dirty word, gesturing toward makeshift homes scattered on harsh, barren soil. "Years ago, the city ended at the other side of the dump, so poor people coming from the country wound up here. Now forty thousand live in Anapra. The first ones built homes from wood pallets and cardboard boxes. They flattened soft drink and beer cans to make the roof. Where you see concrete blocks and tarpaper, those people have some money. In summer, it's over one hundred degrees."

"Is this where you live?" He immediately wished he hadn't asked. Instead of showing that he empathized with anyone forced to live in these conditions, his question sounded judgmental.

"Yes. Many people in Anapra work in the *maquilas*. This is all they can afford on forty dollars a week."

Forty dollars a week? He pictured the Palmer brothers in expensive suits paid for by the sweat of these people.

"Now it is getting worse. A big drug cartel has moved in. They set up crack houses where they recruit kids to deliver drugs. Some people say Anapra is like a 'border motel' because so many drug smugglers hide here before they sneak across the border. No one here is safe, especially not women.

"They call Juarez the 'Murder Capital of the Americas.' Men stinking with tequila kill each other like animals. The *narcotraficantes*—the cartels, the police, and the army—they are at war with each other. Thousands murdered. If you get in the way, you die. In the past few years, more than three hundred women in Juarez have been murdered. Most of them raped and cut, mostly dumped by the river, some on the side of a road, thrown out of cars like garbage. Women disappear. One day they're here, then no more."

She was silent for a minute, then continued, "The fat police chief says, 'This one went back to her village; that one went across the border.' For a while, the police blamed the murders on local bus drivers, then on bad men from El Paso. But they don't really want to know. They're afraid they might catch someone from the cartels they don't want to catch. So every case is 'unsolved.' You know those white crosses along the road from the Hotel Rialto? Some father or brother drove each cross into the ground to mark the place where a dead daughter or sister was found. You saw those crosses but you didn't understand.

"In my village, I taught English and history in a small school, but I could barely live on what they paid. So I came here. By God's will, I have no children. When mothers go to the border, children stay with relatives or wind up in places that are like orphanages. Some disappear. People say they are kidnapped or even sold." Her eyes filled with tears. "I hate Juarez, but I have to stay."

Jack had seen poverty in many cities around the world, cities filled with people who were desperate but not defeated, who endured. But the fact that Anapra was only a few hundred yards from the United States made it more shocking. But it was her words "kidnapped" and "sold" that cut deepest. In his gut, he suspected that some of those missing children had been taken from Salina Cruz aboard *Pacific Dawn*. In a flash it all came back: Peck's brains splattered on the law books, Calder's fury in the horse arena, the shame he felt.

To break out of the foul memories, he pointed at the maze of electric wires crossing over each other to connect the houses. He imagined a new arrival climbing on top of a truck after dark to hook his house into any wire he could reach. As they passed, one of the junctions sparked and popped.

She heard it too. "Sometimes a line breaks and burns a child. The city people say, 'Nobody pays, so we don't care.'"

We don't care. Those words summed up so much. He gripped the steering wheel tighter as he drove slowly down the main road that cut Anapra in half. No trees. Nothing green. Summer heat radiating from the tin roofs and barren hillsides.

"At least the city provides water, doesn't it?"

"Water is supposed to come free from city trucks, but if you don't pay *morditas,* bribes, the drivers won't stop at your house. They're supposed to come once a week but they don't come that often. In summer, when we need water the most, they don't come at all."

"What do you do?"

"In Anapra, four families own everything, even the land under our houses. One of their businesses is selling water. Drivers who work for the four families charge much more to fill the *pileta.*"

"*Pileta?*"

"See those old 55-gallon drums? They come from the dump, so they don't have tops. That's what we use to store water."

"Aren't there any wells here?"

"The old wells dried up, and there's no money to drill new ones. Everyone has diarrhea. Some kids die from it. Father Alarcone at Santa Lucia Church prays, but that's all he does. Look." She pointed up the street. "Here comes one of the family's water trucks."

The truck pulled to the curb and the driver swung down from the cab, flipped the switch on a pump, and hauled a hose toward a shack covered in flaking yellow stucco. He wore greasy black trousers and no shirt. Sweat soaked his hairy shoulders. He shouted in the direction of the doorway covered with a length of faded green fabric.

"He won't pump until he gets his money," Ana-Maria told him.

A woman in her early twenties stepped out, one little girl on her hip, another at her side. Jack couldn't hear what she said, but the driver shouted and shook his fist at her. She offered the man a handful of pesos. He stuffed them into his pants pocket, but instead of filling the drum he stomped back to the truck and started shoving the hose into its storage space. The woman ran to his side, crying and pointing to her children, obviously begging.

"What's going on?"

"Her children are sick and must have water. He took the money she had but says it's not enough. He's going to keep her money and sell the water to someone else."

Jack was out of the Town Car in a second. A few long strides took him to the truck driver.

"Fill it up." He pointed to the metal drum. "I'll pay the rest." When he repeated that in Spanish, the driver began yelling and gave him the finger, pumping his right fist up and down.

Ana-Maria ran up. "We need to get out of here. Can't you see he's high?" She pulled hard at his arm.

He hadn't recognized that the man was stoked on something, but there was no backing down. "I want that water delivered. Tell him I'll pay."

Frowning, Ana-Maria did as he asked.

The man wiped his hand across his forehead, whipped the sweat into Ana-Maria's face, and swung a beefy roundhouse right that landed like a club on Jack's shoulder. Jack stumbled sideways, got his feet tangled and fell heavily on his butt. He rolled to his right and up. The driver came at him with a bellow, paws widespread like a grizzly intending to wrestle him to the ground. Jack moved quickly to the side, grabbed a fistful of the man's mat of hair and hurled him forward, driving him face first into the rough gravel. The burly man got to all fours, then slowly onto his feet, shaking his head side-to-side. He wiped blood and grit from his face and backed away, both hands raised, palms out. He was done.

Jack pointed to the drum. The driver snarled, but filled it. As the water level reached the top, Jack saw dead cockroaches floating.

Swallowing hard, he asked Ana-Maria, "How much?"

She told him. He was tempted to throw the money on the ground, but held it out instead. The driver snatched it, climbed into the cab of his truck and rolled away.

Jack had acted fast, without thought. No negotiations. He couldn't remember the last time he'd done that. *Damn, that felt good.*

Hands on her hips Ana-Maria said, "You're a fool. That man could have killed you. Over what? And next week he'll take it out on that woman. You don't understand this place. You can't fix everything."

That was a tough message to accept. He was programmed to fix things.

"Listen, I have an idea. You mentioned Father Alarcone. Will you take me to meet him?"

She nodded and they climbed back into the car.

The church, with narrow rectangular windows and an arched bell tower, was an attempt to imitate a Spanish adobe mission. The thick stucco that covered the two-story building had a fresh coat of white paint. The fenced-in courtyard was immaculate. It made a statement. Even if the church couldn't reverse poverty, it wouldn't yield to it.

A man with bony, hooked shoulders and a fringe of hair around his bald pate like a Franciscan friar stood in the courtyard listening to an animated conversation among several women.

"*Padre* Alarcone," Ana-Maria called. The priest turned away from the group. "This is *Señor* Strider. *Americano,*" she said and stepped back, not-so-subtly distancing herself.

"Good evening, Father. I asked *Señorita* Archuletta to introduce us because I understand the water in Anapra isn't safe to drink."

The priest nodded. "When the children are sick, they can't study. They don't grow strong and tall like you." He looked down at his clasped hands.

Jack's irrepressible fix-it gene triggered itself. "I'll come back with a water purifier later this evening. When people bring their water here and run it through the purifier it will be clean."

"My poor church could never afford such a thing. I'm sorry."

"No, no. It's a gift. And it costs almost nothing to operate, just a little electricity. It's so simple it won't break down. We'll set it up right here in this courtyard."

The priest glanced at Ana-Maria and took a deep breath. "Maybe outside the post office would be better."

"But you're open much longer hours than the post office."

Padre Alarcone spoke rapidly with Ana-Maria. Then with a slight bow to Jack he said, "You are right. It is our responsibility. When you return, you will have help to set up your machine." He walked into the church.

As Jack drove, Ana-Maria talked but he heard nothing. He wanted to strike at those who had created Anapra, whose greed kept it as it was. He'd taught that helping people in need gave meaning to the practice of law. That was one reason why his father's debauchery had hit him so hard. Until now, he'd been angry with Arthur Palmer and Montana on principle. Coming face-to-face with people who were their victims made it personal.

"What are you thinking?" Ana-Maria asked quietly.

"About what I just saw."

"This afternoon I learned that you are a good man, and I would like to help you. But some people at the plant are too dangerous so—" She put her hand on his arm. "—I'm afraid to tell you anything. And I think you should be afraid too."

Chapter 22

"TWELVE HUNDRED dollars for this water purifier? That's steep," Jack said.

The clerk behind the counter at El Paso Plumbing Supplies looked bored. "Supply and demand. Price goes up as long as water quality goes down." He clearly didn't give a damn what Jack thought.

What the clerk didn't know was that Jack would have paid more, if necessary. Providing potable water in Anapra was worthwhile, but it was also his best shot at changing Ana-Maria's mind. The clock was ticking. The moment Montana got back in town she'd clam up for good.

When he crossed back into Mexico and held up his passport, the man waved him through with no interest in the equipment lashed into the wide-open trunk. He found his way back to Santa Lucia Church. Two men ambled up and spoke in rapid Spanish, realized he couldn't keep up, and pantomimed that they'd been instructed to help. After examining the purifier, they seemed confident they knew enough to hook it up so water would flow into it from the church's large water tank.

A crowd formed outside the courtyard fence, talking and pointing, obviously puzzled about what the tall *gringo* was up to. He wished *Padre* Alarcone had stayed around to explain that what he was doing would make their lives better.

When the system was ready, he opened the inflow valve and ran contaminated water from the church tank through the purifier. After a couple of minutes, he got an empty Fanta can from his car and filled it from the outflow faucet at the end of the unit. With a bit of theatrics, he lifted it to the crowd, as if in a toast, then gulped every drop. He waited for a reaction from the crowd—alarm, excitement, something. There was nothing. Of course there wouldn't be. They drank water out of this church water tank all the time. To them, what he'd done was nothing unusual, just crazy for a *gringo* who didn't have to drink it.

He was about to leave when a teenage boy walked up to the rear of the bystanders. He and an old woman whispered back and forth, and then the boy moved gently through the crowd.

"Pardon me, *señor.* I am Rafael. Everyone wonders what you're doing. If you tell me, I'll tell them."

"If you drink the water in that tank, you'll get sick."

"Yes." His shrug said it all. Life in Anapra.

"With this unit, it's safe to drink," he told Rafael. "People can bring water from their own *pietas,* and this machine will purify that too."

Rafael frowned. "But *señor,* how much will it cost?"

"Nothing. It runs on about as much electricity as a light bulb. You pay nothing."

Rafael spoke to the crowd, ending with, *"Nada, nada."* This time there was excitement, especially among the women.

Then an old man at the rear called out something in a raspy voice. He was too far away for Jack to hear, but his words were repeated through the crowd. People began to murmur and drift away, the two workmen among them.

He was left alone with Rafael. "What's going on? What did that old man say?"

"He scared them."

July 3
8:30 a.m.

AS SOON AS HE rolled out of bed and headed for the shower, Santa Lucia Church was on his mind. He was eager to get back to Anapra and see the water purifier in operation. He'd seen poverty in Rio and Johannesburg and many other places, but this time he could make a difference. Why stop with one unit? He'd buy more.

The drive to Anapra was much quicker this time because he accepted bone-jarring jolts from the potholes without slowing down. Haze over the sprawling slum was worse, and there was an acrid smell that hadn't been there the day before. A couple of blocks from the church, the scorched rubber smell was potent. He'd stay just long enough to talk with *Padre* Alarcone and make sure the decontamination unit was operating perfectly. Then he'd follow the directions Ana-Maria had given him to her house.

He turned left onto the side street to Santa Lucia, expecting to see people lined up with buckets of water to be purified. When he pulled up near the church, he couldn't make sense of what he saw.

The church looked like the mortar-blasted rubble in photos of Baghdad. The face of the house of God had been ripped off. Its insides lay exposed. The planks of the altar smoldered.

He walked slowly through the somber crowd, picking his way among shattered debris, speechless at the gut-wrenching sight.

The big church water tank lay on its side, mangled, its precious contents a muddy blotch on the gravelly dirt. No fire could have done so much damage. There must have been an explosion that disintegrated the water purifier and set fire to everything around it.

A man wearing a black and red jacket, face distorted by anger, pointed at Jack and screamed, "Son of a bitch." Everyone turned to look at him. Some shouted and shook their fists at Jack. An old woman picked up a rock and threw it. Jack twisted away and it missed.

"Señor, you must get out." Rafael appeared at his side, guided him quickly past the edge of the crowd and hurried him to the gold Town Car.

"What happened?" he asked Rafael through the window as he started the engine.

"Big bomb in the middle of the night. All of Anapra was afraid."

"Why are they mad at me?"

"The four families make money selling water. Your machine made them mad. Now we have no church."

A rock smashed the passenger-side window. A bigger one slammed into the trunk so hard it shook the car. A teenager wrenched the passenger's door open and lunged for the keys in the ignition. Jack shifted into drive and hit the gas, throwing the boy to the ground. He hunched over the wheel and didn't look back. His heart was pounding.

Damn! It had all gone wrong. No water. No church. He could have been killed. He was shaken by the sudden twist. Then he thought about Ana-Maria. She'd be in no mood to sympathize, let alone help him. In fact, she'd be mad as hell.

Chapter 23

July 3
9:30 a.m.

ANA-MARIA JERKED the door open so quickly she must have been watching for him out the window. Her tears and red-rimmed eyes made it obvious she'd heard what happened at Santa Lucia.

She didn't invite Jack inside, just gestured for him to follow her. Behind the house they sat a couple of feet apart in blue plastic lawn chairs.

"I feel awful about the church," he said.

"You want me to tell you it's all right? It's *not* all right."

"I thought I was—"

"You thought, you thought," she interrupted angrily. "Maybe you know your courtroom. You know nothing about the street." She wiped her eyes. "But I haven't been crying about the church."

"Then what?"

"It's my friend, Juanita. She was supposed to be here at eight for coffee. She didn't come. She would never do that without calling. So I called her over and over on the phone her boss makes her carry everywhere. No answer."

"Maybe she's sick."

"No, something bad happened. I feel it." She covered her face with her hands and wept.

"Let's go to her house." He stood.

Ana-Maria looked up at him, eyes brimming. "You would do that? After the mean things I said?"

"Come on, let's find out."

She reached out and squeezed his hand, then ran to the Town Car. Ruts and potholes punished the car as he drove as fast as he could. Maybe because she'd lost her usual bravado, Ana-Maria seemed smaller as she sat next to him.

She pointed. "That's her place."

Juanita's house was made of four-by-eight sheets of much-used plywood forming a 12 by 16 foot box. A battered 55-gallon drum stood near one corner. The windows, each barred with a heavy grate, were covered by striped yellow drapes. The only paint was on the front wall, a garish greenish-yellow, a bold attempt at cheerfulness. The small private space in front had been raked smooth. Juanita had done her best to make it a home. A dry wind swirled dust devils around them as they walked toward the front door.

"Oh, God, there's no padlock," Ana-Maria said.

"So?"

"She never leaves her house without locking the door behind her. We all do that."

"Maybe she's inside."

"If she is, the door will be locked from inside."

He motioned for her to step to one side. He looked at the door handle and swiped a sweaty palm against his pants leg. If the door wasn't locked, there could be a body inside—and maybe a killer. He tried to look casual, but the violence he'd already experienced in Juarez made his heart pick up speed. He grabbed the handle, and it turned freely. Instead of opening the door, he banged on it. No response. He pushed the door open and stepped back.

Ana-Maria called out, "Juanita, are you there?" No answer.

He had to go in, no question about that. He took two deep breaths and braced himself for whatever might be waiting and entered the one-room space. A small dining table lay on its side. Shards of dishes and glasses that must have been on the table littered the floor. A flimsy wardrobe rack had come apart, dumping cheap, frilly dresses in front of it.

"Look at this place," Ana-Maria gasped from behind him.

"This wasn't robbery. Her little TV is still here, and there's a purse on the counter. The door wasn't forced, meaning Juanita opened it." *Maybe someone she knew and was afraid to turn away, but he wasn't going to say that to Ana-Maria.*

Ana-Maria wandered around the room straightening things, and muttering, "The bastards!" over and over. She gathered clothes from the floor and laid them on the bed. When she picked up a long red dress, she called to him. "Look."

Lying on the floor was a pocket-sized tool that looked like a heavy-duty wire cutter, totally out of character with Juanita's feminine room.

"That might be evidence. Don't touch it." He used a fork through its grip to pick it up for a closer look. It was heavy enough to turn a fist into a blackjack. "Do you recognize this?"

"They use these in the plant to cut wire straps off incoming waste, like bundles of oily rags. But this one's different." She pointed to leather strips woven in a design around the grip. "The ones the plant gives the men are plain because they steal them. This might belong to a supervisor."

Jack wiped his face. It was already sweltering in the little room. "Where would this be used in the plant?"

"Mostly in Shipping & Receiving, where Juanita works."

"So it could be hers?"

"Of course not. She works in an office for the Plant Manager, Antonio Guzman." She brushed flies away.

"Guzman," he exclaimed. "I ran into him when I first got to the plant." He remembered how the man radiated violence.

"He's vicious. If workers under him don't do what he says, he drags them behind the building and beats them up. Juanita tried to transfer out of his office, but he stopped it and punched her in the neck so hard she passed out."

"Jesus! Did Montana know?"

"He knows everything Guzman does. He makes fun of Guzman, calls him 'The Ape,' but they go drinking together at night. She's always been afraid of Guzman, then something happened that made it much worse." She squinted, remembering. "A few months ago, *Señor* Montana put Guzman in charge of plant security. After that, Guzman treated everyone like they were trying to steal from him personally. He made Juanita keep track of tools, supplies, everything. One day she started thinking that maybe yard workers were stealing company gas and diesel fuel. She recorded how much fuel was pumped each day and how much each truck paid for. The totals matched until a while ago when her records showed that they were pumping more than showed up as going into clients' trucks. She was excited and told me she might get a raise. But when she told Guzman what she had discovered, he screamed at her, 'Say one word about that and I'll kill you!' He took her records away and has been nasty to her ever since."

Jack frowned, puzzled. *That was weird. Guzman should have praised her initiative. Instead he'd threatened her. That had to mean she'd stumbled onto something Guzman wanted hidden. Could he be running a rip-off involving fuel that Montana didn't know about? He'd pegged Montana as the enemy, but maybe Guzman should be at the center of the target.*

"But she told you what happened."

"Not for a few days. By then she'd decided she had to tell *Señor* Montana to protect herself."

"Did she?"

"Yes. *Señor* Montana gave her 100 pesos and ordered her to forget it. Now she's gone. Other women have disappeared from the plant—all young, helpless like baby rabbits—but this is different. Juanita knew something Guzman didn't want her to know."

"Is Juanita's office the one where the sign says Plant Manager?"

"It's just inside that door. You go through her office to get to Guzman's."

So when he'd walked into Shipping & Receiving during the tour a couple of nights ago, Guzman had been yelling at Juanita before he turned on the two intruders. And both Guzman and Montana had been upset that Manuel had taken him into Shipping & Receiving. Why?

Whatever was in there, the den of The Ape was absolutely the last place he wanted to go. At the same time, if he could find Juanita, Ana-Maria was much more likely to help him. But even if he was crazy enough to try, how could he get in?

"What time does Guzman leave his office?"

"Before six, always in a hurry to get to the bars."

"Do you have keys to Shipping & Receiving and his office?"

"No, but Juanita does. She has to get into the office while Guzman is still sleeping off his hangovers." She walked to the counter, opened the purse, and extracted a ring with four keys. "These must be the ones."

He reached out his hand. She drew back.

"You can't go there. The night guards would kill you."

"Believe me, breaking and entering is way out of my usual line of work. But I've been learning a lot of new things lately. I'll be careful."

"Why do you want to do this? Is it to find Juanita?"

It would be easy to say yes, but he wouldn't lie to her. He felt certain Juanita wouldn't be at the office, and finding clues there to where she might be was a long shot.

"Maybe I can find something that will help." He reached out and took the keys from her.

"Please. Don't do this." She was so upset she was shaking.

He guided her outside into the burning sunlight, but she turned and went back in. She came out with a padlock, put it through the hasp, and snapped it closed. Trembling, she made the sign of the cross.

Was she protecting Juanita's belongings, or was she subconsciously admitting that Juanita wasn't coming back?

He said nothing else about needing information from her. Nor did he say anything about the blood he'd noticed on the nose of the wire cutters that now lay on the floorboard by his foot.

Chapter 24

July 4
1:00 a.m.

JACK SAT IN the Town Car where he'd parked behind a bar on the main road near the Palmer plant. He checked his watch, again. Just after one a.m. Now that it was time, he couldn't believe he was really about to break into Guzman's office. This was crazy. How had he gotten sucked in to this? But he hadn't. It was his idea. This was the most dangerous thing he'd ever done. And, oh yeah, it was also a crime. The Professional Standards Committee of the California Bar would yank his Bar card so fast it would smoke. As if he gave a damn. What filled his mind now was The Ape. He closed his eyes to steady his nerves. His eyes popped open when he remembered what kind of a neighborhood he was in. Okay, no more stalling. Time to hit the road.

After a ten minute walk, he reached the plant's vehicle entrance gate. It was secured with a six-inch padlock, but the lock on the pedestrian entrance was hanging loose. He let himself in quickly and started walking a wide arc that would end at the Admin building. For part of the way, there was some cover from rough brush, but the last stretch was in the open and brightly lighted by mercury vapor lights on poles.

When he got to the open stretch, he rehearsed what he'd do if spotted by armed guards. *"Yo soy un abogado,"* he'd say, a lawyer, returning to pick up some documents. *Yo trabajo en el edificio de Administration con Señor Montana."* Saying he worked in Admin with Montana should make them think twice before shooting him. He would even act a little drunk. His plan should work—unless they shot him before he got the words out.

After he passed the Admin building and got deeper inside the plant grounds, his cover story made no sense, so he ran the rest of the way to Shipping & Receiving. He was totally vulnerable outside the door in the bright lights as he tried one of the keys. It almost jammed in the lock and wouldn't work. The second was obviously too small. The third did it. He rushed inside and locked the door behind him. The odor of toxic chemicals was so invasive he took only shallow breaths.

He moved cautiously across the rough concrete floor, trying not to make a sound. In the near-dark, he made out a small crane on a flatbed, a forklift, and several pickup trucks lined up along the far wall.

He unlocked the door to the Plant Manager's office where Juanita worked, ducked inside and closed it. Now he was less exposed, but also trapped. Only one way out. He stopped and tried to settle his nerves. *What the hell was he doing here? Was it really worth it?*

He didn't bother answering the question. Instead, he shielded his flashlight with his palm and saw that both side walls were lined chest-high with file cabinets. On Juanita's desk were small framed photos, a glass holding several pens and a stapler, all neatly placed. The space where a computer would usually sit was empty. Several disconnected wires and cables dangled around its perimeter. *Was it coincidence that her computer was missing? Not likely.* He quietly pulled out the desk drawers but found nothing unusual. That meant he had to do what Ana-Maria had warned him against.

Pointing the flashlight at his feet, he unlocked the door to Guzman's inner office, slowly turned the knob and stepped in. He closed the door fast.

Other than an old desk calculator, there was no electronic equipment in the room. No computer, not even a clock. *No surprise. After all, he is "The Ape."* The metal table was covered with piles of invoices and unopened mail, a platter of congealed refried beans, and several hand tools.

Even if he didn't find anything, Ana-Maria would have to give him credit for coming here. She'd have to talk to him. Like hell she would. Ana-Maria would use her inside knowledge as leverage to keep him searching for Juanita.

In his haste, he almost overlooked the cardboard box full of manila envelopes against the wall on the floor. He set it on Guzman's desk and sat in his chair. Every sound outside the office made him freeze. His ears were playing tricks, interpreting the slightest sound as a footstep. His forehead and palms were damp.

Opening the manila envelope on top, he immediately understood what the contents were because Ana-Maria had delivered similar files to him yesterday morning. They were called "trip files." Each manila envelope bore a number, the name of the client, and the city and state of its headquarters. Inside were details of each shipment to Palmer, including the number of trucks in the convoy, types and quantity of toxic wastes delivered, weight, and trip mileage. They also showed the amount of gas or diesel fuel received at the Palmer fuel pumps. Something about discrepancies in the amount of fuel use had thrown Guzman into a rage—not at the discrepancies, but at Juanita.

Because most entries were numbers, he was able to scan each envelope quickly. Nothing caught his eye until he came to an envelope marked

"Delta Technical Engineering, Portland, Oregon." One difference was obvious. It was the only one where the first page wasn't typed. The information was entered in a handwritten scrawl that couldn't have come from the pen of fastidious Juanita. But it could belong to The Ape himself. If so, this envelope held material Juanita was not meant to see. It was Guzman's private file, and that made it important.

The contents of the Portland envelope also differed in that its pages weren't completely filled in. There were separate pages, one for each convoy. Entries showed only dates of arrival and departure, number of trucks per convoy, which varied between three and six, and how much fuel each received from the company pump. Nothing else. The type of waste on board, mileage, and the other categories were blank. Maybe Guzman left out what he didn't want in writing.

This one envelope was a Rosetta stone, if he could read its code. Flipping through the pages, it struck him how many there were, all from a single source in Portland, Oregon. But maybe they weren't all from Portland. Maybe they came from many locations and Guzman used Portland as a cover. But if that were true, why go to all that trouble? The answer was in this envelope if he could open his mind.

He froze at a sound coming from the cargo bay, sure it was the scrape of a boot on concrete. Motionless, straining to hear, he waited out anyone listening on the other side of the door. After a minute of silence, he decided it was a false alarm.

Holding the flashlight under his right armpit, he scanned Portland again, then a few of the other envelopes. Maybe it was his heightened senses and fear of being trapped that made the clue pop out as if written in red ink. The routine for all incoming trucks was to log into the plant, unload, take on fuel, and immediately leave for home. But every convoy entered in the Portland envelope—and only in that envelope—arrived one day, filled up with fuel, filled up again the next day, and then left.

What was that about?

Maybe those were the simple facts Juanita had innocently pointed out to Guzman. Why would that be so secret that he threatened to kill her if she mentioned it to anyone else?

Each Portland truck used a full tank of fuel overnight which meant it had made a long trip during that time. Why would those trucks make local trips when using a Mexican truck would be much cheaper? The amount of fuel consumed on that round trip, dutifully recorded, could tell him how far they went but not where.

It was important to Guzman, and presumably Montana, to keep these overnight trips out of company records. But then Juanita uncovered a telltale. She didn't understand its significance, but that didn't matter to them. Rather than risk their secret being revealed, they killed her. He'd been sure she was dead from the moment he saw blood on the wire cutter.

A powerful beam of light showed under Guzman's door. Jack shut off his flashlight and rolled under Guzman's desk, almost choking on the stinking debris. He'd been so caught up in playing detective that he hadn't heard the outer office door open. A gruff voice called something to a partner who must still be in the cargo bay. The other called back, something about "Guzman."

The door was jerked open. Light slashed around the room. The guard's dusty boots were visible under the edge of the desk. Jack imagined the guard sniffing, trying to get the scent of an intruder. Maybe not really expecting anyone to have violated The Ape's inner sanctum, he backed out and closed the door. A moment later, the outer door closed. It could be a trick to lure him out. He stayed hidden for several minutes.

After he struggled out from under the desk he used short bursts of light to stack the manila envelopes into the box and put it back in place.

He tucked the Portland file under his arm as evidence, then realized that would be genuinely stupid. When Guzman discovered that the Portland envelope was missing, he'd go to red alert. Since he'd already been suspicious of Juanita, he'd damn sure go after anyone Juanita might have confided in. That would lead him straight to her best friend, Ana-Maria.

Exactly where had the manila envelope been in the stack before? If Guzman noticed it was out of place, he'd know he'd had a middle-of-the-night visitor. He slid it into the stack and hoped Guzman wasn't that observant.

He fished out the key, locked the door of Guzman's office then felt his way to the door leading into the cargo bay. He cracked it open a fraction of an inch at a time. Any second, guards waiting in ambush could fire a hailstorm of bullets. Instead, he heard nothing more than the normal creaks of an empty warehouse. In the cargo bay, he turned back and locked the office door.

Damn it! He'd trapped himself. He should have locked that door behind him when he first went in. The guard who routinely tested the door as he passed by on his rounds had found it unlocked. That's what had alerted him to check inside. If he found it locked on his next round, he'd know it hadn't been left open accidently earlier and would sound the alarm immediately. To buy time, Jack had to leave the door unlocked, but that would only delay the inevitable.

When the guard reported the unlocked doors in the morning, Guzman would know it was no oversight. To make it worse, in the dark Jack had probably disturbed more than he knew. Guzman might spot that, and if he did, it wouldn't be long before he remembered the *gringo* lawyer sent in to snoop on the company. And he'd wonder where the keys had come from.

Nothing to do about it now, so he crept along the wall of the cargo bay and unlocked the outside door. He opened it a crack and listened for guards on patrol. He crouched and stuck his head out. No one in sight, so he bolted for the front gate.

Before turning the corner of a building, he stopped to listen for thuds, scrapes, echoes, anything ahead. Silence. Then from behind him came two voices, low, serious. The patrol. If he stayed where he was in the light from the mercury vapor bulbs, they'd have him. If he ran, they'd kill him. There was no shelter except a trash bin with the top raised. He swung his legs over the greasy rim and rolled inside, landing on his back, cushioned by garbage. If they'd seen him, the last sound he'd hear would be a barrage of slugs penetrating the metal bin.

Their boots crunched gravel. As they got closer, a fierce cramp stung his left thigh demanding that he straighten his leg. He gritted his teeth against the pain. If either guard glanced inside the bin, he was done. The steps slowly receded.

This was his only shot to make it to the gate. He hauled himself out of the bin, smelling like week-old fish tacos, and sprinted, adrenaline at gale force, through the gate.

A half-mile away from the plant, pushing the Town Car past 80 mph, he shouted "Yes!" into the night and pumped his left fist up and down out the car window. He was alive. He'd penetrated enemy lines and escaped.

But he'd left a trail. It was just a matter of time until someone started tracking him.

Chapter 25

THE "CLICK" BARELY registered in his sleep-fogged mind. It had no context until he heard the bottom of the door to his suite brush across the thick carpet then close with another click. Someone was inside. Guzman had found him. Lying in bed, back toward the door, he was totally vulnerable. He'd have to roll out of bed and defend himself without knowing where Guzman was in the room or what kind of weapon he had.

Before he could move, a soft voice asked, "May I come in? My cousin at the desk gave me the key."

He sat up and, in the faint light coming through the curtains, saw it was Ana-Maria. "What are you doing here?"

"I was so worried about you I couldn't sleep. I had to find out what happened." She started unbuttoning her long gray cloak, the uniform many women in Juarez wore to fend off leers and jeers.

"Nothing I couldn't handle." It was easy to talk like a Harrison Ford character now that he'd escaped from the plant. "But I didn't find out where Juanita is." He wouldn't tell her that what he had found made it almost certain that Juanita was dead.

From outside he heard the unmistakable yelps kids make as they jump into a pool. *What time was it anyway?* He checked his watch. Six thirty! Damn short night.

Ana-Maria stopped unbuttoning her cloak. "I know where she is." Her puffy eyes and flat tone said it all. "She's dead."

"I'm so sorry." *He hadn't been able to help Juanita. Had he somehow put her more at risk?* "How do you know?"

"My neighbor works a night shift for the city. He was down by the river when they found Juanita. His wife came to my house and told me. I've been crying ever since."

She undid the last two buttons, slipped the cloak from her shoulders and laid it on a chair. Her dress was dark blue, tied at the waist with a white sash, cut so low that her full breasts were almost bare. No bra. She sat on the edge of the bed, shoulders bowed, eyes downcast.

He felt very naked under the covers.

"They threw her away like she was nothing," Ana-Maria said bitterly. "They made it look the same as the others so people would say, 'oh well, another one.' But I know better."

He reached out and squeezed her hand.

"You're a good man," she said, looking up, "not like the others. I had to see you, to have you hold me." She touched his cheek, stared at him for several seconds, then nodded as if she'd just made up her mind about something.

She moved closer to him. Her fingers slid down the side of his neck then along his collarbone and across his chest, her eyes on his. She lightly touched his nipples, then took his face in both hands and kissed him gently, warmly, then more intimately.

She was Montana's assistant, so he had pegged her as an adversary, someone he had to persuade to reveal what she knew. Now she was a woman who smelled of musk and whose tongue signaled him that . . . what?

She drew away and stood up beside the bed. *Was she having second thoughts? Had he misunderstood?* She looked slowly around the suite, taking in the carved furnishings and the Freda Kahlo print, maybe imagining the extravagance of staying in such a place.

With her left hand she reached inside the dress and caressed her right breast. Her other hand undid two small buttons, and the blue dress opened down to the sash. She reached behind her back, untied the fastening, and the sash dropped to the floor. She shrugged her shoulders. Catching for a moment at the tips of her breasts, the dress became a dark blue puddle at her feet.

Her audacity made her incredibly alluring. He reached out, but she shook her head slightly. She cupped her hands beneath breasts that needed no support; golden skin, aureoles that were a mysterious canvas for erect nipples. She squeezed them gently, as if milk might flow.

Under the sheet, his penis had risen stiff as a totem.

Her hips swayed side-to-side, more primal than dance, not performing, simply being. She brought her middle finger to her mouth, sucked it and used it to circle her left nipple. Her hand slid in slow motion down her smooth belly into the silky hair. She kneaded the knoll of flesh like a cat. Her hips moved toward him and away and toward him again.

He'd never been so aroused, but wouldn't reach for her until she was ready.

Hands on her hips, she leaned slightly toward him. "I will fill your mouth with my breast and lick your nipples. And then, Mr. Jack Strider from San Francisco, you will make love with me until you can't stand."

She drew the sheet away from his body and pushed him back on the pillows. She kissed him deeply, twisting her head from side to side, brushing her body over his. The weight and fullness of her breasts was driving him crazy. Her mouth started to search out his body's secrets. Always, some part of her stayed in touch with his penis. He lost track of time.

With a heroic effort, he tore himself away and dashed to the bathroom for the protection he always carried in his leather Dopp kit.

Then, deep inside her, during seconds when movement was tensely suspended, he said things to her that came from a place he hadn't known existed in him. Every time he was about to explode, she gripped his shaft and held back the tsunami. Then she didn't, and he couldn't maintain control, didn't want to, and he erupted.

Afterwards, he curled up behind her, cupping her body inside his, feeling their breathing slow. As his mind roamed back over where they'd been together, he realized she hadn't climaxed. Her every move had been about him—to arouse him, tease him, bring him to a peak and hold him there and, finally, to let him cross over. He wanted to give her the pleasure she'd given him, so he put his hand on her thigh and slowly drew his fingers up between her legs. Heat radiated from her center. His finger rose into the silk.

Her hand covered his and brought it back to rest on her thigh, her eyes open, watching him. He kissed her forehead. "You didn't enjoy this as much as I did. Was it me?"

"Not you. It's something other men did, men who just took what they wanted. I learned to not be in the room when it was happening."

"I'm sorry." He wanted to comfort her, wanted to erase those experiences from her memory, but he knew words couldn't do that. But something bothered him so he asked, "Ana-Maria, why did you come to my room?"

She turned her head away again. "To see if you were all right."

"Please tell me the truth. Did you have this in mind?"

"All right, you want the truth, but maybe the truth is not so nice. Guzman will come for me next. I feel it in my belly. I can't stop him. Unless you help me, I will die. You don't know what it's like to be helpless."

She was right. He'd lost a lot in the past weeks, but education, money, and a lifetime of success were firewalls between him and feeling helpless. It was a chasm between them he wasn't sure he could cross.

He wrapped his arms around her, felt the satin of her skin, kissed behind her ear. He wanted to admit the real reason he'd courted her at lunch, but couldn't risk telling her. She was okay with using him, but she might resent the hell out of him using her. "I'll do everything I can to keep Guzman from hurting you."

She smiled slightly, fluffed up the pillows and lay back against them, hands clasped behind her head, bed sheet at her waist. "Then I'm ready."

After the intimacy they'd just shared, he was barely able to focus his eyes, but if she was ready again so was he. He leaned forward to kiss her. And this time he'd find a way to help her enjoy it.

She gently pushed him away. "No, I mean I'm ready to tell you what I know about Palmer Industries."

The quick shift into the moment he'd been working toward surprised him. She was about to be his GPS.

"That's good news. Do you know if Juanita had a computer on her desk?"

"Yes."

"It's gone."

"Then Guzman took it. The workers are terrified of him. They wouldn't go into that office if the door was wide open with a million pesos piled on the floor."

"The power cord was still there, so he didn't care about using the computer." He paused, considering where the logic took him. "He wanted to prevent anyone from getting into the hard drive and reading the files. But that doesn't help us."

"Why not?"

"Because I don't know what was on it and can't prove he took it. It's no more proof than the wire cutter, which I still have, that we can't prove was Guzman's. Even if his fingerprints are on it, he can say it was stolen. Think hard. Can you remember anything else Juanita told you about Guzman?"

As she ran her fingertips through her hair, his eyes kept sliding to her breasts. Recent memories were about to get him way off track. He felt a stirring and shifted to hide it from her.

"Maybe I know more than Juanita did," she said. "When she told me about the missing fuel, it didn't mean anything to me. Now it does. I know where it's going. The fuel pumps are right outside my office window, so I see all the trucks coming in and going out. A while ago I noticed some trucks that were different."

"Different how?"

"They're all black and come into the plant close together, nose to tail. Nothing is unloaded from them except the crews that bring them in. There's always a van waiting with new crews. They refuel and leave right away. They're back the next day, sometimes early, sometimes later. The first crews, always hung over, take on more fuel, and leave. Then about a week ago a convoy of trucks began arriving in the morning too. They change crews, get fuel, and keep going. I don't know when they come back because

I'm off work by then."

Her description helped explain what he'd read in the Portland envelope, except that frequency of trips was increasing. "Anything else?"

"Those black trucks are the biggest I've seen at the plant. At first, there were only three trucks at a time. Now, sometimes five or six. I tried to look them up in the trip files, but I couldn't find them."

She couldn't find those trip files because they were in a manila envelope in Guzman's office. "How often do the trucks show up?"

"I don't keep track, but they never load or unload anything at Palmer."

"Where could they go and get back the next day?"

"Quien sabe? Who knows. Chihuahua City? Even farther."

"Did anyone else notice them, maybe talk about them?"

"The men work shifts. Anyone on duty when the trucks arrive wouldn't be working when they come back. Only me, working all day, staring out the window when I get bored."

The mystery trucks only existed in hidden files. Now he had descriptions and schedules. In the meantime, he had to get back to what Montana was doing on-site.

"I asked you before whether Montana keeps two sets of records, but you wouldn't tell me."

"I didn't trust you then. Now I do. There *are* two sets. One is in his office. One he keeps somewhere else. The set you saw shows purchases of equipment needed to treat hazardous waste. Some of those purchases never happened. And it shows payments to dump sites for disposal. Some of those payments were never made because nothing was sent."

"Don't the government inspectors realize that equipment is missing?"

"They walk around the plant for a few minutes, do a few tests, make some notes, then come to the air-conditioned Admin building to get out of the hot sun. They hit on women and tell stories until *Señor* Montana sends for them. All four inspectors are smiling when they leave his office. We don't see them until the next month."

"Montana bribes them?"

She gave him a look that said "only a blind pig wouldn't understand what's going on" and didn't answer.

"If the inspectors aren't filing negative reports, why is PROFEPA going after Palmer?"

"I overheard *Señor* Montana on the phone saying some local company that Palmer Industries takes business away from must have paid PROFEPA to get him in trouble."

"Could the PROFEPA lawyers have gotten a copy of the real records?"

"No. All the data that goes into the real books, I enter into my computer. Then he stands over me while I transfer those files to a DVD. He takes it and watches me delete those files from my computer."

This information tied Montana to bribery and fraud, but so far, the evidence was all indirect. Montana had covered his tracks well. That's why he was so cocky.

"Anything else?"

"A couple of weeks ago, a man came to the office with an envelope stamped "Confidential." He had been ordered to deliver it only to *Señor* Montana's hand and wouldn't tell me who it was from. After an hour, *Señor* Montana returned and took the envelope. Later, while he was out of his office, I saw the envelope and what looked like some sort of form on his desk. I read it as fast as I could. It was a copy of a PROFEPA report that said the Palmer incinerator was sending out too much di . . . something."

"Dioxins?"

"That was it, dioxins. The report said the fumes cause birth defects and poison the breast milk of some mothers." She pressed her fingers against her own breast.

In Alvarez's hands, that letter could be the smoking gun he planned to use to nail Montana. "Did you make a copy?"

"I was afraid. *Señor* Montana was still in the building."

How had PROFEPA gotten incinerator readings? Maybe one of the inspectors had taken a reading and accidentally let it slip through to a supervisor. What mattered was that PROFEPA had the information. Maybe that explained why Alvarez was being allowed to go forward.

Ana-Maria's oral testimony would be far less than conclusive, but for his purposes, she'd confirmed what Montana was doing, part of it anyway. He made a silent vow to take that miserable son-of-a-bitch down.

An awkward moment settled on them. Ana-Maria had what she'd come for, his promise of protection. He squeezed her hand.

"You need to be very careful. Juanita told Guzman about the missing fuel, and now she's dead. Guzman knows you and Juanita were close friends, so he'll think she told you. On top of that, they know by now that someone broke into Guzman's office. Guzman and Montana will be mad as rhinos in heat."

What he needed to say next would change her life forever, but he had no choice.

"You can't go back to work. Don't even go home. You said you want me to protect you. Then let me get you out of here. I'll give you money and take you to the airport right now." Then he saw the problem. "Do you have a passport?"

"No." She took a deep breath and let it out.

"Then flying is out." He started to say he'd take her across in his car, but she'd have to have a visa—and they'd check for sure.

"Do you have a visa for entry into the U.S.?"

"No, not even a driver's license," she whispered. She bowed her head and he imagined her thinking about Juanita, and about leaving her home and her country for the unknown.

He knew she couldn't get a visa at the border. It had to come from a U.S. consulate, and there was no time for that. If he tried to sneak her in and they were caught, Ana-Maria could wind up in the Juarez jail where Montana would have her killed if he found out. And if the U.S. authorities took Jack into custody, he couldn't help her and couldn't stop Montana. He couldn't risk that.

"There is a way," she said, and determination replaced despair on her face. "My cousin knows a *coyote* who gets people across the border. But it is—"

"I know. It's expensive. I'll pay for it."

She gave him a long look, as if measuring how safe she would be depending on a *gringo* who didn't understand the streets. Then she rose from the bed, turned away from him, and got dressed.

He hated having to trust a *coyote*, but it was the only way.

ANA-MARIA SPOKE through the metal grate guarding the front door of a well-kept house on a Juarez side street a couple of blocks south of the Rio Grande. From what he overheard, the stout woman inside, wearing a shapeless yellow dress, seemed to be expecting them.

"My cousin called her," Ana-Maria said to him. "She says to come in. It's not safe to stand on the front porch."

Ana-Maria and the woman left him alone in the front room. The three windows were covered with dark fabric thumb-tacked to the frame. The only dim light came from a metal lamp. He looked around. This *coyote* must be getting fat on the money he gets from people desperate to flee to the States, but he sure didn't flaunt it.

He had a bad feeling about the place. The *coyote* would assume he was carrying a large amount of cash, and no one knew they were there. They could be ripped off, even killed. In Juarez, that wouldn't make a ripple. He cased the room for ways to defend them if he had to.

He checked his watch. This was taking too long. He touched his wallet, as he had several times since leaving the bank where he'd withdrawn $6,000 U.S.

He felt a little creepy. He was here to hire someone to smuggle a beautiful young woman into the U.S. Too damn close to what Peck had done. If they were caught, Rick Calder would rake him over the coals.

106

Ana-Maria returned from deeper inside the house. "It's done."

"Where will you be taken?"

"She won't tell me."

"I want to meet the man."

Ana-Maria spoke to the woman, who disappeared into the next room. After a minute or so, from the shadows in the next room, a man said, *"Buenos dias, señor."*

The man didn't intend to be identified, and it would be a bad idea to push it. They needed him.

"I'll pay you half now, the other half when I know she's safe."

"No, *señor.*"

The man's footsteps receded across the inner room.

"Wait. Here's all the money." He handed $5,000 to the woman. And here's a card with my cell phone number. Call me as soon as she's safe, and I'll pay you another $500."

The man returned to the other side of the doorway, and the woman handed him the money and Jack's card.

No response from the other room. *Did they have a deal or was it a scam?*

"Sí, señor, con mucho gusto," the man said and withdrew into the dark.

"Let's go," he said to Ana-Maria. "What time do you have to be back here?"

"I told her I was going to my house to get pictures of my family and the small ring my mother gave me. It's the only thing I have from her. But she said I can't leave this house. It's for their protection."

"Protection? What's she talking about?"

"One time somebody left and decided to make money by bringing the police here. They demanded a big bribe or they would take her husband to jail. So they make everyone a prisoner until they cross."

"When will that be?"

"They say maybe tonight, maybe three, four days. I hope it's tonight." She pointed to her blue dress. "I can't wear this for three more days."

He took her to the front corner of the room, blocking her from the view of the woman. "Keep this money out of sight," he said, handing her $1,000. "Get far away from the border and call me as soon as you can. I'll set up a bank account where you can draw money to live on."

Maybe this would work, but a lot could go wrong. The *coyote* could take the money from her. So could someone else being taken across. Or there could be trouble on the other side. But it was the only way.

She leaned forward and kissed him. "I wish . . . I wish." Tears filled her eyes.

Chapter 26

July 4
4:30 p.m.

THE PHONE ON his desk at the condo finally rang. *About damned time.*

"Jack, I was with a client when you called earlier." Sinclair's booming voice forced Jack's ear away from the receiver. "Mrs. Pounders told me you're back in Mexico City."

"I got in from Juarez a couple of hours ago. I called to tell you that Palmer Industries doesn't have a prayer at that PROFEPA Hearing."

"That's not what I want to hear."

"That's the way it is. Montana gave me nothing. No help with a defense. The records he provided are phony. Palmer Industries will look even worse if it gets caught introducing those bogus records at the Hearing." It was time to be blunt about what Sinclair had to do to help him pull this off. "Tell Arthur to let me throw Palmer Industries on the mercy of the Hearing judge. Admit failures. Offer to pay a fine. Make a written pledge that Palmer Industries will fix everything."

"I doubt if Arthur will—"

"One more thing. He has to fire Montana. If Arthur won't do all that, he should notify clients that he's going out of business."

"If he won't go along, what's your strategy?"

Sinclair had never before asked him about his strategy. Maybe that was because Arthur was counting on Montana to bribe the judge. What they didn't know was that the PROFEPA lawyers were fanatics and would never let the judge get away with it. So why ask about strategy now? Maybe fishing to find out what he intended to do.

Either way, he and Sinclair shared a goal: keep the plant operating. Sinclair wanted that for his client. Jack wanted it to save his career. But he had another goal they might or might not share. That was to stop Montana from breaking the law.

"I don't have any other strategy. Palmer Industries *should* be forced to clean up its act. Montana's fake books make it look like he's treating hazardous waste properly, but he's not."

"That's a serious charge. Have you seen the so-called real books?"

"No, but I—"

"But you know where they are, right?"

"They're on DVDs, and Montana has those."

"So this is all conjecture, but let's suppose—" He dragged out the word. "—for the sake of argument that Montana has been faking some records. Maybe he did it to avoid taxes. That doesn't merit the death penalty, by which I mean shutting down the plant."

"For God's sake, Justin, this isn't about tax evasion." He took a deep breath to keep from venting his frustration. "You remember when Edward Palmer claimed Montana couldn't be generating such high profits unless he was cutting corners and bribing people? Edward was right. That's the reason for the fake records. Besides that, the PROFEPA counsel, Alvarez, has test results showing that the plant incinerator is emitting dioxin fumes that can poison breast milk and cause cancer. Montana saw that report and didn't modify the incinerator. Those test results may be part of the reason Montana's in Mexico City right now."

The gravity of that possibility must have gotten Sinclair's attention, because he didn't respond right away. "Fax me a copy," he finally said.

"I don't have one, but my source has seen it."

"Who is this source?"

If he exposed Ana-Maria, Sinclair might tell Arthur, and it would get back to Montana. Even after she was safely out of Mexico, he'd never reveal her name.

"I have a reliable source. I'm going to leave it at that."

He could tell Sinclair about Montana's bribery of inspectors and that the plant manager was probably a murderer. He could also tell him about the mystery trucks. But without solid proof, there was no point.

"Then," Sinclair said, "I'll be blunt. No Mexican judge wants to put a big American company out of business, and government ministers aren't going to give up the big cars and beach homes that come from appreciative *maquila* owners. This Hearing judge won't shut the plant down unless you're a no-show and he gets cornered into granting an injunction. Here's my problem. You've made it clear you don't like this client, so I need your word you will register your appearance to prevent a default against Palmer Industries. And I urge you to remember that for a successful partner in this firm, as you could be, all things are possible in the future. Do you really want to let people think you can't get the job done?"

If Sinclair had been subtle when he was a diplomat, he wasn't bothering with that now. But he still knew how to dangle a little temptation—become a leader in a powerhouse firm and everything, even SCOTUS, was possible.

"I'll be there, but you could send Clarence Darrow in as counsel and he couldn't win this, unless you follow my recommendations."

Away from the phone, Sinclair said, "Come in, Mrs. Pounders. Excuse me, Jack, I have to sign something."

Jack leaned back in his chair and closed his eyes, feeling as if he were watching a slide show. Click: an infant being bathed in filthy ditch water. Click: thugs with semiautomatic rifles patrolling the Palmer grounds. Click: a mother suckling her child with carcinogenic breast milk. His way forward was absolutely clear.

"I'm back," Sinclair said. "Do we understand one another?"

"We certainly do."

"Good man. I knew I could count on you. By the way, when word got to Rick Calder that you'd left the country on short notice, he went ballistic. He knew better than to call me after he smeared the firm's name in that *Chronicle* article, so he got his message to me through one of our partners. He said he has you in his sights."

Calder was like a bad-tempered pit bull who couldn't let go. But he was a problem for the future. Right now, Jack had his hands full with people who might literally have him in their sights.

Chapter 27

July 4
8:00 p.m.

"YOU HAVE A visitor, *Señor* Strider." It was the reception clerk for his condo. "It is *Señorita* Vanderberg. Shall I send her up?"

"What?" Jack said, startled. "Are you sure about the name?"

"Yes, *señor*, shall I send her up?"

"No, I'll come down to get her." He felt as flustered as a teenager.

"She didn't wait. She's already in the elevator, *señor.*"

He was standing at the elevator door when Debra emerged, stunning in a khaki suit and dark green blouse, laptop case in one hand, tether of a rolling suitcase in the other.

"Buenos tardes, señor." She dropped the tether and gave him a mock salute. "Reporting for duty."

He stared at her, confused. "What are you doing here? I'm glad to see you, but . . ."

"Our exalted leader sent me. That meant he also took me off the biggest securities offering I've ever worked on. At first I was angry, but on the flight I decided this might not be such bad duty after all."

My God, this morning he'd been in bed with Ana-Maria, and yet he was so happy to see Debra he wanted to take her in his arms and show her how glad he was. He hoped Debra couldn't hear the collisions of his conflicting emotions.

Inside the condo, she looked around. "Wow! Not exactly a hardship post. Driving from the airport through this huge city is a little intimidating, but this neighborhood is beautiful. Now, how 'bout leaving my stuff here and finding some place that serves killer margaritas?"

LIGHTS WERE beginning to flick on as they followed his usual path down Calle Michoacan. He stole sideways glances at Debra, still flabbergasted that she was actually walking beside him in La Condesa. Maybe she wouldn't notice how many of the big sedans and SUVs cruising down the street were armored. Or how many armed "watchers" stood on corners. He put his right arm around her shoulder and gave her a squeeze. But despite his feelings, he'd put her on a plane to San Francisco first thing tomorrow.

He chose La Bomtagne because it specialized in margaritas. The *mesero* led them past a dance floor to a horseshoe-shaped booth with leather cushions. A waiter, smiling and bowing slightly, appeared within seconds to take their drink orders.

A few minutes later, Debra sipped a margarita from a salt-rimmed glass the size of a small punchbowl and checked him out.

"Navy blue shirt, pressed khakis, polished loafers. You're out of your 'I'm-a-serious-lawyer' uniform. I might not have recognized you if we'd passed on the street, but I certainly would have smiled."

She had no idea who he was—that he sometimes wore a leather bracelet given him by a Masai chief, had kayaked through the Grand Canyon, and a lot more she wouldn't expect. But that was a conversation for a different time.

"Now that you've recognized me," he said, "maybe you'll tell me why Sinclair sent you here."

"I honestly don't know. At first I assumed it was to help you prepare for the Hearing, but it's too late for that. He gave me some work to do in Juarez for Palmer Industries, but that made no sense since you're already here. Anyway, Mrs. Pounders had booked the flight and reserved a suite at the Four Seasons. I barely had time to get to SFO. Now here I am, listening to a hot mariachi band."

She delicately licked salt off the rim of her glass. "Sinclair did say that in case you missed the Hearing for some reason, I was to be there and introduce myself as representing Palmer Industries. He said, 'Just sit there and let the judge handle it.' He didn't even give me the Palmer file to read, so I know exactly zip about the situation."

"What did you think he meant when he said I might miss the Hearing?"

"That at the last minute you might refuse to defend the Palmers on principle. In case you boycotted, he didn't want Palmer to lose by default."

If Sinclair really thought he might take a hike, sending Debra as backup was what any smart lawyer would do. Jack wasn't offended.

"Thinking I might dump the client could also explain why he asked you to go to Juarez," he said. "What did he tell you to do there?"

"Draft hazardous waste treatment contracts with three new Mexican clients. So I'll be meeting the mysterious Mr. Montana. Tell me about him."

"Short answer: he's a toad. I went to Juarez because I needed information from him. But soon after I got there, he announced he was leaving for Mexico City. Later on, I found out he keeps two sets of records. That has to be because the real books would torpedo any defense. There's a lot more, but nothing I can prove yet." Time to change the subject. He'd already said too much. The less she knew, the safer she'd be.

He got the waiter's attention and tapped the rim of his glass, then turned back to her. "What were you about to tell me just before you walked out on dinner at Boulevard?"

She looked at him quizzically. "Sure you want to know?"

"Ever since that night."

She hesitated, as if unsure that she wanted to answer. Then she shrugged and said, "Okay. Once upon a time there was this second year law student who took an extra course because she needed the units and heard the guy who taught it was brilliant. At the time, that student had the highest GPA in her class and was odds-on favorite to be editor-in-chief of law review. But the grade she got was just low enough to knock her out of the job."

Oh, no. He got the picture. "Was that my course in advanced international economics?"

She nodded.

"I had no idea. To be objective in grading I always avoided knowing the personal circumstances of my students." *My God, he sounded like a cold fish wrapped in a stuffed shirt.* "But why didn't you talk with me about it?"

He knew that the scathing look she gave him summed up the reasons a very smart, proud young woman doesn't go to any professor to try for a higher grade.

"There was nothing to talk about," she said. "The grade was fair. I just took too many courses that quarter, and did so much work on law review I was always behind. I caught up in the other courses, but didn't quite cut it in yours." She paused and swallowed hard. "I got a great clerkship, but since I hadn't been editor-in-chief it wasn't the Supreme Court. The memory still bites me at unexpected moments. That's what happened during dinner at Boulevard. Don't worry about it."

Jack got it. Even though she thought the grade he'd given her was fair, that hadn't silenced the "what-might-have-been" demon. It probably never would. He knew that demon too well.

"You should see your face," she said and smiled a little. "Did you hear me? Don't worry about it."

The server set down several steaming platters of food. His helper placed three Tecate beer bottles in the center of the tile tabletop.

"Excuse me," Jack said, "we didn't order any of this."

The server gestured vaguely toward the bar and bowed himself away.

"Good Mexican food deserves cold Mexican beer." The male voice came from beyond the halo of light from the lamp hanging above the table. *"Con permiso,"* he said as he stepped into the light. "You are *Señorita* Vanderberg. I am Tomás Montana. Call me Tomás." He took her hand without shaking it, held it for a couple of seconds too long, then slid into the booth next to her.

Still rattled by Debra's revelation, Montana's arrival caught Jack flatfooted. He didn't like it one damned bit.

"Surprised to see me, Jack? You shouldn't be. I can find you anywhere, day and night. No problem."

He wouldn't take the bait. "I'm sorry you didn't find me sooner. Actually, I thought you might be avoiding me."

"But you're my lawyer, no? Why would I avoid you?" His smirk was arctic. "Come." He distributed the glistening bottles of beer. *"Salud y pesetas y amor y tiempo para gustarlos.* Health, money, love, and time to enjoy them."

Jack didn't drink. Why had Montana shown up here? Did he suspect his lawyer had been trespassing at the plant? Well, to hell with him. Instead of forcing him to leave the table, he'd try to get something out of him. He'd just wait for the right opening.

"Your beauty is a blessing on the city, *Señorita* Vanderberg," Montana said. "What brings you here?"

"To do a little legal work for Palmer Industries."

"That will be a pleasant change for me. You must know our friend Jack was sent to Juarez as a spy." Despite the nasty word, his smile didn't change. "But I think he found nothing. Was the trip worth your time, Jack?" He leaned forward, eyes a little glassy.

"Time well spent," Jack said.

"Fortunately, we're making so much money that even your fee won't dent our profits. But let's not spoil our dinner with business talk. I'd much rather talk with *Señorita* Vanderberg." Quickly draining his Tecate, he ordered three more for the table.

He let Montana act like the host, monopolizing Debra's attention with local folklore and humorous stories. Montana would fend him off if he asked questions, so he'd lay back and give Montana time to make a mistake.

After Montana delivered the punch line of an off-color joke, Debra glanced at the floor filled with couples and said, "That's a great band."

Montana leapt to his feet, hand outstretched. "It would be my pleasure to be your partner. May I call you Debra?"

When Debra rose and slipped out of her suit jacket, Jack noticed that her move was appreciated by every man around them.

He watched Debra dance with Montana, her dark hair swirling like the cloak of a whirling dervish. After sitting through several tunes, his wait-and-watch strategy had put him in a sour mood. He ordered another tequila. When she still hadn't returned to the table after several more minutes, he tossed back the tequila and headed for the restroom. When he returned, they weren't on the floor. He looked at the other tables and the bar. They had disappeared.

The server tugged at his sleeve. "The *señorita* said she was going dancing and will see you later." He stepped away quickly, as if he feared Jack might deck him for bringing the message.

Jack got the bill and found it included everything Montana had ordered. Paying quickly, he walked out of the restaurant full of men who believed they knew exactly what had happened. No sign of them outside. Debra had vanished in one of the largest cities on the planet with an unscrupulous bastard who was probably a killer. He confronted the doorman and two valet parkers.

"The woman who came in with me, where did she go?" Their faces were blank. "She left with a man in white pants."

At this, the two valets snickered and exchanged elbow-digs.

"A thousand pesos if you tell me where they went." He held the bills up, more than a month's pay.

The doorman said, "They got into a taxi and went that way." He pointed down the street.

"That's no help at all. Nothing more?"

"*Nada mas, señor.*"

He turned away.

"*Señor?*"

He turned back. The man had his hand out.

"Give me the names of five clubs in that direction, expensive ones, that have dance bands," Jack said. After he got the names, he handed over one hundred pesos and grabbed a cab.

He searched place after place, all huge, crowded and loud. He got more names and tried some of them before he admitted it was pointless.

JACK PACED across the condo's living room, as he'd been doing for more than two hours. That son-of-a-bitch had made a move on Debra the moment he walked up to the table. Then he sweet-talked her into going off with him. She had no idea what she was getting into. He imagined the worst.

There must be thousands of dance bands in the city, but he couldn't wait any longer. He had to go back to La Bomtagne. If he couldn't pry information out of someone, he'd start hitting the night spots one by one.

As he headed for the door, he heard three quick raps. He jerked the door open so fast that Debra, slightly disheveled and unsteady, stumbled inside. He grabbed her by both shoulders, more relieved than angry.

Still, there was anger in his voice when he said, "Are you crazy, taking a chance like that? And without saying a word to me."

Smiling, she put two fingers to his lips. "Shhh. I'm okay."

"Where's Montana?"

"He tried to push his way onto the elevator, but the desk clerk recognized me and saw what was happening. He yelled to a security guy who hauled our *Señor* Montana onto the street. He was furious, like he'd never been dumped before." She wandered across the room and pushed the drapes aside, letting in the glow from tiny lights in the trees in the park across the street.

"Where have you been?"

"He was hot to teach me to salsa." She did a slightly wobbly twirl. "I pulled the plug when he started in on the tango after the band had packed up. Look." She leaned forward and kissed him on the cheek. "If I'd told you what I was about to do, you'd have tried to stop me. I didn't need protection. I have more than enough martial arts fire power to take him out."

She walked past him, tossed her purse onto a chair, and turned to face him. "I left the restaurant with him so he'd think he was Mr. Super Cool, like he'd aced you out. I had a plan, which is why I planted the idea I wanted to see some other clubs. He never felt the hook as he swallowed it. Men!" She shook her head with a rueful glance at him. "You guys aren't very hard to move around. Anyway, you weren't getting anything out of him, so I decided to try a more indirect approach." She collapsed on the couch, kicking off her shoes and pulling her legs under her. "I'm pooped, so we have to talk before I crash. Can you offer a girl a drink?"

He poured a little tequila into a lot of grapefruit juice and handed it to her. She took a sip and wrinkled her nose. "Do you know why he showed up at the restaurant?"

"No, but he knew we were there and called you by name."

"He was letting you know that he's well-connected, doing a little chest thumping. The question is, why would he bother? Maybe he thinks you stumbled onto something and was warning you not to mess with him. If that's it, his surprise visit tells us he has something important to hide. That's why I decided to dig deeper."

"You went to God knows where just to play detective?"

"Relax, *amigo.* You ought to be thanking me. If you'll stop puffing up, I'll tell you what I found out."

He took a deep breath. "Okay, tell me."

"He's intelligent, articulate, a great dancer—"

"Don't give me his resume," he snapped. "I'm not going to hire the bastard. I want to know what he's up to."

Instead of taking offense, she grinned. "It's hard to do much research when a band's blaring away and the guy's got faster hands than a sushi chef.

Ground Truth

So I laid some hot dance moves on him as an investment in the future. During the taxi ride here, he was trying to play the big sophisticate, so right away I needled him about winding up in Juarez working with garbage. He didn't like that one bit and said he'd be out of that, his words, 'shit-hole pretty damn soon.'"

"He's about to quit Palmer Industries?"

"Don't know, but he bragged that the company is going to exceed a certain profit figure, and that will earn him a huge bonus. Millions. So I asked, what will happen if the Palmers won't pay? He glared at me and said, 'They don't have the balls.' If the Palmers cross him, they'd better check under the hood before they start their cars. That guy wasn't kidding."

"Why would he tell you all that?"

"Let's just say he wasn't thinking of me as his lawyer. But he must have had second thoughts because he shut up about the Palmers. That's when I looked at him with Bambi eyes and said, 'Tell me more about yourself.' After that, he couldn't stop talking. Underneath his smooth facade, that man has been a basket case since he was a kid. Do you know where he's from?"

"He's Hispanic, but his accent isn't Mexican. I can't place it."

"Cuba. He talked about how humiliated Cubans felt when Khrushchev caved in to Kennedy and removed the Russian nukes. His father was killed during the invasion at the Bay of Pigs. He blames the U.S. embargo for everything that's wrong in Cuba today. He hates the countries around the Caribbean who didn't help Cuba, especially Mexico." She took another sip of her drink. "He was so bitter, so intense, he was scary." She rubbed her eyes, yawned and stretched.

"Last question. Did he ask if I'd discussed the plant with you?"

"Nope. I don't think you were in the front of his mind." She smiled and promptly fell sound asleep on the couch.

Jack had to admit that he hadn't been outsmarted by Montana. He'd been outsmarted by Debra. But Montana would be out there on the streets, on his own turf. And right about now, he'd be mad as hell at Jack Strider.

Chapter 28

July 5
8:30 a.m.

SITTING IN HIS posh La Condesa condo, Jack signed a suicide note that would be read only after he'd done the deed, when it was too late to stop him. He was about to disobey direct orders from his senior partner and betray his client. He was willing to commit professional suicide if that's what it took to nail Palmer Industries.

The letter said that if it looked like justice was not going to be served at the Hearing, he intended to put Alvarez on the trail to Palmer's real books, a string of bribes, and the mystery trucks. Since Sinclair would know what Jack had done even before the letter reached San Francisco, the real purpose for the letter was to make clear that Debra had not known what he intended to do. He folded the letter and inserted it into the envelope.

"Hard at work already?" She came out of the guest bedroom wrapped in a bulky white robe with the Mexican eagle embroidered on the left breast pocket, her hair an ebony waterfall over her shoulders.

He slipped the envelope under the edge of a newspaper. "I heard the shower stop and called room service for their best breakfast."

The doorbell chimed. Debra hurried into the bathroom as a young man in a dark green uniform entered and spread a feast across the table. With a small flourish, he placed a vase of fresh red roses in the center of the table, checked his creation and left.

Debra returned and settled into the chair across the table from him, looking fresh and bright-eyed. After bolting down several bites of eggs scrambled with *queso fresco*, peppers and salsa, she took a sip from a tall glass of orange juice and said, "You're still planning to go to the Hearing, right?"

"I am. Did you doubt it?"

"Nope. Sinclair was worried that you'd boycott to force a default judgment against Palmer, but I figured out he was wrong. You never intended to skip the Hearing. Your plan is to tell the judge everything you suspect, in public, forcing him to stop the music long enough for Alvarez to follow your leads to the hard evidence." She glared at him. "You're planning to do what your father and the dean of the law school couldn't quite do—cut your throat. You'll be disbarred. You can't throw away your future like that."

He smiled, admiring her mind. At any other time, he'd tell her so. Instead, he said, "I'd be nuts to do that. How are those eggs?"

She scowled at him. "Don't be so damn evasive. Just tell me I'm right."

"If I did, you'd be an accomplice and get tossed by the Bar. That won't happen so long as you can swear you had no part in it. You can even say you tried to stop me when I sprang it on you at the Hearing."

"I'll make my own decisions, thanks." She left her breakfast and strode back into the bedroom.

He dressed quickly in his standard black suit, white shirt and maroon tie, and put the letter in the inside breast pocket of his suit coat. The sexy woman who'd captivated the dance floor last night now wore a dark gray pinstripe suit and white shirt. Her hair was primly coiled.

"You're dressed the way I remember," she said. "Stuffy." She glanced at her watch. "Let's go. We wouldn't want to miss the kick off."

"Look, you can still skip this Hearing. Catch a cab to the airport and get the hell out of Mexico."

"If I left now, Sinclair would have my head on a pike. You may be ready to dump your career, but I'm not. Lead the way."

In the lobby, he stepped away from her long enough to drop the envelope through a slot for the desk clerk to mail. There was no turning back.

The car waiting for them at the curb was a stretched Cadillac with a sequined crucifix swinging in the center of the windshield and Day-Glo fringe across the tops of the side windows. Mercifully, the driver was getting his hip-hop injection via headphones instead of from six speakers.

As the Cadillac pulled to the curb at the courthouse, Debra took his hand. "I have one thing to say, counselor. Get out of line in there and you'll have me to deal with. I'm not letting you commit hara-kiri because of that sleaze ball, Arthur Palmer. Don't do anything crazy. If the judge doesn't put Palmer down, we'll find another way later."

They hurried up the broad stone steps to the second floor of the courthouse and followed signs to the Hearing room. As they approached the door, a guard with a rifle in the crook of one arm scanned Jack with a scowl, then smiled broadly at Debra and nodded that they could enter.

Inside, dust and cobwebs were illuminated by light streaming in through high windows. The floor between rows of seats was covered with the litter shed by bored spectators. The site where justice was dispensed was filthy.

At the front table to the right of the aisle, instead of Alvarez and Santiago, sat two thickset men in their fifties wearing suits that looked like they were made from tweedy carpet remnants. One with heavy jowls and a bushy mustache glanced back at him, then whispered to the other.

What was going on? Jack kept his expression impassive as he walked to where they sat. Both looked up with blank expressions. Neither offered a greeting.

"Good morning gentlemen," Jack said. "Where are *Señor* Alvarez and *Señorita* Santiago? *Donde estan los dos abogados de Departemiento de* PROFEPA?" One raised his eyebrows and shrugged.

They weren't going to talk with him, so he crossed the aisle and sat next to Debra. "Tweedledum and Tweedledee won't tell me what happened to Alvarez. I don't like this. I smell a *ratón.*"

"Jack, I just met our interpreter." She nodded back over her shoulder. A woman in her early thirties rose from the front row of chairs and walked to their table.

"Good morning," she said, "would you like me to sit with you?"

He pulled out a chair for her. "Yes, but first ask those two—"

Before he could finish, the bailiff jumped to attention and opened a door to the right of the bench. There was a rustle of movement as everyone stood. The judge emerged and laboriously lowered his immense body into his chair behind the bench. With no preamble other than the halfhearted smack of his gavel, he called one of the government lawyers by name. The man rose, spoke rapidly, and used his left hand in chopping motions to punctuate the points he was making. Then, with a bow to the judge, he sat down.

"Quick," Jack prompted the interpreter, "what did he say?"

The interpreter smiled. "Congratulations. He said the government has dropped its complaint. They have no case, and no injunction is needed."

That was nuts! Had she misunderstood? He leaned closer to her and asked her to repeat what she'd heard. Puzzled, she repeated it word for word. *Time to put Plan B into action fast.* He stood and turned to the interpreter. "Please translate this. Pardon me, your Honor, let the record show that I am speaking over the objection of my co-counsel because I have certain important facts to place in the public record." The interpreter rushed to keep up. "To begin with—"

"Stop!" the judge bellowed at the interpreter. The bailiff straightened from where he'd been leaning against the wall and took several steps toward Jack. The judge angrily waved the second PROFEPA lawyer to his feet. That one spoke earnestly to the judge, gesturing several times in Jack's direction. Then he turned to Jack, smiled, and clasped his hands together at shoulder level and shook them like a victorious boxer at the end of a fight.

The judge spoke one sentence then stamped a document in front of him in three places and signed it at the bottom. He repeated the process with a second document.

Jack turned to the interpreter. "What's going on?"

"The other lawyer apologized for the government torturing your client."

"Torturing?"

"Sorry, I think his word meant 'tormenting' your client. Then he made a motion to the judge that the complaint be dismissed with prejudice. That's what the judge just did."

"No plaintiff would ask that their own complaint be dismissed with prejudice," Debra said. "That means they can never raise the complaint again."

Seeing his adversaries packing papers into their briefcases, Jack approached the bench. "Your Honor." The judge ignored him. "Your Honor. I have a right to be heard."

Before the interpreter had time to speak, the judge banged his gavel hard, as if force added finality. Ignoring Jack, he heaved himself up and lurched side-to-side through the door, which the bailiff closed behind him.

"Come back here, goddamn you!" Jack shouted. The door remained closed.

He turned to look for the other lawyers. They were gone, but Tomás Montana stood at the back of the Hearing room with a mocking sneer. Instead of rushing up to congratulate his lawyer after a big win, Montana turned on his heel and left.

There was no doubt about who had choreographed the outcome.

Chapter 29

July 5
9:45 a.m.

JACK POUNDED his left fist into the palm of his right hand and swung to face Debra, still in her chair at the counsel table. "I should pay tuition for the lesson I just got. Let's get out of here."

When he got to the street, Debra right behind him, he looked around for the Cadillac. It had left without them.

"Yeah," he grunted, "that driver smelled a loser."

He took aim on a wire mesh litter basket at the curb and punted it into the street in the path of a pickup truck overflowing with cabbages. An arm stuck out the passenger window waving a middle finger. Then the truck stopped. Two men in farmer's coveralls got out. One checked the truck for damage. The other taunted Jack to come over.

Debra put her hand on his arm. "You need to cool down. Let's go over there before you get arrested." She pointed at the baroque Metropolitan Cathedral across the street, then glanced at the two farmers. "Right now."

They crossed the street as a bride and groom came through the carved doors. Well-wishers filled the air with a rainbow of confetti and flower petals. The bride gathered her long train and slid into a limousine while the groom waved to their friends. As soon as the groom was in, the car pulled into the sluggish traffic.

Jack chose a pew in the last row and Debra slid in next to him, brushing petals out of her hair. "At least there's a consolation prize." She said. "Sinclair will give you a corner office. He really wanted this one."

It was hard to do, but he held his tongue. Out of the corner of his eye he saw three little girls running up the aisle, snatching the bouquets of flowers the wedding party had left in the pews. The girls were scooping up everything in their path like tiny whirlwinds.

As if responding to an alarm, a paunchy priest shouted at the girls and rushed through the gate in the altar rail. They back-pedaled, still gathering flowers. The red-faced priest snatched a hymnal from a pew rack and hurled it at the nearest girl. It struck her hard in the back. She stumbled but stayed on her feet. Even though all three fled down the aisle, the priest wasn't satisfied. He called out to a younger priest near the arched entrance who blocked their way, grabbing the smallest child by her thin upper arm. Her pitiful bundle of flowers spread across the marble floor.

Jack stood. "Let the girl go," he called. The priest released the girl's arm, but slapped her on the back of her head. Nose in the air, hands clasped at chest-level, he walked past the holy water font without a backward glance.

Jack sat back in the pew and shook his head. "Unbelievable. He thinks that white cassock gives him immunity. Too damn many people in this world think they have immunity. Millions of Mexicans live in shacks while priests in places like this wear red velvet and guzzle vintage port. It's disgusting."

"I agree, but can we talk about what happened in that Hearing room?"

He turned in the pew to face her. "At the first sign the judge had been bribed to throw the Hearing in favor of Palmer Industries, I was ready to bombard him with evidence against Palmer to get it on the public record. That would make it impossible to stop Alvarez's prosecution. That's where I screwed up. Since Alvarez's superiors had never interfered in this case, it didn't occur to me that the prosecution would be in on the fix. Someone high up, maybe even cabinet level, yanked Alvarez off the case, and that wasn't cheap."

He paused and let his anger strengthen his resolve as he thought about all that had taken place since he'd arrived in Mexico—including Juanita's death and the poverty caused as much by greed as by circumstance. He looked at Debra and said, "By the way, I won't be getting that corner office you mentioned, or any office at all. The second the judge swung that gavel and let Palmer off the hook, I quit working for Sinclair & Simms. Someone has to do something about Palmer. I'm that someone."

She frowned. "There's more you haven't told me, isn't there?"

"Well, I did leave out a few things." He told her about his nocturnal visit to Guzman's office and the mystery trucks. And about the carcinogenic incinerator exhaust and how Montana bribed the PROFEPA inspectors.

"Oh my God. No wonder you—"

But he kept talking, needing to get it all out. He finally finished with, "And not long after Guzman threatened his assistant, she was found strangled on the river bank." He gave her the details.

He saw the shock in her eyes, felt it in her silence. In her world, things like that couldn't happen. "The poor girl," she whispered.

"Now you understand why I'm going back to Juarez. As soon as I get more proof, I'll kick some ass. And it won't be just Montana and Guzman. Arthur Palmer has to be totally involved, so I'll go after him too."

She rolled her eyes up at the celestial murals overhead. "Let's see if I understand this. Classroom professor who just got his own ass kicked thinks he can morph into James Bond or Rambo." She returned her gaze to him. "Are you crazy?"

"Not crazy. Motivated."

Easy to say, he realized, but the truth was that he had no training for going up against killers. The reasonable thing to do was walk away. No one would blame him. No one except himself. Sinclair had told him to get the job done, and that's what he'd do. Just a different job.

"Then I'm in too," she said. "I hate what these people are doing, and I know more about Arthur Palmer than you do. I can help."

He laid his hand on her arm and gave it a gentle squeeze. "Help both of us by going back to San Francisco."

She shook her head. "I can't do that. You remember that Sinclair told me to go to Palmer Industries to write some contracts. If I don't, Montana will know something's really wrong. That would definitely get his guard up."

He knew she was right. "Tell Montana you're staying in close touch with Sinclair. Draft the contracts and get out. Don't do anything to make Montana suspicious, and keep his damned hands off you."

She gave him a knowing smile. "I'll congratulate him on how clever he was in outmaneuvering the PROFEPA lawyers. I can play that bozo Montana like a kazoo."

"Yeah, well, just remember that the bozo is also a killer." He was silent for a moment, then said, "He'll ask about my reaction to what happened."

"I'll say you were very angry and quit. I wasn't really paying attention, but I think you mentioned sailing to Buenos Aires."

They watched a procession of boys and girls pass on their way to the stairs that led to the choir loft.

"Don't go anywhere near the Shipping & Receiving building," he warned. "If Guzman comes to the Admin building, keep away from him. And never leave the plant with Montana. No impulsive stuff like last night."

"Look, I'm worried about *you*," she said. "I'll keep my head down, but if I have a chance to help I'm going to take it. And if Montana's pecker makes him careless, I'll make him pay big time."

There were no good options, but her attitude reassured him. "Montana will probably have a room reserved for you at the Rialto Hotel. I'll call you there."

God, don't let them put her in the El Presidente Suite. He hadn't had the time, and certainly not the clarity, to sort out his feelings about both Ana-Maria and Debra, but he couldn't stand the thought that Debra might sleep in the same bed he'd shared with Ana-Maria. He also knew instinctively that

Debra wouldn't be able to stand it either.

BACK AT THE condo, they packed quickly and caught a cab for the airport. Now the real battle was about to start. By tomorrow afternoon, he'd be up on the ridge overlooking the Palmer plant.

Even an expert might not have spotted the man who tailed them to the airport—and Jack didn't.

Chapter 30

July 6
6:00 p.m.

JACK HAD KEPT a keen eye out for rattlesnakes from the moment he started the steep climb up the flat-topped ridge that served as the west boundary of the Palmer Industries site. Then he stepped over a log into some dry brush, and a creature exploded next to his foot, hissing and spewing gravel behind it like a drag racer. Twenty feet away it looked back and flicked its tongue, as if Jack might be a giant delicacy.

A damned Gila monster.

Jack's heart rate dropped back toward normal. In the past half-hour he'd come to hate the creosote bushes that covered the gravelly ground and stank in the boiling sun. But this ridge was his best chance to study the Palmer plant as a whole.

He'd worn tan twill trousers, a long-sleeve khaki shirt, and broad-brimmed canvas hat to blend into the landscape, but he was still a bird on the ground if there were any Palmer guards patrolling the valley behind him. The foliage was sparse, but there was plenty of undergrowth that could conceal an experienced guard. The only thing Jack had that resembled a weapon was a Swiss Army knife.

When he finally reached the top of the mesa, he got his first close look at the mammoth, decrepit oil tanks he'd seen from the Palmer parking lot far below. They marched north in two rows ending where the mesa dropped off toward the border.

He sat on a length of timber, pulled off his left tennis shoe, and dumped a shower of gravel. While sliding his foot back into his shoe he felt an itch on the back of his right calf. Reaching down, his fingers encountered something squirmy. He slapped at it then jumped up from the timber. A scorpion crouched in the dirt, poisonous wand cocked menacingly. Instinctively, Jack attacked, stamping on it again and again to make sure he'd killed it. Not a great start.

He moved slowly across the flat top of the mesa, getting some cover as he passed between the two rows of tanks. He ran the last thirty yards in the open then scrambled on hands and knees to the edge of the mesa overlooking the plant. He scanned the ground closely, looking for scorpions or other poisonous critters, before stretching out full length to check out the complex of buildings a couple of hundred yards below. A steady stream of delivery vehicles rolled in and out. Maybe he'd get lucky and spot one of the mystery truck convoys.

He saw right away that it wasn't business as usual at the plant. In addition to the roving patrols, Montana had posted armed guards outside the entrances to three of the buildings, revealing the locations he most wanted to protect.

Snap. He jerked his head around at the sound, but saw no one. He looked over the top of his reflective sunglasses. Still nothing. False alarm? He held his breath, listening for sliding gravel on the slope.

Down below, some of the trucks delivering hazardous waste were being routed to Shipping & Receiving, others straight to the incinerator. Outbound trucks stopped for fuel, but none resembled the mystery trucks Ana-Maria had described. He crayfished back from the edge, saltbrush scratching his arms. Sweat stung his eyes.

Near the end of their last meeting at the law school, Sam Butler had told him it was time to get his hands dirty in the real world. Well, that time had come. He'd made the tough climb because he was determined to crack open Montana's shell, to spill the guts of his rotten scheme.

He lay there in the still-hot sun for long minutes, examining and evaluating what was going on below. Other than the extra guards, nothing stood out, nothing suspicious, certainly nothing that would nail Montana. Regretfully he admitted he might as well head back to the motel in El Paso and figure out how to get around the plant guards.

He didn't want to go down from the mesa the way he'd come up. If he'd been followed, they could be waiting to ambush him on the original route. Looking for another way down, he picked his way through scraggly tangles of weeds between the two parallel rows of giant oil tanks. When he reached the last pair, the eleventh and twelfth, he had a clear view down to the flatland between the base of the hill and the U.S. border. On the far side of the border were Sunland Racetrack and the *gringo* world. He looked back at the tanks in two rows longer than a soccer field.

He pressed both palms against tank number twelve and extended one leg behind him, then the other to stretch his hamstrings for the climb down. In front of his face, a foot-square plate was welded to the tank. The first line showed the tank's capacity. Below that it read, *"Hecho:* 1958."

Uh oh. Built in 1958. It must be decades beyond its safe life span. Next to the plate a more modern sign read, "Out Of Service." He saw the same message on other tanks. The oil company, PEMEX, must have considered them too dangerous and abandoned them.

On impulse, he rapped the side of number twelve. A solid "thunk" returned. Not what he'd expected. It certainly didn't sound empty. He walked across to number eleven. His rap produced a hollow "boing" followed by a soft internal echo. He tried both again. The difference was unmistakable. He tried number ten. Another "thunk." The result was the same for every other tank. All except number eleven sounded full.

It couldn't be petroleum. No way PEMEX would have left this much behind. It could be water, but that seemed unlikely. But could it be hazardous waste?

Back at number twelve, he gripped the spokes of the metal valve wheel and tried to wrench it to the left. It was frozen. He picked up a plank, rapped the valve several times then stuck the plank through the spokes for leverage. Standing to one side, he twisted slowly until yellow-green fluid dripped out. He spun the wheel in the opposite direction to cut off the flow. He wrinkled his nose at the vile smell, like hydrogen sulfide but worse.

Even if Montana was temporarily storing liquid biochemical waste here until he moved it to government facilities, these tanks had no secondary containment system. Only a jackass would take such a risk.

According to the records Jack had seen, transporting liquid hazardous waste to a government facility was one of Palmer's biggest expenses. But was it really? Palmer profits were sky-high. Maybe this wasn't temporary storage at all. Montana could be using these tanks to store toxic waste permanently, covering that up by reporting phantom expenses.

If one of the old tanks ruptured, it would send a lethal brew on a relentless journey to the groundwater below. Thousands of people who lived below the ridge and two million residents of Juarez and El Paso wouldn't know what had hit them. This was a catastrophe in waiting.

Moving cautiously to the other side of number twelve, the side more exposed to plant workers below, he saw immediately how the tanks had been filled. Four parallel trunk line pipes rose up the ridge from the plant and culminated in a low metal building between tanks six and eight. From there, a network of pipes, each about a foot in diameter, followed orderly paths to the twelve tanks. He'd noticed the pipes as soon as he'd reached the mesa, but they hadn't meant anything then. Now they did. They were how PEMEX had pumped oil up to be stored in the tanks. The building's door was padlocked.

To get a closer look at the metal building and avoid the line-of-sight from below, he crawled up and over a mound of freshly-turned earth that stretched like a mole track along the row of tanks. Everything else on the mesa looked untouched for years, yet this was a clear sign of recent human activity.

Already spooked about scorpions, digging bare-handed into the soil made his skin crawl, but he had no choice. About six inches down, he uncovered something shiny. He scooped away until he'd exposed a fat section of new glazed ceramic pipe. He cleared several more feet of its length before stopping. No point going farther. His eyes could follow its low profile as it continued north in a straight line.

He scrambled back between the rows of tanks and pushed north through the underbrush. *Slow down. Don't make a mistake.* He stopped behind tank twelve. The mound continued another fifty feet where it turned right at a 45-degree angle and headed down the steep mesquite-covered hillside.

The thought of moving closer to the guards at the plant made his edgy nerves shout at him to get the hell back to his car. He needed to think about what he'd discovered, what it meant. But everything he had on Montana was based on deduction. Without more hard facts, no official would take him seriously much less enter the Palmer site to search. This ceramic pipe led to answers he had to have. *Follow it or quit. It was that simple.*

First he had to take samples of the foul stuff in the tanks so he could have it analyzed. He looked around for something to use as a container but found nothing. Sitting on the gravel next to tank twelve, he took off his tennis shoes and socks and then put the shoes back on. The socks could work as sponges. He gradually opened the valve and let the slimy goo drip onto one sock.

Different tanks might contain different chemicals, so he needed more than one sample. He checked the valves on other tanks until he found one that would turn. As he eased the valve slightly open, the intense odor made his eyes smart. Squinting, nostrils pinched closed, he let the thick fluid drip onto the next sock. Now what? He couldn't carry the stinking socks down the ridge. There was nothing unless . . . he took off his broad-brimmed canvas hat and dropped the socks into it. He still needed more samples, so he took off his T-shirt and used the Swiss Army knife to hack it into four pieces. After he soaked each piece, he added it to the hat. It was a totally unscientific way to collect samples, and some of it would co-mingle, but it was all he could do.

Adrenaline pumping, hat at arm's length, he followed a Cat track probably made by the crew that had installed the new pipe. Before he'd gone fifty yards, he slipped on a leaf-covered patch of shale, landed hard on his butt and slid downhill. Jamming one shoe against a tree trunk stopped his slide. Nothing broken . . . unless . . . he checked his pants pocket to see whether his digital camera was intact. *No problem.*

After the slope leveled out, the barely-concealed ceramic pipe continued into a grove of scrub trees less than a hundred yards ahead. He could sprint across to the trees, but moving fast would attract attention. He crouched and edged forward in slow motion, hoping he'd blend into the landscape until he ducked into the grove.

Suddenly, not far ahead, a motor started up followed by several voices. *Damn it!* When was he going to catch a break? Heart hammering, he ducked from bush to bush until he spotted where the pipe ended abruptly at the edge of a clearing.

A dozen yards in front of him six workmen muscled a section of pipe into line. Another stood by, ready to cement it to the section behind it. Farther away, dozens of sections were stacked, enough to extend the pipeline into the center of the clearing.

Bit by bit he made sense of what he saw. There were three clusters of equipment, each at a separate corner of a triangle about twenty-five yards on a side. A pipe led from each of the three corners into what might be a large pump in the center of the triangle. The ceramic pipe coming from the mesa was heading straight for the pump. It looked like the piping could be operational very soon. He pulled out his camera, took several furtive shots and stuffed it out of sight.

This equipment didn't look like anything PEMEX would have used in the oil business, but he'd seen rigs like this on farms near Sacramento: water well heads and pumps. That figured. When PEMEX built this plant it would have been far outside Juarez city limits so they needed wells to supply water.

If the pump in the center directed water from the wells to the plant, there had to be a main line leading in that direction. To check that out, he edged a few yards to a new vantage point. Beat-to-hell sections of pipe lay on the ground disconnected and pointing in random directions. The line to the plant was clearly out of commission, and there was no replacement pipe in sight. There was no connection from this site to the plant.

He set down the hat he'd been keeping as far from his body as he could while still holding it tightly closed. He took the camera out, snapped twice, stowed it, then picked up the hat, recrossed the main pipeline, and squeezed through the brush to deeper cover. Hunkered down, barely breathing, he understood. There was no line running from the wells to the plant because the plant no longer needed well water. Arthur had boasted about how Montana had coerced the city into diverting a dedicated water supply line straight to the site.

The 'ah ha!' in his mind was so loud and clear it was like listening on headphones. Montana had built this system solely to drain the tanks *into* the wells, sending all that crap deep underground. He'd converted the former PEMEX wells into injection wells.

Oh my God! That would be a catastrophe. He hadn't imagined anything this bad.

He'd taught his water law students that Federal Disposal Restrictions prohibit sending hazardous waste down an injection well unless the waste had been thoroughly treated and couldn't migrate away from the injection zone. But this was how Montana was going to squeeze out the profits that would get him the multimillion dollar bonus.

Montana's idea was clever—run the wells in reverse. Instead of bringing water up, he'd send toxic waste down. The equipment for pumping oil up to the tank farm was already in place so Montana used it to transport toxic waste. Draining the tanks required only a new ceramic pipe and gravity. No one would suspect, because everyone thought the tank farm had been shut down years ago. If the tanks leaked and contaminated the ground, it could take years for the poison to reach the water source. But if Montana poured poison down an injection well, it could hit the water supply like a bomb.

He took quick photos of the wells and turned to sneak away. His first step landed on a dry branch that snapped loudly and slid out from under him, forcing him to grab a parched mesquite to keep from crashing to the ground.

He was facing the clearing so he saw a workman point toward him. The man's eyes widened in surprise, and he shouted an alarm. He'd be able to describe Jack's face in detail to Montana. Jack ducked and moved away fast.

The game was on.

Other workers started yelling. From behind a tree, a plant guard appeared instantly, as though he'd been expecting an intruder. He swung his AK-47 to his shoulder and fired two quick bursts. The slugs ripped through the dry limbs several feet over Jack with a sound like a chain saw. Debris rained on his head.

One man waved at the others to fan out on the slope between the pipeline and the plant. A second guard moved cautiously toward Jack's miserable hiding place then stopped, listening, scanning the brush.

The moment the guard looked back toward the clearing, Jack hurled a stone to land away from the pipeline. As it skittered across the rocky ground, the guard fired a volley in that direction.

Jack plunged into deeper brush. If they caught him, they'd find the camera and his toxic waste samples and beat him to death on the spot.

Branches tore at him, but he held back curses and yelps of pain. An automatic rifle fired somewhere behind him, followed by more angry shouts. After running more than half a mile from the wells, he bent over, hands on knees, gulping air, but ready to drive himself on if he had to. The hunt had flipped. No longer the bloodhound, he'd become the quarry.

He moved more slowly through the thorny brush, trying to protect his face from dangling branches. Finally, he saw a raised roadbed ahead. He stopped at the bottom of the slope leading up to the road. Sweat stung in his nicks and scratches. He couldn't stay where he was. They could still catch up, maybe using dogs. His car was too far away. He'd never get there.

A slowly approaching vehicle rattled like an old truck, maybe carrying a farmer and his girlfriend to a local bar. Or it could be full of armed men scanning the brush for him. By the time he knew for sure who it was, it would be too late to run. If he stepped up onto the road, there was still enough light for them to get him in their sights. He had to decide, and he had to do it now.

Chapter 31

July 6
9:30 p.m.

THE PICKUP STOPPED. The driver leaned across and squinted at Jack through the passenger-side window. With deep, down-turned wrinkles and his few remaining lower teeth protruding from between his lips, he looked like a bad-tempered beaver. After a cold look he turned away, clearly ready to move on.

"Wait, I can pay." Jack stepped in front of the truck. He pulled out his wallet and held up a handful of peso notes. *"Yo pago,* I'll pay. After long seconds of hesitation the driver stuck a .22 pistol out the window and sighted on Jack's nose. If the old man fired, he'd die for no reason on this miserable back road. Jerking the barrel, the driver gestured for him to come closer.

As Jack came alongside, the driver snatched the whole stack of bills out of his hand. He narrowed his eyes, waiting to see if Jack would object. Jack raised one hand, palm facing the driver to signal agreement. He kept the hand holding the hat at his side. The driver waggled the gun barrel at him, a mute threat. Then he wiped his nose with the back of his hand, and pointed the barrel back toward the open bed of the truck where two hog snouts were sniffing over the side rail.

"Muchas gracias." Jack pulled himself over the side into the truck bed, pushing the curious hogs out of his way. Unable to stand as the truck bounced violently across ruts and potholes, he slipped to the metal floor plates with his back to the driver's cabin.

His right hand had been clamped down on the hat full of samples for so long he could barely loosen its grip. He pushed the hat out in front of him and pinned it to the floor with his heel using it as a barrier between his body and the hogs. The hogs backed away, grunting disapproval.

He needed this break to recharge, to let his mind stop racing. This was no spy game. The guards would have reported to Montana that there'd been an intruder, and one workman would earn a bonus for describing that man. Montana would identify Jack Strider in seconds and mobilize all his forces to track him down.

That brought Ana-Maria's safety to mind. It had been two days, and he hadn't gotten a confirmation from the *coyote*. That sucked. She wasn't safe until she was out of Juarez. He'd go to the guy's place and make sure.

After about twenty minutes, the pickup stopped at a paved, two-lane highway. It was evident the driver intended to turn right, the wrong direction for Jack. So he tapped on the rear window and pantomimed that he wanted off. The hogs snorted and jerked their heads like bulls as he hastily climbed over the side of the truck.

He ran and jogged until he reached his rental car where he'd left it off the main road on the backside of the tank farm. He stuffed the stinking hat into the trunk, sped into Juarez, and drove toward the U.S. border. *He could have been captured—or killed.* This was real. But he gave himself a pat on the back for having figured out Montana's scheme when he could easily have missed it. And for having taken some damn big risks. He'd keep going, whatever that meant.

In El Paso he stopped at a hardware store and bought a metal bucket with a top held on tightly by four clips. Outside the store, he opened the trunk and turned away when noxious fumes went up his nose. He walked several steps away, sucked in deep breaths of fresh air and returned to use his thumbs and forefingers to pick up the hat and drop it into the bucket. That immediately cut, but didn't eliminate, the smell. Even after he'd washed his hands vigorously in the hardware store's bathroom, his fingertips looked chapped.

He quickly spotted the El Diablo Motel, a one-story, cinderblock trucker's dump that would be a fine hideout. Meeting Debra at the Rialto would be a bad idea, so he asked the desk clerk for the name of a very out-of-the-way place to eat in Juarez. He implied that his companion would be someone he shouldn't be seen with, so he couldn't take her to any popular restaurant.

"You want the Casa Lupo," the clerk said. "Only locals go there."

Next, he called the Rialto in Juarez. Debra answered immediately.

"Hello," Debra said in a cautious tone.

"Hi. Meet me at Casa Lupo restaurant. It's a local hangout, so dress accordingly. Call a cab and leave as soon as you can. I'll be waiting."

"Hold on." Her voice rose and she sounded exasperated. "I've been trying to get you all afternoon, but your cell was off. I have something important to tell you."

"We'll talk there."

He was eager to tell her what he'd learned, and to have her challenge his reasoning. They could plan a strategy together, but he didn't want to do any of that on the Rialto's phone.

A hot shower washed dried blood out of scratches and made him feel better until he noticed that the water circling the drain was tea brown. He didn't know whether the unpleasant color came from the El Paso water system, the dirt from his cross-country run, or from his own blood. *This sure wasn't the Stanford faculty lounge.*

The clothes in his luggage would make him stand out like a Mormon missionary, so his next stop would be a clothing store. Scanning shops as he drove, he saw Digby Western & Work Clothes Exchange. Suits and jackets hung around the walls of the long room. All the other clothes were piled in huge wooden crates resting on saw horses. Above each table hung a hand-printed sign announcing the contents of the box.

He found a pair of 34 x 34 jeans and, from the next crate, chose a wide leather belt with the words "Fort Worth" spelled out in flat metal washers riveted across the back. Next, he pulled a navy blue work shirt and a Levi jacket from hangers and headed for a dressing room to change. On the way to the checkout desk, he saw the "hats" crate where a broad-brimmed black Stetson floated on top of the pile waiting to be liberated.

"Twenty eight bucks," the indifferent teenage cashier stated. Her bored expression didn't change when he handed over the cash.

Driving across the bridge into Mexico reminded him that decaying Ciudad Juarez wasn't El Paso South. They were very different cultures separated by a few hundred yards of dirty sand and a trickle of polluted water.

Following the desk clerk's directions, he drove along a seedy commercial street in north Juarez: shops, bars, men hanging out. When he turned onto Casa Lupo's street, activity stopped. The neighborhood seemed almost abandoned. The single naked bulb at each street corner barely illuminated the garbage from overturned cans. Most of the buildings, dark as tombs inside, were barricaded with bars and multiple locks. He spotted the yellow neon "Casa Lu o" sign. Apparently, no one had felt a need to replace the missing "P."

Because of "No Parking" signs along both sides of the narrow street, he had to park around the corner a couple of blocks away.

As he walked back toward Casa Lupo, the alleyways that bisected the blocks were such black holes he instinctively moved away from them as he passed. This restaurant was looking like a bad choice.

He wanted to be waiting on the sidewalk when Debra's cab arrived, so he decided to use the time to call his friend George McDonald at Stanford on his cell. He should be home from teaching hydrology classes by now.

Four rings, and McDonald hadn't picked up. Was his plan going to crash just because McDonald was out for dinner?

Then there was a click on the line and a man said, "McDonald."

"Hey Mac, it's Jack Strider calling from Juarez, Mexico. Got a moment?"

"Sure. Great to hear your voice. Giselle and I were talking about you just—"

"Look, Mac, I'm sorry to interrupt, but I need some information, badly. Can we catch up on what I've been doing some other time?"

"No sweat." Mac's tone went sober. "What's up?"

"I'm about to violate the hell out of lawyer-client privilege, so I need your word that this conversation will stay just between us."

The pause that followed was long enough to tell him Mac was troubled at making a blind promise.

"You got it," he said at last.

"My former client is a California corporation with a plant here that processes hazardous waste."

"Not my idea of fun, but someone has to do it."

"That's the problem. They *aren't* doing it. The Mexican government was about to shut them down, but my former client bought its way out of trouble. I spent this afternoon snooping around on the plant site, and I think I have proof that what the company is doing is much worse than the government knows. I'm talking about poisoning people, maybe a lot of them." He related what he'd seen on the mesa and at the injection wells.

"Wow! That sounds serious. What's your next step?"

"I took samples of the chemicals in some of the tanks. I need to know what's in those samples."

"You need to get them to UTEP first thing in the morning."

"UTEP? University of Texas at El Paso, right?"

"That's it. Contact Dr. Ed Rincon, head of the Center for Environmental Resource Management; they call it CERN. We worked together at EPA. I'll call ahead. He'll let you know exactly what chemicals you have."

"Can I trust him?"

"Absolutely, he's very straightlaced. He's also brilliant, which means he's bored in El Paso and would love to work on something unusual. But he'll try to tell you more than you want to know about everything. He's a little . . . eccentric."

"If he can do this job, I don't give a damn how eccentric he is."

"What else can I help with?"

"I need to know what will happen if that poison goes down those wells."

"I'll research the geology down there—soil conditions and absorption rate into the water supply. That will provide clues as to whether your chemicals will have no effect, make people nauseous, or kill everyone. I just hope Juarez isn't sitting on an aquifer."

"This region is a desert, so it probably is."

"You pour cyanide into a swimming pool and you can drain or neutralize the water, but an aquifer would stay toxic for years, maybe decades. Shouldn't you go to the police about this?"

"I believe the man behind this has the cops in his wallet, and no one in El Paso has jurisdiction in Mexico. For now, I'm on my own."

"In the old westerns, isn't this when the townsfolk call in the Texas Rangers?"

"I may have to go a lot higher than the Rangers, but first I need more facts."

"Where can I reach you?"

"Call my cell—before noon, if you can."

He clicked off as a cab pulled to the curb. Debra stepped out wearing black, trim-fitting pants, a burgundy, long-sleeve blouse, and a black leather vest. Her black hair was in a single braid, Mexican style, under a cap with a bill. Two other cars passed, and the cab drove away after them.

She took a look at his Western gear and the Stetson. "Very sexy." She looked up and down the street. "I was wondering whether the cab driver knew where he was going."

"Yeah, the guy who recommended this place didn't mention that the neighborhood was so rundown."

"Did you come by cab, too?"

"Rental car. I had to park a couple of blocks down there." He pointed. "Anyway, I'm glad you're safe. Did Montana give you any trouble?"

"Didn't even see him, but I sure heard about him. That's what I need to tell you."

"Let's talk at the table. I don't want to risk being spotted standing out on the street."

He pulled open the green and red paneled door and inhaled the unmistakable odors of cilantro and chips frying in hot oil. Hundreds of photographs of solemn men seated at the restaurant's tables covered the walls. Wood tables in the single large room had been painted with Aztec designs now covered with plastic. Instead of mariachi music, speakers delivered 1960s Frank Sinatra. Behind the bar, a teenager in a yellow shirt stacked cases of Tecate and Corona.

A passing waiter paused next to him. *"Señor?"* His brow was wrinkled, as if they might have come here by mistake. When Jack pointed to a table in a dark corner at the rear, the waiter waved him in that direction and pushed through the swinging door into the kitchen.

He felt okay keeping his Stetson on as he walked to the table since most of the men in the room wore various types of hats. They'd just seated themselves, Jack with his back to the wall, when a waiter ambled up.

"Buenas tardes, señor. Quieres algo de beber?"

Jack turned to Debra. "Ready to order a drink?" She nodded.

"Margaritas. Con Don Eduardo Anjeo, *por favor."*

Screwing up his mouth, the waiter shook his head side to side. *"No lo tenemos."*

"No problem." He shouldn't have asked for a top-end brand.

The server returned immediately with a pitcher the size of a quart paint can, enough margarita to fuel a revolution.

He filled Debra's glass and then his own. They tapped rims and he took a deep sip and felt a rush.

"Okay, what did you want to tell me?"

"I was in the break room at the plant getting coffee when two young women came in. They must have assumed I understood no Spanish because they talked about how the extra guards Montana had posted saw *el abogado* trespassing. Montana was so mad they hadn't caught *el abogado* that everyone tried to stay out of his way. He was still up on the ridge next to the plant when I left."

El abogado, the lawyer. "Yep, that was me."

"Jack!" she said so loudly that a couple at the next table turned toward them. "What were you thinking?" She reached under the table and squeezed his thigh hard, right on a deep bruise. Surprised, he squawked in pain.

She eyed him in alarm. "What's wrong?"

"Nothing. Okay, only a few scratches and bruises. I took a fall climbing around on the ridge. It was worth going up there, though, because I figured out what Montana's doing, at least some of it." After another swallow, he told her about the oil tanks and the injection wells in the grove near the plant. "Unfortunately, I stepped on a branch. The workmen started yelling, and one of them saw me, close enough to describe me. Then a guard popped up and fired AK-47 bursts my way. I had to pick a little mesquite shrapnel out of my hair. No big deal." *Yeah, right.* And yet he felt a rush of excitement as he recalled those moments.

"So Montana will know it was you."

"Remember in Mexico City when he said he could find me anywhere? I figure he had a tail on me from the beginning. As soon as he heard I was flying to El Paso he knew I hadn't given up, even though the PROFEPA charges were thrown out. That's why he posted extra guards. Here's the thing. As soon as the setup in the grove is finished, Montana will drain the tanks down the wells. That's going to be within a couple of days. I took samples from several of the tanks. They're in the car. I'll have them analyzed and find out from my friend George McDonald how much damage Montana will cause when he starts dumping into the wells."

"I need to stop you right there," she said, looking pensive. "Maybe I should turn this whole thing over to Sinclair."

"That's a dead end. Here's how that would go. You tell Sinclair you're not sure what's in the tanks and you're guessing what Montana intends to do with the stuff. At that point he orders you to stay away from his client." She didn't look convinced, so he said, "Listen, if McDonald says there's no big problem, I'll write memos to PROFEPA and Sinclair, tell them everything I know and suspect, and let them do their legal dance. But McDonald *is* going to say there is a potential disaster. I know it."

From under the brim of the Stetson, he checked out the other diners. One man sitting at a table with three other men caught his eye and quickly looked away. A middle-aged man just walking in looked half-familiar. Maybe after hearing what happened on the ridge, Montana had staked out Debra at the Rialto. If they'd followed her cab, Montana already knew they were inside Casa Lupo. Then he remembered the two cars that had passed her cab on the otherwise deserted street. He was getting a very bad feeling, all his senses ramping up. This wasn't paranoia. This was a bad scenario in real life.

"I'm going to the bar to pay, then we're getting out of here." He tried not to let his voice give away the urgency he felt. He didn't want to spook her.

When he got back to the table, a muscular truck driver-type was leaning over Debra, red face thrust only inches from hers. Jack looked down at the stocky intruder with a look that said, "This is over." The guy straightened, scowled, and rolled his shoulders like he was loosening up. He looked Jack in the eyes but, after a couple of seconds, shrugged and walked back to a table across the room.

"If that guy had leaned just one inch closer to me," Debra said, "I was going to turn his right knee into mush."

Jack couldn't help it. He grinned. "I'll remember that. Right now we're going to El Paso International Airport, and you're getting on a flight to San Francisco."

"Like hell I am. You need my help here." She looked more pugnacious than the departed truck-driver. "I'll tell you again, Cowboy, I can take care of myself."

"Yeah, and I was on the boxing team in college, but we're both way out of our weight class here. And we're not safe in this place. Let's go."

He led her to the door, pushed it open, and stepped onto the dimly lighted street.

Chapter 32

CARLOS GARZA HAD been an assassin-for-rent half his life and had nothing to show for it.

Only $750 U.S. for this job. That sucked. He'd tried to get double for taking on a rush-rush order, but the man said he'd find somebody else. And he could. Competition forced Carlos to work cheap.

He glanced at the "Casa Lu o" neon sign a block and a half down the street. He loved lying in wait, even in a filthy alley like this one, to ambush a target. The man who'd hired him said to watch for a tall guy, black hair, blue eyes, probably the only *gringo* leaving the restaurant. He said the man's name was Strider, like Carlos might give a shit about that. They were all the same to him. There would be a woman too, with long black hair, but he hadn't bothered with her name.

A couple came out of Casa Lupo and walked fast in his direction. The guy looked pretty fit, but Carlos didn't give a damn. He stroked his fat gut. It had fooled quite a few people, made them overconfident. Years in prison had made him tougher, and lifting weights had made him stronger, than any target. Besides, no one was faster than his pig sticker.

He didn't need Vincenzo and Raul for this one, but the man had said to bring help, take no chances. He just hoped they weren't too wasted on the crack they'd done in the van. He'd seen Vincenzo go crazy on one job when he was flying high, sticking a guy over and over long after he was dead, screaming at him to fight back. Raul didn't get that bad, but sometimes he let his dick make stupid decisions.

Carlos squinted down the street. With the restaurant lights behind him, and the man's Stetson pulled down, Carlos couldn't see the face at all, couldn't even be sure he was a *gringo*. But he was tall and had a black-haired woman with him. That was enough. He'd been ordered to make this look like a crack-head street robbery, so he could keep the wallet except for the ID that would prove he had wasted the right man.

The stingy bastard was giving him only half-pay for doing the woman. He'd take her with them to the old Calderon Building and fuck her before he did her. Raul would love that.

Back pressed against the brick wall, he whispered over his shoulder, "They're coming."

Raul pushed forward to take a look. "Hey, Carlos, that chick looks bad, man. This goin' to be some good shit." He cackled softly.

"Shut up. Vincenzo, you and me take the *gringo*. I'll front him."

He liked to kill from behind before his target even knew he was in trouble. This time, to be sure this was the right guy, he had to see his face. No point doing the work then finding out it was some other bum.

"You take the back. Give him plenty of room so he don't get around you if he tries to run." It pissed him off to have to chase some dude down the street. "You hear me, man?"

Vincenzo's glassy eyes looked dead. "Shit, yeah, man. This ain't nothin'."

"Raul, you get the woman. Keep her quiet. We'll take her with us after." He felt loose. It was time. "Vincenzo, *vámonos.*"

Vincenzo strolled out of the alley toward Casa Lupo, paying no attention to the couple across the street walking in his direction. He turned his face away as they passed, continuing farther before angling across the street behind them as if heading for dinner at Casa Lupo.

When Vincenzo was in place behind the couple, Carlos edged out of the shadows and crossed to the opposite sidewalk, arriving about thirty paces in front of them. When they noticed him, he gave the man a half-wave and a smile. They slowed, but kept walking. *Good, I won't have to run him down.* Then the man put his hand on the woman's forearm and whispered something. They both looked back at Vincenzo standing still on their side of the street. They stopped. *Shit, they know something's up.* He immediately gave them his full gold-filled smile and called, *"Perdón, conocen donde esta un medico?* A doctor?"

The man answered, *"No conocemos.* We're tourists," and he pointed back to the restaurant, taking another look at Vincenzo.

Same old shit. He didn't need a doctor, and they weren't tourists. He was within a few feet now and able to see the man's face. A *gringo*, for sure. Black hair. Too dark to tell if his eyes were blue, but he had the woman with him. He was the target all right. Carlos slipped his right hand behind his back, fingers closing around the grip of the eight-inch double-edged blade in the sheath on his belt. He'd step forward fast, swinging the knife in an arc to slash the target's face. From the front, he always started that way. It hurt like hell and poured blood. While the target was screaming and clawing at his face, Carlos followed with a stick straight into the heart.

But Strider seemed to expect the knife and blocked Carlos' swing with his forearm. Out of the corner of his left eye, Carlos saw only the blur of

Strider's fist before terrible pain exploded on the left side of his face. The knife flew from his grip. He knuckled blood out of his eye, stumbling backward to get out of range. Suddenly, a kick in the back of his right knee buckled his leg. A second later, an elbow slammed into his neck. *Shit!* The goddamn bitch was on him too.

"Behind you," Strider shouted to Debra.

Carlos saw Raul sling her off her feet and into the barred door of a pawnshop. He got an arm around her chest. His hand clamped over her mouth.

Carlos blocked Strider's hook with both arms, but a fist hammered into the left side of his face. *Get the son-of-a-bitch on the ground. Crush him.* Driving forward, fists high to protect his battered head, he threw his weight into the man's chest, carrying them to the pavement. He was on top, but the *gringo's* arms wrapped around him in a bear hug.

A head butt in the face would do it, but the fucker kept jerking his head side-to-side. If he could get a hand free, he'd grab a fistful of hair and smash the guy's head into the pavement. Last time out he'd done that and snuffed the target with one blow.

Raul's shriek of pain told him the woman had gotten loose and turned on him. He couldn't believe this was happening. With a bellow he broke his arms free. Again the *gringo* was too fast, hacking him in the throat with his elbow, knocking his head back. Desperate, he threw himself backward, rolled, and saw his knife next to him. He scooped it up.

He glanced toward the pawnshop. Raul rolled on the ground, arms wrapped around his head, knees pulled up to protect his nuts. The woman swarmed around him, kicking him as hard as she could.

The *gringo* was still down, vulnerable. Carlos moved in, weaving the blade back and forth through the air. The move was meant to be hypnotic, but Strider wasn't watching the blade. He was looking straight into Carlos's eyes. Suddenly, Strider rolled on one side. His leg slashed out, knocking Carlos's legs from under him. He landed hard on his right elbow. Pain shot up his arm, but he got his knife between them as they both struggled to their feet. Carlos lunged in, swinging right to left. The blade was so sharp it barely slowed as it sliced across the front of Strider's jacket.

"You're mine now, you shit."

Before he could swing again, Strider moved in fast and got a grip on his right wrist, forcing the knife to one side. Jabs like sledgehammer blows made blood spurt from his nose. By brute force, he jerked his knife-hand out of Strider's grip and backed off.

The madman was about to come at him again, but Vincenzo got there on the run, shouting as he stuck Strider in the lower back. Carlos heard the blade hit bone.

"Ahhhh!" Strider cried out.

Yeah, Vincenzo always went in waist high. As the *gringo* pitched forward, Carlos unloaded a short uppercut that snapped Strider's head back. He landed hard and didn't move. Vincenzo straddled him, knife raised to strike down like slicing open a sack of wheat.

The woman leaped away from Raul and screamed. She swung her leg like she was kicking a field goal. Her shoe drove into Vincenzo's crotch so hard it lifted him off the ground. As he jackknifed forward, the woman's knee caught him squarely under the jaw. Carlos heard teeth splinter and then a *whack* as Vincenzo's head hit the asphalt. *Jesus, he'd never seen any woman fight like that.*

While she was still focused on Vincenzo, Raul clubbed her on the back of the neck with both hands. Her knees buckled, and she collapsed to the pavement. Raul kicked her weakly in the thigh and whined, "Fuckin' *puta* tried to kill me."

The high-pitched sound in the back of Carlos's consciousness got louder. *Hoo-wah, hoo-wah, hoo-wah.* It was the damn *policia. Hoo-wah, hoo-wah, hoo-wah.* They were close.

"*Vámonos,*" he called to the other two.

Vincenzo, barely able to get to his feet, limped back into the alley cupping his balls in one hand and holding his other hand across his mouth. Raul dragged the woman to her feet and painfully slung her across his shoulder. She was dead weight, head bobbing.

"This bitch owes me big time." He followed Vincenzo, staggering under the woman's weight.

Hoo-wah, hoo-wah, hoo-wah. Even closer. If the cops turned onto this street and saw him standing over a dead man he was cooked. He wanted to run, but he needed the ID to get his money so he ripped the wallet out of Strider's rear pocket. Sirens shrieking in his ears, he ran into the alley after the other two.

The man had said the *gringo* would be a pushover. *Shit! Vincenzo was so busted up he'd scream for a bigger split of the money. What a fucked up deal.*

But at least he had the woman.

Chapter 33

July 7
12:30 a.m.

HOO-WAH, HOO-wah, hoo-wah.

Jack's eyes popped open. For several seconds he was totally disoriented, lying in a heap on the asphalt. His jaw throbbed, and his back ached like hell. He felt along his jawbone and ran his tongue around his teeth. Nothing broken. As the siren's wail diminished, he gingerly pushed himself up until he was on his hands and knees, then on his feet. He staggered when a sharp pain pierced his right ribs.

The three punks were gone. He looked around for Debra. *Oh God, they have her!* He looked down the street toward the restaurant and then in the other direction. The street was empty. He had to do something.

From the alley behind him came a distant scream—cut off abruptly. He ran into the alley. No way into the buildings on either side. Had they turned into the next street or crossed into the alley on the other side? He pressed his forehead hard. *Damn, his head hurt.* He had to get this right. Kidnapping a woman, they'd stay in the alleys.

He came to a door on his right, but the trash in front of it was undisturbed. The next door was padlocked. There, to his left, a door with no lock. He looked up. Shattered upper windows. Abandoned. A thug's hideout. He slowly pulled the handle and entered a long, empty storeroom.

To his right, inside a glass-fronted office, one of the attackers sat in a chair, legs spread wide in front of him, whimpering, hand covering his mouth. The big man Jack had fought sat on the edge of the desk, clapping a steady beat. Both men had their backs to him, and Jack edged closer to the glass.

Debra was on her back on the floor. The smallest of the three men was on top of her trying to pry her legs apart, his trousers and underwear around one ankle. He ripped open her shirt. One breast came out of her bra. She tried to knee him, but he had her pinned.

Jack looked around for something to use as a weapon. Nothing. He flung the office door open and exploded across the room, driving his shoulder into the man on top of Debra, knocking him into shelves that collapsed, dumping dozens of cans on him. Jack hauled the man's head back and pounded his neck, knocking him senseless. Jack threw him to one side and saw a man lurch out of the room, holding his crotch, eager to escape.

The man with the fat gut lunged away from the desk and came at Jack with a knife held low in his right hand. Jack ripped a broken shelf post loose and brought it down like an ax on the man's right shoulder. He yelled, and his arm dropped. The knife clattered to the floor. Jack was on him, beating his head with both fists, driving him to the floor, landing on top of him. With an agonized roar, the man under him landed a roundhouse hook on Jack's kidney. He felt the thud of the blow, but his rage blocked the pain. He threw his full weight into an uppercut to the man's jaw, snapping his head back.

Then Debra was beside him. "Stop. Stop it, Jack. He's done." Hands still tied behind her back, her eyes pleaded with him to stop. He looked down at the unmoving hulk sprawled on his back, arms spread wide.

He pulled Debra's bra back into place and freed her hands. She collapsed against his chest with a groan, arms hanging at her sides.

The punk who'd tried to rape her hadn't moved, and Jack heard no sounds from the storeroom. They were safe, at least for the moment.

"He stabbed you in the back," she said. "I thought you were dead."

"I feel a burning back there, but I wasn't stabbed."

She slipped her arms around his waist to feel for herself. "There's a slash in your jacket. Turn around so I can see."

He turned and felt her lift his shirt.

"I can't believe this. He did stab you but it didn't penetrate. You owe your life to 'Fort Worth.'"

"What?"

"That's what's spelled out in brass rivets on the back of your belt. His blade hit the "H" so hard it popped off. The knife tip must have skipped across your ribs at an angle." When he turned back, she gave him a weak smile. "God, that was close."

The crease in his ribs stung, but knowing it wasn't serious made him feel better. He asked, "How did you get away from that guy who grabbed you from behind?"

"I flipped him over my shoulder and played hacky-sack with his head."

"The last thing I saw, he was rolled up like an armadillo. I've never seen feet move as fast as yours."

"When you went down, I came to help, but one of them whacked me from behind so hard I passed out." She held out her hand. It was trembling. "In two minutes, I pumped more adrenaline than in a whole karate tournament."

"You saved my life."

"We're even. Out there on the street I didn't have time to be afraid. But when they got me in here on the floor, I was terrified. They were really pissed. If you hadn't found me when you did . . ."

"If the sound of police sirens hadn't somehow gotten inside my head, I might still be out cold."

He pulled her to his chest and stroked her hair.

"What about these two?" she asked, looking disgusted.

"We have to leave them here. Otherwise, one of us would have to guard them while the other looks for a cop. That's a loser."

She looked at the two bleeding, inert bodies. "At least we did more damage to them than they did to us."

He found enough wire and cord around the office to tie both men to a metal railing. "This will keep them from following us."

He opened the door into the alley and looked both ways. Seeing no one, they ran toward his rental car. At the last corner he flattened against the wall and looked around it. No one near the car, but the hood yawned open, and the driver's side window had been smashed. The door hung open a few inches. He ran to the car.

"Battery's gone." He peered inside. "CD player too. If they broke into the trunk and took the toxic waste samples we're screwed."

The trunk was almost closed but it had been pried open. When he lifted the cover, a faint but distinctive odor wafted out, and he smiled in relief. "The smell in the trunk is left over from when I was carrying these samples in my socks. But the thieves thought it was coming from the bucket. That's why they left it." He grabbed the bucket's handle. "We have to get out of sight fast."

But how? No car. No public transportation. He couldn't call a cab and stand around waiting for it. He looked up and down the street, and then pointed to the lights of the commercial section he'd driven through a few blocks down the street. "That way. We'll find a place to hole up."

They stopped at a small *farmacia* to buy bandages and antiseptic. The pharmacist looked over their soiled clothes and raised one eyebrow, but filled their order without comment. Jack reached for his wallet and came up empty. "That thug ripped it off while I was out cold." Turning his back to other customers, he unzipped his money belt and took out a stack of five hundred peso notes. He paid the bill and put the rest in his pocket.

A few doors down the street, Debra stopped at an open-fronted clothing shop with racks of dresses, blouses, and men's shirts.

"I'll find something clean for us, but I'll need some of that money. I left my purse in the hotel room."

He handed her five hundred pesos and waited on the sidewalk, scanning every pedestrian and every car. He didn't know what to look for but he had to spot anything he could.

She returned in less than five minutes with a paper bag full of her purchases.

"Not a great selection, but they'll do." Her tone was subdued. The shock of the attack had caught up with her. He felt the same. He'd never been attacked so violently, never fought for his life before.

"There are no all-night movies," he said. "Hanging out in some restaurant or bar is too risky. Maybe we can find a hotel."

They tried the only one in sight, a very rough looking place.

"This is opening week at Sunland Racetrack," the desk clerk said. "You won't find a vacancy in this part of town . . . unless La Boca has a room." He winked and pointed. "Two blocks that way."

La Boca was sandwiched between a dark warehouse and a grocery store closed for the night. Each quarter of its two-story façade was a different color: yellow and green below, blue and red above, like a faded quilt. The beat of salsa music thumped through the open door.

"This is such a dump even the Lonely Planet guidebook wouldn't list it," Debra said. She glanced at the metal bucket. "Just as well with that weird luggage of yours."

The lobby was bare except for a reception counter on which a couple of dozen empty beer bottles stood. Next to it, the legs of a padded armchair splayed outward under the colossal bulk of the old woman who filled it. Beneath a rose-colored housedress, her great breasts rested comfortably on her upper thighs; her frizzy bleached hair rose in a cone above her skull. A half-knitted shawl lay across her chest and one arm of the chair. Eyes closed, she moved rosary beads through her fingers. To her left, a staircase angled up out of sight, its treads as worn as those in an ancient temple.

As he got closer to the woman he noticed the barrel of a pistol sticking out several inches from under the shawl, so he stepped to one side before tapping on the counter to get her attention.

Her fingers stopped. She looked at him as if he were selling something she definitely didn't want. She tucked her chins into her chest in disapproval. Maybe she was surprised to see *gringos* looking for a room in this section of Juarez. Maybe it was because they looked like they'd been dragged behind a bus.

"Do you speak English?"

No response. She couldn't or wouldn't.

"*Tiene usted un cuarto?* Do you have a room?"

"*Por supuesto. Por cuantas horas?*"

"She wants to know how many hours we'll be here," he said to Debra.

"I know. I understood her."

"We should get out of here by six." He looked back at the woman. *"Por la mañana, hasta las seis."*

"Se paga ahora." The woman held out a pizza-sized palm in an unmistakable gesture.

"Cuanto?" he asked.

"Quinientos pesos."

He took five hundred pesos from his pocket and handed it over. *Forty dollars for this dump?* He wanted to know why it cost so much. *"Por que es tanto dinero?"*

The woman shrugged, sending waves rippling across her breasts. She counted the money then smiled, flashing several silver triangles, and gave him a key attached to a brass ring a foot in diameter. She held out clean sheets and a somewhat gray towel. *"Numero veinte uno."*

"Is this place okay?" Debra whispered.

"We won't be meeting any debutantes, but it has two things going for it. First, it has a vacancy. Second, no one will look for us here."

"But she's renting rooms by the hour so this must be—"

"You got it."

Emerging onto the landing at the top of the stairs, they walked through a door and stood on a veranda that encircled an open-air courtyard at the second floor level. Below, men and women danced to salsa music coming from several speakers. In one corner, people were holding skewered hunks of red meat over a blazing pile of trash. The sweet smell of marijuana smoke filled his nose and brought back memories. It was like arriving late at a fraternity party.

Farther along the balcony in front of them, a woman was leaning over the railing shouting at someone below in the courtyard. A man sucking on a beer bottle was vigorously fucking her from behind. They squeezed past the energetic man and Jack unlocked room twenty-one.

"Here we are, ma'am, the honeymoon suite. Just call the concierge if you need anything."

He followed Debra into the room. In addition to the swayback queen-size bed there were two scarred wooden chairs, a corner hand sink on a pedestal, and several large unframed posters of snow-capped volcanoes thumb-tacked to the walls. Hanging parallel to the wall to his left, a hammock was suspended from bolts in the ceiling. In his travels, he'd never before seen a hotel room with a hammock, but it wasn't hard to picture its role.

He dropped his Levi jacket onto one of the chairs and helped Debra put the sheets on the bare mattress. He eased onto the bed and drew in a deep breath. "Damn long day."

"Roll over on your left side so I can clean out the wound on your back.

The blade of that guy's knife has probably been places you don't want to think about." She opened the paper bag from the *farmacia*, took out a square of gauze and soaked it in hydrogen peroxide. "You'll hardly feel a thing," she said, dabbing the gauze on the shallow slice that ran across his lower ribcage.

It stung, but it didn't matter. They'd survived the attack. They were safe—for now. In the morning they'd get back on the horse. At this moment, nothing mattered except closing his eyes. At the same time, with the thugs from Casa Lupo on the loose, the last thing he wanted to do was close his eyes.

Chapter 34

July 7
7:00 a.m.

HE FELT HER IN the bed with her back to him.

Hypersensitive to her closeness, he turned so his body curled around her backside. He remembered vividly the couple they'd squeezed past on their way to the room. In seconds, his penis was hard against her. Her fanny was warm but not nearly as hot as the small furnace he sensed ahead. He reached forward under her arm, cupping her breast in his hand. He lifted it, relishing the weight and tautness. He took her nipple between thumb and forefinger and gently squeezed it. She turned her face to him and he captured her mouth, expressing emotions that had grown ever since she'd walked into his suite in La Condesa.

The intensity he felt came from more than having survived near-death together. Along with lust, he felt overwhelming tenderness.

She eased backwards, drawing his penis deep inside her, moving very slowly back and forth, squeezing him. Suddenly, her hips started bucking out of control and he drove forward. His hand never left her breast as she moaned and spasmed seconds ahead of him.

He wakened suddenly and sat straight up. The sharp pain across his back instantly reminded him of the attack. *"Damn,"* he exclaimed with a grimace.

Debra, wearing a yellow sundress with a long skirt and sleeveless top covered in white daisies, came over, sat on the edge of the bed, and kissed the corners of his eyes. "I've been watching you for the last few minutes, thinking how much you've changed since San Francisco."

Her beauty made him catch his breath—and brought back the fantasy he'd just had about her. "You look great."

She smiled at the compliment. "It took a few minutes to pick the rest of the grit out of my hands and knees. The towel looks like a discard from the stock car races, so I used gauze and bottled water to scrub off. Then I air-dried before I changed into this stunning creation. So, how's my patient?"

"My jaw aches, and I feel like I have a row of staples across my back. How about you?"

"Fine except that I'd fight a lion for breakfast. But first, let me look at that cut." He rolled onto his side. "This bandage isn't going to come off easily," she said as she slowly peeled it away. "Good, no redness. The hydrogen peroxide did the trick." She brought tape and a bandage, sat beside him on the bed, and carefully taped a new bandage in place.

She stood. "Time to take a look at your new wardrobe." She handed him his new shirt, pale blue with prints of a variety of cacti, undoubtedly a mocking commentary on his usual dress. She gently kissed him again.

Wishing their lovemaking had been more than a dream, he said, "I want to know you for a very long time."

She beamed. "Whatever that means, I like the sound of it. I must say, you've certainly wakened in a good mood."

He nodded, but he was having trouble hanging onto that mood. He was shaken by how savagely he'd beaten the men in that storeroom. He'd always believed what Gandhi said: "An eye for an eye makes the whole world blind." But when he'd seen Debra on the floor with that guy on top of her, adrenaline kicked in like a hurricane. Violence had been the only way to save her, but what worried him was that he'd lost it, couldn't stop hitting the man. If Debra hadn't intervened, he might have killed him.

"Yeah," she said, "today's pretty sure to be better than yesterday. Speaking of yesterday, there's something you should know. Fighting off Mr. Smooth on the dance floor the other night, I felt real muscles under that fancy silk shirt. If you ever get into it with him, swing first."

"We *will* get into it. Montana sent those thugs to kill us. There was no 'Give us your money or your life.' It was a hit."

She frowned. "How could he get those guys into that alley so fast?"

"Maybe he had someone listening to calls on your hotel phone, or just staked out the Rialto in case you left. Either way, someone followed you to the Casa Lupo and saw me waiting on the sidewalk in front."

Debra nodded. "Montana will find out they didn't get us." She paused and stared at him soberly. "Jack, they almost killed us. It's time for a reality check. We need help."

He swung his feet over the side of the bed and stood. "I'd *love* some help. Look, I'm no action hero. I'm a lawyer. But even if the samples are toxic, I can't prove where they came from or prove chain of custody. I took them because I need to know what's in those tanks and because they might persuade someone in authority to search the Palmer plant. But who? Alvarez touched the third rail and he's toast. El Paso police and the FBI have no jurisdiction in Mexico. They've been scorched several times lately for crossing the border. And everyone says the Juarez police are corrupt. If I call them, they'll invite me in for an interview, call Montana, and lock me up, maybe kill me. I've already warned Sinclair, but his goal is to keep that plant operating. I'll think of something. I have to pry into Montana's head. I need that edge."

TEN MINUTES LATER, eager to leave La Boca and get started on their tasks, they retraced their steps along the interior balcony. The deserted courtyard below reeked with the smell of bleach. They stepped into the street, hot and humid, even though it was not much past seven a.m.

After several blocks, he found a vendor selling plastic-wrapped fried egg sandwiches and warm Cokes in bottles. They walked to a dusty park and sat at a metal mesh table with a bench facing a concrete war-horse ridden by a scowling Benito Juarez. He checked his cell phone, got an adequate signal, and called McDonald.

Mac talked nonstop at high speed, giving him a quick breakdown of the geology of the area, and ended by saying, "So you can see that the water supply there is incredibly vulnerable. If those samples you collected are highly toxic, they would be like injecting poison into an artery. Get them to Ed Rincon at UTEP."

He'd expected bad news, but not this bad.

"Listen Mac, I don't want to get you into trouble, so if anyone asks about our conversations, deny they happened. I'll call you later." He hung up and took a bite of his cold sandwich.

"Don't leave me hanging," Debra said. "What's up?

"Because he's a hydrologist McDonald looked first at water supply and demand. He found out that Ciudad Juarez and El Paso depend on water from a single aquifer. It has two parts, the Hueco *bolsón*—*bolsón* means basin—and the Mesilla *bolsón*. The huge *maquilas* that opened in Juarez suck up that water like thirsty camels, but the real drain comes from the hundreds of thousands of people who migrated here for jobs. To keep the boom going, local governments didn't restrict water use at all until just a few years ago."

"Back up for a moment," Debra said. "I've heard of aquifers, but how do they work?"

"This one is like a giant sponge made of sand, gravel, and silt that accumulates water draining down from the surface—and it's very susceptible to contamination. Only about the top fifteen percent of the water is drinkable. The water below that is too salty. Keep in mind that both these cities are in a desert, maybe seven inches of rain a year. And, as their populations grow, they pump more out of the aquifer than nature replaces. That's called 'mining,' and it draws the salty water deep in the aquifer up to contaminate the fresh water closer to the surface. The water level in the Hueco *bolsón* has already dropped more than one hundred feet."

Debra looked startled. "That's appalling. What are they doing about it?"

"In El Paso, they've cut water consumption by half and opened the largest inland desalination plant in the world to make some of the salty water from the *bolsón* drinkable. That gives them temporary breathing room. The authorities also got tougher on disposing of waste that could contaminate water."

He stopped and looked around. The park was busy now, and the air was rich with aromas of frying food. An annoying *beeb-beeb-beeb* came from a dump truck backing up. Several passersby paused and stared at them, then moved on. He was still watching for the one who might be about to make a hostile move on them.

"I'm guessing that Juarez hasn't been that proactive," Debra said.

He shook his head. "In Juarez, the population is exploding, and they've done very little to conserve water. There used to be a law that required hazardous waste created by *maquilas* to be sent back across the border into the U.S. for disposal. McDonald said that when that law expired, pressure in the right places kept it from being renewed. Now, that toxic waste stays in Mexico."

"Sounds like a great source of business for Palmer Industries and its competitors," she said.

"I'm sure they get some business, but the rumor is that some of the *maquilas* dump their toxic waste in remote backcountry in the middle of the night. In terms of what Montana is planning, that's like comparing a hand grenade to a hydrogen bomb. He's converting ordinary water wells into injection wells to pump extremely hazardous waste underground. In the past, wells that injected material between 4,000 and 8,000 feet deep were permitted in the U.S. The theory was that they were so deep the poison wouldn't affect the ground water and also that they were safer than using landfill, ponds and tanks. In reality, oil and chemical companies used injection wells as a cheap way to put an expensive problem out of sight."

"So if the wells on the Palmer site are that deep, there's no problem, right?"

"But they aren't that deep. McDonald said PEMEX drilled those wells down only a few hundred feet, just enough to draw water from the aquifer."

She tossed the remnant of her sandwich to a crow hopping nearby. "So what happens when the toxins hit this aquifer?"

"If toxicity is high enough, even small amounts will destroy the entire aquifer, killing kids and old people first. Sometime after the aquifer is contaminated, the public—" He gestured at people cutting through the small park. "—will be the walking dead before they know what's happening."

"Dear God," she said, "we have to stop it."

"First step, we get a taxi back to El Paso and deliver the samples to UTEP to be tested. As soon as results are ready, we have them sent to McDonald."

Now that he had a profile of the problem, his pain and fatigue fell away, replaced by urgency. Instead of spinning his wheels waiting for the results to come back, he'd use the time to investigate the mystery trucks whose trips Guzman had worked so hard to keep secret.

He jumped up. "Let's go."

While Debra rose to follow him, he raised his hand to signal, and a 1967 Mercury Monterey taxi swerved to a stop in front of them. As they climbed in, he looked back over his shoulder, distrusting every face in the park.

Chapter 35

July 7
9:00 a.m.

BUSTED. THE AIR conditioning in the F-150 pickup truck Jack had rented in El Paso didn't work. He felt like a lobster boiling under the blazing Texas sun as he inched toward the border crossing into Juarez. Damn that Rent-a-Wreck.

Without Ana-Maria at the plant to let him know when the injection wells would be operational, he was flying blind. And when Ana-Maria didn't show up for work and didn't call, Montana might sense she wasn't coming back. He'd wonder why—and in about ten seconds he'd wonder whether it had something to do with Jack Strider. He'd worry about what secrets she might have revealed. Knowing by now that his ambush near Casa Lupo had failed, Montana would be as berserk as a rodeo bull.

That reminded him that the *coyote* still hadn't called to collect his $500 bonus. He needed to go back to the man's house and check on Ana-Maria.

He drove past the Palmer plant and then doubled back to be sure of what he thought he'd seen. Yes, they were there, a row of black trucks parked in a line on one side of the yard. When they leave the Palmer gate they have to turn left to return to Juarez. When they get there, they could turn north to head across one of the bridges to the States. Or they might turn south to pick up Highway 45, the fastest route toward Chihuahua City. Either way, he had to follow them.

As he drove, he looked around for a place where he could park and wait for the trucks without being seen. The skeletal vegetation within a half mile of the plant wouldn't provide cover for a colony of fire ants, much less his pickup truck. Finally, he parked mostly out of sight in the shelter of a ramshackle fruit stand, able to see a stretch of road. They'd have to go by his hiding place.

Sweat soaked his shirt as he scrunched down in the seat and squinted against the glare. Jack Strider, law professor and Supreme Court wannabe. Okay, ex-wannabe at this point. What was he doing acting like a one-man posse? He checked his watch. Too much time had passed. They must have turned to the right out of the plant and headed for God knows where.

His pickup's engine cranked over and over but wouldn't catch. *Damn it.* Then it caught, and he jammed his foot down on the accelerator. The Ford bounced onto the road heading to the right, back toward the plant.

No sooner had he gotten up speed than the lead truck of the convoy came barreling in his direction, the others right behind. They thundered past, six of them, like Brinks armored trucks on steroids. They sped past, but he had no difficulty reading the large yellow signs: "Danger—Hazardous Waste."

He whipped off onto the sandy shoulder and swerved back on the asphalt behind them. He knew better than to tailgate, but, except for what he'd seen in movies, had no idea how to trail them without being spotted. There was plenty of traffic, and that gave him some cover. That also raised the risk of being trapped and losing the trucks.

After about fifteen minutes, they turned south onto Highway 45 for Chihuahua City, the nose of each of the five trailing trucks within a few feet of the tail of the one ahead of it. They appeared identical except that the last in line had a short crane mounted on a heavy frame on the roof of the cab. Mysteriously, the presence of the massive black convoy brought order to the highway. Speeders suddenly slowed down.

He settled into a rhythm, staying alert, keeping several cars between him and the last truck. An hour passed, then another.

Who was in the trucks? Were they drivers-for-hire who'd run away if challenged? More likely, *pistoleros* hired to fight.

Because of the secrecy, he assumed they were doing something illegal. But he also knew that trucks from the U.S. loaded with hazardous waste were permitted to deliver it to selected places for treatment and disposal, places like the Palmer site.

But Ana-Maria had said these mystery trucks never unloaded at Palmer, just fueled up and switched crews, so they had to be dumping their cargoes somewhere else in Mexico. So why go out of the way to stop at Palmer just for fuel? Palmer Industries had to be getting more out of this than a few bucks at their gas pumps. And why did they switch drivers?

Heat and monotony must have dulled his brain because he hadn't seen the other possibility until this moment. What if these trucks were actually empty and on their way to pick up a cargo to smuggle *into* the U.S., maybe drugs, immigrants, even terrorists?

His mental focal length had been too short in concentrating on Montana. Organizing an operation this big was above Montana's pay grade. Somewhere there had to be a puppeteer pulling his strings. He remembered Arthur Palmer's scornful eyes and sharp tongue.

He was so absorbed in trying to figure out what was going on that all at once he was too close to the rear truck. He cut sharply behind a Coca-Cola

18-wheeler for cover. It looked like the convoy was heading into Chihuahua City, famous as the hangout for Pancho Villa and Benito Juarez, but near the big city the trucks veered southwest onto Highway 16. He followed. The convoy rolled on for an hour and a half, climbing high into the Sierra Madre Mountains. Pinto beans and prickly pears were replaced by Ponderosa pines and *vaqueros* on horseback herding cattle.

He'd been watching the fuel gauge on his gas hog slide toward empty, expecting to see a gas station where he could slam in a few quick gallons. Mile after mile there had been none. Now, with the pointer hard on empty, he nursed the Ford up every climb and coasted the few downhill stretches. He wasn't going to make it. His hot pursuit was about to end with a whimper, leaving him to shake his fist after them. They'd never even know he'd been there.

When he cut his speed to fifty to conserve fuel, he lost sight of the convoy, spotting it once far across a side canyon, then not again. He finally passed a roadside sign: "Town of Creel." Under that, "Entrance to Copper Canyon, Deeper and Longer than the Grand Canyon." He limped into Creel at twenty miles an hour. It had the feeling of the kind of place where loggers come out of the pine forests on Friday night to get drunk and fight with chainsaws.

The town was falling apart, but its two-pump gas station looked beautiful to him. He got out and stretched—and immediately felt a sting across his lower back where the knife slice was only partially closed.

He was filling up when a metallic silver coupe making a growling sound pulled up to the other side of the pump. It was a Mercedes SLS. That meant 550 horsepower, 7-speed transmission, and a price tag above $200,000. The gull wing doors flipped up. Two men got out and glared at him, as if they expected their mere attention would make him evaporate. His gas tank was close to full so he cut the flow and paid the man who'd quickly appeared to serve the Mercedes.

They must be *narcotraficantes*. Copper Canyon was probably a haven for men like these twenty-something, stone-cold killers.

Talk about out of the frying pan, into the fire. He was in country where anyone he didn't know might be a danger to him. And he was chasing people he knew damned sure were.

Back on the road he pushed the old Ford faster than it could handle safely. If he was gaining on the convoy, it wasn't by much. The truckers were better drivers, and they knew the road. Deep inside the Barrancas del Cobre National Park a sign pointed to a turnoff to the town of Batopilas, but the dirt and gravel road looked too puny for the convoy. Nevertheless, he pulled over and walked back to the turnoff.

Within a dozen steps he saw marks that could have been left by giant tires. Logic told him the convoy would stay on the faster asphalt road, and these marks might belong to logging trucks. He was about to go with logic when he saw a plume of dust in the distance in the direction taken by the gravel road. He sprinted back to the pickup.

The gravel road immediately dropped off the high ground, descending in a series of switchbacks scratched into the steep slopes of the mountains. No shoulders, no guardrail. He drove too fast, trying to keep the wisps of swirling dust in sight. One mistake, a moment of distraction, would send him plummeting down a thousand feet. The crisp atmosphere of higher altitude was replaced by air as humid and hot as the tropics. Pines gave way to bushy acacias, papayas, and mangos.

On a steep downhill stretch, he wrestled the Ford around a blind corner and was almost on top of several scrawny cattle straggling uphill. He jerked the wheel left, banging the front fender on the rock face. The truck rebounded back into the center, fishtailing, heading straight over the edge of the cliff. He forced himself to cut the wheels opposite from the way his instinct screamed for him to do, but the pickup couldn't straighten out fast enough.

A spooked cow bolted in front of him. No chance to avoid it. The Ford rammed it, sending the flailing animal over the edge. The collision stopped the truck cold, front bumper hanging over space. *Damn, that was close.* He sucked in a deep breath, checked twice to be sure the Ford was in reverse, and punched the accelerator. Back on the road, he continued downhill after the vanished convoy.

When he finally reached the valley floor, the field to his left was lush with low-lying cannabis. In the distance was a boarded-up entrance to an abandoned mine.

"Batopilas," the wooden sign read, "Silver Center of Mexico." The gravel road became the main street of a town wedged between a cliff and a river. Batopilas appeared to be a wealthy mining town that had decayed into poverty. Several stately old Spanish-style homes had obviously been vacant for a long time. A huge theater was a statement made by suddenly-wealthy mine owners, like the grand opera house erected in Manaus, halfway up the Amazon, during the rubber boom.

The rest of the town looked like a set for a low-budget western. On shaded porches, men leaned back in hard chairs, watching and judging from under tilted *sombreros*. Batopilas was the kind of place where no one showed up without a reason.

The haze in the air showed he was only minutes behind the convoy. Driving along the valley floor, he saw the telltale plume turn right, continue a few hundred meters and disappear. Now he had to be much more wary. If they were close to their destination, they'd be more on guard.

He turned off the road, following the tread tracks until he reached the mouth of the side canyon. A steel pole gate barred the road. Boulders prevented him from driving around it. He backed up until his pickup was out of sight behind another boulder, and sat there for a few moments, breathing air so humid it made his lungs feel like wet sponges.

He knew he was pathetically unprepared for what was coming up. He also knew he couldn't stop now, so he climbed out of the truck.

When he got back to the gate and ducked under the bar, he crossed the line into a much more dangerous world. After a few hundred yards, the side canyon broadened to become an oval bowl a half-mile across and two miles long, a *cul de sac*. He bent low and dodged from one scrap of cover to the next. At each stop, he scanned the landscape for a guard posted to pick off intruders. He knew that in the Sierra Madre, where some of the most esteemed citizens run international drug cartels, trespassers are not tolerated.

Piles of rocks that had fallen from the canyon walls blocked his view, so he clawed up a slab of stone and crouched just below its crest. Peering over the top, he saw mine shafts running into both side walls of the canyon. He counted ten. The enormous mounds of tailings around the entrances looked like the work of giant moles from the age of dinosaurs.

Shading his eyes, he scrutinized the rest of the bowl. The trucks had vanished. He saw enough of the valley floor to know they couldn't be sheltered by boulders or brush. The only other possibility was the mine shafts, but the entrances he could see were too small to admit even one black truck. The group of men sitting in a patch of sparse shade must be the truck crews, but where were the damn trucks?

If he tried to get closer, his movements would give him away. No need to take the risk. He already knew the trucks would be going back to Palmer Industries. He could pick them up there and follow them to the other end of their run.

He worked slowly back toward the narrow exit, crouching, watching the canyon floor to see if he was being followed. As soon as he was out of sight of the truck crews, he stood upright to ease his back. Before he took his first step, he spotted a man standing on a ledge ahead to his right, work clothes almost blending into the rock. The sentry was so close it was too late to find cover. At this range, if the guard looked his way, his shot wouldn't miss. Then the man bent his head lighting a cigarette, clumsy because of the rifle crooked under his arm.

Jack moved quickly and quietly until he ducked under the gate bar, sweating and tense, and ran to his pickup.

RETRACING HIS route, he demanded more from the pickup than it had to give, imagining that the black trucks were behind him, catching up. After seventy-five or eighty miles of careening around curves and skidding across corrugated sections of road, he was approaching the town of Creel when he saw a sign that pointed to Chihuahua City to the right and Divisadero to the left. Past the intersection was a tiny grass airstrip, the kind used by drug smugglers and bush pilots for hire. He'd read about *gringo* hunters flying around in the Copper Canyon and leaning out of the window to take pot shots at jaguars. Or maybe this was some drug cartel's private strip.

He looked back at the sign again. Divisadero. The name jogged his memory. The pilot who'd sat at his table in Bar Nueva Leon in Mexico City was from Divisadero. And that solved a problem that must have been bouncing around in his subconscious. A pilot was exactly the man he needed now. But how could he find this one? The guy had said he had a permanent seat at the bar of some hotel on the canyon rim. Jack didn't remember the name of the hotel, but how many could there be?

He burned up the thirty miles to Divisadero and went on the hunt for a cliff-side hotel. The first one he found, Posada on the Rim, full of German tourists, was a dry hole. His only other shot was the Hotel Divisadero Tarahumara, some distance out of town. It was a rustic place of stucco, stone, wood beams, and red roofs.

Gano LeMoyne lounged in a hand-carved chair on a deck that had a panoramic view of Urique canyon. He wore a black T-shirt, faded Levis, and had his cowboy boots crossed on the railing. The forward tilt of his head made him look asleep behind dark aviator glasses.

"Gano, I need to talk with you," Jack said when he walked onto the deck.

"Umph," Gano grunted without looking up. "Who are you?"

"Jack Strider. We met at the Bar Nuevo Leon in Mexico City a couple of weeks ago. I'm—"

Gano's slid his glasses down and gave him the once-over "Oh, yeah. Lawyer, right?" He picked up a mug from a table next to him and took a swig.

Jack nodded. "Yes. Listen, I'm short on time. Can we talk?"

Gano looked suspicious. "First tell me how you happened to come to this out of the way place to talk with a guy you met for fifteen minutes in a Mexico City bar?"

"No mystery. You said, 'If the money's right, I'll deliver anything, absolutely, positively anywhere.' Well, I need to be delivered to a canyon just beyond Batopilas."

"I know that countryside. There's only one canyon you could fly into, and it's tighter than a tick's ass. What's so interesting about it, if you don't mind me being nosy?"

He did mind, but if Gano took the job he'd know a lot more than that before long. "I think several trucks are being loaded in that canyon right now. I need to know their cargo."

"Hmm. Since they're loading there, they want privacy. That means they'd be upset by someone flying over to spy on them. Maybe even get ugly, right?"

"You mean you won't do it?"

Gano grinned. "Sure I will. I'll just factor that into my fee. But there *is* one problem. What we need is a chopper. I can rent one from Raramuri Tours down the road, but they charge me a premium because I've been known to be sorta rough on their birds."

"What's the price for you and the chopper?"

"Five grand, U.S."

Because of Gano's aviator glasses, Jack couldn't read his eyes, but the price sounded like a rip-off. "We're only talking about an hour or so," he said, but he knew he didn't have much bargaining power.

"I ought to charge more than that for doing a hurry-up job. Hell, that's why I hang out here, to avoid rushes. And don't be thinking you're paying too much. Something will go wrong. It always does. Want a beer? It's in the price."

Jack had serious reservations about the helicopter. He was fine on commercial flights, but had an irrational aversion to small craft. The fact that Gano had probably already downed several beers made him feel even less secure.

"No time for a beer. The price is right. Let's get moving."

THIRTY SECONDS after the little chopper cleared the ground, Gano whipped it into a right bank so steep Jack was looking almost straight down until Gano reached his course and leveled off.

Twenty minutes later, Gano pointed at Batopilas ahead of them. "Looks like a dump now, but in the old days it was surrounded by the richest silver mines in Mexico. Pancho Villa robbed their mule trains loaded with silver so often he was on a first name basis with the drivers. In the 1890s, a lucky bastard from Washington, D.C. got hold of the mines and became one of the richest men in the world." He pointed up at the rotors. "With this racket, we can't sneak up on them, so I'll fake 'em out. They'll be watching the open end of the canyon. We'll come in from the other direction."

Gano skimmed the rock-strewn surface of a wide mesa, then jammed the stick forward and dove over a cliff, plunging hundreds of feet in seconds, entering the canyon from the *cul de sac* end.

"Eyes sharp, laddie. We don't have a lot of time."

Jack noticed the men under the trees scrambling to their feet, several pointing at the chopper and shouting. The chopper was past the men in a flash. Still not a truck in sight, but he'd seen something that hadn't been visible on foot. At the base of the canyon wall was a crack, thirty-feet wide and as tall as a three story building.

"Hold on, tiger. Stunt coming up." The chopper, now almost at the canyon's exit slot, shot straight up, hung for a moment and then fell off to port and swooped back down just above the valley floor, zipping among obstacles like a race car in a video game.

White puffs of smoke popped from the barrel of the guard at the entrance. Jack gritted his teeth, bracing for the impact of bullets. They missed. Gano had a tight smile as he flew directly at the tree cover, scattering the men. Apparently he didn't take to being shot at and wanted payback.

At that moment, a black behemoth slowly emerged from the crack in the wall like some Paleolithic beast. Just then, a man on one knee started firing a semiautomatic weapon at the chopper. Gano waggled the stick hard from side to side, then hauled back and curved to starboard to get out of the canyon.

"Damn, we made it," Jack shouted. "I don't see how they missed at that range."

"They couldn't, which means they weren't trying to hit us, just scare us away. Signs all over this bird say Raramuri Tours. Those suckers assumed I was some asshole pilot giving a tourist a thrill. They know the shit would hit the fan if they shot us down. And they aren't the kind to call attention to themselves by complaining back in Divisadero. They played it just the way I was counting on."

"You've been shot at before?"

Gano grinned again. "Things can get a little rowdy when I have to land at some pissant backcountry airstrip at midnight with no runway lights. I can't see who's down there, but I know they may want to take what I have on board. Or they don't want me to see what they're up to. Not a lot of trust in these parts."

"So you shoot at each other?"

"Usually, but friendly—sort of."

As soon as he'd landed, locked the bird, and driven them back to the Hotel Divisadero Tarahumara, Gano settled himself on the deck and quickly drained a bottle of beer in a series of gulps, belched, and took a sip from a second. "So, *hombre*, get what you wanted?"

"Still no idea what the cargo is, but I saw where the trucks go to be loaded. Do you know anything about that crack in the cliff face?"

"That's a lot more than a crack. It's a sacred place for the Tarahumara people. Story is, their greatest chief cast a spell on it a thousand years ago, putting a curse on any outsider who might enter it. During the silver rush, some of the miners went in. Not one ever came out."

"What's it like inside?"

"Tarahumara legends say there's a maze of caverns with spikes in the ceilings that fall and impale intruders. Then there are black-water lakes full of croc-like things with fangs and packs of scorpions the size of Chihuahuas. Every midnight, weird beings they call 'guardians' run footraces deep inside the mountain. Anyone working inside that cave should be looking over his shoulder every few seconds."

Gano set down his empty beer bottle, and a server set a full one in its place.

"Both times I've been there," Jack said, "the truck crews were sitting in the shade instead of doing the loading. That's so they don't know what's being loaded and can't blow the whistle. Damn smart."

"So the little tour was worth $5,000 after all, just like I said."

Jack still didn't know what the cargo was but he knew what to do next. He stood, walked to the railing, and turned. "I want you to fly me to El Paso."

"That's easy," Gano said. "Five hundred plus gas both ways for the trip. If you want me to hang with you after that, it'll be because things have gotten complicated. That'll be $1,000 a day, plus expenses for the plane. No offense, Goldfinger, but let's see if we can get some laughs out of this."

The price was stiff, but Gano was the only game in town.

"Don't know about the laughs, but the money's right."

He wasn't about to mention that this flight was just the first step. He intended to hook Gano into a lot more than that.

GANO PULLED UP in a steep climb from the private airstrip. Jack didn't like flying in a small plane any better than he did in a helicopter, but he had no choice. He'd expected Gano's plane to be utilitarian and old. Instead, it was a shiny new high-wing, four-person Cessna. "You must have hit the lottery to buy this thing."

"Better. I hit three gents who had to get out of Dodge in a hurry, life or death you might say, and they weren't in a position to fly United. My fee was 300k. After I set them down on a Colombian country road in a rainstorm, I hauled ass to Wichita and bought this baby. It's the turbo version of the Skylane, and it'll climb faster than anything I'm likely to come up against in my line of work. Intuitive avionics. Flies like a bat in Carlsbad Caverns."

"What's that?" Jack pointed to a long-barrel weapon in a bracket bolted to the dash.

"Benelli R1 semiautomatic rifle. Almost no recoil, so it's easy to keep on target. Depending on what I expect, I may swap it with my Mossberg 935 loaded with three and a half inch 12 gauge magnum shells. It's back there." He indicated a weapon strapped above the rear seat the way it's done in an Alabama pickup truck. "One burst from that baby can cut a grove of banana trees in half."

In his shades and cowboy hat, Gano reminded him of Hunter S. Thompson, the gonzo journalist who had a lifelong romance with firearms and drugs. Gano's impulsive nature made him a loose cannon Jack would have to watch every second. On the other hand, going after the mystery trucks was leading him deeper into a swamp where Gano would come in very handy.

If he'd driven the pickup back to El Paso, he'd have been on the road until after three a.m. Flying with Gano would get him there in time to grab a few hours of sleep and gather some essential information in the morning. During his pursuit of the mystery trucks, Debra would have delivered the samples to Rincon and been working on the other assignment he'd given her.

They landed at the El Paso airport just after nine p.m., and he hailed a taxi to take them to the El Diablo motel. Along the way, he gave Gano a sketchy outline of who Debra was but nothing about what she'd been doing.

He knocked on the hotel room door to let Debra know she had company. No answer. He let himself in. No Debra, just a note which he read.

He told Gano, "Debra flew to Austin to do some research. She'll go to Professor Rincon's office at UTEP tomorrow morning and then brief me on what she finds out."

"What kind of research—"

Gano's question, which Jack didn't want to answer, was cut off by the phone ringing. He snatched up the receiver and listened to Debra's questions about his safety. As soon as he reassured her, she switched into a commentary on his recklessness. He interrupted to fill her in on what he'd learned about the black trucks and the cave near Batopilas.

"I brought back someone who'll be working with us for a few days. Gano LeMoyne. He's a private pilot who does . . . special deliveries."

"Who recommended him? Do you know him?" She sounded skeptical.

"We've done a project together that worked out fine. You'll like him.

Now I have to go. I'll call you tomorrow, and we'll choose a place to meet." He hung up.

"That was interesting," Gano said, filling a plastic cup from a bottle of dark rum. "You forgot to tell her about the bullets and the bad guys. What's she going to say when she finds out about that?"

Chapter 36

July 8
6:30 a.m.

IN TRUDY'S Restaurant across the street from the El Diablo, Jack watched as Gano wolfed down the Breakfast Burritos Salsa Special and a plate of refried beans.

Gano looked up. "What you lookin' at?"

"Nothing."

Gano looked down at his tight black trousers and black-on-black embroidered western shirt with pearl buttons. "This is my El Paso pimp look. Glad you like it." He turned his attention back to demolishing the giant burrito.

Waiting for Gano to finish, he had to make a decision. He could stake out the plant again and try to follow the trucks north, knowing he might be trapped in traffic or at the security checkpoint and lose them. Or he could try to pick them up on the U.S. side of the border.

"Gano, if a convoy of black trucks, like the one we saw yesterday, was heading north from Ciudad Juarez, where do you think they'd cross?"

"Bridge of the Americas stacks up like a parking lot. Same for the Zaragosa and Stanton Street bridges. Smart truckers avoid them like the clap. The Ysleta crossing is less crowded, but truckers with questionable loads stay away because it has a gizmo that uses Pulsed Fast Neutron Analysis. It's a scanner that detects smack, pot, explosives, mustard gas, even bags of cash. But it takes so long they scan only about one in twenty trucks, and they just guess which ones to pick. On the Mexican side, they pay some grunt $50 a day instead. Anyway, your black trucks wouldn't go through at Ysleta." He scraped the plate for a last fork full of beans.

"Okay, so that's where they wouldn't cross." He tried not to sound exasperated. "Now tell me where they *would* cross."

"At Santa Teresa in the New Mexico boonies. Trucks coming *from* Mexico are supposed to be inspected on the U.S. side, but that's a joke. A serious inspection takes two hours, and they don't have enough trained people. Only about ten percent of trucks get checked at all, and that's mostly for worn brakes or tires and for whether the load is secured right.

"As far as trucks going *into* Mexico at Santa Teresa, neither side gives a damn. U.S. shippers file a bill of lading and an export declaration, and that's it. After the Customs grunts get to know certain companies and their trucks, they just wave them through. Of course, serious players never take a chance. We, I mean they, lay some *dinero* on the Customs officers at Santa Teresa so they'll start inspecting the clouds."

"So trucks that cross into the U.S. at Santa Teresa are home free?"

"Unless they're terminally stupid. If they head toward El Paso on I-10, they'd hit a checkpoint at the New Mexico/Texas border where trucks are spot-checked with an X-ray to catch illegals. Trucks with any kind of no-no on board stay in New Mexico and drive north without being touched."

He made his decision. "Eat up, and we'll rent a car in your name."

"Hold on, pard." Gano mopped up the last of the burrito sauce and ate it. "Okay, now let's hit it before all this lard slams into my heart."

Jack drove to within fifty yards of the Santa Teresa crossing and stopped to watch. From the American side of the border, the light that was supposed to flash red if a Mexican Customs officer wanted to signal a vehicle to stop, seemed to be stuck on green. Cars barely slowed.

There were only five trucks stopped in the northbound lane entering the U.S. Instead of vigorously inspecting the first truck, an officer leaned against the cab and chatted with the driver.

When he'd seen enough, Jack entered the Mexican Customs office and flashed a Sinclair & Simms business card at the officer in charge. "I'm conducting a routine audit for Palmer Industries to confirm how many trucks have come through here in the past thirty days carrying hazardous waste to our plant in Juarez. I especially need to know how many large black trucks in groups of three to six have come through. They have yellow 'Hazardous Waste' warning signs on their sides."

The officer, who wore gold-braid epaulettes and a galaxy of brass stars across his chest, chewed one corner of his mustache and waved away a colleague who had stopped to eavesdrop. "No trucks like that have passed this checkpoint, *señor.*" He broke eye contact and shook his head side to side several times.

"Maybe you could check your records. I'm willing to pay a fee for your service." Jack took out his wallet and withdrew several 100 peso bills.

"No such trucks, *señor.*" The official raised both hands in the universal gesture of *que sera sera.*

Gano pulled Jack aside and whispered, "Okay, your honor, this bureaucratic weasel is lying so bad it must make his teeth hurt. What say I take him around the corner and beat the crap out of him until I get a straight answer?"

Gano's mouth was smiling, but his voice wasn't. Because of his black shades, Jack couldn't tell how serious he was.

"Not this time. If he's been bribed to keep those convoys invisible, he's probably been threatened big time. We can't turn him around."

As they got back into the car, Jack said, "We don't have time to wait around hoping a northbound convoy shows up. Besides, I have a better idea, a long shot." He pulled back onto the road north and pushed down hard on the gas pedal.

"Way to go, champ," Gano said. "When in doubt, drive faster."

"Very funny, but it just hit me that while the Customs guy was giving us the runaround, I looked out the window and saw a man working on the adobe wall around the building. When we came out, he was driving away in an old Taurus. I want to talk with him."

"Your wish is granted." Gano pointed to a Taurus parked in a Serv-U gas station.

"Buenos días, señor," Jack said as he walked up to the man filling his tank. He described the convoy. "Have you seen trucks like that?" He held out a $20 bill. The man shrugged. Jack added another $20. No response, so he turned and started back to the car.

By the third step he heard, *"Señor,"* behind him.

In broken English, the man described the black trucks crossing the border two or three times a week while he worked on the grounds of the Customs offices. He said the head Customs official on duty spoke only with the lead driver and waved the trucks through within a minute. Trucks like that had passed through just a half hour ago, heading north.

Jack climbed back into the car and punched the steering wheel. "Damn it! We missed them." He looked at Gano. "Unless . . ."

GANO PEERED out the side window of his Cessna. "Looks like the foxes have gone to ground. We've flown along three highways and come up dry."

"We're not quitting."

"May have no choice. We've already violated half the FAA rule book. Been in and out of Fort Bliss air space for half an hour. I guarantee they're tracking us. You might say Bliss is following us."

Jack suppressed a chuckle at Gano's little joke and said, "But I haven't seen anything that looked like a military base."

"It started just outside El Paso. At seventy miles by thirty miles, it's bigger than Rhode Island. Those ol' boys specialize in air defense and get downright cranky about visitors. I'm surprised they haven't scrambled a fighter to ground us. Anyway, if they come up, we go down in a hurry."

Jack tilted a road map toward Gano. "There's a back road from Las Cruces to Alamogordo then up to I-40. Let's try that."

"We have to be careful. See that long line of white gypsum dunes off to the left? White Sands Missile Range is over there. They play games with guided missiles and high energy laser weapons and don't put up with drop-in company. We're also right over the UFO capital of the universe. Maybe that's where those big trucks came from." He grinned. "Hey, flying this low isn't makin' you nervous is it, chief?"

"No sweat." But he wouldn't have minded pulling up a few hundred feet. They were so close to the ground he could easily read the signs on the concrete block buildings below: American Legion Post, Crystal Ballroom, and Black Cat Fireworks. Straight ahead he saw the Mendoza Tortilla Factory, the New Image Beauty Shop, and a large sign that read "Income Tax Service & Window Tinting."

"Shame your friend Debra's not along for this joy ride," Gano said.

"Maybe, but she's working on a project for me. We'll see her when we get back."

"Cool. Okay, we'll follow Highway 54, that's the back road you were pointing at. If we get as far as Alamogordo without spotting them, they lost us."

"No way. We'll keep looking until we're out of fuel."

Gano glanced over. "Tell me this, *compadre*, what's got you so riled up? You've got it made in the shade. Why go through all this shit?"

Jack didn't answer right away. Gano assumed he had it "made in the shade." Yeah, maybe if you don't count seeing everything he'd worked for destroyed in a week, including his reputation and dreams.

"I'm going through all this shit because in the last few days I've cared more about what I'm doing than in the last ten years. You'll understand more about that after we hear from Debra." He didn't mention the new fear he carried like a great stone.

Gano poked his dark glasses half an inch down the bridge of his nose to look over them with black-ink eyes. "Heavy shit, Sigmund." The glasses went back into place. "Good thing you have a lot of experience at this sort of thing."

"Yeah, from Boy Scouts."

Gano banked the Cessna into a slow turn. "Unfortunately, we're not going to pin the tail on the donkeys today. I haven't taught this thing to fly on fresh air yet."

Jack caught the glint of sunlight off a windshield below and grabbed Gano's arm. "There they are about a mile up the road." The closely bunched trucks looked ominous, even from 1,200 feet above.

"Targets acquired, lieutenant." Gano grinned but continued north, not changing course. "If they see us they won't be suspicious unless we do something dim-witted that makes them pay attention. We'll let them get out of sight for a while. That's Mescalero right ahead of them. If they don't stop there, they must be going to Ruidoso Downs to bet on the ponies."

But a few miles past Mescalero, the trucks turned off on a well-maintained road that wasn't on the map. After another mile, they stopped at a wide gate made of a lattice of heavy steel bars. A razor wire fence three times the height of a man stretched miles from the gate in both directions. A long-barreled weapon mounted on the roof of the gatehouse immediately trained on the lead truck. No one dismounted from the trucks. Looking back over his shoulder, Jack saw the gate swing inward and the trucks move up the road like six ducks in formation.

Gano whistled. "Wow! That's a 120mm cannon, like the one on an Abrams battle tank; thermal imaging gun sight and a laser rangefinder. It's probably remote controlled by some geek in an air-conditioned office. I don't like that one damn bit. I'm going to lose some altitude before we get turned into a puff of smoke." He didn't pull out of the dive until the Cessna was a hundred feet off the ground. "Harder to target us down here."

The cannon was out of sight behind them, but Jack sensed its black snout tracking the plane. If it fired, they'd never know what hit them.

"With firepower like that at the gate," Gano said, "they've damn sure got more inside. This is getting interesting." He stroked the Benelli semiautomatic rifle, then reached back and brought the Mossberg shotgun forward.

Jack frowned and said sharply, "You're not going to need those. We're not going to kill anybody."

"That's the captain's call, swabbie. Aboard this ship, that's me. I'm going to circle out of sight for a minute to give them time to get where they're going, and then make a high speed pass right on the deck." He reached under his seat, pulled out a mini camcorder, and handed it to Jack. "Be ready. A fast moving plane is a bad platform, but that has a 35X optical zoom with an image stabilizer. We're only going to make one pass." He pulled the Cessna into a steep climb. Puffy white clouds filled the windscreen.

Minutes later, dropping out of the sun, Gano started his dive. "Look at that baby down there, one hell of a private airstrip. And that road must lead to—yep, there's home plate."

The plane banked slightly, giving Jack a clear view of warehouses, 18-wheelers, several low buildings that could be offices, and rows of apartments. Whatever was going on, it was big.

Gano brought them so low they lost sight of the compound behind a ridge. "When we pop up over that ridge we'll be maxed out at 175 so get with the 'lights, camera, action.' We ain't comin' back." He whipped the Cessna up a few feet and over the ridge line. "Yahoo!"

The landscape shot past, a blur of cacti and rock. Jack got a clear look through the camcorder's viewfinder.

"Oh my God!" they said in unison.

Chapter 37

July 8
4:30 p.m.

"WHY DID THAT air traffic controller call you 'Crash'?" Jack asked as they taxied across the Tarmac and away from the dust-caked glass domes of El Paso International Airport.

"She's a smart ass, that's why," Gano answered. "Forget it. See that gizmo by your right hand? Pull it off the Velcro strip, point it at the sign on that hangar ahead and click the button."

After several seconds, the hangar bay doors of Aerolitoral Airlines slid open. Gano steered the Cessna inside and shut it down. With another click, Jack closed the big doors behind them.

When he jumped to the asphalt he saw a person, a backlighted silhouette, entering the hangar through a small entrance to the left of the hangar bay door. As the figure got closer, he saw it was Debra carrying her laptop case.

"If you're finished playing air commando," she called, "I have a lot to tell you."

When he'd called her from the plane to let her know where to meet them, her tone had an edge, letting him know she thought he should have stayed in El Paso. Instead of giving her a hug, he waved to Gano to join them.

"Gano LeMoyne, this is Debra Vanderberg."

"Howdy, ma'am." He made a half-bow.

Debra gave him a quick handshake with no comment. Apparently she wasn't buying his backcountry Cajun pitch.

Gano walked to a wall cabinet and came back with a bottle of Cuban rum.

"You're certainly at home here," Jack said.

"When Aerolitoral isn't using this hangar, they let me park here. I use it when I have, hmm, sensitive cargo, whether it's animal, vegetable, or mineral." He poured three fingers of rum into a cup and drank half of it.

They settled into chairs around a worktable in the corner, and Jack described for Debra the buildings, weapons, and black trucks they'd seen on their flyover. "But there were no signs, so we couldn't tell who owns the place. That's why I called you with the GPS coordinates. Any luck?"

"I pulled up a state map and plotted the coordinates. Then I called the emergency number of the Public Service Company of New Mexico and said I'd been hiking and smelled gas. When I gave the operator the location, she said, 'Oh jeez, you're on D-TECH land. You better get out of there fast. How did you get through the electrified fence?' I said I hadn't seen a fence, so we agreed I must be confused about the location. Anyway, the owner of that site is named D-TECH.

"I looked on the New Mexico Secretary of State's web site and found out D-TECH wasn't incorporated in New Mexico. Next, I called the chief of police in Mescalero. He claimed he'd never set foot on the site and knew nothing about D-TECH."

Raising his cup, Gano said, "I've got a scrap of info to kick in. There's this joint in Las Cruces, the Aces Inn, where they play a little poker. Hotshot quarter horse owners come slummin' from Ruidoso Downs, so I drop in when I feel democratic, you know, like redistributing their wealth." He took a swig of rum. "One night a fella sounded off about some big operation not far out of town. He was pissed because it hires no locals and spends no money in the county. He said it was like a spaceship. Everything they need is beamed in, and workers never leave the place. And if you believe him, that fence around the property has fried more cattle than ever got rustled in these parts. He never mentioned the name, but he had to be talkin' about this D-TECH."

Jack handed the memory card from the camcorder to Debra. "Run it at one-quarter speed, and let's take a better look at what we saw."

On the laptop screen, five of the giant trucks were lined up next to each other near a warehouse. The sixth truck was parked directly in front of the cargo door of the same warehouse.

"Now go to super slow motion and zoom in," Jack said.

Watching frame by frame, he saw outsized forklifts removing pallets carrying green barrels from inside the warehouses and placing them into the big truck.

"Stop there, Debra. See the markings on that first barrel? If those are three yellow prongs inside a black circle, that's a radiation warning."

"And look at this one." Gano touched the screen. "It looks a lot like the symbol for an atom. That must have something to do with radiation."

"My God," Debra said, "that could mean there's radioactive material in those barrels."

"That ups the stakes," Jack said, "but from the way they're handling them, it's probably low level nuclear waste. Debra, will you make a print of the frames that show the cargo?"

She nodded.

In the next frames, he picked out another detail. Two long hatches on top of the truck with the crane were open. The cargo compartment was empty. *Why would it come north without a load?*

"Look guys," Debra broke in, "we don't know much about what's going on at D-TECH, but we know for sure that Palmer Industries is . . ." She stopped.

Jack knew what she was thinking. She didn't know how far he had brought Gano into the circle and didn't want to spill anything. Gano picked up on that too.

"Let's stop the pussyfooting," Gano said. "You don't trust me. Maybe you think I'm just some gun-totin' pothead. Even if you're right, I'm also a little brighter than your average prairie dog. So here's the deal. I'm in this game of cops-and-robbers all the way, or I'm out. Jack came to find me, not the other way round, and it seems like he's going to need me. Hell, the money's right, and this is shaping up as a lot more interesting than my usual dump-and-run gigs, so I wouldn't mind playing the hand."

"You're in, Gano," Jack said, "as long as you accept my ground rules. First, keep all this absolutely secret. Second, don't kill anyone."

"My lips are sealed."

"And the other?"

Gano took off his shades and looked at him steadily. "Let's play the hand."

Debra glanced at Jack, eyebrows raised.

He nodded "Yes." It would be up to him to keep Gano in check.

"As I was about to say," Debra said, "since your home movie doesn't prove anything about those trucks, Palmer will be your highest priority after you hear what I learned from Professor Rincon. The first shock came when I walked into his office. The man looks like a praying mantis in a white lab coat and white Nikes. His eyes are round and flick around the room, like they're operating independently.

"He knew I was in a hurry to get the information he had, so he jumped right in. And that was the second shock." She consulted her notes. "He said the toxicity is 'off the top of the scale.' Here's what he found in the samples—trichloroethylene, carbon tetrachloride, chloroform, benzene, toluene, xylene, and dioxin, plus crude oil, lead, mercury, and medical waste."

"Holy prickly pear," Gano said.

Debra's grimace dismissed his attempt at humor. "There's more. He found compounds that probably came from outdated chemical weapons—traces of blister agents such as mustard gas, phosgene, which is a choking agent, and even AC and CK that prevent blood from carrying oxygen. After he told me that, he went off on a rant about how Congress let utilities, mining companies, oil drillers, airports, and incinerators release *seven billion pounds* of toxic waste directly into the air, water and land last year alone. He called the samples 'murderous' and said whoever put that stuff together should be shot. By the way, every time he made a big point, he cracked his knuckles like a string of firecrackers. After a while, that really got under my skin. Anyway, I asked him whether counteragents could be mixed with this stuff to make it less toxic. He said it's too complex. And there's also no antidote."

"What if it were diluted?" Gano asked.

She flipped through her notes again. "He said if you took a few milliliters and mixed it into Lake Powell, no problem. But as you increase the amount and decrease the volume of the solution into which it's mixed, it would be fatal."

"Did he ask where the sample came from?" Jack asked.

"He never stopped trying to pry information out of me, but I gave him nothing."

"At least he did everything we need," Jack said.

"I'm afraid he might do more than that. After he recited all that stuff he got a weird look in his eyes and announced he was going to call the police to tell them about the samples."

"I was worried about that," Jack said with a sigh. "He doesn't know whether we're the good guys or not."

"Since he doesn't know about Palmer Industries, he tied the toxic samples to you and me. I pointed out that the samples could have come from anywhere, even a UTEP chem lab. I also said that a terrorist wasn't likely to come to UTEP to have samples tested. Then I shifted into 'I'm a shit-kicking lawyer' mode and warned him that slandering people would have serious consequences for him."

"Did he back off?"

"He started popping knuckles again and said he'd hold off because George McDonald had vouched for you. But if he hasn't heard from us within four days, he'll take everything to the authorities."

"You handled that well," Jack said with a quick smile.

"Thanks, and I have more. I now have a good idea how Montana has been getting away with this. Here's how the EPA tracking system works. Suppose Alpha Petroleum in Texas ships ten tons of hazardous waste to Palmer Industries for treatment, but it reports to the EPA that it shipped five tons. Then Palmer Industries reports to the EPA that it received five tons. Problem is, it's all paperwork with no on-site inspections. So Palmer is free to dispose of the difference any way it wants, say by dumping it down a well. EPA people know that the producer of waste and the disposal site can easily collude, but they say, 'Well, it's the best we can do.'" She paused and looked up. "Are they that stupid? No, they don't like to approve dumping in U.S. landfills, so they're fine with it going to Mexico. Even if EPA catches someone in violation, a big fine might be $15,000. So nobody cares."

The way Debra laid it out made the scam obvious. By keeping it off the books, tons of hazardous waste flooding into Mexico didn't have to be properly treated. Instead, it could be dumped illegally. The greedy bastards who produced the stuff saved big bucks. Lazy bureaucrats weren't the watchdogs they were paid to be, and the Palmer brothers and Montana were the biggest rats of all.

"What else did McDonald say about the aquifer?" he asked her.

"I gave Professor McDonald the rough dimensions of the tanks on the ridge. Assuming they're full, he calculated the volume of toxic waste. Then he gave me what he called a SWAG—scientific wild ass guess—on the volume of water in the Hueco *bolsón*. He'd used those figures to build some quick mathematical models that considered various flow rates, viscosities and other variables. His calculations showed that the water in the upper levels of the aquifer would become fatal to humans and livestock and unusable for farming for miles downstream, maybe for more than a century. It would be a disaster."

"How soon would it be deadly?"

"He said he'd need more details before he could answer that."

They sat in silence. Debra's face was pale. Gano's hand had stopped with his glass halfway to his mouth. "Holy shit."

"That's an understatement," Debra said. "Jack, there's something else eating at me. When I got mad at you back in law school, I didn't say anything." She took a deep breath. "I won't make that mistake again, so I have to say that you were irresponsible wasting all day yesterday tracking those damned trucks across northern Mexico, then most of today on a wild goose chase over New Mexico making spy movies." She jerked her thumb in Gano's direction. "You're flying around with Doc Holliday when you should be stopping that weasel Montana before he pulls the lever. What the hell were you thinking?" She scowled, crossed her arms over her chest and leaned back.

His face felt hot, so he took a breath before answering. "I had a damn good reason to be worried about those trucks. I was afraid they were smuggling biological or chemical weapons out of Mexico into the U.S. But that video shows the forklifts coming *out* of the warehouse and loading an empty black truck for a trip south. That made me remember how those trucks sounded when I followed them south from Palmer Industries to the cave. It was a low rumble. That means they were fully loaded."

"Not that I have any personal experience," Gano interjected, "but that's a real switcheroo on the usual south-to-north smuggling routine. Those are huge trucks. This could be a big deal."

"It's a big enough deal for Guzman to commit murder to keep the trips from being revealed." He looked at Debra. "Nuclear waste is being loaded at D-TECH and transported to that cave. And Palmer Industries is involved."

"If the Mexican government finds out someone in the U.S. is using Mexico as a dump," Gano said, "that will go over like a turd in a *piñata*. Might make 'em mad enough to sell their oil to China instead of to the good old U.S. of A. They're already pissed that the U.S. security obsession has brought border traffic to a standstill. Then there's that wall they're building along the border." He stopped for a swallow of rum.

Jack turned away from the conversation to mull over what he knew. Fact: the toxic waste at Palmer was deadly enough to poison the aquifer. Fact: Montana had the mechanism and motivation to do that. Fact: a high volume of nuclear waste was being smuggled into a remote cave in Mexico.

"Okay," he said, "I know who to call to find out about D-TECH. We rowed crew together in college." He pulled out his cell phone and entered a number.

"Hello. I'm calling for Senator Toby Baxter."

"Sorry sir. Senator Baxter is—"

"Please tell him Jack Strider is calling. Say we're in the final hundred meters, and I need his help. He'll understand."

Toby came on the line a minute later. "I have to get to the floor for a roll call vote, Jack, but I'll always take a call from you. My secretary said something about the 'final hundred meters,' which means you must be under some kind of pressure. How can I help?"

"Thanks Toby." *That's the thing about old friends. They step up when you need something.* "I want information about a company doing business in New Mexico, and I'm under enormous time pressure."

"I represent Wyoming. I'm not likely to know anything about—"

"You sit on the Senate Intelligence Committee, so you may know this one. It's called D-TECH."

Several seconds passed before Toby said, "Why do you ask?" This time, his voice was wary.

"Because it affects one of my clients, and I can't find out anything about the company."

Toby lowered his voice almost to a whisper. "It's what spooks call a 'gray company.' They operate behind smokescreens, doing things that no politician is going to vote for in public."

"For Christ's sake, Toby, I didn't ask for a civics lesson. I need specifics. This is serious."

"Okay, but you didn't hear this from me. D-TECH works on Department of Defense Special Ops projects. Designing miniature nuclear weapons is one of them. Its Board includes Pentagon alums and associates of the Carlyn Foundation, so it's wired into every administration." He cleared his throat. "That's as far as I can go."

Jack was stunned. D-TECH was such a heavy-hitter that even a U.S. senator was on eggshells.

"Damn it, I'm calling on our friendship. I need more." He heard the anger in his voice and knew he had to dial it back.

"Jack, I'm up for election, and bad things happen to people who snoop into gray companies. Now I have to get to the floor for that vote."

He could keep pushing, but the tone in Toby's voice told him he'd get nowhere.

"If you change your mind, give me a call." He broke the connection. Toby Baxter had lost the strength he'd had as stroke on the Stanford crew. Politics had turned another good man into a jellyfish.

"That sounded like a dead end," Debra said dryly. "So much for college friendships. Can we get back to the catastrophe we *know* is about to happen?"

He massaged his forehead. She was right. "Yeah, but there's one stop I have to make right now. While I'm gone, I hope you'll start getting some essential information I need. I'll drive you to the El Diablo."

"Drop me at the Blanco Bar & Grill near UTEP," Gano replied and stood.

"I'll go with you, Jack," Debra said.

He shook his head. "I have to do this alone."

The stop he had to make was to be sure Ana-Maria was safe somewhere north of the border. Just in case she was still at the *coyote's* house, he didn't want Debra with him. Bringing the two of them together would be like filling his shorts with gunpowder and handing each of them a box of matches.

Chapter 38

July 8
6:00 p.m.

JACK PARKED DOWN the street from the dilapidated home of the *coyote* and walked past kids getting in some kickball before they lost the light. As before, the windows were covered with fabrics, and it took several raps on the metal grate before the same stout woman answered.

"Buenas tardes. I came here four nights ago with a young woman. You know her cousin. We made arrangements—"

"What you want?" she said through the grate.

"Is my friend still here?"

The woman shook her head 'no,' her mouth tight.

That was a relief. Ana-Maria had crossed. "Your husband said he would call me when my friend was safe on the other side, but he didn't."

She glared at him. "No money back."

"I don't want any money back. What's wrong?"

"All week, the police attack the Muñoz cartel in Juarez. My husband can take no one across."

"She's *not* across? Then where is she?"

She looked over her shoulder and then she looked at him, as if deciding how much trouble he'd cause if she refused to answer.

"While I was making lunch," she said, "she found the back door unlocked and ran away. All afternoon, I hope she comes back, but no."

A feeling of foreboding swept over him. "I need to talk with your husband."

"Not here."

"When will he be back?"

"Quien sabe?" she muttered, meaning that her husband didn't intend to be confronted by the *gringo* about the woman he was supposed to safeguard.

"Look, I don't want my money back. I need—"

"Good-bye, *señor."* She closed the door behind the grate. The lock clicked.

Where *was* Ana-Maria? Was she afraid the delay had given Montana time to track her down? Was she so impatient that she'd try to get across on her own? No, she would have called him. What if she'd gone back to her house for some reason? That would be a crazy risk. Montana could have staked out her house, or bribed a neighbor to call him if she showed up. Uneasiness shot into alarm. If she was in Anapra, he had to get her out of there.

LESS THAN HALF an hour later, he ran across the scraggly grass to Ana-Maria's front door. There was no padlock, so she must be inside. Thank God, he'd found her. He knocked. She didn't answer. The situation was eerily like standing at Juanita's door a few days ago, except this time he hadn't really expected anyone to be at home. There was no response to his knock, so he turned the handle. It wasn't locked from the inside so he pushed it open and stepped in. The room seemed normal until he saw a cardboard suitcase on the bed, half-filled with clothes. Next to it was a thin stack of photographs, a little costume jewelry and a few personal treasures. Near the head of the bed was the dark blue dress and white sash she'd worn at the hotel.

She must have gotten fed up with living in the same clothes for four days and made a dash home to get her own stuff. No, he realized, she'd come for the photographs and the ring from her mother. She wasn't willing to leave Mexico without them. So why had she stopped her packing? Where was she?

On impulse, he ran outside and around to the back of the house where they'd sat in the morning sun . . . and fell to his knees next to where she lay on her back. A small-caliber bullet had drilled a round hole in the center of her forehead. Blood, now dried and brown, had run in threadlike streams down both sides of her beautiful face.

Hot July wind burned across his face, and tears filled his eyes. "Oh, no. Oh, God, no. Ana-Maria."

But maybe . . . he pressed his ear on her chest. No heartbeat. He reached for her hand, and then her neck. No pulse. Her skin was red from lying exposed for, how long, an hour? Five hours?

He lifted her head and cradled her in his arms. He touched her face, caressed her hair. She'd been so full of life when she'd come to him in the *El Presidente* Suite.

Then he saw blood clotted on her left palm. He looked more closely. She had raised her hand in a futile attempt to fend off the slug.

As far as he could tell, she hadn't been beaten or raped. She'd been assassinated. Montana, or whoever he had sent, had been bold enough to kill her out in the open to show they had the power to do whatever they wanted.

When his tears finally dried, he gently laid her back on the ground and stood, bone-tired. He didn't want to leave her on the ground, but if he moved her he'd be disturbing a crime scene, interfering with the police investigation. What a joke! Even if Montana had left his business card on her body, the cops would give him a pass.

He tenderly scooped Ana-Maria up in his arms, carried her inside, and laid her on the bed. After sponging her face clean and covering her with a light bedspread, he kissed her on the cheek.

He looked at a photograph of her younger sisters in their village, loving and depending on her. He picked up the photos and slid the thin ring from her finger. They belonged to her sisters. He'd make sure they got them.

Thinking of her family made him remember the money he'd given her. She wouldn't have left it at the *coyote's* house, so it must be here. He checked what she was wearing, then the blue dress, the suitcase, drawers, shoes, everywhere likely. It was gone. The murderer had come to kill, but was a common thief as well.

He inspected her small home in hopes of finding anything that would identify her killer. There was nothing. He took the ring with two keys from Ana-Maria's pocket to lock the door behind him, hoping that would keep anyone from disturbing her until the police got there.

Time to go. He looked back at Ana-Maria on the bed. Without thinking, he swung his fist into the wall. It hurt like hell. He closed his eyes, but not from pain. He was breathing hard. He'd make Montana pay for what he'd done.

He stood on the harsh gravel in front of her house, unable to walk away, and looked down the street at the shacks with bars on their windows where *maquila* workers fought to survive. A guy rolling slowly past on an old Harley gave him a look that said, "What are you doing in Anapra, *gringo?*" It took a moment to register that the biker was also a witness who could place a tall *gringo* at the scene of a murder.

He waited until the biker was out of sight before going to his car. He had to report the murder, but didn't want the cops to have his cell phone number, so he drove out of Anapra, past the city dump, and found a bar. His first stop was the pay phone. To convince the cop on the line that Ana-Maria was dead, he had to describe the wound and her condition. That hit him hard again, and his voice became hoarse. The cop demanded to know who was calling. He felt guilty and quickly hung up. He needed a drink badly.

A wood chair scraped loudly as he pulled it back and sat at a corner table. A bartender set a bottle of Corona in front of him. Jack waved it away. He needed something a lot stronger. He ordered scotch.

The bartender came back, poured a triple shot glass full to the rim and left the bottle on the table, obviously the custom in the place. The label read "Chivas Regal" but the label was so stained he knew the bottle had been refilled more than a few times. It went down rough, but it stayed down.

He silently toasted Ana-Maria and refilled the triple shot glass. In just a couple of days, she'd helped guide his transition from the ivory tower to reality on the ground. The image of her ruined forehead filled his brain. He drained the glass, hoping it would dim the image. It didn't. He'd tried to get her to safety and failed. She'd be buried in a pauper's field, and there was nothing he could do about that now. When this was over he'd make sure she didn't remain in this place she'd hated. He'd find her sisters and return Ana-Maria to her village for proper burial.

As time passed, the bar got crowded and was filled with stinking billows of cigarette smoke, tinny mariachi music, and the shouts of small men angrily bumping chests like banties. Three men in T-shirts with cutoff sleeves eyed him openly, as if looking for an excuse to start trouble. He felt like a farm-raised chicken in a cock fight.

He poured more scotch. When he set the bottle down, it landed hard on the rim of his glass and smashed it. Well, shit, he didn't need a glass. He drank from the bottle. Ana-Maria had left her innocence behind when she came to Juarez, and he'd lost his, too.

The bit of his brain still functioning warned him to get out of the bar before he got too drunk to defend himself. He paid and weaved his way to the door, hitting the frame hard with his shoulder. He found his car, but it wasn't where he'd left it. Or maybe it was. After a little fumbling he got it started and pulled into the road.

Damn it. Just when he had to get back to the motel, get some sleep, he couldn't find a road to a bridge across the Rio Grande. Somehow he'd gotten into an industrial area, far from the river. A truck swerved and almost hit him. In his rearview mirror he saw a red traffic light. Had that been for him? The river must be to his right so he made a last-minute turn, swinging wide into the oncoming lane before straightening out.

Hoo-wah, hoo-wah, hoo-wah.

His reaction to the siren screaming right behind his car was visceral, taking him back to the violence outside Casa Lupo. He pulled over to get out of the police car's way, scraping his tires on the curb. In his side mirror, he saw three cops erupt out of the cruiser's doors.

One pulled him out of his car. They all shouted at him. Another one shoved him in the chest and he stumbled backwards, lost his balance and fell hard.

JACK'S BRAIN SWAM slowly back into consciousness. He was lying on his side on a rough concrete floor, but where? He squinted. Men around him. Uniforms. Oh my God. A jail cell. He vaguely remembered being dragged from his car. The alcohol still fogged his thoughts. He had to do something, so he pushed himself up onto his hands and knees.

The *guardia's* boot crashed into his ribs, driving him sideways into the wall. He slid down the concrete block surface, pain searing his lungs as he tried to grab a breath. The guard stepped back, a broad smirk on his face.

A squat man wearing gold braid on his shoulders strode into the cell, his officer's hat tilted so far forward his face was a dark shadow. The guards edged quickly out of his path.

"Hey, *gringo*, they say you claim you're some big shot. You tell me, *gringo*, how big a shot are you now?"

"Jack Strider," he gasped. "I'm a lawyer. San Francisco."

"Hah! Bloody mess. Whiskey stink. You don't look like no *gringo* lawyer I ever saw."

"I'll give you a number in San Francisco. You have to call it. They'll vouch for me."

The officer thumped his own chest with his fist. "Chief of Police, Ciudad Juarez. I don't *have* to call San Francisco."

"Then call my room at the El Diablo Hotel in El Paso. Look, I'll pay a fine, anything. I won't say a word about what's happened here."

A contemptuous snort told him what the Chief thought about Jack's total lack of bargaining power.

"But nothing happened here. You have no cuts. No broken teeth. You just fell on your ass in the street. My men hauled you in because they think you're *un común borracho*, a common drunk. But maybe you're worse, maybe you raped and killed *las mujeres jóvenes que trabajan en las maquilas,* the girls working in the *maquilas.* So I'll keep you locked up."

"You're crazy! You have no evidence."

The Chief's eyes flashed at the insult. "If we need evidence, we'll get it for sure. Don't you worry." He winked at his men and drew laughter.

"I want a lawyer." He started coughing.

The Chief nodded at a guard who slammed his open palm across Jack's right ear. Head ringing, Jack collapsed.

The Chief leaned over him. "My men make sure you're ready to tell me about the killings when I come back." He walked away. The last guard following him flicked off the lights for Jack's cell and the hallway. In the dark, Jack heard the sound of claws scurrying on concrete. Despite them, and the pain, he pressed his back into a corner and plunged into sleep.

A moan from the next cell woke him into the blackness. He had no idea how much time had passed. He edged up, gritting his teeth. He heard voices and loud laughter from farther away. They sounded drunk, so they must be guards.

If he survived the beating they planned, the Chief would pin a string of murders on him. He'd never get to trial. The Chief would kill him without ever knowing why he'd been drunk.

He also saw that getting drunk in a sleazy bar, even because of grief, had dishonored Ana-Maria. Maybe she'd been killed because of her close friendship with Juanita, but there could have been more to it. Right after Montana assigned her to assist Jack, she'd stopped coming to the office. The thought of a connection between Ana-Maria and Jack would have made Montana furious. And that connection had been Jack's idea. He owed it to both women to stop the Palmer Industries' gang.

The hall light came on, followed by the heavy tread of guards heading toward his cell. He braced himself to handle what was coming. One guard stepped out of the group, unlocked the cell, and dragged Jack out of the cell by his arm. *"El Jefe,"* he said, and pointed down the hall.

July 9
2:30 a.m.

JACK HAD ONLY a hazy memory of signing some papers and Debra hustling him out of the jail and into her rented Mustang. He ached all over—his head from alcohol, ribs and thighs from being kicked. Deep inside his ears there was a buzzing that wouldn't stop.

Without opening his eyes, he asked Debra, "How did you get me out?"

"I was at the El Diablo, worried sick that you weren't back. Then around midnight, three guys with Juarez Police Department badges showed up. One of them, acting like he was worried, said you'd been in an accident and wanted them to bring me to the Juarez central hospital. They described you perfectly. I went to Gano's room to get him to come with me, but he was still out drinking. Instead of taking me to a hospital, they parked at the Juarez jail and took me to the Chief. He informed me that, and I quote, '*Señor* Strider is a serial killer, one of the worst criminals in the history of the state of Chihuahua.'"

"I said there had to be a mistake. He sneered and said, 'No mistake, but if I keep this man in jail for killing so many women, someone will kill him. Bad publicity. So I will let him out on bail until the trial.'"

"I took it for granted," she said, "that he didn't expect you to come back, and he'd pocket the money."

"How much did he want?"

"Fifty thousand."

"Don't tell me you—"

"Not a chance. I came on like the late Johnny Cochran. I promised to make flaming meteors rain down on him and would produce witnesses to prove you were in Zanzibar on whatever dates they claimed the killings occurred. That's when he decided that you were only a common drunk and could go home for a mere 2000 pesos. Cash only, of course."

"So you paid it?"

"Yeah. I couldn't come up with any defense to the common drunk charge." She gave him a disgusted look. "For heaven's sake, Jack, it's D-Day, and you're falling down drunk in the street. Why?"

He really didn't want to go there, but she deserved an explanation. "Ana-Maria was supposed to have been taken across the border. That didn't happen, so I went to her house hoping to find her. She was there, in the back yard, shot in the forehead."

"Oh my God." She covered her face with her hands. He knew the death of another young woman hit her hard. There was no need for her to say so. And she had no idea how hard it had hit him.

"Yeah, and a biker saw me at her house. In Anapra, everyone watches the streets, so others probably saw me and the car. The cops could get those descriptions any moment and make the connection." He rubbed his eyes. "And that police chief would love to send his goons to the El Diablo to snatch me. We need to get out of there fast, find a new hotel. I just hope they aren't already waiting for us."

Chapter 39

July 9
8:00 a.m.

"PROFESSOR STRIDER is calling," Mrs. Pounders announced through the speaker. "What would you like me to tell him, sir?"

Justin Sinclair hesitated. Strider's threat to sell out Palmer Industries had been mutiny. Well, at the Hearing he'd gotten a lesson on how the classroom differs from the real world. Surely he wasn't calling to complain. So what *did* he want?

"Put him on, Mrs. Pounders."

Impatient to get to the reason Strider was calling, he skipped pleasantries and pushed the conversation forward.

"Good to get that Hearing behind us," he said. "Dismissal with prejudice. Best possible result."

"Justin, this *isn't* over. You need to listen to me."

Odd. That sounded like a threat.

"No, you need to listen to *me*," he replied in his best "don't-fuck-with-me" voice. "I promised I'd tell Arthur to clean up their environmental practices. I did, so that's the end of it." He didn't mention that Arthur had let fly a string of curses and said the only thing he'd tell Montana was not to get caught again.

"There's another problem at Palmer Industries," Strider said sharply. "And it's much bigger than the ones PROFEPA knew about."

"Forget about other problems. You're off the case. Time to walk away."

"Justin, you have no idea how much is at stake here—and it affects you personally."

He wanted to slam down the handset, but held back. If Strider was about to cause trouble, better to know about it so he could head it off.

"I'm listening."

Strider described oil tanks, a pipeline, injection wells, and toxic waste, and made it clear he intended to bring the roof down on Palmer Industries.

He broke in. "Stop right there. All your conclusions are based on speculation." That was true, but the bombardment of details was troubling.

"The shots they fired at me when I was at the wells weren't speculation."

"Probably just a warning. By your own admission, you were trespassing."

"They were more than a warning. Montana doesn't want anyone to know that he's about to dump the contents of those tanks straight into the aquifer that provides water for El Paso and Juarez."

Son-of-a-bitch. That was a firebomb out of left field. Montana couldn't possibly—he took a deep breath. He'd made a career in diplomacy by carrying on smoothly when shocked by a nasty surprise. He had to do that now. Strider had the bit in his teeth. He had to find a way to make him let go.

"There must be a good explanation for that pipeline and well contraption."

"There is *not*. I have reports from a biochemistry professor about toxicity of the chemicals in the tanks and from a hydrology professor about the vulnerability of the aquifer."

Reports? If Montana dumped those chemicals and these reports went public after that, the fallout would be like acid rain—and it would fall on him. He'd spend the rest of his career defending Palmer Industries in court. This could bankrupt the Palmers and blacken his own reputation. He had to deal with this before Strider did.

"You're saying Montana is a monster. I just don't believe that."

"You should. A week ago, a secretary with information that would expose plant secrets was murdered. Three nights ago, Montana hired punks to ambush me outside a restaurant in Juarez. They damn near killed me. And last night, Montana's assistant, who he thought might betray him, was murdered at her own home."

"Accusations are easy. What's your proof?"

"Montana had the means, opportunity, and sure as hell had motive. For God's sake, Justin, face it. Montana is a psychopath. All he cares about is that bonus Edward complained about. He'll collect his money and disappear, leaving Palmer Industries—and you—holding the bag."

Sinclair looked at rows of testimonials hanging on his office walls, every one validating his self-image, his power. He'd been threatened by the best. He wasn't going to be fucked with by the "new" Jack Strider. But what the hell was really going on down there? Was Montana completely off the rails? Arthur would have to control him—or dump him. Sacrifice Montana to muzzle Strider. Just good business.

"You're right, Jack. Maybe I've been too much of an advocate for this client. So what's the next step?" He had to flush out Strider's plans.

"Call Arthur and tell him to stop Montana. If he won't, I will.

Whatever else he does, I know Arthur will call Montana to warn him. If that stops this disaster, I'd rather let Montana cover his ass than have him destroy an entire ecosystem."

Justin thought about what Strider had just said. Strider knew there was no point in him calling Arthur Palmer directly. But why hadn't he called the EPA? Easy, because it had no jurisdiction in Mexico. Why not PROFEPA? Because those two red-hot lawyers had been canned. And Juarez cops would side with Montana. So Strider was calling him because he had no other options.

"Of course I'll talk with Arthur," he answered, "but he's no fan of yours and won't believe what you've just told me. I'll need some time to think this through."

"There *is* no time. Montana will dump that poison as soon as he can. Listen, I'll read you what the biochemist said will happen to the aquifer."

"Just fax that to Mrs. Pounders. You've already convinced me. I'll figure out a way to stop Montana."

"I've already thought it through. Hire private guards in El Paso to remove Montana from plant grounds this afternoon and lock him up. Start dismantling the wells immediately. Then bring Montana to San Francisco and have him arrested. If I don't see evidence of the first two steps before five p.m. today, I'll blow the whistle so loud they'll hear it in Candlestick Park."

"Don't bullshit me. If going public was your best shot, you wouldn't have called me. So back off." He was probably right about that, but Strider might not be bluffing, and he didn't want to find out. "Give me a chance to convince Arthur. Is there anything else you should tell me?"

"I'll tell you more when I have more facts."

"Jack, come back to San Francisco. We should talk this over face-to-face." He used the deep imperial tone he rolled out when he wanted to sound like God commanding Moses. "We also need to talk about Rick Calder. I've been holding him off, putting myself on the line for you, but I don't know how long I can do that." That was a lie, but Strider would get the message.

"I'm not finished down here."

Justin blinked in disbelief. The blunt refusal was a slap in the face. But something was going on, and that meant he couldn't afford to break off communications with Strider.

"That's a mistake, but I suppose it can wait. By the way, I'm worried about Ms. Vanderberg. I sent her to Mexico City to help you. Then she spent a day at the Palmer plant doing some contract work, but Montana hasn't seen her since. She's not answering her cell phone, so Mrs. Pounders checked this morning and found out she wasn't at the Rialto Hotel in

Juarez. Any ideas where she is?"

"Probably on her way back to San Francisco. Look, I'll call you to confirm that Arthur did the things I outlined." Strider hung up.

Justin set the receiver on its base and leaned back. From his first meeting with Strider, he'd been able to read him like an eye chart. That had changed. Strider had become opaque. Worse, he was sounding like he'd turned into a pit bull. That worried him, because pit bulls can bite.

Chapter 40

WHEN HE AND Debra got back from Juarez in the middle of the night, they'd cased the El Diablo carefully to make sure no cops were waiting for them. Then he'd shaken Gano awake, they'd all grabbed their gear, and fled.

Jack joined Gano in the small restaurant of the Buena Vista Motel, the place they'd chosen after their hasty exit from the El Diablo.

"Okay, that's the gist of it," he said to Gano. "If Sinclair doesn't come through by my five p.m. deadline, we have to take action ourselves as soon as the workers leave the plant."

"You think Sinclair will call Palmer? And will Palmer do anything anyway?" Gano was clearly skeptical.

Jack shrugged. "I don't know, and that's why I have a backup plan."

"Damn, you're good," Gano said. "No wonder they pay you the big money. What's your vision?"

"Attack the wells, but first we have to get onto the plant grounds without being stopped."

"Deep thinking, Plato. Maybe some kind of magic cloak?"

"Exactly." Jack smiled. "I know how to make us invisible."

"Spell it out."

"I'll do better than that. I'll show you."

They drove the rented Mustang for less than five minutes before he spotted what he was looking for. He pointed down a side street. "That's our magic cloak."

"Can't see a damn thing. That garbage truck is blocking my view."

"That garbage truck *is* the magic cloak."

"And I'm the Wicked Witch," Gano scoffed. "Give me a break."

Jack gave him a smug grin. "Guards at the Palmer plant see garbage trucks every day. They blend in because they're not a threat. We'll drive around the plant yard like we were on a job. When we're close enough to the wells, we speed up and ram the main pump and as many wellheads as we can. Get it?"

"You've missed your calling, my man. That's brilliant." Gano gave him a mock salute. "Well, except for a couple of tiny flaws."

"What?" Jack asked, frowning.

"After all hell breaks loose and we're sitting in a smashed-to-hell garbage truck, how do we get away?"

"Got that covered. Even if it's not out of commission, it's too slow. Which is why we leave this Mustang parked outside the gate and take off in it during the excitement. You said there were a couple of flaws. What's the other one?"

"No biggie. Just that we don't have a garbage truck, and I don't think Hertz carries them. So where do we get one?"

"Steal one when we get to Juarez."

"Hard to believe I'm listening to Mr. Law & Order. But I do have something to add. I always feel more prepared when I bring my own fireworks to the party." There was a maniacal glint in his eyes.

"What are you talking about?" Jack asked warily.

"I need to do a little shopping so, in case the Sinclair/Palmer team doesn't come through, we'll be ready. I'll give you directions."

Ten minutes later Gano was admitted into a corrugated metal warehouse with no sign. When he returned, he carried several bundles wrapped in rough burlap and a six-pack of empty beer bottles in a carton.

"Get everything you need?"

"Nah," Gano said. "They were out of rum."

Later, back in the motel room waiting to hear from Sinclair, Gano looked up from his work. "I'd rather use C-4, but if we go that heavy we'd blow ourselves up. So I put together some small stuff with timers to use as diversions. And I've rigged these Molotov cocktails to carry for self-protection. How's that sound?"

Molotov cocktails? How the hell did Gano think it sounded? Like a stroll through the park? Before he answered, the phone rang. Sinclair.

The call was short and consisted mostly of Jack listening. When it was over, he took a deep breath and let it out slowly.

"What excuse did the former Secretary-of-Weaseldom use?" Gano asked.

"That he couldn't reach Arthur Palmer for four or five hours after we talked this morning. When he did, he said Arthur argued but finally agreed to get back to him tomorrow. Sinclair was lying. I heard it in his voice." *Damn Sinclair for covering for Arthur Palmer. And damn Palmer for everything.*

Gano frowned. "Was he lying about what Palmer said or about calling Palmer at all?"

"I don't know, but, either way, Arthur Palmer is standing pat. They're not dismantling the wells, and Montana's still head honcho." He stood and began to pace. "If Sinclair did talk with him, Arthur undoubtedly warned

Montana that he's being watched. If Montana's really spooked, he may start trucking the toxic crap in the tanks to some remote canyon. If he's not spooked, he'll do nothing until he's sure I'm gone. Then he'll dump it into the wells. The worst case is if Montana dumps before he hears from anyone."

He stopped pacing, looked at Gano and made his decision. "We have to take care of this ourselves."

Gano's wide grin showed he was ready for action. "Easy as scratching a grizzly bear's ass."

6:00 p.m.

AFTER DRIVING along Juarez back streets for thirty minutes, Jack found exactly what he wanted—a battered Waste Management Freightliner trash collection truck making its sluggish rounds in a low-rent commercial district. They passed it, parked a hundred yards ahead and waited. When it stopped near them, Gano walked casually around the massive front bumper, then jumped on the metal step under the driver's window. Holding on with one hand, he pointed his silver revolver through the window and ordered the driver to leave the keys and get out.

When they hustled the driver to the rear, expecting to find one assistant who operated the truck's hydraulic lift, they found two rough looking crewmen, instantly angry at having a gun pointed at them. When Gano ordered them to climb into the green trash bin they hadn't yet emptied, they looked willing to fight rather than cram themselves into the reeking bin.

Gano grabbed the chubby driver by his shirt front, pointed the muzzle of the revolver at his balls, and cocked the hammer. Cursing under his breath, the man gestured to one of the others to help him over the side.

The second all three were inside, Jack slammed the lids down and slipped a stick through two eye bolts to lock the lids closed.

"They won't suffocate," Gano said. "As soon as they think they're alone, they'll shout for help. Then the search for the missing Trash Taxi will be on." He pointed to that name painted on its side. "I'm psyched."

"I'll drive this thing," Jack said. "Follow me. I'll stop near the gate where you can stash the Mustang. Let's go." He was flying so high on adrenaline that the fear any rational lawyer should be feeling was a no show.

A few minutes later, a quarter-mile east of the entrance to Palmer Industries, Gano parked the Mustang and climbed aboard. The sound of Gano's door slamming snapped Jack back to the reality of what he was about to do. He'd taken risks on the plant grounds before, but then he'd done everything he could to avoid being noticed. This time he was taking on the whole damn place out in the open. Even an adrenaline rush wasn't enough to dissolve the knot he felt in his gut.

Gano buttoned the Trash Taxi jacket he'd taken from the driver and they both put on caps they'd found in the cab. "I don't suppose you've got a gun?" he said to Jack.

"No."

"So if we run into guards with AK-47s who try to turn us into confetti, you're going to negotiate until they're unconscious, right?"

Jack was glad Gano was using sarcasm to lighten the mood just before they went to battle. He slowed at the gate, waved at the guard and didn't stop. The guard didn't challenge him, so he drove slowly across the parking lot in front of the Admin building, stopping at its southeast corner.

Gano jumped out and raised the lid of the Dumpster, as if inspecting the contents, lowered it, and then swung himself back into Trash Taxi. Jack stopped at Dumpsters next to three other buildings where Gano, taking one of the burlap-wrapped packets with him each time, repeated the process. As Jack had predicted, guards ignored them.

Gano climbed back into the cab. "Phase One complete, *comandante*. Ready for Phase Two."

Jack rolled past the last row of warehouses and turned west, staying close to the buildings, paralleling the Rio Grande less than a half mile north. He stopped in the shelter of the building at the end of the row. Ahead, a dirt track with deep ruts led to the grove of trees where the wellheads and pumps were hidden.

"This don't beat flying into a dirt field along a row of flashlights held by Chiapas rebels, "Gano said, "but it comes close." He handed Jack a couple of beer bottles. "Treat these like they were 18-year-old scotch."

Jack wiped his hand on his sleeves before taking the bottles. His mouth was so dry he didn't think he could talk. There was nothing left to say anyway.

Gano rolled up the window and checked his watch. "Three seconds until Dumpster *numero uno*—"

Ka—BOOM!

The wall of the building next to them lit up in a brilliant flash. The air rattled like hail hitting a metal roof. There were shouts everywhere, even a couple of cracks from a rifle.

The blast was more powerful than he'd expected. His voice was gruff when he said, "Jesus, Gano, what did you use?"

"Best incendiary money can buy. Semi-plastic gel. Stuff ain't cheap when it comes out the backdoor, so don't forget to reimburse me." He checked his watch again. "Right about now."

Ka—BOOM!

This one sent a message that the first explosion was no accident. Now everyone knew the plant was under attack. Four guards ran out of the grove of trees toward them at breakneck speed. They crossed the path of the Trash Taxi without registering it as a source of danger.

"Forward, Don Quixote," Gano shouted, "into the fray!" He rolled down the window and banged his hand on the truck cab.

Jack jammed the accelerator to the floor, making the truck lumber forward like a crazed hippo, gaining speed on the dirt track.

Ka—BOOM! A fireball lit the darkening sky behind them.

"Yee-haw!" Gano yelled. "Might have overpacked that puppy."

Not much had changed in the clearing since Jack had been there three nights before—wellheads at the corners of a triangle about 25 yards on each side; pipes leading from each of the three wellheads to a pump in the center of the triangle. But there was one crucial difference. The fat white ceramic pipe coming down from the plateau was now fully connected to the pump. Montana's time bomb was set to blow.

He'd planned to plow the huge truck straight over the pump, the nerve center feeding all three wells. After that, he'd circle around and take out the wellheads. The Trash Taxi would flatten them like Tonka toys.

"Son-of-a-bitch," Gano shouted.

Jack stared ahead in disbelief, then jammed both feet on the brake pedal and hauled back on the emergency brake lever. Montana had barricaded the big pump with a circle of concrete slabs at least two feet high.

"Got a backup plan, boyo?" Gano asked.

Not for this, but he said, "I'll get that wellhead on the left first. Hold on." He released the emergency brake, raced the engine and shoved it into gear. Like a locomotive pulling uphill, it rammed into the nearest wellhead which screamed in protest as it was crushed into a tangle of steel beneath the truck's undercarriage. As the truck surged forward, the wreckage lifted its front wheels off the ground. Jack gunned the engine, trying to rock it forward and back, but it was crippled for good.

"Grab your bottles," Gano yelled.

Ka—BOOM!

The halo of light from the explosion revealed that their diversions hadn't worked well enough. Two guards were racing toward the truck. He and Gano had agreed what they'd do if they had to deal with guards. They looked at each other. Now was the time.

Jack's door jammed. He rammed it with his shoulder until it opened and he half fell out. He got back up on the metal step and grabbed his two bottles.

Gano was already out. "Fire up that wellhead over there, Scoutmaster, and the other one if you have time. Do it the way I said. Screw up and it'll kill you. *Now!*"

Jack pulled the cork from the first bottle and smelled gasoline and white phosphorus. He took a strip of cloth that had been wrapped around the neck of the bottle, soaked half of it in the flammable mixture, and re-tied it around the neck of the bottle. He stuffed the cork back in place. The cloth lit immediately from the flame of the lighter Gano had given him. *One . . . two . . . three.* He looped it in a high arc toward a wellhead where it shattered. Brilliant flames shot into the air, with enough heat to take out gaskets, switches, and a hell of a lot more. He lit the wick and tossed his other bottle in the direction of the second wellhead. It exploded with a blinding flash.

They hadn't destroyed the wellheads, but Montana would have to make some heavy repairs.

Gano's gasoline bomb sailed above the dirt track and exploded directly in the path of two men who frantically fled back toward the plant. "That's enough good deeds for tonight," Gano shouted. "Let's *vamoose!*"

Jack studied their surroundings. They could attempt to get to the river, but there was almost no cover. If they tried to get away up the ridge, guards would come up the other side of the mesa and trap them. That left the escape they'd planned, a run back among the plant buildings to the Mustang, with only the fire and confusion to shield them.

"Not so good, Smokey," Gano said somberly, as they looked across the open ground between them and the northern row of buildings.

Jack had to face facts. They couldn't make the gate on foot. Time to improvise.

"See the sign reading 'Shipping & Receiving'?" Jack pointed to the building. "Montana's head goon works there, a man he calls The Ape. I've seen vehicles parked inside. We can grab one and power out to the gate." That might also give him a chance to break into Guzman's office and steal the mystery truck records to prove Palmer Industries' involvement.

"Let's roll on, buddy. You go first," Gano said. "I'll hang here and use this last bottle bomb to cover you." He held up the Molotov cocktail. "As soon as you're inside, I'll follow."

Jack put his head down and sprinted for the building fifty yards away. He pressed himself against it for a few seconds, then rounded the corner and pushed through the door, leaving it ajar. He ran across the open space and grabbed the door handle next to the *Director de Planta* sign. *Damn!* It was locked. He grabbed a three-foot section of pipe leaning against a workbench and raised it over his head to smash the handle.

"I wouldn't do that, *señor*," said a calm tenor voice coming from the dim space.

Two men stepped out of the flickering shadows and walked toward him, their unhurried pace radiating cockiness. Jack couldn't make out their faces, but he didn't have to. The voice told him Tomás Montana had found him. Even in silhouette, the sloping shoulders and round skull of the other man identified Guzman. The two stopped twenty steps away. Montana's arms were crossed, and Guzman's gun was pointed straight at Jack.

"Jack Strider." Montana's tone sounded as if he were identifying a species of bug. "Come here."

Why in God's name was Montana here? He must have guessed Jack was the arsonist, then reasoned that whatever had caused him to sneak into Shipping & Receiving before might bring him back.

"I'm fine where I am," Jack replied. Staying away from them was his only chance.

"Get your ass over here, Strider," Guzman said, and waved his gun in a hooking motion, "or I'll kick your balls into *refritos.*"

"Drop it or you die." Gano's voice came from the darkness to Jack's right. Guzman's arm froze, his weapon pointing at the ceiling.

Crack.

A slug hit the concrete next to Guzman's boot and ricocheted into the metal wall. He dropped his gun.

Gano stepped into the light, his .38 Special snub-nose pointing midway between Guzman and Montana. "Maybe you'd like to pick on me instead, you fat tub of shit."

Guzman's brow furrowed, apparently amazed that anyone would dare challenge him. "I'll take you apart," he snarled.

"Shut up," Montana barked at Guzman. "My plant wouldn't be on fire if those fools you sent to Casa Lupo hadn't screwed up." He turned to Jack. "You've cost me more than you can imagine." His lips were tight, and his eyes burned. He looked ready to kill.

Gano stepped closer to Montana. "I know you're holding, so pull it out slowly with two fingers, set it on the deck and kick it my way. You see this?" He held out the Molotov cocktail. "Get tricky and you'll be a toasted marshmallow."

Montana took a Beretta from a pocket inside his jacket and dropped it at his feet.

"So you're The Ape," Gano said to Guzman. "You've got quite a reputation down in Divisadero. A woman who works at Casa del Amor told me about the bully who likes to punch young girls. Tell me, fatso, you really got a pecker like a baby *jalapeño?*"

Jack watched Guzman's face reveal that he understood exactly what

Gano was referring to at the Casa del Amor. Then comprehension was replaced by rage at the reference to his pecker. But Gano's .38 kept him from doing anything about it.

Gano moved quickly to Jack's side and set the bottle next to him. "Take my popgun and watch Mr. Slick, *comprende?* If he moves, shoot and keep shooting until you put a hole between his eyes." He turned his attention to Guzman. "Now, ugly Green Giant, I'm going to settle a score for those girls in Divisadero. Bring me what you got."

Guzman looked at the gun Jack held and didn't move.

"Take him out, Ape," Montana ordered. "Don't worry about white bread here. He's harmless."

Guzman's right hand shot behind his back and whipped out a switchblade. He pressed it with his thumb and a long blade clicked into place. He let out a guttural bellow and charged, slashing side-to-side. Gano sidestepped like a matador and hacked his fist on the back of Guzman's bald skull. When Guzman turned and charged again, Gano grabbed a bucket and hurled oily waste into his face.

Guzman clawed at his eyes. "You son-of—"

"Gano!" Jack shouted, and tossed him the pipe.

Guzman swung wildly with his knife. Gano stepped in, blocked Guzman's arm with the pipe, and chopped the rigid side of his hand like a cleaver on the bridge of The Ape's nose. The snap sounded like green pine in a campfire.

Guzman wiped gouts of blood from his nose and roared like a wounded beast. He charged again, and the upward thrust of his knife ripped through the left sleeve of Gano's jacket. Gano jumped back.

"Try again, fart face."

Guzman got control of his rage and transformed back to the cagey street fighter he was. He used the back of one hairy hand to mop blood off his mouth as he advanced cautiously, weaving his blade in sideways figure eights. Suddenly, he lunged. Gano parried with the pipe and followed with a swing to Guzman's ribs. The *"thunk"* sounded like a left hook to a tree trunk.

"Cabrón!" Guzman faked a thrust from the right. Gano countered with the pipe, but that let Guzman dive in close and hurl Gano to the concrete. He crashed hard and lost his grip on the pipe. As he stumbled to his feet, Guzman right-hooked him to the shoulder and knocked him into a tool bench against the wall.

"Stop screwing around, Ape," Montana called. "End it."

Guzman flicked a look at Montana. "Fuck you," he grunted.

Using Guzman's second of distraction, Gano snatched a long screwdriver from the tool bench. He danced around Guzman, darting in and out, jabbing him again and again with the screwdriver. He was punishing Guzman, not trying to end the fight, making him bawl in pain and rage.

Jack's finger tensed on the trigger. Gano was taunting Guzman. That was stupid.

Guzman changed tactics. After a slash at Gano's face, he dropped to one knee and punched the tip of his blade into Gano's thigh.

"Goddamn," Gano cried, falling back, looking at blood staining his pant leg. Gripping his leg, he half-turned and bent forward. Guzman charged with his knife raised high. Gano whirled and drove the screwdriver through Guzman's belly to his backbone.

"Ugh. Ugh," Guzman gurgled. His knees buckled, and he fell at Gano's feet.

"Payback for my friend Helena in Divisadero, the woman whose face you cut."

Jack took a quick look to see how badly Gano was hurt. When he turned back, Montana had his silver Beretta aimed at Gano.

"Drop it," Jack ordered.

"Shoot the fucker," Gano shouted.

"Strider doesn't have the guts," Montana said scornfully, "so let's you and I do business. That's why I didn't stop you." He nodded toward Guzman, butt in the air, face on the concrete. "That was a job interview. He failed. You passed."

"Big fuckin' deal. You have nothing I want."

"I have a cash cow here." He waved, taking in all of Palmer Industries. "When these fires go out, I'm back in business. You do what I need done, and I'll cut you in."

"Sure you will, until you change your mind like you did with your subhuman life form here. So fuck off."

Montana pursed his lips and frowned. "You're right. It wouldn't work out. You've got a bad attitude." He lifted the Beretta slightly.

"No time to be a pacifist, Jack," Gano said quietly.

"He won't shoot," Montana said. "What would the gentlemen at the yacht club say?"

A .38 slug tore into the back of Montana's hand and shattered its web of small bones. He screamed. The Beretta skidded across the floor. Gano snatched it and slammed its butt into the side of Montana's head, who fell forward with a groan and lay still as his blood colored the concrete.

"Damn lucky shot, Bart." Gano looked at Jack and grinned. "What were you aiming at anyway? Something bigger than his hand, I hope. Hell, I'll bet you've never fired a gun before."

"Expert Marksman in the Navy. I never said I didn't know how."

Gano gave him an appreciative smile. "That's profound. Now give me back my nonviolent .38." Gano took the revolver. "What do we do with these two? I'm guessing you don't want to be rational and burn 'em both."

Jack looked at Montana hunched over his wounded hand. "We'll take Montana as a hostage to help get us out of here. Guzman, too, if he can move."

"A hostage does no damn good. If we go out that door, we'll get hosed down by the guards' AK-47s."

The yard outside filled with the wailing sirens of fire trucks arriving.

Gano smiled triumphantly. "We lucked out, Sure Shot. Our cover just showed up." Gano walked to where Guzman lay inert, rolled him over with his boot, and peered at his face. "This one will be dead meat in a few minutes." He pointed at a Ford F-350 pickup with a crew cab and a front bumper like a battering ram. "There's our chariot. I can hot-wire that baby in ten seconds flat."

Jack looked toward the truck. He wanted to run to Guzman's office and grab the records on the mystery trucks, but that could cost them their lives. "Crank it up, Gano." He turned to Montana. "You better pray no one tries to use those wells."

The Ford's motor roared to life. Gano ran to where Montana squatted, cradling his pulverized hand. Montana never saw the uppercut coming from Gano that knocked him against the wall. Gano jerked him up, dragged him to the truck, and shoved him headfirst into the back cab. Gano straightened up. "Jack, the day may come when you wish I'd smoked this piece of garbage."

Jack climbed into the driver's seat. "Punch the button on the wall that opens the cargo door, and then mount up fast. I'll ease out and see what's going on."

Outside was chaotic—flashing lights, sirens, jets of water arching through the air. Guards held their automatic rifles with one finger on the trigger while they watched the frenzied firefighters.

He pulled slowly out of the building and was picking up speed when a guard stepped from around the corner and waved his rifle at them. *"Detenerse!"* he shouted. *"Detenerse!"*

"Head down," Jack said. "It's show time."

The guard got off a wild burst before diving to save himself from being run over as Jack floored it.

From near the gate, a Nissan pickup rolled forward, angling to cut them off. As they closed, Jack swerved and rammed the Ford's massive bumper into the smaller Nissan, sending it careening into the fence. The big Ford shuddered, then got moving toward the gate again. A bullet shattered the rear window; others slammed into the tailgate.

Suddenly, the passenger-side door of the crew cab flew open and Montana tumbled out. Jack had to choose. Leave Montana behind, wounded and venomous, or escape.

Chapter 41

July 9
10:30 p.m.

DEBRA, ARMS CROSSED and mouth tight, sat across from Jack at the small table in the Buena Vista Motel room. Gano lay on one of the beds, injured leg propped up on a pillow, drinking Jose Cuervo tequila from the bottle.

Jack told her a version of what had gone down at the Palmer plant in a way he hoped wouldn't freak her out. But each time Gano interrupted and exaggerated the already outrageous events, making both of them sound like comic book heroes, she frowned, barely holding back her annoyance.

"So," Jack said, "a couple of miles from the plant, black smoke poured out from under the hood. When the engine locked up—"

"Why did that happen?"

"Hell," Gano put in, "that ol' truck was hit by so many bullets it felt like we were in a hailstorm. It's a wonder—"

"It didn't matter," Jack said. "Gano was right behind me in the Mustang you rented."

"Damn it. You weren't going to tell me you'd been shot at?" She was pissed.

"No big deal. They hit the truck, not us. Anyway, I drove the Mustang straight to an emergency room in El Paso. The intern didn't ask any questions and patched up Gano's leg right away."

"And did a good job," Gano said, "even though he was wasted from smoking weed."

"Gano, tell Debra about the time you delivered those three guys who paid for your new plane," Jack said. He was damn well going to change the subject. "I'm going to take a shower."

In the isolation of the shower, the raid on the plant filled his mind. Everything from stealing the Trash Taxi to running from the burning wells now seemed dreamlike. But he remembered every second of Gano's fight with Guzman. And the moment he pulled the trigger to shoot Montana. Like a lot of violent acts, there had been no time to think. He'd never forget it.

He pushed those images from his mind and imagined the hot water washing away his tension. *Tomorrow was going to be a bitch.*

As soon as he went back into the other room, Gano jumped up, saying, "My turn."

The moment the bathroom door closed behind Gano, Jack said to Debra, "I think they're filling up that cave near Batopilas with nuclear waste. We're going back there in the morning."

"You were almost killed tonight at the plant." Her eyes were wide with alarm. "Please don't go to that cave."

"It's not my first choice either, but there's no other way to find out what I need to know."

"Why tomorrow?"

"Our attack on the wells failed. We only crippled them, and Montana got away. He can't get them operational tomorrow, but it won't take much longer than that. I only have a few hours to fly to the cave and get back here in time. Besides, he'll be as mad as a buffalo with a spear up its backside. He'll have people searching for me, kicking down doors. And the Juarez cops will be after me for what I did to the plant. Maybe even for the murder of Ana-Maria. I can't let that psycho police chief at the Juarez jail get his hands on me again."

When Gano reappeared in clean clothes, Jack said, "We need special gear for tomorrow. The only place we can get it by then is from Ed Rincon. Debra, will you call and persuade him to meet us at UTEP as soon as he can get there?"

She cut her eyes at him, still angry. "I may not be able to persuade him to do anything. He's already right on the edge of calling the cops."

"Tell him we'll feed him some information. Maybe he'll be curious enough to come."

"And maybe not." She stalked out of the room to make the call.

DEBRA'S DESCRIPTION of UTEP professor Ed Rincon had been dead on. Ghost thin, glancing incessantly around the room.

"Thanks for coming, Dr. Rincon," she said. "I'd like you to meet Jack Strider and Gano LeMoyne." They shook hands, and Rincon sat on a high stool, waiting.

"Now," she said, "if you agree to strict confidentiality, Jack will fill you in."

Jack watched Rincon think that over, knowing he didn't have enough facts to take to any authorities. Rincon popped the knuckle of his middle finger and said, "Very well."

Bone weary, Jack leaned against the edge of a table. The point of telling

Rincon anything was to set him up for the request he planned to make in a minute.

"The samples Debra brought you came from huge tanks in Juarez that are full of those chemicals," he said. "Someone is about to dump them down injection wells into the aquifer. Gano and I tried to destroy the wells, but we were attacked by armed guards and barely got away."

"Ah," Rincon breathed, in what seemed to be his equivalent of excitement. His restless gaze stopped and focused on Jack.

Jack walked across the room to where Rincon perched on his high stool. "The damage we did gives us a small window of time while the wells are being repaired, but that same person has another scheme that could be even more disastrous. Early tomorrow, Gano and I are going to a secret site where I think he's been dumping huge quantities of nuclear waste. Dr. Rincon, we need your help to stop him. I'm depending on you to get us the right equipment to test for radioactivity."

Rincon's pupils again started bouncing around like pucks in a pinball machine.

"Nuclear waste. Hmmm. How could you possibly know it's nuclear waste?"

Jack pulled out a print Debra had made from a frame of the video he shot over D-TECH. "Look at the markings on those barrels."

"The black and white one that looks like an atom is the sign for nuclear power," Rincon said, "and the yellow and black one, the trefoil, is a radiation warning symbol. But even if you're right, I don't have any equipment that would be useful to you."

What was with this guy? He must be afraid that if he helps he'll be blamed for something.

"Look, Dr. Rincon, we'll use this equipment exactly the way you tell us to. If you want, I'll write up a statement holding you harmless. Now, even if you don't have what we need here in your lab, it must exist somewhere in this university."

Rincon looked thoughtful. "Mr. Strider, you haven't even told me the locations of the tanks or the cave or who's behind this. I need to know all of that."

Jack read the bluff. Rincon didn't "need" to know anything more. He was just a slave to his curiosity.

"If you can help us but refuse to do so," Jack said quietly, "you'll have the consequences on your conscience."

This time Rincon didn't hesitate. "The physics lab storeroom is on the floor above this one. Be right back."

Rincon returned with his arms loaded with gear. After he set the pile on the table, he held out a fiberglass case, about the size of a pulp paperback, with a small red bulb on top. "This is an Eberline Personal Contamination Monitor. The faster it clicks, the higher the radioactivity. It's like a Geiger counter. It uses a string electrometer and ion chamber to detect gamma rays and—"

Jack shook his head, conveying "you're telling us more than we need to know."

"Yes, well," Rincon went on, "you'll also need these HEPA filter masks. They should protect you from inhaling airborne alpha-emitter particles from nuclear waste. Inhale too much of that, and you'll die. Do not take the mask off." He popped the knuckle of his index finger.

He held out a half dozen of what looked like convention name tags. "These badges measure how much radiation you've been exposed to. Unfortunately, if the reading is high, it's already too late to save yourself. You won't be wearing an overcoat made of lead, so your only protection against Gamma rays is to get the hell away from the source as fast as you can." He raised both skinny arms, palms up, as if committing Jack's and Gano's fates to the gods.

Debra's face was grim as she listened to Rincon describe threats more deadly than bullets. Even Gano made no wisecracks.

They left the lab with Rincon, and Gano carried the gear in a sack as they walked across campus. Rincon pointed out the trapezoidal four-story main buildings made of stone blocks. "They're replicas of *dzongs* in Bhutan, part fortress and part Buddhist monastery. Of course, nowadays almost no one knows or cares what they represent. That's why—"

"Ed," Jack said, "we have to get going."

Rincon nodded to each of them and walked away, shaking his head.

"Gano," Debra asked, "what do you think of Jack's plan?"

"Totally nuts!"

"So he shouldn't do it?"

"Of course not."

"And you won't help him with it."

"I'd have to be crazy." He grinned and pinned on a badge.

Chapter 42

July 10
10:00 a.m.

GANO AMUSED himself playing chicken with treetops in a two-person helicopter that looked like a Plexiglas dragonfly. "This EchoStar is the cat's ass," Gano called over the sound of the rotor. "You should see me whip one of these suckers through the Grand Canyon."

They were headed for the Big Silverado mine shaft located on the other side of the mesa from the cave near Batopilas. As they flew, Gano told him a story.

"The miners who dug the Big Silverado a hundred years ago accidentally broke into the Tarahumara sacred cave, the big crack you saw. They tried to keep it secret, but word of the desecration leaked out, and the Tarahumara shamans hurled curses and hexes at the Big Silverado. Soon after that, the thick vein of silver ore played out just as the shamans had promised, and the mine shut down."

"Is that story the reason you think the Big Silverado is a back door to the cave?" Jack asked. "Are you sure about that?"

"Does a bird shit on your freshly washed truck?"

Even though it was a long shot, Jack had to know whether there was radioactivity in the cave. "Back door it is."

"Here's the way we do it," Gano said. "I'll bring this baby in as quiet as I can, but in this still air you can hear a pine needle drop. We have to figure the trolls over in that cave will hear us." He throttled back. "Probably the last helicopter they heard was us snooping around. When they hear a chopper on this side of the mesa, they'll come looking pronto. The road from the cave goes all the way 'round the end of the mesa. That gives us forty-five minutes max before they roll in here." He pushed the control forward. "Elevator going down," he said, and dropped below the rim of the mesa toward the mine opening.

This was his third time with Gano in a tiny aircraft, and despite the acrobatics, he was beginning to feel okay about it. They hovered about thirty yards in front of the Big Silverado, looking at dozens of massive boulders piled up to block the entrance.

"Son-of-a-coyote," Gano exclaimed. "Those ol' boys in the canyon have locked the back door. Look at the cat tracks of the machine that did all that. Those tracks are pretty new, too."

"Land anyway. We'll take a closer look." Jack checked his watch. Forty-five minutes wasn't much time.

When they climbed out of the EchoStar, the boulders rose thirty feet above their heads. Bolted to a 4 x 4 cedar post driven into the rocky soil was a metal sign bearing one word, *"Peligro!"* and the international symbol warning of falling rocks.

"They've shown us their hole card," Jack said. "They wouldn't have gone to all this trouble unless they had something important to keep secret."

"Yeah, but we're still locked out."

"Maybe not. Before we landed, I thought I noticed an opening under one of the biggest boulders." He pointed near the top of the left side of the pile. "Could be a way in."

"I should have mentioned this before, oh Great Spelunker, but I have a bit of the ol' claustrophobia. Squeezing in under a boulder that could shift and squash me is way more than I signed up for."

"No problem. I'll take the gear and go in alone." Jack wasn't looking forward to fumbling his way through an abandoned mine shaft full of bats and scorpions, but he wasn't turning back. He reached into the chopper, retrieved his gear, and slung the strap of the Eberline contamination counter case over his shoulder. He clipped the dosimeter to his belt and stuck a couple of HEPA filters into his pocket. He'd put one on at the first sign he was nearing the intersection with the cave.

"Hold on, pard," Gano protested, "I'm not explaining to Debra that I was out here sitting in the shade and having a belt of tequila while you were inside getting fried. Know what I mean?" He clipped on his dosimeter, stuffed the HEPA filters away, and hung a coil of rope over his shoulder. He tossed a flashlight to Jack. "Stealth LED, best there is." Then he checked his .38.

Jack walked to the boulders and started pulling himself up until he reached a horizontal fissure a couple of feet high, maybe two and a half, between monster rocks. He shined the powerful flash inside. The beam revealed nothing. He had to commit himself without knowing what was on the other side of the pile, which could be a sheer drop—or he might get wedged in part way, unable to back out.

Jack checked his watch again. Ten minutes had passed since they'd landed. "I'll go first." He edged ahead, clawing with fingers, pushing with toes. The clearance quickly narrowed to just a few inches. He felt as if he were in a stone coffin with tons of rock poised to settle and flatten him into a wet spot. He began to hyperventilate. His chest expanded. The space closed in. *Get a grip.*

He forced his breathing to slow, and, after inching forward over a second boulder, then a third, his beam of light showed he had reached the mine's main tunnel. He kept scooting until he was hanging head down on the angled surface of a boulder about 15 feet above the tunnel's floor. He gave a last push to free himself from the crevice and swung to his left for a handhold. He got it, but couldn't hold on, and dropped, barely getting his feet under him. The momentum threw him onto his back, and his skull banged against the tunnel's floor. That pain was nothing compared to his relief.

A beam of light appeared above him, then Gano's head. "Damn, I hated that. I closed my eyes and made like a crayfish all the way. Couldn't have done it if you hadn't gone first, Old Scout. You're not so bad, even if you don't pack heat."

"Push yourself out and get your feet under you. I'll break your fall."

Gano did as instructed. Then, with Gano close behind, Jack moved down the tunnel slowly, using the slimy wall as a guide, flashing the Stealth only long enough to reveal the next few steps. When he rapped a century-old timber support beam, it sounded hollow, as if dry rot had eaten it. A few feet farther, and the ceiling began to slope down to his shoulder level, forcing him to bend deeply.

"Maybe it's breathing air that smells like rotten fungus," Gano said hoarsely, "but I'm good for about one more minute before I need to head out of here. I'm no goddamned mole."

"Can't be much farther." Seemed like the best thing to say even though he had no idea how far they had to go. He guessed that the side shaft that intersected with the cave would branch off to their left. If he was wrong and they had to retreat and try another shaft, men driving from the cave could show up in time to trap them in the mine.

Just then, his beam of light picked out a side shaft partially blocked by a crude wooden barrier. That had to be it, so he edged past the barrier. The ceiling of the side shaft remained low, and the width narrowed. The mountain was closing in. His back ached, but if he complained, Gano would use that as an excuse to bail out.

He stopped to listen. The faint sound of running water that had been with them for a while was getting louder. Now it was joined by the low hum of a motor and muffled voices. He fitted a HEPA filter mask to his face, signaled to Gano to do the same, and inched forward, feeling his way along the rough wall.

The ceiling rose abruptly, so far up he couldn't touch it. A faint light began to illuminate their shaft, growing stronger as they advanced. Voices grew louder. They had reached the sacred cave.

He rolled his shoulders and shook his arms a few times to loosen up and then peered around the last corner. A floor-to-ceiling wire mesh barricade bolted to the stone walls blocked their way. Beyond the mesh, more than a dozen men were at work, every one wearing knee-high rubber boots, rough work clothes and a face mask. A man shouting orders to the others wore gloves and a protective suit that looked like it was made of aluminum foil.

A great chamber opened up ahead of him, its scale far greater than he'd imagined. The section he saw was filled with hundreds of metal drums stacked in neat rows. Off to the left, cement cylinders the size of mini-submarines were lined up behind red warning tape.

He couldn't fully interpret what he saw, but those cylinders weren't for low-level waste from hospitals or university labs. They looked exactly like pictures he'd seen of containers for high-level nuclear waste.

Two forklifts idled, drivers talking with one another, and then one drove in their direction. He told himself there was no way the operator could have spotted them, that they were safe behind the wire mesh, but the machine coming at him was unnerving. Fifty feet away, the driver wheeled ninety degrees to place another metal drum in its row.

Gano tapped his back to get his attention, then tapped the glowing face of his watch. Thirty minutes had passed. They were out of time, but a radioactivity reading was the whole point of taking this risk. He swung the Eberline counter around in front of him and felt across the control panel until he found the "On" switch. Ed Rincon had described the low buzz the machine would produce if there were any radioactivity; slow clicks for a low level, faster if the level was high. Fortunately, the sound should be masked by the machinery in the cave.

He flipped the switch to "On." It started as a slow hum and immediately rose to sound like a rasp drawn across the edge of sheet metal. Within ten seconds the rapid-fire clicks blurred together in a whine that reverberated back into the mine shaft. He slapped at the switch, missed, and had to fumble to shut off the racket, too late to prevent workmen from hearing and knowing where it came from.

Gano pulled him away from the mesh barricade and gave him a shove to propel him back to the shaft's opening. He stumbled forward, banged his forehead on the lower ceiling, but managed to keep his flashlight on as he shuffled, bent over, at triple their pace coming in.

"You okay?" he called back to Gano.

"Yeah, but now I'm worried more about the artillery comin' by road."

They reached the boulder barrier. Jack pulled himself up, diving into the crevice head first and wriggling thorough like a salamander.

Just before the opening, he stopped, remembering that Gano was armed and should have gone first. But if the guards were already there, Gano's gun couldn't save them. He poked his head out of the crevice. No vehicles in sight, and the chopper appeared untouched. He moved out of Gano's way and scrambled down the boulders.

"Guess we're not as popular as we thought," Gano said. "Let's take off before the party starts." Then he pointed to Jack's belt and said, "Son-of-a-bitch! Does that dosimeter reading say what I think it does?"

Before he could unbuckle the dosimeter to read it, a dust plume rose near the end of the mesa. "They're here."

They raced to the chopper. Seconds later, a pickup with a bed full of men barreled down the dirt road toward the Big Silverado.

"Time to make like a flying saucer," Gano said.

The engine of the EchoStar started. Rotors whirled slowly, then faster and faster. The craft began to get light on its skids. But it was all too slow. The pickup raced at them, bouncing crazily, but the men aboard were firing every weapon they had. The low hanging chopper couldn't climb fast enough to get out of range.

Instead of trying to gain altitude, Gano spun the bird around to face the pickup, just a foot off the ground, and revved the engine. In seconds, a thick cloud of sand and dust engulfed them, and Gano whipped the chopper around 180 degrees to fly in the opposite direction, still hugging the deck. Several hundred yards away, he hauled back, and the EchoStar climbed out of the dust cloud, and out of firing range of the pursuers' pickup, now buried in the dust.

"Well, that was almost kiss-my-ass-goodbye time," Gano said.

Jack looked down at his Eberline contamination counter and dosimeter. He'd heard the buzzer go mad under the *blitzkrieg* of electrons from the cave, so he was worried. What would Rincon say concerning the strength of the radioactive emissions? Had they absorbed enough radioactivity to start glowing?

Chapter 43

July 10
4:00 p.m.

BACK IN THE El Paso airport, Jack reflected on what he'd seen. The markings on the barrels at D-TECH, the shapes of the containers in the cave, the contamination counter—everything told him that cave was packed with nuclear waste, at least some of which was high level. That made up his mind to take drastic action. He could contact the CIA or Homeland Security, but both were flooded by reports from alarmed citizens promoting conspiracy theories. There was no time to fight his way through their bureaucratic mazes. The only move left would be the most radical thing he'd ever done. Persuade Jason Gorton, President of the United States of America, to take control. Once Gorton heard about the pending disasters in El Paso, Juarez and Copper Canyon, he could stop them.

So how could he reach the President in an emergency? The White House switchboard wouldn't put him through, but maybe he could reach a high-ranking staffer and persuade him or her to contact the President.

He called the White House and asked to speak with President Gorton. As expected, the operator politely offered to take a message. When he insisted the call was important, she routed him to a secretary in the Communications Office who, even more politely, offered to take a message. Again he insisted it was urgent. This time he was transferred to Alvin Thomas, Assistant Counsel to the President.

Thomas at least asked for his *bona fides*. As he recited the buzz words—Professor, Stanford Law School, Sinclair & Simms—he was very aware they were all past tense. Even though Thomas didn't know that, he was unwilling to forward the call to President Gorton. "Send a registered letter, please" he said, and hung up with Jack in mid-protest.

Jack called Senator Toby Baxter, reasonably confident Toby could get a call through to Gorton. But his friend, or former friend, was deer hunting in northern Wyoming, unreachable unless he called into the office which, his assistant said, he never did. Another dead end.

That left Justin Sinclair as his only other conduit to Gorton. He would, by God, pressure Sinclair into contacting President Gorton for him.

When he called Mrs. Pounders she gave him a verbal stiff-arm, treating him like a paperclip salesman instead of a partner—former partner—in the firm. After he stressed the urgency, she said, "He's booked solid except for one opening. His eight a.m. appointment tomorrow just passed away. You could call Mr. Sinclair at that time." Jack said he'd be at Sinclair & Simms in person at eight.

MRS. POUNDERS, usually indifferent to anyone waiting to be admitted to Justin Sinclair's inner sanctum, had delivered several frowns in Jack's direction. She made no effort to hide her distaste for what she saw.

He didn't blame her. Wearing a dirty twill shirt and boots caked with mud from the mine shaft, he looked like a vagrant tossed off the train from Fresno.

He'd left El Paso on time last night, but dense fog at SFO had diverted his flight to Reno for an overnight. By the time the morning flight reached San Francisco, it was too late to get home to Atherton to change into fresh clothes before meeting Sinclair.

When two law clerks came by, they looked first at him and then at the two armed Shorenstein Security guards posted in the hall. Were they there because Sinclair was worried that his former partner might do something crazy? *Little did he know.* Jack looked at his watch. Already 8:20.

Without looking at him, Mrs. Pounders said, "Mr. Sinclair called someone else in who arrived earlier. He'll send for you presently."

His idle glance down the corridor took in antique Tabriz carpets resting on enough black marble to pave a cathedral. On his first visit for the Sunday morning job interview, he'd been impressed by the emblems of accomplishment in the world he knew well. They'd made him feel at ease. Today, after all he'd been through, this office had become an alien place.

"He'll see you now," Mrs. Pounders intoned, just as the door to the inner office swung open. Justin Sinclair strode out, still the legal world's facsimile of Charlton Heston—craggy features, intense blue eyes, and swept-back white hair. The instant he took in Jack's appearance, his expression became decidedly less congenial.

"I'll be damned. A couple of days ago I invited you to come meet with me, and you got prickly as a hedgehog. Now here you are. Well, come in. I've just been talking with someone about you."

He followed Sinclair into his office where his eyes were immediately drawn to the east window wall and the gaunt frame of Arthur Palmer. The scowl and crossed arms said clearly that he'd heard from Montana about the attack on the plant.

What the hell? Why had Sinclair brought Palmer in? Maybe Sinclair had anticipated that Jack would be on the warpath, so he'd set up a dogfight scenario between Jack and Palmer, leaving him untouched on the sidelines. Whatever Sinclair's reason, Arthur's presence would make it much harder for Jack to get what he'd come for from Sinclair. *Damn him.*

"You're one crazy son-of-a-bitch, you know that?" Palmer snarled. "You set fire to four buildings. You stabbed the plant manager. You shot Montana, tried to kill him. I'll see that you're in the slammer for the rest of your miserable life!" Palmer was so mad his voice cracked.

"Here's what really happened," Jack said. "We started fires in metal trash bins to divert the guards. And I didn't stab anyone. Your manager, Guzman, pulled a switchblade and attacked my friend. In self-defense, he stuck Guzman with a screwdriver. Montana was about to kill my friend, so I shot the gun out of his hand."

"The Juarez police are after you for trespassing, destroying property—"

"It was an emergency. I tried to destroy the wells so Montana couldn't use them to dump toxic waste into the local aquifer. He doesn't give a damn that it will kill people and destroy the only water supply for Juarez and El Paso. By the way, you'll be liable if he pulls it off."

"Liable, bullshit." Palmer pointed at him with both index fingers. "You just confessed to a felony. Justin's a witness."

"I had to go to the plant because you didn't do the two things I told Justin you had to do to stop Montana."

"What are you talking about?"

"I called Justin two days ago and told him I'd take action if you didn't get Montana off plant grounds and dismantle those wells."

"You sent *me* an ultimatum? You're joking." His tone reeked with scorn, but he glanced at Sinclair with a question in his eyes. "I heard nothing from Justin until I called about the fires you set. That's when he said you'd given him a wild story about Montana planning to poison some aquifer. He also said he'd fired you after the Hearing and ordered you to stay away from Palmer Industries—which you obviously did *not* do."

Jack noticed Palmer's glance at Sinclair and thought he heard a slight change in his tone. Had he caught Palmer off guard? It didn't matter. Palmer's default response was to lie.

"I don't believe you. You're in this with Montana, and I'll nail you for it." He opened his wallet and withdrew the folded printout from Ed Rincon that listed the chemicals and carcinogens stored in the tanks on the ridge. "Here's what Montana is ready to dump into the Hueco *bolsón*. You either ordered him to do it or looked the other way." He tossed it on the desk. Sinclair picked it up and read it.

"You're full of shit," Palmer snorted. "I told Montana to make money for Palmer Industries. That's all."

"And that included bribing PROFEPA and the Hearing judge? I saw what happened at that Hearing."

"For God's sake! Has Montana ever bribed somebody in Mexico? Of course, but I've never heard of the Waco whatever-it-is and didn't authorize him to dump anything into it. So get off my ass."

"If I hadn't gone after him, Montana would already have opened the valves and buried your company in bankruptcy. You'd be heading for prison. You want me to get off your ass? I *saved* your ass. Until now."

Palmer turned his hawklike eyes on Sinclair. "I detest this son-of-a-bitch, but what if he's not hallucinating? Bankruptcy? Prison? You're supposed to be protecting us, and you're not doing it."

Sinclair leaned back in his chair, unruffled. "Turning on me would be very unwise, Arthur. I've supported Palmer Industries when other attorneys would have backed away. And," he smiled grimly, "just in case your hands aren't entirely clean in this matter, you'll continue to need my help. You wouldn't want me on a witness stand, would you?"

Palmer scowled, and his face reddened. "Don't threaten me, Justin. Who the fuck do you think you are?"

Sinclair didn't respond, but his narrowed eyes said, *You damn well better remember who I am.* Aloud, he said, "Strider has upset you, Arthur, so I won't take offense. Now, who are you better off listening to, him or me?" He turned to Jack. "Mr. Strider, you've overstayed your welcome."

"What welcome? You only agreed to see me because you wanted to know my reason for coming."

"I'm no longer interested."

"Hold on," Palmer snapped. "I'm the one he's threatening. Besides, he's a felon. I'm not letting him just walk away."

"All right, damn it, what do you want?" Sinclair said gruffly with no pretense of civility.

Jack met Sinclair's glare with one of his own. "To prevent a disaster, I need to meet with President Gorton immediately. I want you to set that up."

"Jesus," Palmer said. "Meet the President? That's the last—"

"Quiet," Sinclair barked.

Palmer ignored him. "I'll go down there and kick Montana's ass to China. I'll make sure he won't—"

"What Montana *won't* do," Jack said, "is take any more orders from you. He's cornered, so he's thinking about how to save himself. My guess is that he's so mad he'll poison the aquifer on his way out of town. And that will be on your head."

He turned back to Sinclair. "President Gorton is the only one who can reach across the border and act fast enough."

That shut Palmer up. He stepped back, deferring to Sinclair. Sinclair's expression was pensive, looking at neither of them.

Jack knew exactly what was in Sinclair's mind. Exposing the crisis to Gorton would put Palmer Industries squarely in the line of fire. Sinclair had a fiduciary obligation to protect this client, but that wasn't a valid excuse for refusing to set up this meeting. He'd boxed Sinclair in by demanding something he had the ability to do and knew needed to be done. If Sinclair refused to make the call, he might have to defend his refusal in public after the disaster happened. If Gorton declined to meet with Jack, Sinclair could later say he'd tried. Jack wanted Sinclair to believe that the greater risk to him personally would be refusing to try.

Sinclair leaned back, tucked his chin and looked at Jack over his glasses, his face a mixture of amusement and scorn. "You're asking me to use my relationship with the President to draw him into this grudge match between you and Tom Montana. You accuse Montana of all kinds of evil intentions, but the only actual damage has been done by you. You haven't made your case, so I'm not disposed to call the President."

Jack stared at the man, taken aback. Sinclair's decision was contrary to his own best interests. Was he being illogical? Not likely. Therefore, he was bluffing. That forced Jack to choose between two last-ditch options, both bad. So far, he'd been careful to say nothing about D-TECH, the mystery trucks, or radioactivity in a Mexican cave. Those issues might persuade Sinclair of the urgency of this situation, but Jack hadn't yet connected the dots. Sinclair would mock it as a conspiracy fantasy, cutting the legs from under the solid case he had about hazardous waste being dumped into the aquifer. He intended to tell Gorton everything he knew about D-TECH and the cave, but right now, he needed Sinclair to focus on the aquifer.

His alternative strategy was provocative and insulting, and the consequences were unpredictable, but it was the better choice.

"If you don't set up a meeting with Gorton," he said coolly, "I'll call a press conference. You and Arthur can figure out how you're going to answer questions from dozens of reporters." He made his tone as matter-of-fact as Sinclair's.

Sinclair's head went back, chin up. "A couple of days ago you threatened to blow the whistle—but didn't. You only get one bite of that apple. Besides, no reputable reporter would walk across the street to hear what you have to say."

"Really? I race my boat against my friend Ronnie Patterson every week. As you know, he owns the *Chronicle*. When I give him this story, he'll put it on page one."

Jack felt like he was inside Sinclair's head. If Sinclair wasn't personally involved in what Montana was planning, Jack meeting with Gorton wouldn't hurt him. If he doubted whether Arthur Palmer could stop Montana, meaning that the aquifer might actually be poisoned, Palmer Industries and everyone else would be better off if Gorton stepped in. And a media firestorm involving a major client would certainly tarnish Sinclair & Simms. Sinclair must see all that.

Sinclair took off his glasses, polished them, restored them to his nose and looked at Jack. "Well played, young man. My friend Jason Gorton will take my call, and you'll have your meeting." He stopped Arthur's objection with a chopping motion of his hand. "Don't say a word, Arthur. I'll explain later." Turning back to Jack, he said, "Now I'm going to send you away with something to think about. When you walked through my door the first time, you were in sad shape. You thought you'd hit bottom, but that was nothing. If you can't prove every word of what you've just said, you'll curse the day you met me."

As Jack walked down the long hall, away from Sinclair's office, he had no doubt that Justin Sinclair would try to destroy him no matter what happened with Gorton.

JUSTIN SINCLAIR SAT motionless, staring out the window at, but not seeing, Alcatraz, the prison-fortress in the middle of San Francisco Bay.

He hadn't seen this move by Strider coming, and that worried him. Years ago, he would have been ready to block it. Now he was left with damage control and damn little time to perform it.

A diminutive celadon urn, one of a priceless pair on his desk, caught his eye. He picked it up, revolved it in his fingers, and hurled it across the room. Its thin shell evaporated on impact.

He stilled his anger and turned the possibilities over in his mind until a strategy took shape. He poked his speakerphone button. "Mrs. Pounders, get Frank Miller on the phone, Chief of Staff, the White House."

Chapter 44

July 11
11:15 a.m.

JACK LEFT SINCLAIR'S office, headed south from the city on Highway 101, stopped in Atherton for a shower, shave, and clean clothes, and drove to the Stanford crew boathouse, all with his mind in neutral. The meeting with Sinclair and Palmer had been like combat, and he needed to recharge. His strategy had worked, and he'd scored a vital victory—unless Sinclair reneged on calling Gorton. But the meeting had also raised troubling questions. Had Palmer really been surprised by some of what he heard? Why hadn't Sinclair called Palmer about Jack's ultimatum?

He parked and walked down the pier toward the boathouse. At the end of the pier, eight tall young men were gently lowering their shell into the water. When all were aboard with oars ready, the coxswain gave them a quick pep talk, and they pulled away to start their many practice runs. Jack remembered how exhausting those practices were. He'd participated in them many, many times.

After they were gone, he sat on the pier where he could listen to the lapping of waves and watch cloud-shadows on the surface of the bay. Being around water always helped him think, and right now he had to reason through some complex puzzles.

Before he could start thinking about them, the cell phone buzzed in his pocket.

"Mr. Sinclair is coming on the line," Mrs. Pounders announced.

"It's set," Sinclair said, tone indifferent as if he were discussing a tennis date. "President Gorton will see you tomorrow at noon aboard Air Force One. He'll be at Travis Air Force Base to present awards to a transport air group. You have a fifteen minute slot, which means you won't get sixteen. Your security pass will be at the front gate." He hung up.

Jack pumped his fist in the air. *By God, he'd pulled it off.* Now all he had to do was argue the biggest case of his life.

He called Debra in El Paso and asked her to handle two important tasks. One required her to make a five-minute phone call. The other was much tougher, and a lot depended on her pulling it off.

In his next call, he gave Gano a task that was straightforward and dangerous. Gano said he was ready to roll.

As soon as Jack clicked off, his phone buzzed. "This is Ed Rincon calling."

Jack's mouth went dry, letting him know how apprehensive he was about the radioactivity report from Rincon. For a few seconds, he watched a sloop with a billowing yellow Genoa tack around a race marker buoy. Well, if it was bad news, he'd deal with it.

"Dr. Rincon, thanks for calling."

"I got the results from the lab on the readings on your Eberline contamination counter. Many factors affect the readings like distance from the source, intervening shielding such as rock, and so on, but there's definitely intense, ambient radioactive material in that cave."

"So that showed up in our personal dosimeters too?"

"It's a matter of degree. For reference, a person gets about ten millirem of radiation from a chest x-ray. If you work around nuclear material, you're allowed a max of five-thousand millirem a year, which is five rem. At around twenty-five rem, you'll experience serious health problems."

"Where does that leave me, and Gano?"

"Your readings were four rem. Both of you should be fine as long as you don't add much to that in coming months."

Jack let out the breath he'd been holding. The sun seemed brighter. He closed his eyes and gave himself a moment to absorb the good news.

"Can you tell what kind of radioactive material is in the cave?"

"That little Eberline can't discriminate. But for you to accumulate four rem that fast, some of it was probably Cesium-137 or Cobalt 60. Could even be high-level radioactive material out of nuclear reactors, but that stuff is stored on-site at power plants or government weapons-making facilities. I don't see how it could have gotten into Mexico. By the way, if the workers you saw weren't heavily protected and working very short shifts, every one of them is probably dying."

Jack had a clear image of the men working in the cave. "Then they're dead men."

"How critical the problem is," Rincon said, "depends on whether what's in that cave is low level nuclear waste or high level nuclear waste."

"Please explain."

"Low level waste, referred to as LLW, is generated by all kinds of businesses. Hospitals pump out radioactive lab waste, carbon-14, tritium and a lot more. Almost none of these businesses have adequate room or security to store the LLW on-site so they have to ship it by rail or truck to treatment facilities—if they can find one that will accept it. Inspection of treatment facilities is unbelievably slipshod. Inspectors are poorly trained, and most are so spooked they want to get off the property two minutes after they get there."

"Out of morbid curiosity," Jack said, "is that stuff driving past me on the highway?"

"Of course it is. When they're carrying Class A, B and C radioactive cargo, the drivers take any route they want. If the cargo is more dangerous, it's supposed to be route-controlled. But if that's not the shortest route, some shippers ignore the rules. The biggest problem is that every state refuses to be a dumping ground for nuclear waste from the rest of the country. That's why there are so few approved storage sites and why they charge exorbitant fees."

"So what about high level waste?"

"Government facilities that build nuclear weapons are the biggest sources of high-level nuclear waste, or HLW. Next are nuclear power plants. Some of that HLW is so dangerous they enclose it in glass cylinders inside stainless steel barrels inside concrete blocks. Sometimes the containers look like long sausages."

Jack's mind went back to the cave. *Or maybe like mini-submarines?*

"Where is that stuff stored?"

"Historically, it's stored on site because there's nowhere to send it for permanent storage. For example, Oak Ridge National Laboratory tried hydrofracture, meaning they dumped HLW into 1,200 foot deep wells. After a while, radiation started escaping up the well shafts so they had to cap and abandon every single well. Next, they tried disposing of radioactive liquid waste in seepage pits in beds of shale on the theory the shale would absorb the radioactive material. That failed, too, and they had to cap the pits with 30 feet of cement. Scary stuff. And that's why businesses, power plants and places that build nuclear weapons will pay almost any price to get rid of their nuclear waste."

Suddenly, everything became clear. *That's what motivated someone to use D-TECH and Palmer Industries to funnel nuclear waste into Mexico. As always, it was about the money.*

"So," Jack said, "you're saying there could be some HLW in that cave?"

"Based on the readings, I'd say so, except that regulations would prevent that. For example—"

"Dr. Rincon, thanks for calling about the readings." Jack knew the regulations hadn't prevented anything, and didn't have time for a recital. "You're a great help."

"Hold on a minute. You sure you're on top of this?"

Damned good question. "I think so."

"Remember that if I don't hear from you, I'll have to do something."

"I remember. I'll keep you in the loop."

He hung up and bowed his head for a moment, letting the tension flow out of his body. He wasn't about to start glowing in the dark after all. The presence of some amount of high level nuclear waste meant he'd been right to worry about the mystery trucks. But they were just the mules in a system that was still unclear to him. George McDonald could help, so he made the call.

McDonald's secretary said he was teaching a class but would be free after four o'clock.

"Please ask him to meet me at the Sculpture Garden on campus. I'll be there at half past four.

Just after he clicked off, caller ID showed an incoming call from Sam Butler. He didn't want the interruption. He'd return it later.

He watched as a long shell finished practice, and the oarsmen settled the graceful shell back on its rack. When the pier was quiet again, he centered his thoughts. He had to have everything well-organized when he met with the President.

First, dumping nuclear waste into an unprotected cave would result in a catastrophe if he couldn't persuade President Gorton to intervene. To convince Gorton, he needed to identify the person, or entity, behind it. So who the hell was it?

The most logical candidate was D-TECH. Its executives would know that more and more generators of radioactive waste are forced to shut down because they can't dispose of it. They'd know that expanded reliance on nuclear power was dead in the water for the same reason. D-TECH's executives were sophisticated enough to come up with this solution and make it operational. They could easily persuade generators of nuclear waste to ignore the law to solve the problem. Certainly, the immorality of dumping nuclear waste in Mexico wouldn't deter a "gray" company like D-TECH, not with hundreds of millions in profits at stake. At least now he knew for sure that trucks from D-TECH were transporting nuclear waste to Mexico via Palmer Industries.

It added up, but it didn't feel right. The D-TECH Board would have to be crazy to initiate a scheme that, if discovered, could cost it every one of its profitable government contracts and put the company out of business. Much more likely that D-TECH was just one stop along the line, maybe without the knowledge of its Board.

Could Tomás Montana have pulled this off on his own? He had a big motive and could have organized the logistics of the D-TECH-to-Juarez-to-Batopilas piece of the action. But he didn't have the connections to implement the whole plan. It was more probable that someone had brought the idea to him to help implement it.

That left Arthur Palmer. Because of the business he was in, Palmer had contacts with companies desperate to get rid of nuclear waste. He controlled the equipment and personnel needed for the logistics. Plus, he was a greedy son-of-a-bitch who would dump nuclear waste in Mexico and never look back. But when he'd confronted Palmer, the man hadn't stuck with his usual bullying tactics. Of course he was a liar, but he'd seemed genuinely surprised by what he heard about the aquifer.

What Palmer lacked was the essential ingredient. The strategic vision needed to operate a complex international scheme. Only a few people had that. People like . . . *Justin Sinclair.*

The thought slipped into place so easily that it was there without him even realizing it. And it rang true.

Sinclair was a master at seeing and solving complex problems. He had the credibility to set up the network of suppliers of nuclear waste, and he would certainly know about D-TECH.

He'd also made a big issue of keeping the plant from being shut down, had been ready to hand one million dollars to PROFEPA. That was to protect his client, he'd claimed, but was he also protecting the lifeline of the black trucks?

Sinclair was already rich, but Jack knew that for people like him no amount of money was ever enough—and maybe there was more to it than that. But whatever the reason, it all fit.

Then Jack had caught the master game player off guard when he'd marched into his office. Wielding facts and the threat of going public, he'd maneuvered the man into setting up the meeting with Gorton.

Sinclair didn't suspect that Jack knew anything about smuggling of nuclear waste. If he had, he would never have set up a meeting where Jack might tell Gorton about it. After all, he'd never said a word to Sinclair about the nuclear waste. In retrospect, that had been a very smart move. And now, thank God, he could give the President the identity of the mastermind—and fight to make that stick.

"Hey," called a young man coming out of the boathouse, "didn't you used to be the guy who rowed in the Olympics, like a long time ago?"

"I guess I used to be that guy," he answered, barely looking up. He didn't want a conversation right now.

"Yeah, saw your picture on the wall in the boathouse. Well, cheers." With a half-salute, the young man walked toward the parking lot.

Jack had lost respect for Sinclair during the last few weeks, but it was still hard to wrap his mind around the conclusion that a former Secretary of State was his enemy. Sinclair had undoubtedly already covered his tracks, including setting up Montana or Arthur to take the blame. They'd never see that coming. He reminded himself that Sinclair would do the same to him in a heartbeat.

Chapter 45

July 11
4:30 p.m.

How had he gotten into this situation? Jack wondered. Only six weeks ago, he'd been elated at winning a sailboat race that seemed like a big deal at the time. Professionally, he'd been on the fastest track. Then Peck died. No, Peck *shot* himself. Suddenly, the sky had crashed on his head. That had been a dark time, but he'd changed course, chosen a path that would help him recover. But it sure as hell hadn't worked out that way. His choices had led instead to the coming confrontation. Or was that the result of his evolution in the way he saw the world—and himself?

Many times over the years, he'd walked among the larger-than-life bronze figures in the Stanford Sculpture Garden, the biggest collection of Auguste Rodin outside Musee Rodin in Paris. This time he walked from the "Burghers of Calais" to the "Gates of Hell" before seeing George McDonald striding across the courtyard toward him.

McDonald's face hadn't changed much since his undergraduate days when he'd been PAC-10 light-heavyweight boxing champion. It was still a geometric assembly of flat planes, like a Cubist version of Jack Palance.

"Good to see you, Jack." He stuck out a hard hand. His face remained solemn. "I came as soon as I finished teaching."

"Thanks. I need to get right to business. Did Debra Vanderberg get through to you with our questions?"

"She said a lot of lives depended on my having certain information ready for you for a critical meeting tomorrow. Nothing like a little pressure. But when she read her list of questions, I told her I'm a hydrologist not a nuclear physicist, and the information she wanted was way out of my field. She didn't take that too well. In fact, she was pretty damn snappish."

"It's stress," Jack said. "But do you mean you don't have the answers?" He felt his blood pressure rising. He'd taken it for granted that Mac would come through for him. Now he'd have to meet the President without being able to quantify the danger in Batopilas.

"Take it easy," Mac said sharply and with a frown. "I had to scramble, but I have more than you need. I'll give you the short, short version."

"Great, but we need to go someplace private." Ever since Casa Lupo, he'd been looking over his shoulder. "Let's drive out to the Stanford golf course and talk there."

In less than ten minutes, Mac pulled his Land Rover into the golf course parking lot and killed the engine.

"Okay," Mac said, "you asked for an overview of what's done with nuclear waste in the U.S. Here goes. It wasn't until 1970 that the federal government finally accepted responsibility for building a permanent geologic repository for disposal of high-level nuclear waste. That means someplace to bury it forever.

"But it wasn't until 1999 that the Department of Energy opened the Waste Isolation Pilot Plant—WIPP—a facility in the desert near Carlsbad, New Mexico. It's a disposal site for transuranic waste left over from nuclear fission. Now picture this: they created a series of rooms 2,100 feet deep in a salt formation. But there's a big drawback. WIPP can't accept high level nuclear waste because it's so hot it attracts water that could corrode the containers holding transuranics, even cause them to explode.

"I know this is kind of dry, but here's the part you'll love." He grinned as if about to tell a joke. "That Carlsbad site is meant to store that stuff for at least 10,000 years, so DOE is erecting granite pillars to warn extraterrestrials who drop in after humans are extinct. The pillars were designed by linguists, anthropologists, and science fiction writers who call them 'passive institutional controls'. There's even an image of 'The Scream' by Edvard Munch. Honest, I couldn't make this up. You with me so far?"

Jack nodded. "Keep going."

"When the uranium in nuclear reactors stops producing energy efficiently, they call it 'spent nuclear fuel.' They shut down the reactor and the SNF goes into a cooling tank that's like a deep swimming pool. It takes at least five years before its temperature cools down enough for it to be stored someplace else. Right now many of the cooling pools are crammed full. Several nuclear-powered electric utility sites have shut down because they're out of storage space. More will close in the near future."

"So this crisis has been building for a long time," Jack said. "What's the government been doing?"

"For decades, DOE has been shipping nuclear waste from one temporary site to another, hoping someone will figure out what to do with it. They try to keep these shipments secret, but it took me about ten minutes to sniff out pending shipments to DOE's Savannah River National Laboratory and the Idaho National Lab. So far, they've dodged any catastrophes, but now they also have to protect nuclear waste from terrorists.

"As I said, high level waste must be placed in permanent isolation in an approved geologic repository. Since every state raised hell to keep any nuke dump far away, Congress avoided making a decision on a site year after year. In the end, DOE was ordered to focus on Yucca Mountain, Nevada, as the site for the repository."

McDonald reached into the rear seat and produced a couple of containers of bottled water. He handed one to Jack, opened his bottle and took a long swig.

"There must be a dozen task forces studying what would happen in case of an earthquake near Yucca Mountain. In one study, DOE projected what the environment will be like in the Yucca Mountain tunnels for the next 40,000 years. How crazy is that?"

"Does that mean," Jack asked, "that Yucca Mountain will solve the problem?" *If so, why would Sinclair think his Mexican alternative was such a big deal?*

"Not a chance. First, it could take another ten years and $80 billion more before it could open. Second, Yucca Mountain is designed to hold only 70,000 tons of nuclear waste. The existing backlog at nuclear power plants would fill it up in no time. Third, there's a big concern that water will seep into the tunnels and lead to chemical reactions that corrode the storage casks. If that happens, the contents could leak into the ground water. You may remember the Hanford atomic bomb building plant in Washington. The government is still storing over 50 million gallons of HLW in below-ground tanks. Some of those tanks are leaking and migrating to the Columbia River. It's a disaster."

Which is exactly what will happen at the Batopilas cave where not even one study of the water table has been done.

"But all that doesn't matter," Mac said, "because DOE has dropped funding for the project from the budget while they look for an alternative. Yucca Mountain is sacred land to the Western Shoshone. I think they put a hex on the project."

Another parallel with the Batopilas cave, Jack thought before he said, "So for political reasons this could go on indefinitely."

Mac nodded. "In desperation, the private sector took a swing at it. Eight nuclear power utilities got together and paid the Skull Valley Band of Goshute Indians to use part of its land as a site for temporary storage of nuclear waste. But since the site is only 60 miles from Salt Lake City, politicians stopped the project. Now a court has given it the go ahead. If it ever opens, utility companies will use the site for short term storage until they ship their nuclear waste somewhere else for permanent storage. Okay, there you have it," he concluded.

Jack shook his head in disbelief. Mac had just described the conditions that had inspired Sinclair to fill the void. "What a nightmare."

"And now," Mac said, "it's time you level with me. When you called me out of the blue a few days ago, you asked me to research the geology and hydraulics of an aquifer under El Paso and Ciudad Juarez and for a reference to someone who could analyze samples you'd taken. I did as you asked, and you outlined what the impending threat was. Then you asked me how nuclear waste is disposed of. I've explained that, but you haven't told me why you want to know."

"Okay. You deserve an answer. There's now an alternative to Skull Valley and Yucca Mountain. It's a remote cave in Mexico where U.S. companies, for huge fees, can ship whatever radioactive waste they want, in whatever containers they choose. I think when that cave is filled, it will be sealed up, leaving thousands of tons of nuclear waste simmering inside."

Mac's head jerked back. "That's nuts! Stored like that, radiation will leak into the atmosphere or into the groundwater. That stuff can generate enough heat to explode like a dirty bomb, bigger than Chernobyl."

"It could get worse," Jack said. "The grunts who operate the cave could sell nuclear waste to terrorists. Or terrorists could break in and steal what they want. Think what a panic that would cause."

Shaken by the parade of horrors, Mac's face lost color. "You think the same group is behind the cave and the threat to the aquifer? How can we find out who it is?"

He wanted to answer Mac's question, because if something went wrong he needed someone of stature who could make the facts public, tell the story. But that knowledge could also put Mac at great risk. Mac was a family man with two kids and a good life.

"Mac, I'm not sure I should answer that. I'm worried that telling you more could put you in danger."

Annoyance flashed in Mac's face. "Look, I've done what you asked, and I deserve to be in for the whole ride."

Jack considered what was at stake, and said, "You're right. You're in. Tomás Montana, manager of the Palmer Industries plant in Juarez intends to poison the aquifer. And I'm certain the entire smuggling scheme was organized by—" He paused, knowing how his words would affect Mac. "—former Secretary of State Justin Sinclair, managing partner of the law firm I used to work for."

Mac's jaw dropped. Twice he started to speak and couldn't get words out. He shook his head, swallowed hard, and said, "My God, you have to get the FBI, CIA or Homeland Security in on this before—"

Jack shook his head. "Too late for that. I have a meeting set for tomorrow at noon. That's when I'll blow the whistle."

"A meeting with whom?" Mac's squinted eyes broadcast his skepticism.

"The President of the United States, aboard Air Force One up at

Travis." He watched Mac's expression turn to total surprise.

"Whoa! You can do that?" Then Mac frowned. "But if Montana or Sinclair knows you're going to expose them, they have to stop you from getting to that meeting."

"I don't think Montana can reach this far, and Sinclair wouldn't have set up my meeting with Gorton if he had a clue I'm going to accuse him. Listen to me. I can handle this, and I don't want you involved any more than you already are. By the next time I see you, this will be over."

Mac gripped the steering wheel. "Look, the bad guys will have people watching your home in Atherton, all the airports, even the buses."

"They aren't the Mafia with a platoon of thugs on standby."

"You don't know what they have, so I'll ride shotgun for you up to Travis."

Ride shotgun. That's what Gano would have done. And Mac was leaving him no choice.

"Okay, but no heroics." He shook Mac's hand. "Now I have to go. Sam Butler called earlier wanting me to meet him in his office."

Mac frowned. "Butler can wait. You need to get out of sight. Now."

"Nope, I can't miss this one. I want to hear what he has to say." The only way Butler could have known he was in town was for Sinclair to have told him. He needed to find out why Sinclair did that.

"Then I'll park outside Butler's office and keep my eyes open."

Jack nodded, but as they drove back to the Sculpture Garden, he had an ache in his gut about letting Mac stay anywhere near him. If anything happened to him . . . But Mac was a tough guy. He knew this was risky and had *demanded* to be part of it. That didn't make Jack feel any less anxious. Somehow he knew that what he'd been through so far was nothing compared to what was coming up.

Chapter 46

July 11
6:00 p.m.

MAC PARKED HIS Land Rover about fifty feet away from Jack's BMW on the curve of Palm Drive, not far from the entrance to Butler's office. No longer a stodgy hydrology professor, Mac had morphed into a grim-faced bodyguard.

Jack left Mac in the Land Rover and took the stairs to Butler's office two at a time. At the door, instead of the usual tap-tap of the Olivetti, he heard a Mozart piano sonata. He rapped the glass firmly.

"Come in, Jack," called the familiar scratchy voice.

At first glance, the room was unchanged. Files, casebooks, legal publications, and clutter everywhere. Uncharacteristically, Butler was already on his way to the door. As they shook hands, Butler adjusted his glasses and peered intently at Jack's face, as if searching for something.

"I'm glad you could come by, my boy. You're just in time for a sip of some fine single malt. Be a good lad and pour, will you?" He pointed to a bottle and glasses on a bookshelf.

"Thanks. I'll take a rain check."

"Then pour one for me while I settle here in my favorite chair."

Sipping scotch, Butler made a few comments about a recent Supreme Court appointment and then halted abruptly. "Sorry Jack, I didn't stop to think that the Court might be a sore subject for you. I know you had hopes . . . well, let me tell you about a law review article I'm writing on the need to reform current practices of gerrymandering."

Jack noticed that Butler made no reference to Sinclair & Simms or Mexico even though he was certain Butler and Sinclair had discussed his departure from the firm. As he half-listened, he glanced around the office. Butler's love affair with Gauguin paintings had not lessened. Just below the two women carrying mangos was a new landscape, a rich brown field and a man wielding a hoe. It had a special radiant quality.

"Ah," Butler interrupted himself, "Gauguin has spirited you away from my prattle."

"That landscape is a beauty. It's new."

"Your memory must be failing. It's been here for some time. A reproduction, of course, but a good one. An old academic could never afford an original." He looked at Jack over the rims of his glasses with a self-deprecating smile. "You know, Gauguin fled to Tahiti for inspiration. Did Mexico work that way for you?"

Clever transition, but why had he lied about the landscape? It had definitely *not* been in this room the last time he was here.

"Mexico was no inspiration," he replied.

"Quite a few California businesses have a presence in Mexico. Were any of them your clients?"

Butler was sandbagging him—again. He must know about Palmer Industries. Okay, he'd play along. "Yes, one with a big operation in Juarez. As it turned out, I caught them planning some criminal activities."

"What did you do about it?" Butler asked casually.

"Not much . . . yet." He wasn't about to tell that story.

"But you confronted the company?"

"When I told the CEO what I knew, he pretended to be shocked and denied any involvement." He wanted to hear what had caused Butler to call the meeting, but decided to troll a little. "What do you think I should do?"

"Turning against your client can have a damaging effect on your own career. Are you willing to step into the spotlight again? As one sage said, 'You need to know when to hold them; know when to fold them.'" Butler leaned back, sloshed his scotch on the insides of the glass and took a deep sniff of the aroma. "My advice is to look out for yourself." He absentmindedly drained his scotch.

So that's why Butler had called, to talk him into walking away from Palmer Industries.

"Sam, I have to go now." He stood. "I'll think about what you—"

"Sit down, Jack. We're not done here." Without raising his voice, Butler had issued a blunt command, totally out of character. "After you left Justin's office earlier today, he called me because he knows you and I are good friends. He brought me up-to-date and said he was afraid you were about to make a very serious mistake. He was referring to—"

"I know exactly what he was referring to."

"I see. Well, you might say I'm acting as *amicus curiae*, an advisor, a messenger between two friends to help avoid an unnecessary conflict. Justin authorized me to say that he feels he's in the best position to resolve the issues in this Palmer matter. He would appreciate your agreement to let him take full responsibility for his client. He knows you have strong feelings about it, so he made the following proposal." As if sensing Jack was about to object, he said, "Listen carefully. It would be in no one's best interest for you to return to Sinclair & Simms. And the chairmanship of the international law department has been awarded to Professor Greenwald, so that's no longer available. However, I will arrange for you to regain your tenured position on the law school faculty, get you back in the teaching rotation next quarter, and have you appointed assistant Dean, presumptive replacement for Dean Thompson when he retires. All of this will take considerable effort on my part, but I'm willing to go out on a limb for you." Butler gave him a grandfatherly smile.

He sensed Butler wasn't finished, so he held his tongue.

Apparently unruffled by Jack's silence, Butler continued, "Or if you prefer to remain in private practice, choose one of the top firms in New York City, and we'll give you an introduction and references that will assure a partnership. Since your specialty is international law, I recommend Debevois & Plimpton in Manhattan with offices in London, Paris, Moscow, and the other usual places. If you want to be where the action is, take their Shanghai office."

After making his pitch, Butler seemed almost shrunken in his worn leather chair. He interlaced his fingers and looked at the Benjamin clock, head cocked, listening to it. After a dozen or so more ticks, he grew impatient.

"Well, my boy, which do you prefer?"

They'd been so slick, trying to read his mind, ready to switch bait until he bit. Slick and damned insulting, thinking they could buy him. Sinclair was so corrupt that he assumed corruption in everyone else.

"I'm impressed by the leverage you have with Thompson—" He was neither impressed nor surprised, but felt like making the dig. "—but I have a job to finish."

Butler's mouth tightened, as if he had to squeeze out the next words against his will. "Justin predicted you might say that, so he wanted to stress that he can return that situation in Mexico to the *status quo ante*. His only goal is to make things right. To do that, he'll reverse all arguably unlawful actions taken by the general manager that are the cause of your concern. Some actions can be reversed immediately. Others will take longer but can begin at once. Within an hour after you accept this package, Montana will be fired and removed from the plant. In return for all this, you agree not to pursue Arthur Palmer or Palmer Industries. You'll sign an oath of absolute confidentiality. And, of course, there would be no point in meeting with President Gorton tomorrow—or anytime.

"It's time," Butler said firmly, "for you to examine your motives in this matter. If you're in this for publicity, or revenge against Arthur Palmer, or even for the thrill of the chase, you should consider the damage you're going to do. If you really want to repair the situation in Mexico, you can't predict whether President Gorton will believe you or, if he does, feel that any action by him in Mexico is warranted. In fact, you may find yourself in some cubbyhole talking to an intern instead of the President. In contrast, Justin can guarantee the results you say you want and give you your life back. It's not my style to be blunt, but if you don't accept this proposal at once, it will be withdrawn. In that case you will fail to improve the situation in Mexico and will incur certain substantial liabilities."

Jack almost laughed. *First the carrot, then the sledge hammer.* It seemed rational to take the deal. Sinclair could make good on all the things he offered. If Jack refused the offer, he'd have to persuade the President to condemn Sinclair, his friend for decades. And Sinclair would put the Sinclair & Simms machine in attack mode against Jack Strider. So it would be rational, *except that the offer was a total hoax.*

If he accepted, Sinclair would cancel the meeting with Gorton with enough innuendo that Jack would never get another one. That done, Sinclair had no intention of doing what he promised. Sinclair was bargaining for time to silence Jack. With a start he realized that Sinclair might target Debra, too. She was safe at the moment, but he had to let her know how things stood.

Somehow, all the threats weren't having much effect on him. Maybe he'd been threatened too often recently. Or maybe he now felt he could handle anything they threw at him. Maybe they were just too late, because he'd set his course and damn the torpedoes. Whichever, it was time to bring down the curtain on this act.

Without looking up from his glass, now empty, Butler said quietly, "I remind you that time is of the essence."

Butler had pressured him to decide on whether to take the job with S & S, and Jack had made that decision within the time limit. This time he'd march to his own beat. He stood and looked at Butler for several seconds.

"I'll think about it." He walked across the old wood floor and out the door. Even though the time when Butler had been friend and mentor seemed long ago, he felt a sense of loss. He knew he'd never be back.

AS HE WALKED toward his car, Jack saw Mac get out of his Land Rover, look around, then head his way. As soon as they were both in the BMW, Mac said, "What was so important to Butler?"

Jack told him about the offer.

"My God," Mac said, "you must have Sinclair cornered."

"Yeah, well, everyone knows a cornered beast is extremely dangerous. Look, Sinclair orchestrated every step of his scheme brilliantly so far. He hasn't suddenly gotten stupid. If I get Gorton to stop Montana from poisoning that aquifer, that won't burn Sinclair at all. He's just their corporate lawyer. So why would he make me such an over-the-top offer when negotiating with me must piss him off? There's something wrong with that."

"Maybe he just wants to avoid the hassle."

Jack shook his head. "No, there's only one explanation. He must have gotten a report that there were intruders at the cave. Maybe he even got inside information from D-TECH too. That would tell him the smuggling and the cave are in play. That *he* is in play." The logical extension of that insight shocked him into silence. Sinclair's only move was obvious. "He knows I won't back down and that he can't bribe me, so he has to prevent me from getting to Air Force One. And even that won't be enough. He has to stop me from going public anywhere, or dropping out of sight to resurface later."

"That means *killing* you," Mac said in a hushed voice. "Would he go that far?"

"Of course," Jack said with certainty. "Only God knows how much violence he authorized as Secretary of State, but I suspect he developed a taste for it. He sees himself as a righteous king, justified in crushing anyone who tries to knock him off his throne. He'll do everything he can to kill me before noon tomorrow."

Jack saw in Mac's pallid face that he was getting all the implications.

"Let's have a reality check," Mac said. "Suppose there's no meeting at all, that Sinclair's playing you to get you out in the open."

"I checked with the White House, but the public relations people won't confirm or deny appointments. Could Sinclair be faking it? Possible, but I'm sure he hadn't made the connection between me and his smuggling scheme when he made the appointment. I think it's still on, and I will be there. Besides, Butler stressed that I had to make a decision quickly so the meeting could be cancelled. He thinks it's real."

Mac frowned and drummed his fingers against his knee. "I still don't see why Sinclair set up that meeting."

"I surprised him and forced him to make a quick decision. We were discussing only dumping toxics into the aquifer, and he probably doesn't have exposure on that. And maybe he's confident he's kept his fingerprints off everything, even the smuggling. He thought that lack of evidence, coupled with his long friendship with Gorton, would let him skate. So he made the right decision for himself even though it will sink his client. What he really didn't want was for me to hold a press conference that would smear him. So he arranged for Gorton to give me only fifteen minutes. Not much time to get my story told. I'm sure he's already stacked the deck against me, but I'll deal with that."

"Okay, that's why he'd set up a meeting, but he's had second thoughts big time or he wouldn't have had Butler offer you the moon. By now, Butler has told him you won't back off, so it's too dangerous for you to spend the night at home. Get a room at the Westin on El Camino Real. I'll come with you."

"No," Jack said. "I'll get the room, but you go home to your family. And don't show up tomorrow, my friend. I'll handle this on my own."

Mac slammed his fist on the dashboard.

"Shit." Jack said as he jumped, taken completely by surprise.

Mac glared at him. "You're talking about *my* country, *my* family. You have no right to let what you know get buried with you."

"I have no intention of being buried."

"And you won't be, because I'll have your back." His eyes were blazing, challenging Jack.

Mac was right, and they both knew it.

Jack didn't like it, but he relented. "Pick me up at 7:30 tomorrow morning. We'll drive together to Travis."

"I'll be there. Keep your eyes sharp between now and then."

Mac walked back to his Land Rover, and Jack pulled away. In his rearview mirror, Jack saw that Mac didn't get in until he was sure no one was following the BMW.

As the university campus faded from sight, he resented going into hiding. But being attacked by Montana's thugs only a week ago was vivid in his mind. Even a quick stop at home to pick up fresh clothes was too risky, so he turned down El Camino and into the Stanford Shopping Center where Brooks Brothers had everything he needed to be presentable on Air Force One. Next, he picked up a pepperoni pizza at the Oasis. It felt weird to watch for a face that might look suspicious in the familiar student hangout.

He checked in at the Westin and worked until after midnight, organizing his presentation to Gorton. He kept expecting a call from Gano with the information he'd asked him to get, a piece of the proof he needed for Gorton. The call didn't come. When he finally stacked his notes and clicked off the light, he was ready to step onto a high wire without a net at tomorrow's meeting.

Chapter 47

July 12
7:00 a.m.

THE UNRELENTING beep finally drilled into Jack's brain. It took a moment to locate the phone and fumble it to his ear.

It was the voice of the hotel's impassive mechanical concierge. "Good morning. It is seven a.m. The temperature is sixty-two degrees. Your personal copy of the *San Francisco Chronicle* is outside your door. Have a nice day."

A nice day? Not likely. And the night hadn't been very nice either, full of stressful dreams. He felt wrung out.

In the bathroom, he forced a smile to improve the weary expression he saw in the mirror. After a hot shower, he used the towel like a shoeshine rag to stimulate his body into full consciousness. Within minutes, he was in his new Brooks Brothers black suit, white shirt and burgundy tie. His objective was initial credibility with the President of the United States.

His cell phone started buzzing. Caller ID told him it was Gano.

"Morning Gano. You're just in time."

"Yeah, well, you owe me four hundred bucks, Mr. Paymaster. That's U.S. money." The Louisiana accent was like molasses. "The damn Mexican highway patrol claimed they clocked me at 110. Fined me, payable on the spot."

Jack didn't even bother to ask if the police had been right. "I'll pay. What did you find out?"

"Don't get your knickers in a knot, old boy. I figured if I started tracking those trucks anywhere near the cave the crews would be on me like woodpeckers on a June bug. So I parked on a side street in Batopilas to ambush 'em. Sure enough, four of those big mothers rattled past. I got a few photos but they're not great. I'll send them to your cell phone. Anyway, as soon as they passed me, in tight formation like the Blue Angels, I let some other folks get between us, then settled in for the trip back to the Palmer plant. It was all good 'til we got close to Chihuahua City. You said all four trucks would turn north onto 45D toward Juarez."

"Right."

"Wrong. Only the first two went north on 45D North. The other two split off, so I swung into the middle lane to stick with them. When one of them suddenly turned onto 45D South, I was way out of position to follow. All I could do was chase the last one into Chihuahua City."

Something was wrong. "The one that turned south, any idea where it was headed?"

"Could be Monterey, Guadalajara, even Mexico City. *Quien sabe?*"

"Who knows" wasn't good enough. He needed proof of the route the trucks took, and Gano didn't have it. The fact that the trucks split up meant something. He had to figure out what.

"You didn't lose the last one did you?"

"Hell no," Gano said. "I ain't no amateur. As soon as he turned toward the city, the truck jockey pulled over next to an all-night burrito joint. It looked like they were settling in for a while, so I jumped back on the highway and gunned it after the two trucks heading north."

A soft knock on the door was followed by George McDonald's voice. "Jack? You ready to roll?"

"Just a second, Gano." He opened the door. "Hey, glad to see you, Mac. As soon as I get off the phone, I'll move my BMW to underground parking. It was full when I got here last night."

"I scoped out the parking lot. No unfriendlies in sight. I'll move your car, then pick you up at the side exit in my Land Rover."

Feeling rushed, he gave Mac the BMW keys and got back to the conversation with Gano. "Where are you now?"

"After I followed the trucks to the Palmer plant, I crossed into El Paso."

"Great. I need to know where Montana is."

"I'll track him down and give you a shout. Have to go now. I'm losing bars on the phone. *Hasta luego.*"

JACK PUSHED through the Westin's side exit door onto the parking lot. The air was crisp, the sky clear and sunny. Quite a contrast with his mood. He expected to see Mac in his Land Rover, but he wasn't there. Maybe he was having trouble with the BMW. He walked closer to where he'd parked the night before and saw the BMW, motionless, partly backed out of the numbered space where he'd left it. That was odd. Engine trouble? Still a row away, he heard the motor running so he walked toward the passenger's side—and stopped in his tracks.

The passenger's window was a sagging web of safety glass, opaque because of a pink mist washing down the inside surface. Heart pounding, he rushed around to the driver's side.

Through the open window, he saw Mac slumped at a sharp angle to his right, the seat belt keeping him from falling over. His thick hair looked like a blood-soaked sponge. The left shoulder of his jacket was bloody from a second wound.

Fighting not to throw up, Jack spun around, looking for the shooter. A middle-aged man was helping an elderly woman into a car. A man in a gray uniform stood behind a grocery delivery truck. None of them was acting as if they'd just heard gunfire.

He stood by his car in shock, unable to process what had happened, unable to move. He couldn't take his eyes off Mac's brutalized brain and inert body.

Mac had insisted on coming along as his bodyguard, flexing the warrior nature that had made him a champion boxer. With apparently no warning, not even a split second to get his guard up, he'd gone from being a brilliant professor and powerful man to being dead.

But maybe Mac wasn't dead. He forced himself to lean forward and press his fingers to the side of Mac's throat. No sign of life. Then his left wrist. Nothing.

"Oh my God, Mac." He felt completely responsible. He'd drawn Mac into this. Let him get too close. But he had to hold back his grief. He should call 911 or notify the hotel staff to get the police. But if he was detained and questioned, he'd miss his crucial meeting with the President. He hated leaving Mac to be discovered by a stranger, but he had no choice. It wouldn't be long before some hotel guest walked up to the car to ask the driver to move it.

The wallet would identify Professor George McDonald, but ownership of the car would be traced to Jack Strider, and the hunt would be on. He had to get to Travis Air Force Base before they could catch him.

He thought about taking Mac's Land Rover, but there was no way he'd try to dig the keys from his friend's pocket. Glancing around, he started across the parking lot toward an Enterprise car rental office across the road. From force of habit he asked the clerk for a convertible, but switched to a black Honda sedan. He needed to be inconspicuous. He tried to pay in cash to avoid leaving a trail, but the agent insisted he use a credit card. Walking to the assigned car, he fought against a surge of nausea.

He drove north on El Camino for a few minutes, then turned east and caught the 101 on-ramp north toward San Francisco. The most common route would be to stay on it to the City and cross the Bay Bridge. Instead, he turned east in Menlo Park to use the Dumbarton Bridge to cross the Bay, a much less predictable way to Travis.

As soon as he settled into a groove on the freeway, his mind filled with images of George McDonald in the BMW. Given the high crime rate in the

Bay Area, the CHP would think it had been a botched robbery. But then they would notice what he had—a bullet embedded in the frame just above the driver's window. That meant at least three gunshots, and they had *not* been fired by someone standing next to the car. They'd come from farther away. He remembered seeing a dense grove of sycamores beyond the last row of parked cars. From there, a sniper would have had a clear line-of-sight to the BMW. The assassin had found him at the Westin and staked out his car. He and Mac were similar enough in build that, from a distance, a shooter expecting Jack Strider to be getting into the BMW hadn't realized the target in his sights was a different man. Jack had no doubt that Justin Sinclair had hired the hit man. Question was, had the hit man stayed close enough to the hotel to realize his mistake? And, if so, where was he now?

If Jack called off the meeting with Gorton, the President would forget the name Jack Strider by sunset. But Sinclair wouldn't forget. It had been in Sinclair's best interest to set up the meeting with Gorton. But everything had changed since then. Sinclair now knew he was in great danger, so he'd never permit Jack to reach Gorton, and he'd never let Jack escape. That's why he'd issued a death sentence.

A red Ford sports car swerved past on his left, horn blaring. He deserved it. He'd drifted halfway out of his lane, nearly sideswiping the Ford. That forced him to pay attention to the dense freeway traffic as he sped north past Berkeley.

His eyes flicked repeatedly to the rearview mirror, scanning for any vehicle appearing to be trailing him. He should be anonymous in a rental car picked up less than an hour ago, but he felt as though his caution lights were flashing to attract attention.

Just beyond Vallejo, highway signs led him to the small town of Fairfield and the mammoth Travis Air Force Base. He stopped several hundred yards short of the main entrance and watched. Lots of people walking, most in uniform, many parked cars with couples in them. *Trying to identify a shooter was nuts.* Shooters made themselves unnoticeable. He tried to convince himself that Sinclair had called off the assassin because he thought he'd been successful. That didn't work. What did work was telling himself that security was so tight around this base that an assassin would have to be suicidal to start shooting.

He had another problem. A big one. The two people he needed with him in the meeting were missing. He called Debra, but got her voicemail. He said, "I hope you're almost at Travis because the meeting starts in a few minutes. I was planning to bring both you and Gano in with me, but now I'll have to leave passes at the gate for you. If you're still where I sent you when you hear this, stay there."

He waited another few minutes, then drove to the gate. The guard stepped to the car window and asked stiffly for his identification and destination.

"Jack Strider. I have a meeting aboard Air Force One. Here's my driver's license."

The guard took it and disappeared inside the guardhouse. When he hadn't returned after several long minutes, Jack grew suspicious. By now the CHP had his name. Could they have already connected him with the rental car and put out an APB?

Suddenly, the man returned. "You're cleared to go aboard, sir." He returned the license.

"Thanks. I also need you to get passes ready for two people who'll be joining me on Air Force One."

"Beg your pardon, sir, but you're just a visitor yourself, so I have no authority to write a pass like that. It would have to come from the Commanding Officer of the Base or from the White House."

This was a fight he wasn't going to win in the few minutes he had left. "I understand. When they arrive and mention my name, please contact Air Force One immediately. The President will want to see them."

"I'll tell the Captain of the Guard about your request, sir. Now please park over there. Master Chief Williams will drive you to Air Force One." He snapped a crisp salute and held it as Jack drove to the small parking area.

By God, he'd made it here. Then the pain hit him. *But Mac hadn't. If it was the last thing he ever did, he'd make Sinclair pay for that.*

Chapter 48

July 12
11:30 a.m.

MASTER CHIEF Williams drove up beside Jack in a black sedan, saluted, and asked him to hold out his left hand. The Chief looped a self-locking plastic strip around Jack's wrist and pulled it snug. From it hung a multicolored badge with strings of numbers and an imbedded holographic design.

They drove past several office buildings into an area of huge hangars. Following a trail of red markers in the asphalt, Williams turned past the last hangar and there, less than fifty yards ahead, was Air Force One, gleaming in the sunlight. It looked as he'd seen it in news clips showing one president or another descending the roll-up staircase, waving at real or imaginary crowds. The giant Boeing 747-200B, white with powder blue trim, stood at the center of a ring of armored vehicles. There was the Presidential seal on the nose, the words "United States of America" on the side of the fuselage, and the American flag painted on the tail. It was called Air Force One when the president was aboard even though its tail number read 28000.

The layout of the interior of the plane was classified, but he knew that the cockpit and communications center were on the top level with the bottom level used for cargo and equipment. The presidential suite was all the way forward on the main deck.

Williams escorted him to the bottom of the flight of steps used by the President. "Sorry for the inconvenience, sir, but I'll have to keep your cell phone and any other electronic devices before you go aboard." He smiled, even though his implication was that Jack might be about to blow up Air Force One.

Jack handed them over, and Williams placed them in a leather pouch, locked it, saluted, and got back into his sedan. While Jack was climbing the stairs, hypothetical shifted to cold reality. He had fifteen minutes to gain the trust of the President and motivate him to stop two looming catastrophes. It was all on him.

A Marine sergeant standing behind a stainless steel podium at the top of the stairs examined the wrist badge, scanned it with a hand-held device, and used a headphone to confirm Jack's identity. He then searched Jack's briefcase. Only then did he snap a heel-clicking salute.

A Chief Communications Officer joined them. "Good morning, Mr. Strider. I'll take you to Sitting Room B. The President will send for you when he's ready."

They walked past a galley and a large room nearly the width of the plane. "That's the President's conference room," the officer said. "Those paintings are of earlier presidential aircraft. The one at this end with the label Sacred Cow is FDR's C-54 Skymaster. Farther down is President Nixon's Spirit of 1976. And, of course, those black and white photos are aerial shots of President Gorton's ranch."

Farther aft, beyond a movable barrier, he saw a few rows of seats marked for reporters, all empty.

"Where is everyone?"

"They aren't permitted to board until the President passes the word that he's ready to depart. Most of them wait at the Officer's Club."

Just past the conference room, he was shown into Sitting Room B which was set up as a working office space with computers and phones. He checked his watch. 11:45 a.m. Perfect timing for a noon appointment.

He breathed deeply, trying to steady his nerves. This setting was much less imposing than the Oval Office would have been, but the President was no less the President. He visualized a minute of small talk followed by Gorton asking what made it so important that they meet. He was ready with that answer.

At noon he stood up, expecting a knock at the door. It didn't come.

By 12:15 p.m. he was mentally bouncing off the walls. Had this delay cancelled the pitiful fifteen minutes he'd been allotted? Had Gorton forgotten him? He picked up a phone but realized how out of bounds it would be to complain that the President was keeping him waiting.

At 12:20 p.m. his internal clock was ticking so fiercely that each second had become an electrode shocking his brain. Something must be wrong. He tried the door handle of Sitting Room B. It opened. Seconds after he poked his head out, the Chief appeared.

"May I help you, sir?" He conveyed respect for anyone on the President's calendar, along with disapproval of that person for having left his assigned space without being summoned.

"I was supposed to meet President Gorton at noon."

"Yes, sir. I'm sure it won't be long." He smiled and nodded as if sharing inside information.

Jack retreated and continued pacing. Less than five minutes later a knock came and the Chief opened the door.

"Sir, I just took coffee service in to the President and handed him a note that his twelve o'clock appointment was here. He said you should come right in. Please follow me, sir."

When he entered the conference room, President Gorton was coming toward him from the far end of the gleaming redwood table. Medium height, a few pounds overweight, his black leather flight jacket had a "Commander-in-Chief" insignia embroidered on the chest, surrounded by a circle of five-pointed stars. He looked like an image on a wartime recruiting poster.

"Damn good thing the Chief told me you were out there." He flashed his trademark grin, shook hands firmly and gave Jack's shoulder a squeeze followed by a friendly slap. "My friend here told me you must have decided to cancel." He waved an arm casually in the direction of the other man in the room who stood next to a porthole, facing them.

Justin Sinclair stayed where he was, brushing a speck of lint from the sleeve of a dark gray suit that radiated genteel extravagance.

Jack had considered the possibility that Sinclair would show up at this meeting, so his game plan prepared him to counter. But that was before the son-of-a-bitch had tried to have him assassinated; before he'd had Mac murdered in a parking lot. He felt a rush of rage, his face hot. He wanted to run across the room and beat the coldhearted bastard's face into the bulkhead, pound that cynical smile off Sinclair's face. He could feel his hands gripping the man's throat. But that would end the meeting with Gorton. Too high a price.

At Jack's first step forward, Sinclair took a reflexive step back.

Years of training enabled Jack to get control of himself. He had to keep his anger from knocking him off his game plan. He could do that. The moment of danger had passed. Gorton might not have noticed the moment he'd lost it, but Sinclair had—and that was good.

Sinclair had a big edge. He'd been in the room alone with Gorton, peddling his poisonous fiction. But now Jack had an edge too: Sinclair's heart must have skipped a few beats when Gorton told the Chief to bring in a man Sinclair thought was dead. It was a shame the intervening minute had given him time to make his face impassive.

To most people, Sinclair's bushy eyebrows and slightly drooping lids made him look a little sleepy, but Jack knew he was as alert as a cheetah poised to pounce on a gazelle. Sinclair's prey, in or out of the courtroom, seldom escaped. The floor of the legal jungle was littered with the bones of lawyers who had antagonized Sinclair, but Jack was ready to take him on, right here, right now. This was no longer a matter of making a carefully crafted argument to a skeptical President. *This was war.*

"In your absence, Mr. Strider," Gorton said, showing no intention of resuming his seat at the end of the table, "Justin briefed me on those allegations of environmental violations in Mexico you wanted to see me about. I agree with him that any infractions can be handled by—was it Palmer, Justin?—yes, by Palmer Industries with the firm guidance of Justin's law firm. Best all around to keep the public out of this thing. I'm sure you agree."

"No, sir. I don't agree, and I don't think you will either if I may speak with you for just a few minutes."

From the far end of the room, Sinclair broke in. "Time to drop it, Strider. I gave the President all the salient details. Obviously he's satisfied."

"That's about it, Mr. Strider," Gorton said. "Justin also mentioned that you've been under considerable strain and tend to grow overly alarmed about what are quite manageable situations. Sorry you made the trip to Travis for nothing. I'll have the Chief arrange a VIP tour of the Base for you."

Sinclair had done his work well. No wonder the bastard was always the last man standing. *But not this time.* Jack had scores to settle for Mac, Ana-Maria and Juanita. Gorton could take his VIP tour and stuff it.

Gorton's hand returned to Jack's shoulder, this time to steer him toward the door. Jack braced himself and stopped his motion. Gorton stepped back looking perplexed.

"Mr. President. It's vital to you and our national security that I outline this situation for you myself. Since this meeting is supposed to be between the two of us, I respectfully request that Mr. Sinclair wait outside."

"You ingrate." Sinclair's voice rose. "Don't you dare suggest I haven't told the President everything he needs to know. A man with a reputation as disgraceful as yours has no credibility in this room."

"Hold on, Justin," Gorton broke in, looking perplexed. "You didn't tell me he has a disgraceful reputation. If that's true, why the hell did you insist I meet with him in the first place?"

"I set this up only because Strider threatened to go public with his crazy stories. I thought it was worth investing fifteen minutes and getting him off our backs. As far as what I said about him earlier, I was trying to be kind. The fact is that he was fired by the law school where he taught."

"That's not true," Jack protested.

"But you told me you hired him for your firm," Gorton said.

"That was a mistake. I had a specific job to be done in Mexico that I thought he could handle. Instead, he caused so much trouble I had to fire him. He—"

"Mr. President," Jack interrupted, "there are two situations that need your immediate action. The first involves poisoning a major aquifer that two million people depend on. If it's destroyed, El Paso and Ciudad Juarez in Mexico will turn into ghost towns."

"Just a damn minute," Gorton said. "Destroy the El Paso water supply? Are you saying there's some terrorist plot? We've always been worried about the vulnerability of—"

"Pardon me, sir," Jack interrupted. "It's not terrorism. It's the greed of an American company. That's what I need to tell you about."

Gorton grimaced and glanced at Sinclair. "All right, I'll listen for a minute. Take a seat here at this end of the table." Gorton sat at the other end of the conference table. Sinclair sat at his right.

The conference table seemed as long as a bowling alley. The psychological distance felt even greater.

"Mr. President, Palmer Industries, a California corporation, set up a facility on the outskirts of Juarez to treat and dispose of extremely hazardous waste trucked in from all over the U.S."

"All perfectly legal," Sinclair said.

"Only as long as Palmer Industries obeys Mexican laws . . . which it doesn't. That's why PROFEPA, the Mexican environmental protection agency, tried to get an injunction to shut it down. Mr. Sinclair ordered me to defend Palmer whether they were guilty or not. Then Palmer Industries bribed the prosecuting attorneys and the judge and got the complaint dismissed with prejudice. But it gets much worse. Rather than spend the money to treat some of the lethal chemical and biological waste, the manager of the Palmer Industries plant, Tomás Montana, has been pumping it into huge tanks on top of a mesa near the plant. From there, he built a pipeline to three injection wells. Those wells drain straight into the aquifer that serves El Paso and Juarez."

Sinclair snorted. "Strider, you're delusional."

Jack took a folder from his briefcase and held it up. "This statement, prepared by a Stanford hydrologist, describes the geology of the area and the vulnerability of the aquifer." He took out a second folder. "I also have a statement from a scientist at the University of Texas at El Paso. It's an analysis of the contents of the tanks on the mesa that shows how deadly they are. And here are photographs I took of the tanks and the wells."

He walked the length of the table and held them out to Gorton. The President merely nodded and indicated that he should set them down.

He returned to his seat and continued, "The wells were damaged three days ago, but Montana could have it operational almost immediately. After he dumps that toxic material into the aquifer, El Paso and Juarez will be uninhabitable. The Mexican government won't stop him, and the Juarez police are in his pocket. When Montana pulls the lever, there will be an international catastrophe with an American corporation as the proximate cause."

"Good God!" Gorton exclaimed and looked at Sinclair. "What's going on here? You told me you're their general counsel. How could you let this happen?"

Sinclair looked indignant. "As I told you earlier, I can handle it."

"The President won't think so when I tell him the rest of the story." Jack consulted his yellow pad. "After I met with PROFEPA on June thirtieth, I told Mr. Sinclair that Palmer was guilty as charged by PROFEPA. Four days later, I told him that Palmer should settle and comply in full."

"On July 9th, three days ago, I informed Mr. Sinclair how Montana intended to poison the aquifer and that he should be arrested and the wells dismantled immediately. I also told him that Montana's people had shot at me and that two women who could have testified against him had been murdered. Mr. Sinclair could have stopped Montana right then. Instead, he did nothing."

"You're lying," Sinclair shouted. "You gave me that cockamamie story with absolutely no proof. Against my better judgment, I passed it on to Arthur Palmer to take whatever action he saw fit, if any. But the one I should have stopped was you." He withdrew a folded sheet of paper from his inside breast pocket. "Justin, this is a letter Strider wrote me just prior to the Hearing pertaining to the minor charges made against Palmer Industries by PROFEPA. He'd become so fanatical in his belief that Palmer Industries was doing terrible things that he was determined to make the company suffer. He said that if the judge didn't penalize Palmer, he would betray his own client and put them out of business. When the judge decided in Palmer's favor, Strider and some other thug trespassed on plant grounds and tried to burn the place down. He's wanted for a dozen felonies in Mexico. He's here because he wants revenge."

Damn it! He'd known Sinclair might use that letter to get him in trouble with the Bar, but he hadn't expected to be confronted with it on Air Force One.

Gorton scanned the letter and leaned forward. "Mr. Strider, this letter certainly undermines your credibility. Do you challenge its authenticity?"

"No, sir."

"And when you said the pipeline system had been 'damaged,' that was a result of your taking the law into your own hands?" He pulled open a drawer under the table, took out a black cigar, and lit it. "I may have to hand you over to the Secret Service until we sort this out."

"Sir, I decided to act in the public interest even though the Bar association might question me about it later." He felt conflicted. If they kept talking about the aquifer, his time would run out before he could warn the President about the nuclear waste smuggling. He had to change the subject and keep talking.

"Mr. President, my time with you is limited, and there's another extremely urgent matter you need to know about."

"Stop it!" Sinclair exploded. "This fellow simply cannot be believed. You know the aphorism, 'Like father, like son.' Jack Strider is the son of H. Peckford Strider who was responsible for the deaths of innocent young girls and the scourge of AIDS he imported across our border. The San Francisco District Attorney is investigating Strider to determine whether he would be prosecuted for involvement in the multiple felonies committed by his father."

"Judge Peckford Strider," Gorton said. "I hadn't made that connection."

Jack saw uncertainty in Gorton's eyes as he took a long draw on his cigar. The smoke he blew at the ceiling immediately swirled back down toward the table.

"Mr. President," Jack said, "may I respond?"

Gorton waved his cigar in reluctant acquiescence.

"Mr. Sinclair said I was fired by Stanford Law School. That's not true. I resigned from the school to accept an offer from Mr. Sinclair to become a partner in Sinclair & Simms. The Dean of the law school will confirm my resignation."

"I made that offer," Sinclair said, "before his father's crimes were splashed all over the front page of the *San Francisco Chronicle*. You have no idea—"

Gorton silenced Sinclair with a stern look and nodded for Jack to continue.

"Mr. Sinclair knew my father well for more than thirty years, knew him as a highly respected judge. Yet he has the gall to use guilt by association to try to discredit me, the same tactic used by the late Senator Joseph McCarthy."

Despite Jack's rebuttal, Sinclair looked composed, obviously confident that his status as a trusted advisor was enough of a shield.

"Justin, your attempt to impugn Mr. Strider's character was less than successful," Gorton said caustically. "Mr. Strider, before we were interrupted you wanted to raise some other issue. Keep it short so I can get back to Washington before my term expires."

Jack checked his watch. 12:40. *Still no Debra.* At any moment Gorton might give the signal to get Air Force One ready for takeoff.

"What I'm going to tell you about is potentially more dangerous to the United States, and to you personally, than the threat to the aquifer."

Gorton took several short drags on the cigar, and another cloud of smoke added to the miasma in the conference room. "That sounds very unpleasant, Mr. Strider, which means I should hear about it. Go ahead."

"It's about illegal disposal of high level nuclear waste." *It was done.*

"Stop!" Sinclair roared. "I won't stand for this. Jason, don't let him take us on another wild goose chase." Red-faced, nostrils flared, he looked like he was about to have a stroke.

"Justin—" Now Gorton was angry. "—be quiet. I am damn well going to hear this."

Jack was ready. "For at least several months, power plants, hospitals, research labs, and maybe some government weapons facilities have been illegally shipping high level nuclear waste to a place called—" He paused and watched Sinclair. "—D-TECH."

Sinclair's face tightened.

Gotcha.

"Where is this D-TECH?" Gorton asked. "Who owns it?"

"It's a 'gray company' near Mescalero in the New Mexico desert. I don't yet know who owns it."

"Look," Gorton said impatiently, "we have a half-dozen agencies dealing with nuclear waste issues. If you see some problem, take it to one of them and they'll do . . . something."

Jack shook his head. "This is way out of any bureaucrat's league. You're the only one who can deal with it. The nuclear waste I'm talking about doesn't stay at D-TECH. It's loaded into trucks that are driven across the border into Mexico."

"Impossible!" Gorton exclaimed and sat up straight in his chair. "There's no way the Mexican government has approved that. It would take five years of negotiations and hundreds of millions in sweeteners before they'd help us like that. But wait a minute." His brow furrowed. "How do they get it across the border without being stopped?"

"Bribes. Or maybe the guards won't inspect trucks with hazardous waste symbols. Inspections may be tight on the U.S. side when cargo is coming north, but heading south the Mexican guards don't care much. After the trucks cross the border, they go straight to Palmer Industries in Juarez where they take on fuel."

"Palmer Industries?" Gorton's voice rose in pitch. "You mean all this stuff is connected?"

"To Strider everything is connected to Palmer Industries," Sinclair scoffed. "He's obsessed by it."

"Sir," Jack said, "may I lay out the rest of this?"

Gorton made some notes on a previously untouched yellow pad then jerked his head at Jack to continue.

"They switch crews so no one knows the whole route. With new drivers, the trucks head south past Batopilas and offload into a heavily-guarded cave at the closed end of a box canyon. Then the trucks go back to Palmer Industries, pick up the original drivers, and return to D-TECH."

Gorton looked up from his pad. "If the Mexicans had approved a facility for storage of nuclear waste, I'd know about it."

"I've seen that cave," Jack said. "The government can't have approved it for anything. It's filled with piles of metal drums, concrete crates—"

"Did you see any long cylindrical shapes?" Gorton looked worried.

He gets it. He understands there's highly radioactive waste in the cave. Jack felt triumphant. "Yes, sir. Quite a few."

Gorton squinted at Sinclair whose face was as stony as a West Virginia road cut. No doubt he has a cover story ready, Jack thought, but he has to be sweating, not knowing what's coming next.

"Jason, don't let Strider's fairy-tale make you react without thinking it through." Sinclair had changed tactics, using a composed tone to say, *Listen to me. I'm the voice of reason.*

"Are you saying Strider's lying about this?" Gorton asked.

"Of course he is, and for the same reason he made up that story about an aquifer being poisoned. He's lying because Arthur Palmer has been riding him since the day they met, trying to get me to fire him. He claims he was assaulted in Juarez by thugs sent by Montana, but he has no proof of that either. And did you report anything to the police, Mr. Strider?" He barely paused. "Of course not. He's so hostile toward Palmer Industries that he was ready to violate his fiduciary duty and help PROFEPA shut them down. You read his letter." Sinclair managed to look as affronted as if he represented all lawyers everywhere. "And remember, he's a wanted man in Mexico. The Secret Service should take custody of him right now."

"That's such a standard tactic," Jack said to Sinclair. "Attack me because you can't refute anything I said. I'm convinced Tom Montana and Palmer Industries are a menace. If the Juarez police want to talk with me, it's because I tried to stop Montana. When I was attacked in Juarez, a senior associate in your law firm was with me. We were both injured and barely got away alive. Maybe you think she was hallucinating as well. The fact remains that you haven't discredited one word I said."

Sinclair ignored him. "Jason, buying into his ridiculous theories would make a president look pretty damn stupid. That's not what you want." He sounded solemn and judicious, and then turned to face Jack. "You, sir, are a damned liar." This time his booming words filled the room. "We do not require your further presence here."

"Stop!" Gorton snapped. "You two have given me a goddamn headache."

"Mr. President, you have to listen to me," Jack said, and instantly knew he'd misspoken when Gorton's face flushed. Before Jack could soften his words, Gorton spoke.

"No force on this planet can make me listen if I don't want to. Now you listen to me. You haven't shown me anything solid, certainly no smoking gun. You've made your report to your Commander-in-Chief. I'll let you know what I decide to do, if anything."

Jack had been a little intimidated at meeting the President of the United States. He was over that now.

"Mr. President, I can't leave until you hear what's going on down there. By coming here, I've put myself in a no-win situation. If you dismiss me now, Sinclair will try to destroy me. If you believe me, I'll be known as a whistleblower, an outcast. Give me a few more minutes. Then, if you want me to, I'll leave without another word."

Gorton swiveled slowly side-to-side in his chair, looking first down the table at a man he'd met less than half an hour earlier, then to his right at the man he'd known for decades. He cleared his throat.

"Mr. Strider, you pushed hard to get this in front of me, but Justin's right. What you have is speculation. I want you to report all the information you have to the Base Commander and write down your suggestions for dealing with it. As far as everything that's been said in this room, I hereby classify all of it as top secret. If you violate that classification, I'll have the Secret Service take you into custody."

His sober tone told Jack that this wasn't a hollow threat. Jack stood staring at him, trying to decide what to do. If he walked out now, Sinclair would control what happened next. If he pressed his case, someone's blood would be on the deck a few minutes from now, very likely his.

"Mr. President, if you leave me no other choice, I will hold a media conference on the steps of the Supreme Court building. The *New York Times*, CBS, CNN, and the rest will come to hear what the son of Judge H. Peckford Strider might reveal." Ironically, that would be the closest he'd ever get to the Supreme Court now. "Even if you have me locked up afterwards, the media will investigate and confirm that I'm telling the truth. That will be easy because by then it will be too late."

"You've just threatened your president." Gorton's tone was icy.

He didn't respond but returned Gorton's stare, willing himself not to blink, prepared to hold it for as long as it took.

"I've been around long enough to know when a man's bluffing," Gorton said, "and you're not. For Christ's sake, there's no need for a public pissing match. We don't want to spook the good citizens. I think you're even nuttier than Justin says you are, but I'll give you a few more minutes. If you don't convince me, I'll put you where the sun don't shine until we extradite you to Mexico to play games with the Juarez cops."

Sinclair was making no attempt to restrain his merciless smile.

Jack pointed to the photographs on the table next to Gorton. "Those show the black trucks at D-TECH. The report from Dr. Rincon is an analysis of Eberline contamination counter and dosimeter readings from inside the cave. The readings prove there's radioactive material there."

"So there are trucks at D-TECH," Sinclair said. "How amazing. But he can't show what's in them and can't connect them to Palmer Industries. You'll notice there are no pictures of any trucks at the cave, because it doesn't even exist. That's what I mean by speculation."

"I didn't take pictures at the cave because the people on the ground were shooting at us. But I have some photos that show the trucks on the road between the cave and Palmer Industries."

He reached for his cell phone. It was gone. *Oh my God.* Chief Williams had taken it, and he wasn't aboard Air Force One. He had to ask Gorton to send for him. But what if Gano's photos weren't convincing or, God forbid, he hadn't sent them? He had to gamble.

"Sir, those photos are on my cell phone, and it's in the hands of the chief who drove me here from the gate. If you can have him brought aboard—"

"He has no photographs," Sinclair said contemptuously. "And if he had, we probably couldn't even tell what *continent* they were taken on."

"Mr. Strider," Gorton said with a sigh, "I don't have time to chase down some chief. Anything else in your bag of tricks?"

"Yes, sir. This document is a summary of several disaster scenarios that can result from cramming high level nuclear waste into the uncontrolled environment of that cave." He took it to the President.

"As far as we know, that came from a science fiction writer," Sinclair taunted.

"It was prepared by Stanford hydrology professor Dr. George McDonald. He'd be here right now to present his findings except—" Jack paused until Sinclair noticed the delay and looked at him. This was the money shot, and Sinclair was the eight ball. "—he was murdered this morning in the parking lot of the Palo Alto Westin Hotel."

"Jesus, he was *murdered?*" Gorton exclaimed. "Will somebody please tell me what the fuck is going on?"

Jack stared steadily at Sinclair who now knew the name of the man he'd had assassinated.

"Probably shot by a drugged-out carjacker," Sinclair said smoothly.

Sinclair was quick. No phony questions about Mac. No denial. Just a brush off, as though they were discussing a traffic ticket given to a stranger, to keep Gorton from thinking that Mac's murder was relevant.

"I'll get back to that," Jack said, "but I want to stay on point. We have

D-TECH, trucks and a radioactive cave. Those are the mechanics. Now I'm going to tell you how all this started."

"You see what he's trying to do?" Sinclair broke in. "He can't support this nuclear waste malarkey, but he's still going to try to blame it on his favorite villains, Montana and Arthur Palmer."

Jack heard a subtle difference in Sinclair's voice. Now he sensed the deeper danger and realized he was no longer defending a client. He *was* the client and in a fight for his life.

"You know better than that," Jack said. "Montana was a key player. Arthur Palmer probably was too, but they didn't put it all together." This was the climax. Everything had led to this moment. *"You* did that."

"That's outrageous," Sinclair snarled.

"Justin, knock it off," Gorton ordered, before turning his glare on Jack. "Your histrionics don't impress me one damn bit. Mr. Strider, you're obviously a very smart guy, but you seem obsessed with this situation. Now you've crossed the line. I will not tolerate—"

Jack knew it was dangerous to interrupt Gorton, but he couldn't see any way around it. "Sir, Mr. Sinclair came up with a solution to the problem of nuclear waste piling up all over the U.S.—ship it to Mexico. Mr. Sinclair had Montana find a dump site, which turned out to be a remote cave. Next, he lined up D-TECH as a place to collect large quantities of nuclear waste. When companies are secretly approached about reducing their stockpiles of nuclear waste, they're happy to pay exorbitant fees to get the stuff out of their possession before it causes a catastrophe or they have to shut down."

"May I be heard now?" Sinclair asked quietly.

"It better be good," Gorton said.

Sinclair stood slowly, then rose onto the balls of his feet like an old matador poised to deliver the *coup de gras*.

"A common thread runs through the fabrications of this *felon*. No proof of anything. If I'd set up the scheme he's ranting about, I would have had to talk with all those suppliers of nuclear waste, even someone at Palmer Industries. If I had done that, Strider could provide names of all those people." Sinclair looked smug. "Because he can't do that, I'm going to sue his ass off for slander."

"When you were a spy," Jack countered, "you learned to work covertly. I'm sure that's what you did in this case, too. You used an anonymous intermediary to deal with suppliers of nuclear waste. But you left D-TECH off your list just now. That's because D-TECH was different. You had to deal with someone there personally, but you were confident you'd never be exposed. And *that* is your Achilles' heel."

Gorton studied Sinclair pensively, then looked at Jack again. "Put up or shut up, Mr. Strider. Do you have those names, or witnesses, or even affidavits that support the accusations you've made?"

"Sir, taken as a whole my evidence is overwhelming."

"Then your answer is 'no,' so I'll sum up where I stand. You haven't proven that the events you described actually happened, or that the events you predict will happen. In addition, you face a very heavy burden of proof when you accuse a respected former Secretary of State of being a criminal. You haven't come close to meeting that burden. Further, he's someone for whom I have very high regard." He drew on his cigar. "I have to ask myself what is your motive for being here. Maybe you want revenge against Arthur Palmer, this fellow Montana, and Justin as well. The letter from you to Justin saying you intended to turn on your own client shoots your credibility to hell. Lastly, and this is part of real life for any president, the actions you want me to take would sink me and my party politically."

"But sir—"

"I'm not finished," Gorton said sharply. "At the same time, you have spun out two scenarios with considerable detail. You haven't convinced me, but if either is close to reality, the consequences could be severe. Therefore, one of my staff will contact an outside contractor we use and get some boots on the ground down there to take a look—wells, cave, the whole shooting match. Now, stand by outside while I confer with Justin." Gorton's tone was absolute.

Before Jack could react, the phone buzzed.

Gorton started to push the speaker button, but glanced at Jack and picked up the handset instead. "Yes, Chief?" He listened. "Emergency? Then come in."

Jack caught his breath. Thank God. The two people he'd been depending on had finally arrived. This would turn things around.

But instead of Debra and Gano coming into the room, a massive African-American man in a khaki suit was standing close behind the Chief in the doorway. The Chief nodded back toward the man and said, "Mr. President, this is Mr. Corte from the National Security Agency. He says there's an emergency, and he needs to speak with you immediately."

"I'm already waist deep in emergencies," Gorton snapped. "Escort Mr. Corte to a seat in the press section."

Corte stepped forward, nudging the Chief to the side with his elbow. "Mr. President, sir, there's nothing more urgent than the reason I'm here." Corte's bass voice was tight. "We have a *situation.*"

That must have been a code phrase because Gorton immediately said, "Very well, come in."

Corte looked at Jack, nearest to him, then Sinclair. He blinked at each, as if making separate mental files.

Gorton said, "Tell me what this is about."

"I can't do that, sir. Only eleven people in the country have the necessary security clearance. These people are not on that list, sir." He held up an envelope sealed with blue tape. The only marking on the outside read *Top Secret-Crypto: Yankee Fire-Eyes Only*. "This came to your Communications Office and was immediately routed to the National Security Advisor. That was—" He checked a communications device in his other hand. "—eight minutes ago."

"Give me the envelope."

"Sir, with these people here, I'm not authorized—"

"I gave you an order, damn it." Gorton took the envelope, ripped off one end, and pulled out a single sheet of paper.

He read it quickly and gasped, "Sweet Jesus."

Chapter 49

July 12
1:15 p.m.

JACK SAW THE color go out of Gorton's face as he read the paper again and cut his eyes to the chronometer on the bulkhead. His mouth opened and closed. Whatever was written on that paper had stunned the president of the United States.

"Corte, get the National Security Advisor on the phone—and someone from DOE who understands this stuff."

"Sir," Corte said, "I'll patch them through to your secure line. We have to keep this inside the room. And these other two gentlemen will have to be placed in quarantine." Corte straightened to his full height of at least six feet eight inches and took a step toward Sinclair.

Gorton's balm went up. "You're not putting the former Secretary of State in quarantine. Both of them stay here. In fact, I hereby grant everyone in this room whatever the hell crypto clearance you're talking about."

Uh oh, Jack thought. *He's let Sinclair off the hook again.* But Corte's arrival had also kept Jack from getting the heave-ho from Gorton.

"Yes, sir," Corte answered. He tapped numbers into a tiny keyboard. "National Security Advisor on the line, sir. She has a copy of the demand."

Gorton hurried to the end of the conference table and picked up his phone. "What's this about?" He listened. "How long will that take?" After another pause, he snapped, "Don't keep me waiting," and hung up. "Get me the DOE expert," he ordered Corte.

He handed the paper to Sinclair. "Read this."

Sinclair scanned the single page. "Son of a bitch." He read it again, mouthing the words. Then he glanced at Jack and handed it back to Gorton.

To Jack, Corte looked like the type who prides himself on never losing his cool. Yet he was in high-stress mode. Gorton was too. Jack took a chance and held out his hand. Gorton absentmindedly gave him the document.

To: President Jason Gorton

We have hidden a number of dirty bombs in the United States and Mexico. Each bomb contains highly radioactive waste, C-4 and TNT explosives, and drums of JP8 aviation gas.

Our requirements:

Transfer $100 million to us before 7 p.m. today or we will detonate all bombs.

Wire that amount to Union de Banques Suisse, Clearing #230, private account #085-292163-7459650, before the deadline. If you attempt to interfere in any way before we withdraw the funds, we will detonate all bombs.

If you locate a bomb, any effort to tamper with it will detonate it.

When withdrawal is complete, we will reveal the locations of all bombs. A flashing green light will indicate a bomb can be safely disassembled.

We want only money. After receiving payment, we have nothing to gain by detonation and will not do so.

There will be no further communication until we inform you of the locations of the bombs. Do not doubt our ability or our willingness to carry out our threat.

Jack carefully set the page on the table. He couldn't get his mind around the magnitude of this threat. The specificity of detail was chilling and made it credible. But would it be called off even if payment were made?

"Corte," Gorton said, "do the people who wrote this know what they're talking about?"

"No doubt about it, sir. The C-4 will rupture the nuclear waste containers and release intense radioactive contamination. The TNT, detonated a second later, will disperse the radioactivity. Burning aviation gas will create a plume of smoke sufficient to carry radioactive gasses for hundreds of miles."

"Hundreds?" Gorton repeated in disbelief. His face was like a zombie mask. Instead of taking command, he seemed incapable of speech.

"Mr. President," Corte said, "I have Dr. Poindexter from DOE holding on the line. I've given him the parameters of this *hypothetical* situation. Dr. Poindexter is Director of—"

Gorton snapped back into the moment. "I don't care what his title is. Put him on the speaker."

Corte glanced at the others as if about to make another security objection, but apparently thought better of it. "He's on the speaker, Mr. President."

"Dr. Poindexter, Mr. Corte briefed you about a hypothetical situation we've been discussing here. Tell me what would happen if someone set off a dirty bomb with the characteristics Corte described to you."

"Mr. President, there are so many variables that—"

"Take your best shot or get me someone who will."

"Yes, sir. Yes, sir." Dr. Poindexter was clearly agitated by the un-expected call from his Commander-in-Chief. "First, the blast and shrapnel from explosion of a medium-size dirty bomb could flatten buildings and start fires in an area of about eight acres. After that, radiation would be a serious hazard to anyone nearby, including law enforcement and emergency response personnel. Cleanup workers and people living or working in the area would also be at serious risk. We estimate that cleanup of a single urban area would cost more than $4 billion and take three years, maybe longer."

Gorton sucked in a breath, blew it out. "How far would radioactivity spread?"

"In a form people could inhale, not far unless there was a substantial fire in connection with a blast, or high winds. In those cases, radioactivity could be carried in a plume of smoke that could put people within fifty square miles at high risk of irradiation and contamination."

"Exactly what does that mean for people on the ground?"

"Some would inhale radionuclides carried by the plume. Others would be poisoned by gamma radiation deposited on the ground. Drinking water would be contaminated by radioactivity. People wouldn't know anything was wrong until symptoms of radiation poisoning knocked them flat. After that—"

"That's enough, Poindexter. I have the picture. Keep this conversation secret. That's an order." Gorton clicked off the speaker. "We're in a hell of a mess. Corte, can you trace this e-mail?"

"We're on that, sir, but unless the senders are idiots, it won't lead back to them. We also have people analyzing the language to see if it suggests some specific nationality."

"Piss poor help considering the amount of money we give the NSA every year." Gorton rubbed his forehead. "And we're blind. We don't know how many bombs or where they are. There's no way we can stop them."

"Actually," Jack said, "I think—"

"All right, Justin," Gorton said, ignoring Jack, "let's walk through this. The money they want isn't much compared to the damage they can do. We can tap our war slush fund at Defense or disaster relief money at Homeland Security. So why not pay?"

Sinclair, who had been fidgeting, wanting to be called on, jumped in. "If you pay and you never hear from these guys again, the leaders of the other party will call you a patsy."

"My job is to protect the people. Because of 9/11, I'll make hash out of the guy who says I should have gambled. And if I pay and bombs go off anyway, I did my best. So the real downside is if I do nothing and a dirty bomb goes off in, say, the San Francisco financial district. Corte, get me the Treasury Secretary. He'll have someone who knows about the mechanics of transferring funds."

"Mr. President," Corte said, "with all due respect, it would be a mistake to think of this as blackmail. NSA got this e-mail to you so fast because it fits six of our seven criteria for a valid terrorist threat. This has to be treated as—" He paused, apparently to give weight to the word. "—terrorism."

Gorton's upper body recoiled as the implications hit him.

"And in the case of terrorism," Corte went on, "there is an established procedure to follow. You immediately assemble Defense, CIA, FBI, and the Homeland Security team on a secure conference hookup. Terrorist attack protocol requires that Air Force One get airborne without delay in case the attackers have also targeted you. All unauthorized persons must disembark at once and—" His expression changed to a slight smile. "—be detained and isolated to ensure secrecy."

Gorton, eyes fixed on Corte, shook his head and frowned. "But the demand was only about money."

"A trick," Corte stated in his decisive, resonant voice. "After they collect the money, they come back with more demands, including political. They'll try to spook you into going public and starting a panic. Then they'll start detonating bombs, showing that even after a warning we can't stop them. That's how terrorism works."

"But if it is a terrorist attack we have to—"

"Yes, sir, execute Plan Sapphire immediately." Corte sounded eager. He looked like an action guy, ready to start down a track he'd trained on.

Gorton nodded reluctantly. "I have no choice. We're not going to make the same mistakes that—"

"No sir, not on your watch."

"And these United States of America," Gorton said, jaw jutting, "sure as hell aren't paying one American dollar to a bunch of goddamn terrorists. I won't negotiate with them either. That's my policy, by God."

Jack had never seen a tide turn so fast. The instant after Corte gave his tirade about terrorism, Gorton had stopped thinking and started spouting dogma that made no sense. Switching to autopilot made decision making under pressure unnecessary. Once the "terrorist attack" bell sounded, Gorton could be criticized only if he departed from the script. He'd risk disaster before doing that.

Jack decided he had to make Gorton listen to him, so he slammed his palm on the conference table.

Corte's hand snaked inside his khaki jacket and came out holding a black revolver aimed at Jack's heart.

Everyone froze.

"Sorry, Mr. President," Jack said quickly. "I had to get your attention. Look, this *is* blackmail, not terrorism. I know who sent that blackmail note. He can and will carry out his threat."

"How can you possibly know who it came from?"

"You know the answer, too. It's Tomás Montana at Palmer Industries."

"Sir, we have a plan to follow in this situation," Corte rumbled immediately.

"Oh my God, Strider," Sinclair groaned, "you're still beating that drum?"

Jack shot both men a grimace and said, "I'm not guessing. Montana had access to the nuclear waste in that cave and to trucks that can deliver dirty bombs. At least four of those trucks left the cave yesterday afternoon. My man followed them. In the past, all these trucks made the same circuit and returned to the Palmer plant. But this time, one truck went south in the direction of Mexico City. Another headed into Chihuahua City, but it could have gone on to Monterey or even Tampico. Only two went back to the Palmer plant."

"If that's true," Gorton said, "what provoked this e-mail threat?"

"Montana thought he'd get a huge bonus by secretly dumping hazardous waste into the aquifer. He knows that's been 'outed' and he won't get it. Then, as soon as he got reports of someone flying over the cave site and being seen inside the mine shaft that intersects with the cave, he knew that was likely to be shut down too and he'd be the subject of a manhunt. For him, money is all that matters—and this blackmail is his fail-safe plan."

"If this e-mail came from Montana, could he really make good on his threat?"

"The bomb components were available at the Palmer plant or at the cave. All he needed was a few hours to load those trucks. If his ultimatum works, he lives like an emperor. If it doesn't, he takes revenge and disappears."

"Mr. President," Corte held up the communications device he'd just consulted, "there's no Tomás Montana on our Watch List, and we have no intelligence on him. However, we've intercepted a lot of chatter in the last twenty-four hours from a nasty terrorist group called Gundah Resistance that specializes in high explosives. You can't just roll the dice and hope this isn't a terrorist attack."

"Terrorist groups," Jack said, "have political objectives. That e-mail is only about *money.*"

"This *is* political," Corte insisted. "Maybe they'll attack cities in both countries to start an international conflict. Mexico will blame the U.S. Every disagreement over immigration, oil, drug smuggling, whatever, will become more hostile." He glared at Jack. "Don't tell me that's not political." He turned to face Gorton. "Sir, procedure requires you to get Air Force One and the F-18s in the air right now."

"Mr. President," Jack said, "you don't know how many trucks or where they are, so it's too late to stop Montana before his deadline. You have to pay the money now and go after him later."

Sinclair gave a dismissive wave. "Montana's a desk jockey who spends every day processing crap. He doesn't have the balls to pull off something like this threat. Don't let yourself be shaken down by terrorists. Listen to me. I've been down this road before, and Corte's a professional. We don't cave in to terrorists."

Jack read Sinclair's strategy in a flash. In Corte's scenario, if Gorton refused to pay and dirty bombs went off, the bombers would be labeled terrorists. The national security apparatus would launch an international hunt among the usual terrorist suspects—and that wouldn't include Justin Sinclair. If Gorton treated it as blackmail and paid the $100 million, Montana would be a credible perpetrator, especially since he would have disappeared. Sinclair's links to him could be a major issue. Corte's terrorist theory let Sinclair off the hook. So, to focus suspicion away from Montana, Sinclair would back Corte all the way.

Sinclair would let dirty bombs explode rather than have Jack point at him as having put Montana in position to blackmail the United States government.

"Mr. Strider," Gorton said, "nuclear material can come from anywhere in the country, and you don't even know what's in those trucks. Limiting our response to going after Montana would be a fatal error. Besides, if I give in to these terrorists, I'll get another demand from some other group tomorrow. I'd also be undermining our allies who follow our lead in refusing to deal with terrorists." He tilted his head back and straightened the collar of his flight jacket. "That's not my style."

Gorton was in political survival mode, and there wasn't time to turn him around. Jack had to find and stop Montana himself, but there was too little time to fly to El Paso. Wait a minute. He was thinking about a commercial flight, but he was already at an Air Force base.

"I understand," he said to Gorton, "but you won't mind if I try to find Montana on my own, will you?"

"Of course not."

"Then I need the fastest ride there is from Travis to El Paso."

Gorton glanced at Sinclair who nodded in support of Jack's request.

Jack knew he'd just given Sinclair a win-win. If Jack didn't find Montana, that would suit Sinclair fine. If he did find him, Montana would make sure Jack never testified against anyone.

"Mr. Strider, I'm still not persuaded this plant manager is a terrorist, but I'll get you to El Paso. If you want help, I'll round up some of the Special Forces stationed here at Travis to go along."

"Yes, sir, I could use more eyes and muscle."

"Sir," Corte spoke up, "I'm sure the NSA would recommend against sending Special Forces. Mr. Strider's search for the plant manager will take him into Mexico, a sovereign nation. Sending Special Forces in there could be considered an act of war."

First terrorism, now war. Corte had cleverly trapped Gorton. Jack held his breath, waiting for Gorton's response.

Gorton frowned and said, "He's right. After I get you down there, you're on your own. Chief!" he shouted.

The Chief opened the door so quickly he must have posted himself right outside. "Sir?"

"Get Mr. Strider aboard the fastest ride to El Paso they've got on this base. I want them with wheels up inside thirty minutes. Do it now."

"Aye, aye, sir." He saluted and disappeared.

"Strider, if by some miracle you come up with something, contact me. Here's a number that can reach me directly." He wrote a number on a piece of paper and handed it over. "Corte, get our Homeland Security team on a secure conference hookup. If we need to go to Condition Red, that's what we'll do. We're not going to let those bastards get away with this."

Jack thought a blind mole could see that e-mail came from Montana, but Gorton just wouldn't get it. Instead, he'd rather swing at a piñata in a pitch black room. Gorton, Sinclair, and Corte—each for his own self-serving reasons—were guaranteeing that Montana *was* going to carry out his threat.

Chapter 50

July 12
1:45 p.m.

THE C-20B GULFSTREAM jet Gorton had lined up for Jack was still climbing as Sacramento passed below. Jack knew that while he was hunting for Montana, Sinclair would use his guile to discredit him with Gorton. If Sinclair succeeded, Jack would have to consider a career in Uzbekistan.

He tried his cell phone. Good signal, so he entered the number.

"Captain, my captain." Gano's voice sounded relieved.

"Where are you," Jack asked, "and what do you have for me?"

"I'm in El Paso now. When I cruised by the Palmer plant earlier I didn't see any of those big trucks, so I laid a fistful of your pesos on a worker getting off his shift. He said two of the black trucks left early this morning. No idea where they went. What happened at your big meeting?"

"Before I left for the meeting, while I was still at the hotel, Sinclair had a sniper try to kill me. He screwed up and killed Mac instead." He had to stop for a moment and swallow hard.

Gano was silent for many seconds, obviously absorbing the news, knowing how Jack felt about Mac. Finally he said quietly, "So now Sinclair is all in, no holds barred."

"And so am I." He didn't want to say anything more about Mac right now. "Sinclair beat me to Air Force One and undercut me with Gorton. When I got in to see Gorton, Sinclair and I had a free-for-all. He was about to win the decision when Gorton got an e-mail from someone who claimed to have planted multiple dirty bombs in the U.S. and Mexico. He wants $100 million by seven o'clock tonight or he'll detonate the bombs."

"Did the wacko claim responsibility?"

"Didn't have to. I know damn well it came from Montana. He has the nuclear material, the trucks, and the motive—$100 million. But Gorton wouldn't buy it. His intelligence expert persuaded him the e-mail came from terrorists."

"Montana. Yeah, that fits. How did Sinclair play it?"

"He beat the terrorist drum big time. The last thing he wants is for his client's plant manager to be the leading suspect after those bombs go off.

He knows he'd be implicated. Gorton went for the terrorism theory because he's better off politically if he follows the rule book—which means hunkering down and not paying anyone."

"That's plain ol' country stupid. If Montana doesn't get paid, he'll blow up everything he can. I knew I should have snuffed him the night of the big fireworks."

"Don't rub it in. We have to find Montana and stop him in the next two hours, three hours at most. I'm aboard an Air Force jet out of Travis. I'll meet you in front of the Delta terminal at El Paso International in an hour and a half."

"I'll be there. Debra with you?"

"She was supposed to meet me at Air Force One but didn't show. If I can get her on the phone, I'll ask her to be at the airport. Gano, if you can find Montana before I get there, that might be the most important thing you ever do in your life."

"I'm on it, *comandante,*" Gano said and hung up.

Jack loosened his seat belt and stretched his legs. He felt strange being the only passenger on a plane built to serve fourteen VIPs. The crew never left the cockpit, probably under orders.

He sat again and let the day's events unfold in his mind's eye. If he hadn't confronted Sinclair yesterday, pushed him so hard, he wouldn't have sent an assassin, and Mac would still be alive. The image of Ana-Maria's waxen face seldom left his mind, but grieving for both still had to wait. He closed his eyes and took a series of slow, deep breaths, then entered Debra's number into his phone.

She answered after the first ring. "How did it go?"

"Not worth a damn. I really needed you there to help clinch the case against Sinclair. What happened? Are you okay?"

"I'm fine, but by the time I got anything useful it was impossible to get to Travis in time. I tried to call, but apparently you'd turned off your cell phone."

"They confiscate it before you board Air Force One."

"I thought that might be it. Where are you now?"

"On an Air Force jet on my way to El Paso. I need to hear what you have for me."

"I do have news. Some good, some bad."

"Let's get the bad news out of the way."

"I did my damnedest, but I couldn't get the witness you wanted. I'm on my way back to El Paso myself, about thirty miles away."

"Wasn't there some incentive or pressure you could use?"

"I tried everything. It just wasn't possible." Her voice conveyed her exasperation with his question.

Getting the witness he'd asked her to line up had been a long shot, but so crucial he'd convinced himself it would happen. Without that witness, he couldn't make his case that Sinclair was the mastermind behind smuggling the nuclear waste.

Debra spoke into his silence. "You should have asked for the good news first. Then this wouldn't seem so bad."

"Oh, for God's sake," he said, tense and frustrated, "what's the good news?"

"I'm bringing back some great evidence with me."

"I hope it's enough. Meet me at the Delta counter in the airport and tell me about it then."

"I'll be there."

He gave her a high-speed summary of his confrontation with Sinclair and how Gorton had reacted to the e-mail threat. And why he was going to El Paso. He left out the part about Mac. He just couldn't go over it again right now.

He concluded with, "Montana knew the roof was caving in on him. He knew that could happen, so he had a plan to hit the jackpot on his way out the door. As soon as he felt seriously threatened, he loaded the trucks with nuclear waste and explosives and sent them off. Figuring out what he's doing isn't enough. We can't stop this truck-by-truck. We have to find *him.*"

"He'd be crazy to go back to the plant or to his home in El Paso."

"Right. In fact, he could have e-mailed Gorton from a laptop, BlackBerry, iPhone, or anything like that. He could check his account in the Swiss bank the same way."

"I saw a documentary about terrorism," Debra said, "that explained how a bomb could be detonated or deactivated by telephone, calling one number to detonate or another number to disarm."

"Meaning that Montana could already be out of North America, maybe planning to trigger the bombs from someplace like Buenos Aires." He looked out the window along the length of the wing and listened to the roar of the turbofan jets. "If he's gone, this is pointless, so I have to believe he's holed up in El Paso or Juarez. If one of his bombs is there too, he'll break cover before the big bang. I'll have the pilot contact all major airports within a few hundred miles of El Paso to see if Montana has a reservation on any flight. Problem is he could have bought a cheapo passport and ID kit so he could travel under a fake name. Same problem with checking hotels."

"He has to avoid public places," Debra said, "so maybe he dropped in on a girlfriend."

"*That's the answer.*" He felt a flicker of hope. "The address of the sender of the e-mail to Gorton was cloaked, meaning it couldn't be traced. That would be hard to arrange on a cell phone or BlackBerry, but easy on a regular computer. So he's hiding in a place with a computer. But where?"

"I know where—and it's not with a girlfriend!" Her excitement burst through the receiver. "Remember a week ago when I went dancing with him in Mexico City, the night you got so bent out of shape? He invited me to see his etchings as soon as I got to the Palmer plant to do that contract work."

"Come on. He didn't really say 'etchings.'"

She chuckled. "Figure of speech. He was boasting about rare Aztec antiquities he'd bought on the black market. He's obsessed with them. He said he keeps them at a lodge he owns on the mesa north of El Paso."

"I've seen that mesa. There are dozens of homes up there."

"He talked about a spectacular view of city lights at night and said he can see the ridge on Palmer plant grounds in Juarez."

"Anything else, like a putting green, barn, pool—"

"Not a pool. He called his lodge 'El Castillo' because a dry moat runs around it."

"That puts the lodge in a certain sector of the mesa, and the moat will be a giveaway from the air. I'll call Gano and have him get airborne."

He clicked off and entered Gano's number.

"Anything on Montana?" Jack asked.

"Zilch. I called the plant, posing as a client. Montana was a no-show all day. I even took a run by his golf course and through the clubhouse at Sunland racetrack. *Nada.* I don't know where else to look. He's slithered out of sight."

"Get airborne as fast as you can. Here's what you're looking for." He relayed Debra's information. "If you spot it, get out of there fast. Don't spook him. And let me know."

"Roger Wilco. I'm ten minutes from the airport now. Over and out."

He called Debra back. "Gano's on his way. If he finds the lodge, it's our only shot before time runs out." He thought about the black trucks, visualizing explosions ripping the containers apart and spraying radioactivity into the sky.

"What about calling the El Paso cops?"

"Even if they believed me, they'd barge in, and he'd detonate everything. But I'll do this. If we don't find the lodge and Montana, I'll try to convince the cops to search for the black trucks. They'll have to use unmarked cars in case Montana is in line-of-sight of a truck. Maybe I can get Gorton to send in some Special Ops people to help search. But that doesn't help with trucks in other cities."

"Suppose he is at El Castillo. Then what?"

"We have to take him by surprise. I have a plan, but it will put you at risk. I wouldn't consider it if the stakes weren't so high."

"Think back to Casa Lupo. I'm a warrior." Her voice was strong, every bit a warrior.

"I remember. Rent an SUV at the El Paso airport and have it waiting."

"Will do. But what if Montana has his thugs with him when we find him?"

"He won't. He doesn't want witnesses. See you at the airport, Delta terminal."

He closed his eyes, letting the vibrations of the plane wash over him. Even if they cornered Montana in his castle, he would be deadly. Jack knew his plan was much more likely to fail than succeed, and it could cost the lives of two people very important to him.

Chapter 51

July 12
6:40 p.m.

DEBRA BRAKED hard to a stop at an unmarked asphalt drive that curved sharply uphill from Rim Road, the two-lane state highway she had followed north from El Paso. Squatting next to Jack in the cargo space of the gray Ford Explorer, Gano spoke loudly enough for Debra to hear.

"If this ain't the place, I'm turnin' in my GPS. Like I told you, the lodge is in a grove of scrub pines about fifty yards from the edge of the mesa. The moat is dry but it's obvious from the air. There's a black Hummer in the driveway. No other vehicles." He lowered his voice and put his hand on Jack's shoulder. "We're playing for keeps, Mr. Pinkerton Man, so don't give me any nonviolence crap. It takes whatever it takes." Gano patted the gun inside his jacket and rested his hand on the Mossberg 935 loaded with 12 gauge magnum shells next to him. "Let's get that sum-bitch."

Debra turned into the driveway and sped uphill. Before they'd gone a quarter of a mile, they emerged from the trees into a clearing. A white adobe brick gatehouse loomed ahead. She hit the brakes, but it was too late. A motion sensor activated two wide beams of light that flooded the Explorer's hood, likely setting off an alarm at the lodge. The gate was a high grill of heavy gauge steel bars with no lock to be jimmied or cut.

"Damn," Jack said. "That gate must be controlled from the lodge. So much for catching Montana by surprise."

"Standard hard-wired security system," Gano said, "which means there's a speaker and a video camera. I'll bet my left boot he already sees the vehicle."

Jack had planned for Debra to stop out of sight of the lodge so he and Gano could get out and sneak up on it from the rear. Now that Montana could see the Explorer, Plan A was toast. He had a Plan B, but hadn't wanted to use it because it would be much more dangerous for Debra. Now he didn't have a choice.

"We have to make that camera work for us," he said. "Debra, drive up to the gate and smile at the camera. Tell Montana you've just flown in from San Francisco to see his etchings."

"He won't bite," she said. "He's focused on hitting a $100 million jackpot. And remember, last week he tried to have me killed. I think that means his hots for me have cooled a bit."

"You said he never gets turned down by women, but you shut him down cold. Now here you are at his door. He'll grab the chance to improve his batting average."

"Hold on," Gano said, "he'll ask how she knew where the lodge was."

"I can handle that," Debra said.

If she couldn't, Montana would suspect a rat. God knows what he'd do then. But Debra's confident. That's good enough.

"Listen," Jack said, "if he lets you through the gate, keep going until we're near the lodge but still out of sight. Then pop the rear hatch and slow down. We'll roll out and into the brush. Drive in front of the lodge and honk. Don't get out. Get him to come out of the house and toward the car. Hold his attention for a few seconds, and we'll take him down. If anything goes wrong, floor it and get out. We'll get off the mesa overland and meet you on Rim Road."

"Don't keep me waiting, boys. He won't be in the mood for small talk." She gave him a smile that seemed a little forced.

She drove slowly into the full glare of the lights and stopped next to the gatehouse. No communication from the lodge. She edged the Explorer forward until the heavy bumper was tight against the bars of the gate, as if she intended to ram her way in. She honked over and over.

"Stop that." Montana's angry voice came from a speaker high in the adobe wall. "Get out of here."

"It's Debra Vanderberg, your salsa partner."

After several seconds, "Get out of the car so I can see you."

She did, flashing her legs. "Look, I flew down here because it seemed like a great idea, but maybe not." There was no response. "I called your plant. They told me you hadn't been in all day. No answer at your home either, so I figured I'd try up here."

"How did you know about this place?" His voice radiated suspicion.

"You told me about it and about your Aztec stuff between dances." She ran her fingers through her hair. "Is it coming back or were you too drunk to remember?" she asked in a mocking tone.

"I remember," he said, sounding more surly than suspicious. "What do you want?"

"I owe you for running out on you in Mexico City. I'm here to pay up. If you can't handle it, I'll catch the last flight out tonight. No harm, no foul. Either let me hear some enthusiasm, or I'm out of here." She got back into the Ford.

"Come up. Park next to my Hummer." The bars on the gate slid silently away.

As soon as they reached the mesa's flat top, the lodge's lights showed through the trees. "Ground Zero in sight," Debra said and slowed by letting the Explorer roll so there'd be no brake light. She punched the door release for the cargo space. Jack and Gano tumbled onto the driveway. As soon as the Explorer was a few car lengths away, they started circling to approach the lodge from the back.

Jack's chest was tight. *She'll be alone with Montana.* They had to surprise him and take him down before he could hurt her.

They moved swiftly from tree to tree in the dim light until they reached the clearing around El Castillo. A dozen strides ahead of them was the dry moat; beyond it, the back wall of the half-timber lodge. They paused to size up the situation. Gano reached into his jacket and pulled out a black revolver. He held it out to Jack.

"This is my favorite .38 Special. Don't lose it."

There was no time to debate. Jack tucked it inside his belt behind his back. "The main entrance must be around the corner to the left."

He dashed down the sloping side of the moat and up the other side to the back wall of the lodge, Gano following. He edged forward to peer into the parking area just as the Explorer pulled in, passed the Hummer and stopped.

Expecting Montana to be waiting inside the house, he watched in horror as Montana jumped up from behind the Hummer, ran to the rear of the Explorer, and fired four booming shots downward through the rear windshield. He hadn't been fooled by Debra's story and had intended to kill Jack Strider, whom he obviously thought would be hiding in the cargo space.

Debra was screaming when Montana jerked open her door. Shouting curses, he punched her hard on the side of her head, dragged her out of the Explorer, and hauled her across a bridge over the moat toward the front door. She was stunned, off balance, helpless.

Adrenaline blew Jack's plans apart. A split second before he could launch himself after Montana, Gano clamped a hand across his mouth and yanked him backward.

"You're too late to stop him," Gano whispered fiercely, "and I don't have a clear shot. If he finds out we're here, she's dead. Got that? We'll case the place and break in."

"No good. He'll hear us and kill Debra." His mind raced through bad alternatives. "You find a way in the back. I'm going in the front."

"Get real. He'll slaughter you."

"I'll buy time and distract him while you get inside."

The front door closed behind Montana. Jack took a deep breath, ran across the gravel and ducked behind the Explorer.

He yelled, "Montana, it's Jack Strider. We need to talk." No response. Seconds passed. "Montana, don't be a coward. Come out here."

The door opened slowly. "I'm not coming out. You're coming in. Otherwise I'll kill this *puta*. Hands up. Get moving."

She's in there because I asked her to take the risk. Jack knew that following Montana's orders was foolish, but he had to go after her.

A second after he stepped through the door, Montana slipped behind him and snarled, "Straight ahead, into the living room." Jack started forward. "Hold on," Montana said, "you wouldn't be stupid enough to have a weapon, would you?" He reached around in front of Jack and patted his chest and under his arms. Then he patted down his back. "I'll be damned. You *are* that stupid."

Montana yanked the .38 out of Jack's belt and slammed its butt into the back of Jack's head, knocking him to his knees. Sparks flashed in front of his eyes. His skull felt cracked open. He touched the wound, and his fingers came away wet. If he passed out, Montana would kill him, then Debra. Her moan from the next room gave him the strength to pull himself together.

"Get up." Montana prodded him with a boot. "I don't have time to screw with you."

When he struggled to his feet, Montana shoved him into a pine-paneled room with a vaulted ceiling. The light was low, windows covered with drawn drapes. Several wooden crates stood directly ahead of him, one overflowing with what must be Montana's prized Aztec artifacts.

Debra's back was against the side of an open staircase, arms stretched over her head and tied to the iron railing at her wrists. Her ankles were roughly bound together with packing tape, toes barely touching the floor.

"Stand in front of my desk and don't move." Montana waved Jack across the room to within a few feet of where he'd tied Debra.

Montana sat at his desk behind a laptop computer, black eyes riveted on Jack. He was breathing through his mouth, quick and shallow, almost panting, pumped up. His trigger finger might squeeze at any second.

Jack had to say something to get Montana to calm down. "Look, you haven't dumped the tanks so there's no harm. You can unwind all this and walk away."

"I'm way past walking away, and we both know it. You made a big mistake coming here, *gringo*. Were you going to kill me?"

"No, turn you over to the El Paso cops for planning to poison the aquifer." The revolver in Montana's left hand was trained steadily on his chest.

"You thought you could take *me?* On my own turf? You're as nuts as Arthur Palmer." Montana showed a hyena-like grin. "He tried to con me by promising a huge bonus if I met profit goals he thought were impossible. He doesn't know it, but I've had him by the balls ever since I talked him into moving the plant to Mexico."

"You were going to use the wells to jack up the profits."

"Of course. Then you screwed it up and cost me two million bucks."

"You'd destroy two cities to get a damned bonus?"

"Don't look down your nose at me, you rich shit!" Montana shouted. "I grew up in the mud in Cuba. That bonus was my ticket out of the *gringo* world."

"That's why you hired those thugs to kill us outside Casa Lupo."

"And they fucked up. If I'd been there, you wouldn't have lived to set fire to my plant. Now I'll finish their job. You forced me to change my plans, so you're responsible for everything that's going to happen tonight." Montana checked his wristwatch. "I have to do some business on the computer. I'll let you hang around for the good news, then we'll wrap this up."

Jack edged closer to the desk.

"Back off!" Montana ordered.

Montana's right hand rested on the desk, bandaged like a pro boxer's because of the bullet Jack had put through it three days ago. Typing with one finger of his left hand, he laboriously entered something lengthy. The gun rested next to the computer. When the connection was made, Montana consulted a yellow pad next to him and made more entries. Seconds passed while he studied the screen in silence.

The Swiss bank, Jack thought. *He's put in his password and account numbers to see whether he's been paid off.*

"Damn him!" Montana took several deep breaths before turning back to the keyboard. This time he double-checked every keystroke against the yellow pad before punching "Enter."

"Goddamn him," he said again, almost inaudibly. "He's going to wish he'd done what I told him." He looked up at Jack, eyes blazing, then back at the keyboard. He repeated his attempts, face growing harder after each try. His eyes flicked up every couple of seconds to make sure Jack had not moved.

Jack glanced over at Debra. Her tense face showed the pain of agonizing minutes hanging by her wrists, supported on her tiptoes. The packing tape must be like a tourniquet cutting off circulation to her hands. She struggled to breathe and looked ready to pass out. He knew that if he moved to help her, Montana would kill them both.

Where was Gano? The lodge's defenses must have defeated him. It was up to Jack to do something, but a frontal attack on Montana would be suicide. So what the hell was he going to do?

Montana checked the Swiss bank account again. His angry expression showed that no money had been deposited. He grabbed the phone, entered a number, and launched into a conversation in Spanish, far too rapid for Jack to follow—but he heard Montana say "Strider" twice. Montana hung up and dialed again. He listened for about ten seconds and hung up. Then he turned back to his keyboard, poked one key with his index finger, and looked at Jack with a manic, horrible grin.

Jack glanced at his watch. Only 6:15. *Why was Montana losing it?* His deadline was still 45 minutes away. As far as Montana knew, $100 million could show up in his account anytime. Then Jack saw a small digital clock on the wall to Montana's left. It read 7:15. *Oh, shit.* He understood what had happened.

"Montana. Listen to me. The deadline is—"

"You listen," Montana interrupted in a guttural snarl. "A doc sewed The Ape's guts back together in the hospital. He's infected, septic, but he'll live long enough to open the valves and dump that shit down the wells I patched up. I told him that was the way to get revenge on you and your buddy with the screwdriver. He'll be at the plant in a few minutes." His smirk was foul.

"Call him back. There's a screwup. Your deadline is based on Mountain Time, the time on that clock on the wall. Gorton is at Travis Air Force Base. He thought you meant Pacific Time, and that's an hour earlier. He thinks he still has 45 minutes left."

He was trying to keep Montana from setting off dirty bombs for at least another forty-five minutes, but he knew the words tied a noose around his own neck.

"That's bull shit," Montana said. "Gorton is in Denver to give a speech at a regional EPA meeting. I saw it on the news. That's Mountain Time, same as here. I'm not stupid."

"Maybe he *was* in Denver, but he was aboard Air Force One at Travis Air Force Base in California when he got your e-mail. That's Pacific time."

Montana's face registered disbelief, then fury, as he processed what he'd just heard.

"You know about my e-mail to Gorton?" Montana's voice was deadly. "And my deadline? Then you've talked with Gorton and you know about the bombs."

Maybe that's all he'll figure out.

"You bastard!" Montana shouted. He'd obviously figured out the rest of it. "You told him about me." Then he gave Jack a sly look. "But he didn't believe you, or the Marines would have surrounded this place. So now you're really fucked."

"I told Gorton who you are and that you would carry out your threat," Jack said. "If I hadn't done that, you wouldn't have gotten a penny. Contact Gorton again. I have his direct phone number. Give the location of one bomb so he'll know you can do what you say."

And maybe, he desperately hoped, *hearing that will change Gorton's mind.*

"He'll know where the first bomb is at any moment. Right after I talked to The Ape a minute ago, I sent Gorton my Albuquerque e-mail. By God, he'll pay now." He looked back down at the computer screen.

If Montana had threatened to detonate a bomb in Albuquerque, Gorton might panic and wire the money. Looking at Montana's grim expression, Jack was no longer sure that would make any difference. Montana was so angry he didn't care about the time zone screwup. He might blow the bombs just to punish Gorton.

Jack had to make a move. He couldn't get to Montana; the desk was between them. Could he throw something? He glanced around. Nothing within reach except . . . he cut a quick look back at the Aztec antiquities in the open box behind him. Pieces of pottery and clay sculptures rested on top. Worthless as weapons, but priceless to Montana. He glanced at Debra. Her eyes were fixed on him. He had to signal her without getting caught. He glanced back to Montana.

"Casa Lupo," he said loudly.

Montana looked at him. "What?"

"Casa Lupo," he said again, louder.

"Shut up," Montana snapped and looked down again.

Jack reached back slowly, not daring to look, and lifted a pottery double-cup out of the box. He said "Casa Lupo" for the third time. Debra looked puzzled but alert.

When Montana looked up from the computer, Jack tossed the cup onto the floor where it shattered.

"Hey!" Montana shouted. "That's a 15th century—"

Jack snatched a ceramic sculpture of an eagle and held it in front of him at shoulder height. "Shoot me and it drops."

Montana sprang to his feet, grabbed his gun, and rushed from behind the desk to save his treasure.

As Montana passed in front of Debra, she jackknifed her knees to her chest and drove both shoes into Montana's back with all the strength she had left. Propelled forward, Montana landed hard, screaming as his bandaged hand hit the floor. His gun slid across the room and under a couch.

As Montana scrambled to his feet, Jack rammed into him with his shoulder. Both of them went down. Jack rolled and came to his feet to the right of the stairs.

Montana tried to reach the gun and couldn't, so he jerked a curved, double-edged sword out of a tall box. It looked lethal.

Jack spotted a ceremonial sword hanging on the wall whose wooden shaft had shards of black obsidian imbedded in it like rows of shark's teeth. He seized it.

Montana glanced at Debra, who was yelling muffled words into the packing tape. "You're next, bitch," he said, then advanced on Jack. "That's an Aztec sword. Too bad for you, they never got out of the Stone Age. One swing with this," he whirled his blade around his head making a sound like a wind turbine, "could cut an Aztec in half."

Jack doubted his own sword could cut a pineapple in half. For God's sake, where was Gano?

Jack barely got the wooden shaft vertical to block Montana's first slashing blow. It sent splinters of wood flying. Montana's immediate backhanded swing hacked into the shaft, cutting a deep notch. Montana pressed forward, poking short jabs at Jack's midsection. Jack countered, but the weight of the stone chips made his weapon top-heavy and clumsy. He back-pedaled as Montana's next swing chopped another gash in the wood shaft. He blocked Montana's assault, but the shaft had cracked, was about to fail. Another slash at Jack's leg missed, and the steel blade knocked over a light stand.

Jack could tell Montana was toying with him, probably showing off in front of Debra. But he also noticed that Montana was awkward, gripping his sword with both hands, which meant his bandaged right hand was too painful to swing it alone. Jack swung his sword like a club in a horizontal arc and landed the blow on the bandaged hand as hard as he could.

Montana howled in agony.

Jack ducked inside and ripped a row of his sword's razor-edge obsidian spikes into Montana's left thigh. They penetrated his trousers and stuck into flesh. Montana screamed and jumped away. The stone points stuck in the fabric and jerked the wood shaft out of Jack's grasp.

Montana, maddened by pain and anger, moved in, limping, carving the air with the sword blade. Afraid to look away, Jack stumbled backward and tripped over a low table. He crashed down on his side.

Montana straddled him, dripping sweat. He raised the steel sword to deliver the single blow that cut Aztecs in half.

Chapter 52

July 12
6:45 p.m.

JUSTIN SINCLAIR felt Air Force One level out as it reached cruising altitude after its emergency departure from Travis. It was bound for Andrews Air Force Base outside Washington, D.C.

He'd paid no attention to the names of the men who had boarded just before takeoff, but he remembered their jobs: a senior NSA rep, a deputy assistant Secretary of State for Counter-Terrorism who happened to be at Travis, and a Marine Lt. Colonel with special weapons training. They had been hastily assembled in case they could be useful, but they were bit players, unlikely to voice an opinion, much less disagree with anyone senior to them. Locked in a pressure cooker, they weren't used to this kind of heat.

Corte, in a corner tapping away at his communications device, was different. He was both a trained technician and a warrior eager to engage an enemy.

Sinclair glanced at Gorton sitting at the end of the table signing documents, ignoring him. In just minutes, Gorton had lost his usual tanned, robust persona. Now he looked gray and fatigued. He was in deep denial, hiding in routine paperwork instead of dealing with looming danger.

The terrorist threat had given Strider a reprieve, and if he actually found Montana in Juarez, Montana would take him out. If that didn't happen, Justin would make sure Strider never got another shot at Gorton again. *Damn, how had he misjudged Strider so badly?*

He slid back into the chair next to Gorton. "You realize that everything Strider said was a lie," he said in a confidential tone. "Every time you pressed him for proof, he changed the subject. He has a screw loose. Paranoid for sure."

Gorton didn't contradict him so he continued. "It was about revenge. He's obsessed with the idea that Arthur Palmer had it in for him. That probably led to his hatred for that man, Montana. On top of that, Strider's father did those terrible things and Strider got the shaft big time. So he has a hard on for me, you, the whole damn world."

Gorton glanced at him. "I'm not so sure. The details he gave about what Montana is doing were pretty damned persuasive."

"That's because he's convinced himself it's true. I'll assign a dozen of my best lawyers to look into his claims. Nothing for you to worry about."

Gorton set down his pen. "You're the one who pressed me to meet with the guy in the first place. And don't tell me you were being nice to him. 'Nice' isn't your style."

"Strider showed up in my office yesterday and threw out a bunch of wild accusations. Then he demanded I set up a meeting with you. I refused. He threatened to go to the media and, unfortunately, he has some good contacts. He threatened you the same way a little while ago. He'd claim you refused to talk with him about threats to national security. Thinking about what would be best for you, I agreed to set up the meeting."

Gorton looked at him as though appraising him at a first meeting before saying, "I'm the one who decides what's best for me. Now I have to make some calls."

He turned away and gave instructions to the Director of Homeland Security to have all agencies get the word out around the country to be vigilant for anything out of the ordinary, especially in major central business districts.

Anything out of the ordinary? Justin thought derisively, and imagined the Director trying to make sense out of something that vague. The Director would know the President had a reason for being imprecise so she wouldn't press him. Instead, she'd put the whole country on alert to play blindman's bluff. Gorton was walking a tightrope. He wanted to be able to claim, if he ever had to, that he'd put out sufficient warning, but he didn't want to start a panic.

Gorton was ten parts politician and no parts soldier.

When Gorton slumped in his chair and closed his eyes, everyone quieted immediately. Brigadier General Spinner, the senior NSA rep, lowered his coffee cup to the table without making a sound.

Sunlight paled as Air Force One sped east with the jet stream. Justin felt the occasional shudder as the fuselage encountered turbulence. He checked his pocket watch, a Patek Philippe, a gift from a now deceased member of the Forbes family. The timepiece showed there was almost an hour before the deadline. Whatever it took, he'd keep Gorton from caving in and paying the $100 million.

Suddenly, Gorton sat up straight. As he had several times already, he pushed the "Communications Officer" button on the speaker phone. "Lieutenant, have your guys picked up reports of anything unusual?"

"No sir. We've been scanning the country, like you told us, listening in on 911 and major city fire department frequencies. We've also tapped three TV network satellites, and we're working the major Internet service providers. If anything big happens, we'll know about it."

"You're doing a heck of a job, Lieutenant. Keep it up. That's all." He clicked off, looked at his watch, and announced to the room, "Well, guys, this will be over in an hour." Everyone murmured agreement.

Justin studied his old friend and wondered what Gorton, in his gut, really expected to happen. Did he believe it was all a fraud? Or did he expect one or more dirty bombs to explode in major cities? Did he think payment would make any difference?

Gorton leaned toward him and said in a low voice, "I hate to admit it, but I'm still sweating."

"You made the right call." *Yeah, except that Gorton would already have paid off like a broken slot machine if he and Corte hadn't talked him out of it.*

Someone knocked at the door hard, insistently. Everyone stopped talking. Corte opened the door and took an envelope from the Chief. For a moment he seemed about to open it himself. Then he handed it to the President.

Gorton took the envelope and stared at it. Justin knew he didn't want to open it, didn't want to have to deal with anything new. His resilience was gone, like a boxer who wishes the ref would stop the fight. Seconds ticked away as Gorton did nothing.

"Mr. President?" Justin prodded.

Gorton started, carefully opened the sealed envelope, as though he planned to reuse it, and pulled out the single sheet. It was another e-mail. He turned away from the others to read it.

"It's the terrorists." He sounded annoyed, as though someone had stepped on a toe of his newly-shined Sorrell Custom cowboy boots. "They give me fifteen minutes to pay the $100 million, or they'll detonate the rest of the bombs. What do they mean, 'the rest of the bombs?' That sounds like they've set off one already."

"That can't be right," Corte boomed. "We have almost an hour before their damn deadline."

"Shut up, Corte," Gorton snapped. "I have to—"

"Mr. President," General Spinner said softly, as if he didn't want to be heard.

"Not now, Spinner."

"Sir, we may have miscalculated," Spinner persisted, rising and moving toward the door.

"Who's this 'we,' General? Do you mean your gang that can't shoot straight has fucked up again?"

Sinclair saw the shock in Spinner's face at being addressed that way by his Commander-in-Chief.

Spinner swallowed hard and said, "The first e-mail set the deadline at seven p.m. Since we were in California, we assumed that meant Pacific Time, but what if the deadline referred to seven p.m. in some other time zone? In all other U.S. time zones, seven p.m. has already passed."

Around the room, faces of the newcomers showed stunned disbelief that such a kindergarten mistake had been made. Their silence proved that they realized the consequences of the blunder.

"Mr. President," Corte said, "there have been no reports of any explosion. These people are demanding payment within fifteen minutes to keep us from checking it out. It's a bluff."

"Their new deadline is only a few minutes from now," Gorton croaked. He swiped his forehead with his fingers. "I've already had Treasury set up the transfer mechanics. The money could be in Switzerland in a few seconds."

Before the President could collapse completely, Justin walked behind him to read the e-mail over his shoulder. *Could be a real terrorist, or it could be a bluff.* But if the senders were on the East Coast, they would have thought their deadline had passed hours ago. The sender of this e-mail seemed to think it had just passed. That meant they were probably in the Mountain Time Zone, a one hour difference. He realized that he knew something very important. Juarez and El Paso were in that Mountain Time Zone. If this was from Montana, he might think his deadline had passed minutes ago. He looked up. Corte, watching him, shook his head, clearly expecting him to keep Gorton from giving in to a terrorist.

What should he do? His mind raced through the maze. What if it *was* Montana and he wasn't bluffing? If a dirty bomb detonated anywhere, Strider would insist the perpetrator was Tom Montana, and Justin Sinclair had put him in position to do it. Initially, he'd steered Gorton away from the blackmail explanation because it could too easily have pointed to Montana—and to him. Now the greater danger to him was that a bomb would actually devastate some city, and he'd be implicated in that. Time to change horses fast. Time to shut down Corte and talk Gorton into making that payment.

Before he could say anything, Corte spoke. "Mr. President, please listen to this language in the original e-mail. 'Transfer $100 million to us before seven p.m. today or we will detonate *all* of these bombs.' Now they're claiming just one. You called their bluff. Now they're trying to spook you with another fake. There's a saying that a dog with no teeth barks loudest."

"Mr. Corte is being simplistic," Justin said. "In the first e-mail, the claim they could detonate multiple dirty bombs was for shock value. Referring to a single bomb in this e-mail doesn't mean they're backing off or bluffing. It means they know that even one explosion will ensure payment in full. If a bomb has exploded, you'll be blamed for not making the payment to stop others." He paused, then lowered the tone of his voice for greater impact. "Send the money now."

Corte's mouth opened like a fish at Justin's one hundred and eighty degree reversal. He stood even taller, frowned, and said in his deep bass, "Mr. President. You can't deal with terrorists. You have to be strong and stay the course."

"Stay the course," Gorton said in a mechanical voice.

The man from Counter-Terrorism at State said, "Mr. President, from a political point of view, I agree with Mr. Corte. At a Senate Hearing they'd say, 'The President took $100 million from taxpayers and gave it to someone whose only demonstrated capability was sending e-mails. Suppose this turns out to be a fraternity prank? Or it's from some radical in Yemen who will use the money to sink U.S. ships? They'd call you, forgive me sir, gullible. With the election coming up . . ." He didn't need to finish.

Gorton's face told Justin that the discussion was over. Two clever nobodies had just outmaneuvered him and pushed the right buttons to manipulate the vacillating President. All he could do now was hope the e-mail wasn't from Montana.

"Our entire intelligence apparatus is on alert," Gorton said. "If a bomb had gone off, we'd know about it by now. We'll stand pat and this will be the last we hear from these people."

The banging at the door and the ring of the red phone were simultaneous.

Chapter 53

JACK COCKED both legs, ready to lash up at the blade when it chopped down. Suddenly, the air filled with a thunder clap. Splinters of glass rained down. He rolled away as the sword hanging over him crashed to the floor.

Montana stood with both hands pressed to his chest, eyes wide, staring at Jack with a fixed gaze. Gurgling, he stumbled across the room to a side door, struggled to unlock it, and walked slowly outside, hands now dangling at his sides.

"You kiddies okay?" Gano asked from outside. He was looking through the shattered window, the muzzle of the Mossberg 935 now pointing at the ceiling. "Sorry about the delay. This place is like a vault and all the drapes are drawn. I knew Montana would have a gun on you, but I couldn't see him to take a shot until you got him moving around in front of the slit in the drapes."

"He's getting away," Jack called as he scrambled to his feet and ran to Debra. "Stop him."

"Oh, he's just looking for a place to lie down. I'll go get him."

After shaking like a dog to rid his clothes of glass fragments, Jack gently pulled the tape from Debra's mouth. "You all right?"

"I am never, ever, under any circumstances, doing you a favor again. This was—"

He lightly replaced the tape, then saw in her flaring eyes that it wasn't a good joke and removed it.

He unwound the tape from her ankles and said, "Wrap your legs around my waist to get the strain off your arms so I can get them loose."

She did as instructed. When she was free, he carried her to a chair and lowered her into it.

Gano came in through the side door alone.

"Where's Montana?" Jack asked.

"He's lying face down at the bottom of the moat. Didn't look like he was in the mood for conversation. Sorry about that. I know you wanted that pissant in one piece, but those 12-gauge magnum shells . . ." He shrugged.

Yeah, he'd badly needed Montana alive, but then he pictured Gano looking in the window, seeing Montana with the sword raised.

"Not like you had a choice," he said. "And thanks."

"It's nothing. Hey, Debra, how'd you like hanging out with the Chief here."

"Never a dull moment around Jack," she answered.

Jack walked behind the desk. "I hope his computer will tell us something." It took only seconds to open Montana's most recent outgoing e-mail. He read it to the others.

"If you haven't paid in full within fifteen minutes of receiving this, we'll set off the rest of the bombs."

"After he brought us in here," Jack said, "he was on the computer checking his Swiss bank account. Then he sent this e-mail. Let's hope it was a final bluff to get the money without pulling the trigger."

"If he used timers," Debra put in, "all the bombs will go off even though he's dead."

"To use timers," Jack replied, "they had to be set at the cave before the trucks left last night. Montana could never get drivers to do that. And to remain flexible on when each bomb goes off, he couldn't use timers at all."

"You told me," Debra said, "that his first e-mail said the trucks are booby-trapped to explode if tampered with. If he knew how to make a booby-trap, that could still happen."

"A tenth grader could build booby traps using a lift device," Gano said. "That's a simple mercury switch like the wall thermostats in old homes. It's a glass capsule a half-inch long. When it's tilted, which could happen if a cop opens a truck door, the mercury shifts, closes a circuit, and 'boom.' Or he could have picked up passive infrared from Radio Shack, like they use in home security systems and light sensors. That would be bad. Those are tricky to disarm, even for experts."

"I'll call Gorton, tell him what we know, and suggest that he search Albuquerque first," Jack said.

"Why there?" Gano asked.

"Because Montana told me he'd sent what he called his 'Albuquerque e-mail' to Gorton."

"While you call him, I'm going to take a look around this place," Debra said and walked out of the room.

"Now what?" Gano asked.

"After I talk with Gorton, we get to the Palmer plant as fast as we can. Montana has programmed Guzman to dump the toxic waste tanks."

"No way." Gano looked taken aback. "Guzman bled to death."

"Nope. Someone sewed him up in time."

"Damn, I should have used a Phillips head screwdriver. But why would Montana care about the wells? It's way past bonus time."

"Montana lost his cushy job, the bonus, and his cut from the nuclear waste smuggling. He was looking at a lifetime on the run. More than anything, he wanted revenge. Right now, odds are huge that he's going to succeed in taking it out on El Paso and Juarez. Even as a dead man, he's using The Ape to destroy both cities."

RING . . . RING . . . RING.

"Air Force One conference room."

Jack recognized Corte's bass voice. "Jack Strider calling. President Gorton, please. It's urgent." He turned to Debra. "Sounds like a dozen people, all talking at once." He heard Corte say, "Yes sir, and he says it's urgent."

"For Christ's sake, it better be." Gorton sounded hostile as he said into the receiver, "Go ahead."

"Sir, it's Jack Strider."

"I know that."

"It's over. We found—"

"Over? Tell that to Albuquerque! A dirty bomb just went off at Kirkland Air Force Base near Albuquerque. Sandia National Labs, where we build nuclear weapons, is on that base. There's a goddamn plume of radioactive smoke. If a wind comes up it could contaminate El Paso, maybe even Phoenix or Denver."

Oh my God. He covered the receiver and whispered to Gano and Debra, "One of the trucks exploded in Albuquerque."

"We're at Condition Red," Gorton said. "I wired $100 million to the terrorists a few seconds after we got word. No choice. Had to keep more bombs from going off. Can't talk now." He slammed the phone down.

"Gorton has panicked." Jack dialed the number again. This time it was answered immediately.

"General Spinner here."

"This is Jack Strider calling back. Listen carefully. Tell the President this was not terrorism. It was blackmail, and the blackmailer is right here, *dead.* I'll hold." He heard shouts in the background.

Gorton came on the line. "Dead? Who's dead?"

"Tomás Montana. He was the blackmailer." He wanted to add, *Just like I told you.* "We found him."

"Then how did a bomb just go off in Albuquerque?"

It was that second call, Jack thought. *The one Montana made right after talking with Guzman. He didn't speak or leave a message because he hadn't called a person. He'd called a triggering device.*

"He must have set it off by calling a cell phone in the truck," Jack told Gorton. "He was killed a few minutes after that without making any other calls."

"Are there any more truck bombs?"

"At least three, and they are probably booby-trapped. If anyone disturbs them, even a thief trying to break in, they'll detonate." He heard Gorton groan. "But I can make educated guesses about where they are."

"Then tell me, for God's sake."

"El Paso or Juarez, Chihuahua City, and some major target from Monterey to Mexico City. Each truck will probably be parked near high-value targets like a downtown or a national monument. The trucks are large and black with 'hazardous waste' warning signs on the sides."

"I'll get the FBI on it in El Paso," Gorton said. "If Mexican authorities find out American-made dirty bombs are sitting in their cities, their President will rip me a new one. I'll get DoD explosive ordnance disposal experts down there in civvies within hours. Best case, they find them, disarm the booby-traps, and sneak the trucks back across the border. Worst case is worse than I want to think about right now. Can you help in the search?"

"No, sir. I have to get to the Palmer Industries plant in Juarez. Montana ordered his head thug to pump the toxic waste into the aquifer."

"Holy—" Gorton said, and then Jack heard him shout a string of names and order someone to get them on other phone lines. "I'm sending troops from Fort Bliss to pulverize that plant. No one's dumping anything."

Jack shook his head. *Gorton seemed to make the wrong decision one hundred percent of the time.*

"That won't help, sir. Montana's man is programmed to turn the valves no matter what. My friend and I will try to take him down before he knows we're there. It's the only way. Send your people, but tell them to keep quiet and wait outside the main gate. If they hear shooting, have them move in fast."

"Yeah, okay," Gorton said, already distracted, clearly too rushed to argue. "Look, I have one question. You were with Montana when he blew up that bomb in Albuquerque, right? I mean, I'm sure you did your best, but couldn't you have stopped him?" In the background, Jack heard Corte telling the President his other calls were waiting. Gorton told Jack, "Never mind, we'll talk about that later." He was gone.

Ungrateful bastard—but Jack had already asked himself the same question. It was like an echo from Peck's suicide.

"I found the mother lode," Debra said, bursting in from the kitchen. "There's a Land Rover in the garage loaded with boxes. The key was in the ignition so I unlocked the cargo space and found cartons of Aztec stuff and bricks of hundred dollar bills."

"So Mr. Personality probably had a light cargo plane lined up," Gano said, "maybe for a hop down to Panama." His eyes lit up. "Look Boss, I was going to bill you for overtime, but I'll settle for a few of those bricks."

"We're out of here," Jack said to Debra and Gano.

"We're not going anywhere," Debra said, "unless we find the control panel for the front gate. We're locked in."

"There has to be a remote control in his Land Rover," Jack said. "We'll drive that."

"What about the Explorer we drove up here?" she asked.

"Montana shot the hell out of the back end, so it would attract cops like a magnet. We don't need that."

"We're bringing the money, right?" Gano prompted.

That was one of the things Jack liked about him. He always kept his priorities straight—and in plain sight.

As she approached the bars of the formidable gate a few minutes later, Debra pulled the remote control from where it was clipped to the visor above the Land Rover's windshield. She pushed the button, but the gate didn't move. She kept trying as she pulled closer, punching it harder. Still no movement. "I'm going to ram it." Then the gate swung slowly toward them, and she jammed her foot down on the accelerator.

Jack closed his eyes, trying to concentrate on what was coming up. Instead, he heard Gorton's question again. "Couldn't you have stopped him?" Maybe he should have gone in the front door shooting. But that would have been stupid. Montana would have killed him—and Debra—and then detonated all of the bombs. As it was, three cities had been spared—so far. He'd made the right choice.

On the other hand, if their attack on the wells had been successful, or they hadn't left Guzman behind, or Montana hadn't thrown himself out of the truck, this trip wouldn't be necessary. Should he have let Gano have his way and smoke them both back then?

His mind kept grappling with the questions until he smelled the odor of the Rio Grande and opened his eyes. They were at the border. If the Juarez cops had put out an APB on him, he could be grabbed right here. He and Gano feigned sleep while the guard checked Debra's ID. If he ran the license plate, he'd discover the Land Rover wasn't theirs. If he opened the cargo space, well, it would be game over for sure. The guard took long enough that a car behind them in line started honking. With an annoyed look he waved them through.

Minutes sped by as they raced to the plant. No one spoke. The tension in the vehicle had weight and an odor.

"Pull over right there," he said to Debra as they neared the entrance to the plant.

No light shone through any of the buildings' windows. He pointed at dim lights in the distance. "That's Guzman at the wells," he said to Gano. "We'll have to run for it."

"Not this ol' cowhand. That's fifty yards in the open before we get to the first building. There could be guards watching us through those windows. I don't do suicide missions."

"Debra," Jack said, "hop out and get out of sight. I'm taking the Land Rover in."

"I'll drive," she said.

Jack gave a hard shake of his head. "Not this time. Gorton's troops have orders to wait outside the gate. Make sure they do."

She studied his face for a moment, then nodded.

He touched her shoulder as she got out, wanting to pull her into his arms. Instead he took her place behind the wheel and drove the Land Rover in a wide arc before pulling up in front of the Admin building. They waited. No shots, so they jumped out and flattened themselves against the wall, then dashed from building to building through the faint smell from the fires three days earlier. At the last building, they stopped to get a better view of the grove of trees.

"We haven't seen a single guard," Gano said.

"Maybe Montana sent them away. He doesn't care about the plant anymore and wouldn't want witnesses for Guzman's dirty work."

The clearing in the grove was faintly illuminated by a few bare bulbs strung on trees, shining on the wells and up the slope along the pipeline.

Suddenly Gano swung around, aiming his .38 in the direction they'd just come from. Then he let the barrel drop. "Tough chick," he said admiringly as Debra slid in behind them.

"Hey guys," she whispered.

"Get out of here," Jack hissed. "Guzman is—"

"A bad ass dude," Gano put in.

Jack looked at Debra.

"Let me guess," she said, frowning at him. "You want me to stay right here and pretend to be a cactus."

"You got it—and this time, *do* it."

"Train's leaving," Gano said, and moved into the open like a ghost. Jack followed him. In half a minute they were both inside the grove.

Jack saw no movement near the wells, but he heard a low sound. "Someone's singing or drunk."

"Look there," Gano whispered. He pointed up the slope at the pipeline that connected the tanks on top of the ridge. "Something's shining. Looks like water."

Except it wasn't water. Deadly hazardous waste must be leaking from some of the joints between hastily-repaired sections of the pipeline. That meant Guzman was here and had already opened the valves of the tanks on the ridge. The entire pipeline down to the pumps was full of toxic waste. When one of those joints broke loose, thousands of gallons would soak into the ground.

"Gano, you circle to the right. I'll go left." He crouched low as he edged through the scrawny trees toward the singsong sound.

In the center of the clearing, Guzman leaned against an elevated pipe where it entered the main pump. His legs looked like swollen sausages protruding from dark shorts. He'd wrapped a rag around the heavy gut hanging over his belt. Wrench in one hand, a bottle in the other, he sang to himself in a slurred voice. He tried to set the bottle on the pipe and stared at it numbly when it fell to the ground. He cursed and staggered ahead with his wrench, leaning forward in a half-crouch like a Neanderthal, determined to finish the one job he had left in his life.

Gano sprinted straight at Guzman and launched himself in a flying body block, sending Guzman crashing into the pipe and caroming to the ground. Gano grabbed Guzman's legs, dragged the barely conscious man across the clearing, and dropped him at Jack's feet.

"I figured I'd do what you want just this once. You know, bring the bad guy back alive."

Suddenly, a roaring *"WHOOSH, WHOOSH, WHOOSH"* filled the air. Sand on the floor of the clearing swirled, as if caught by a tornado. They looked up through pummeling waves of sound.

Gano shouted, "Black Hawk attack helicopter. No other sound like it. They don't rent those babies out, so this is one of Gorton's toys."

"I told him," Jack shouted, "to keep his backup people outside the gate."

"You're missing the point. They're not backup for us. They have orders to capture this plant. Any minute now the commandos are gonna scale down on ropes and shoot the shit out of anything that moves. If we weren't right under them, they'd already be using machine guns to turn us into ground beef. They've been told everyone on the ground is the enemy."

"We'll identify ourselves."

"In a dust storm? Over all that noise? No way. They'll shoot first and ask no questions later."

A machine gun overhead fired bursts, spraying the trees. Then three narrow beams of lights pointed directly down from the Black Hawk.

"They're coming," Gano said, cocking his .38. "How about we hustle up the slope?"

"No. If they see us and start shooting, they'll rupture the pipes."

"I'm more worried about us getting ruptured. Let's make them a present of fatso here and run for the nearest building."

He'd left Guzman behind once before and wasn't going to make that mistake again. He shouted over the sound of the whirling blades, "Guzman comes with us. Let's go."

The chopper descended a few more yards. The whine of its engine grew even more piercing. Several ropes abruptly dropped, the weighted ends slapping the ground.

Jack hauled Guzman to his feet. "Dragging him will be too slow. I'll take his shoulders, you take his legs." They lugged Guzman through the grove to where Debra was waiting.

Struggling with Guzman, Gano handed Debra his .38. As they crossed the open space, she trailed, gripping the pistol and looking over her shoulder. Jack heard the Black Hawk's engines straining, then saw a black patch rising into the star-filled sky.

"They're heading for the U.S. side of the river," Gano said softly. "That means the troops are on the ground and will be comin' this way fast."

The first two buildings they checked were locked, but the padlock on the third was hanging open in the hasp. They ducked inside. From the acidic odors, the barely-visible steel vessels must be filled with chemical waste.

Jack spotted a structure in the middle of the vast space, about 20 x 20 feet with waist-high wood walls and wire mesh rising above; maybe a supervisor's station.

"In there," he said.

They dumped Guzman inside the cage. Gano kicked his thigh and got no response. Jack turned a metal desk on its side and wedged it against the wall facing the entrance to the building. All three of them squatted behind it, Debra between them.

They were silent, scarcely breathing, eyes fixed on the door.

"Sinclair did this," Jack whispered hoarsely. "He wanted me dead even if a full-scale attack pushed Guzman into poisoning the aquifer. He talked Gorton into changing the plan." He glanced at the other two, and away. "I'm sorry I got you into this."

Debra squeezed his hand. "Maybe they won't find us."

"They *will* find us," Gano said, "They'll search every building. I damn sure hope they've been briefed that this plant is full of deadly gas and flammables. Otherwise, their technique is to kick in the door, toss in a couple of hand grenades, and spray the place with automatic rifles. Then they send in the grunts. Bad for us."

They heard automatic weapons firing nearby.

"They saw what direction we ran," Gano said, taking his .38 back from Debra. "When they get here, whatever happens, don't stand up or they'll cut you in half."

Seconds later, a barrage of bullets slammed into the metal door. Already unlocked, it swung open and banged into the wall, hanging from one hinge. Silence. The attackers were listening, poised to invade the building.

"Ready men," called a gruff voice, "on my signal."

Out of the corner of his eye, Jack saw Guzman clawing at the cage wall to haul himself to his feet. Jack grabbed his ankle with one hand. Guzman jerked loose and lurched out of the cage into the open, screaming with all his strength. His curses in Spanish were punctuated by shouts of, "Fuck you. Fuck you." He shook his fists at the door.

The impact of bullets pounding his body jerked him from side-to-side like a puppet. He swung a defiant left hook, pitched backwards, and landed in a heap. The shooting stopped and the attackers quickly withdrew.

"Son-of-a bitch," Gano said matter-of-factly, "that fat bastard got the last laugh on me." He was holding his upper arm where blood oozed through his shirt. When Debra looked at the wound in alarm, he added, "It's a ricochet, a flea bite. But thanks to Guzman, now they're sure we're the bad guys so they'll come in shooting."

Jack wrapped his arm around Debra's shoulders. Her martial arts skills wouldn't be enough this time.

He said softly, "I love you." She looked at him and winked.

"Gano," he said, "I'm going to tell them who we are."

"Right, like they'll take your word. I'll try something that works in old war movies." From his cramped position behind the metal desk, Gano sang out at the top of his voice, "From the halls of Montezuma to the shores of Tripoli." He paused. Nothing happened. "We fight our country's battles in the air, on land and sea."

A rifle barrel poked around the corner into the space and fired two shots that glanced off a steel vessel.

"Knock it off, damn it, until I tell you," someone shouted outside. The same voice called through the doorway. "What comes next?"

"First to fight for right and freedom," Gano sang out. "And to keep our honor free."

"That proves shit." There was a pause. "Who won MVP in Super Bowl 44?"

"Drew Brees," Jack called. "We're here to *stop* the wells from being poisoned."

"This is Captain McIntyre, Special Forces," called a stern voice. "How many are in there?"

"Three, alive."

"Who's the one on the ground?"

"He was going to poison the aquifer."

"Identify yourselves."

"Jack Strider, Debra Vanderberg, Gano LeMoyne. The aquifer is safe for now, but the pipeline that runs up the hill has to be repaired immediately."

"First I want you to come out single file. No weapons. Hands on top of your heads."

"Tell your men to back off," Gano called.

"We're not backing off. Now move it."

"Don't know about going out there naked," Gano said to Jack. "Those trigger-happy sons-of-bitches turned Guzman into Swiss cheese. I'll just hang on to my ol' .38."

Jack looked at Guzman's corpse. He wasn't worried about McIntyre's men being trigger-happy. He was worried that Sinclair might have made sure three *gringos* wouldn't leave this plant alive—no matter what. Of the options, what they would do if they saw Gano with a gun was more predictable.

"Leave the gun, Gano," he said. "They can take us apart anytime they want. I'll go first." He stepped around Guzman's body into the beam of the Captain's blinding flashlight, hoping that he wasn't making a mistake that would result in all of them dying.

Chapter 54

CAPT. MCINTYRE had seemed relatively sure they weren't the terrorists he'd been sent to kill, but he wasn't accepting Jack's story either. He'd separated and handcuffed them and taken their cell phones. Then he'd radioed the Black Hawk.

"Pick me up in the plant's parking lot. Come in hot, no lights. Do it now."

Twenty minutes later, after marching them to the parking lot and loading them aboard the Black Hawk, McIntyre placed a set of headphones on Jack and disappeared into the cockpit. Jack looked at Debra, seated behind him. She appeared a little worse for wear but gave him a brave smile.

Sometime later, McIntyre's voice came over Jack's headphones. "We'll land at Fort Bliss in a few minutes. A plane will be waiting to take you to Andrews Air Force Base. If you're legit, you'll be a hero. If not, I wouldn't want to be in your boots after what happened in Albuquerque."

Soon after they landed on the Fort Bliss runway a few minutes later, they were transferred to the plane in silence and seated out of conversational range of one another. Jack called a crewman over. "My hands are numb from being cuffed behind my back. How about getting these cuffs off?" He thought the response would tell him a lot about their status, how they were being regarded.

The crewman went to the cockpit, returned and removed Jack's cuffs. Jack was starting to stretch when the man said coldly, "Wrists together in front of your body." The cuffs were reapplied, and the crewman put Debra and Gano through the same procedure. The change made the flight less miserable, but they were still being treated as possible criminals.

It was dark when they landed at Andrews AFB and were led to a gunmetal gray Ford SUV with smoked windows for the next leg of the trip.

The sun had begun to rise just as they reached the destination, a manor house at the end of a half-mile long drive. It was white, vaguely Colonial, flanked by several guesthouses and what looked like a stable. This was obviously very high-end real estate, yet the landscaping was basic, mostly hedges and natural grasses. Instead of Mercedes and horse trailers, the vehicles scattered around were a variety of nondescript black sedans.

To Jack the utilitarian furnishings inside the mansion reinforced the likelihood they hadn't been brought here for fox hunts or pool parties.

A young man took him directly to a bedroom where he removed the handcuffs. No TV, no phone, and the bookshelf was bare. The design of the wrought iron strips outside the large window was decorative but they were still bars. He was sitting on a corner of the bed when the same man reappeared, bringing him a Continental breakfast.

"Where are we? What kind of place is this?"

The man cocked his head to one side. "You'll find that out tomorrow," he said and started for the door.

Jack started after him but the man got out fast and closed the door behind him. Jack heard the lock slide into place and stared at the blank, solid door. He was too exhausted to really connect with the rage that had been building inside for the past few hours. He had put his life on the line to save the damn aquifer, to stop Montana from blowing up three more cities—maybe. So where was the presumption of innocence? Where was Gorton? Too tired to beat on the door to demand answers, he looked down at his filthy clothes and thought he ought to take a shower. Instead, he let the clothes drop in a pile and collapsed on the bed.

July 13
Noon

"MR. STRIDER, TELL us everything you know about the crimes committed by your father, Judge H. Peckford Strider."

That's how the interrogation by two agents, or whatever they were, had begun. The room looked as though it had at some time been a large bedroom, rectangular, a row of curtained windows along the west wall. A short conference table ran parallel to the east wall. The agents sat in two of the three chairs that faced the windows. They'd put Jack in the chair across from them that faced the wall. There was other furniture in the room, but it didn't match and seemed to have no function other than to fill up the room.

The agents wore business suits, government standard. He felt ridiculous sitting across from them wearing a *gi* with the belt called an *obi*. Karate gear. During the night, someone had taken the clothes he'd worn through the battles at El Castillo and the Palmer plant and left these . . . pajamas. The *gi* made him think of prison garb designed to make the wearer stand out in a civilian population. There was no way the people interrogating him would look at him and think he was a hero.

The pasty-faced, middle-aged man in a floral print shirt repeatedly referred to his father as a "trafficker in human flesh." He also pointed out that District Attorney Rick Calder had never exonerated Jack and had implied, instead, that smuggling, human or otherwise, might be a genetic trait.

Their style and implications annoyed him, so after several denials, he refused to play. When they finally switched their line of questioning to the events of the past two weeks, Jack was willing to be more forthcoming. However, he quickly realized that when he answered a question in a way critical of former Secretary of State Justin Sinclair, the agents' eyes narrowed and they abruptly cut him off. At one point, after Jack added another accusation against Sinclair, one man looked at the other and said, "Jesus."

They drilled in on the bundles of cash the Special Forces men had removed from the Land Rover at the plant. Jack pointed out that the vehicle belonged to Montana but, since their questions were based on their belief that the cash was evidence of Jack's participation in Montana's scheme, they disregarded his denials.

After almost six hours with no breaks, the second agent, a pencil-necked man wearing thick horn-rims, asked the same question for about the tenth time. Jack wanted to knock the plastic smile off the agent's chops, but instead he said, "I'm fed up with your innuendos. Either I'm free to leave or I'm going to exercise my Miranda rights."

The agents didn't answer, but made some notes and left the room.

What the hell was going on? Jack stood and stretched vigorously, as he'd done every hour for the past six. He wasn't being waterboarded, but this was no friendly debriefing either. The agents had been trying to provoke him into losing his temper, blurting out something incriminating. Or catch him in inconsistencies. They seemed certain he was guilty of something and expected him to tell them what it was. They seemed ready to keep him in suspended animation until he confessed.

He waited, glad for a break, but was soon bored. He tried the door. Unlocked. He cracked it open and looked out. No one in the hall. Time to look around. He walked into the hall and looked through a window on the far side. Beyond the lawn and a saltwater marsh, a wooden Skipjack sailed past in open water. To any sailor, the Skipjack was the emblem of the Chesapeake Bay. He looked at the sky. From the angle of the sun, he had to be on the Eastern shore. Judging from the time it had taken to drive from Andrews, he was in Maryland.

He walked downstairs and happened onto a solarium, a long room with floor-to-ceiling windows along one wall. Like the window upstairs, the view was impeded by bars with an intricate Arabesque design. A sturdy oak table, ten feet long, ran lengthwise down the room, flanked by four chairs per side. It gave an otherwise casual space the austere aura of an AA meeting. He immediately noticed the door that opened onto a slate terrace and tried the handle. Key-locked. When he turned, a tall man with the fixed stare of a Doberman had entered the solarium at the far end. He shook his head 'no.'

Jack walked back upstairs to the room where he'd spent the night. The interrogators were probably comparing notes, setting traps for tomorrow. Somewhere, Debra was reasoning through what was happening. Gano would be pissed, looking for an edge.

He thought about the karate pajamas, locked doors, and no communication with the outside world. He, Debra and Gano were prisoners. That could only be happening because Gorton had ordered them detained. Since Gorton controlled this remote, secure place, odds were good it was a CIA safe house where they could hide people indefinitely or sweat their guests without upsetting the neighbors.

He tried to put himself in Gorton's mind. By now, Gorton knew Jack had been right about the aquifer and the dirty bombs. Despite that, he clearly did not regard Jack as a hero. Therefore, as a result of Sinclair's poisonous insinuations, he must believe that Jack had been in on all of it with Montana. Some of the questions the agents had asked implied that when Jack saw the scheme collapsing he'd sold out Montana to save himself. The bricks of cash in the Land Rover could support that belief. Gorton could have even bought the bullshit Sinclair fed him about Jack having been involved in Peck's crimes.

Sinclair had tried to program the Special Forces to cut down the three of them at the plant. Because that failed, he knew that Jack could still damage him badly. He'd stop at nothing to make sure that didn't happen.

The President was sinking in quicksand. Having bungled the blackmail threat and let a dirty bomb go off in Albuquerque, he desperately needed Sinclair to back him up. And Sinclair would do that to avoid being blamed for his own role in the fiasco. Each was trading on their thirty-year friendship, and both had reason to fear what Jack Strider might say. Would Gorton offer him an incentive to keep quiet? Would he do something a lot more coercive?

Or would the most powerful men in the world, the man who had snatched him from the real world in the middle of the night, simply make him—and Debra and Gano—disappear for good?

Chapter 55

July 14
8:00 a.m.

THE NEXT MORNING, Jack awakened and checked his watch. Nine hours of sound sleep and not one dream. Despite having been beaten up by the physical and emotional intensity of the past few days, he felt halfway recharged—and completely fed up.

Fortified by coffee, fried eggs and hash browns, he told his inquisitors in the upstairs room, "I'll play your games until noon. After that, not one more word. This isn't Guantanamo Bay. Last I heard, the Constitution still applies in Maryland."

Neither man reacted to his ultimatum. They simply started on their list of questions. At eleven, they declared a fifteen minute break and left. He stayed in the room, bracing for a showdown.

When they returned, the senior agent said, "We're done here." His scowl contrasted with his bright Hawaiian shirt.

"You've been jerking me around for two days and all you say is 'Done here'? How about an apology? Maybe something like, 'We're very sorry for the misunderstanding. You're free to go now. We'll call a cab'?"

The man's scowl deepened. "I didn't say you were free to go. Some people want to see you at four o'clock this afternoon." They both turned and walked out of the room without another word.

After a flavorless lunch on a tray in his bedroom-cell, Jack was left alone behind a locked door. Solitary confinement. Nothing to do but think.

So that's what he did. Less than six weeks ago, his carefully-orchestrated career had been right on track. Then Peck killed himself, the scandal broke, and Jack's future had evaporated. Since then, he'd stood up to several crises, Mac and Ana-Maria had been murdered, and Sinclair, Montana and Guzman had tried to kill him. Had all that changed him? *Bet your ass it had.*

Sinclair, the deadliest of them all, would keep trying to kill him until he succeeded. The only chance he—and Debra and Gano—had was to persuade Gorton that Sinclair was the mastermind behind the smuggling of nuclear waste and guilty of murder.

And Jack had another mountain to climb. To prevent cartels and terrorists from getting their hands on the nuclear waste in the cave, he had to get Gorton to take charge. That wasn't very likely because they were in this CIA safe house only because Gorton had already sided with Sinclair.

By the time he heard the click of the lock in the door at 3:45, he was in a foul mood.

"Stand up," the agent said. "Give me your wrists."

Handcuffs again. His face was hot as he came to his feet, but he took a deep breath and held out his wrists. If the four o'clock visitors were imported interrogators who planned to sweat him, he was ready. Being locked up had lit his fuse.

Being led downstairs to the solarium, he felt like a gladiator entering the arena. *Bring it on.*

Debra and Gano, also handcuffed and in karate gear, stood together by the window.

"Hey," Gano called, "glad you could make it. Looks like we all got the same come-as-you-are invitation."

"You two okay?" Jack asked.

"Let's see," Debra said, "house arrest, nonstop verbal abuse, fashionable jewelry—" She held up the cuffs. "—and you ask . . ."

The door opened. The President of the United States walked in.

Jack was knocked off balance by the man's sudden appearance. When he saw Gorton's unreadable mask, his defenses shot up. He knew instinctively that this was about to be very unpleasant.

"Mr. Strider," Gorton said in a flat tone. Then he glanced at the other two. "Ms. Vanderberg. Mr. LeMoyne. Yes, I've been briefed on both of you, especially on Mr. LeMoyne's unusual background."

Without a word, Jack held up his hands.

Gorton signaled to a man in a brown suit and mirrored sunglasses who had come in right behind him. "Agent, get all those cuffs off."

The agent, his expression reluctant, retrieved the cuffs and backed into a corner where he stood stiffly. Gorton said, "You may leave us now."

"But sir—"

"Now."

The agent left, and Justin Sinclair appeared in the doorway, wearing a black suit and looking completely composed. He walked straight to Jack. When he was within a few feet, he broke into a broad smile and stuck out his right hand. Jack didn't want to shake it and didn't. With no hesitation, the trajectory of Sinclair's hand rose and gripped Jack's shoulder briefly.

"Strider," Sinclair said, "your country is in your debt. Isn't that right, Mr. President?"

Jack stepped away from the hand on his shoulder. He knew Sinclair didn't think the country owed Jack Strider a damned thing.

"Correct," Gorton said, "Let's sit down and talk about that." As soon as Gorton chose a chair, Sinclair hurried to sit on his right.

Jack sat opposite Gorton, joined by Debra, who looked tense, and Gano, who looked ready for a fight.

"I can't stay long," Gorton said, "so I'll get right to it. Jack, there will soon be a vacancy on the 9th Circuit bench, and I'm going to appoint you to fill that seat. Quite a few Supreme Court justices have come from the 9th Circuit."

Jack blinked, surprised. That had come right out of the blue. Gorton was offering him an incentive, but what did he want in return? And why had he chosen the 9th Circuit? Then he got it. Someone had briefed him that a 9th Circuit judgeship would be appealing for exactly the reason Gorton mentioned. He'd never told Sinclair about his Supreme Court goal, but he *had* told Samuel Butler. So the idea of using the 9th Circuit as a carrot was based on information from Sam Butler. Gorton was offering to feed Jack's ambition in return for his silence. To Gorton, the offer made sense—a win-win—so he would expect Jack to go for it.

Now Jack understood why Sinclair was almost jubilant. If the deal shut Jack up voluntarily it would give Sinclair time to silence him permanently. Sinclair couldn't get to him in this safe house, but he could after Jack, Debra and Gano were released and out on the streets. Gorton only wanted to avoid being embarrassed. Sinclair wanted to avoid life in prison.

"Mr. President, I appreciate your confidence in me, but before I respond to your offer, I have a couple of questions about Mr. Sinclair."

Gorton frowned. "I don't think questions are necessary, nor is rehashing our discussion aboard Air Force One. After you left for El Paso, the situation got damned tense, and Secretary Sinclair stepped up. At times like that, a president needs people he can trust around him."

Yeah, especially when you're making the worst decisions of your undistinguished career.

"There's bad blood between you two," Gorton continued, "but I want you to get past that. Secretary Sinclair has my full confidence."

Sinclair nodded his agreement with the benediction he'd just received. He had worked his magic again. Jack pictured a viper hissing in Gorton's ear.

There was another possibility, one that stretched his imagination. Maybe Gorton had actually approved Sinclair's smuggling scheme in advance. If that was true, nothing Jack said would matter. But if it wasn't, he had to confront Gorton before he left.

"Jack, I've made you an attractive offer. I'd like your decision by close of business tomorrow."

"Mr. President, before you leave, will you clear up one thing for me?"

Sinclair, on his feet and turning for the door, said, "Mr. President, you'll be late for that meeting if—"

"What can I clear up for you?" Gorton said with an indulgent smile.

"When I called you from El Paso, you said you would send troops to the Palmer plant and have them wait outside the front gate. We agreed they wouldn't come crashing onto the property and spook Guzman into poisoning the aquifer. Is that how you remember it?"

"Things were moving pretty fast—"

"Instead, Special Forces showed up with orders to shoot any so-called terrorist they saw, basically anyone on the plant grounds. Correct?"

Looking perplexed, Gorton walked to a tall window. "I'm not sure that's a fair way to characterize the orders I gave."

"Captain McIntyre told me those were his exact orders. Here's my question. Did Mr. Sinclair persuade you to give those orders?"

Gorton gave Sinclair a sharp look. "I was told that if I deployed the troops immediately, they'd finish their job before you got to the plant. Justin also reminded me that you and Mr. LeMoyne are untrained civilians who failed to stop Montana from bombing Albuquerque. He even suggested that you might have been helping Montana, but I didn't buy that." He spread his hands. "As President, I'm responsible for that decision."

Sinclair's expression was filled with disdain. "Strider, *you're* the one who insisted that poisoning the aquifer was imminent. The President acted to protect the people of El Paso." He tilted his head back like a preacher concluding an irrefutable sermon.

Jack pointed his finger at Sinclair. *Time to go for the jugular.*

"If Special Forces had killed all three of us," he said, gesturing at Debra and Gano, "you would have been in the clear. That's why you persuaded the President to launch the attack."

Gorton looked shocked. "Hold on. You're saying—"

"It was a crisis," Sinclair spoke over him.

"It was a crisis all right, and you helped cause it. When I forced you to set up a meeting with President Gorton, you were afraid of what I might say. Rather than risk being exposed, you tried to have me assassinated."

He heard a low "Wow" from Gano to his left.

"That's slander *per se*," Sinclair shouted, finally aware of how great a threat he faced. "I'll have you—"

"No, you won't, because truth is a defense. You told President Gorton I'd be a no-show for my meeting with him on Air Force One. You thought I wouldn't be there because your sniper had told you he'd killed me. You reached Air Force One before the media had the correct name of the man shot at the Westin Palo Alto. That's why you thought you were safe in manipulating the President."

Sinclair screwed up his face, radiating outrage, but when Gorton sternly shook his head at him, Jack continued.

"Aboard Air Force One, I said Professor McDonald had been, and I quote, 'murdered.' Right after that, you said he'd been, I quote again, 'shot.' And even though I'd said nothing about my car, you suggested he'd been shot in the course of a carjacking. You knew those details because you heard them from your assassin."

"This is driving me goddamn nuts," Gorton snapped, fury in his voice. "I don't remember Justin's exact words, and we sure as hell don't tape what goes on in my conference room on Air Force One. You say Justin intended to have you killed by sending in that Black Hawk, but I told you I made that call. You say he tried to have you assassinated, but you have no assassin and no connection to Justin. Your accusations, with no evidence, are appalling."

"I have conclusive evidence. Ms. Vanderberg will tell you about it."

"I've already listened to crap I shouldn't have to put up with," Sinclair objected to Gorton and moved close to where Debra sat. "This woman is only an associate in my firm, totally unqualified to say anything." He leaned forward and said very softly, "Say one word about me, and your career is finished."

"Shut *up,*" Gorton barked at Sinclair. "Ms. Vanderberg, please get on with it."

Sitting across the table from Gorton, one seat to Jack's right, Debra said, "Mr. President, because of what I've learned since Mr. Sinclair sent me to Mexico, I hereby resign from Sinclair & Simms."

Right between the eyes. Jack hadn't seen that coming. *What guts. What timing.* Despite what she'd been through, and never having been in such a high-stakes drama, she looked and sounded completely unruffled.

"Now I need to tell you about Dr. Heidi Klein, the CEO of D-TECH. I made an appointment with her by posing as a reporter writing a story about D-TECH. I said I was giving her a chance to suggest corrections prior to publication. When I got to her office I told her the truth, that I'd been sent by Mr. Strider. I then described what I knew about the nuclear waste smuggling she was doing. I also said her business partner would make sure she took the fall by herself. She got an odd look on her face and said, 'I've known from the beginning he'd try that.'"

"Jason," Sinclair interrupted, "only an inexperienced lawyer, and a biased one, would attempt—"

"Mr. Sinclair," Debra snapped, "isn't it true that Dr. Heidi Klein reported directly to you at the State Department?"

Sinclair glared at her and didn't answer.

"Justin?" Gorton pressed.

"The name sounds familiar. So what?"

"Dr. Klein told me she had been solicited to join a smuggling scheme."

"I'd like to talk with Dr. Klein," Gorton said sternly. He obviously got the drift.

"I'm afraid that's not possible. She was afraid for her life." She looked steadily at Sinclair, leaving no doubt what she was implying. "However, because she didn't trust her business partner, she kept detailed notes about every phone conversation between them and about every nuclear waste shipment that passed through D-TECH. I have a copy of those notes."

"That's absurd!" Sinclair scoffed. "Klein could make up anything she wanted. What she *couldn't* fake is correspondence from, or checks signed by, her alleged partner. Show those to us."

"The details in her notes would persuade any jury, Mr. President, but I have more than that. Dr. Klein described an urgent call she received from her partner ordering her to turn away all new shipments of nuclear waste and to ship anything already at D-TECH to Mexico immediately. In other words, her partner shut down the whole operation."

"That can be checked," Sinclair said. "Get her phone records. See who called."

"No need," Debra said. "Dr. Klein said her partner was paranoid about the phone and that his calls were untraceable. She'd already tried. But we do know what was said in that final call because she made what she called a 'get out of jail free' card, a recording of that call."

Sinclair stared at Debra who sat in her simple karate *gi*, no briefcase, nothing in front of her on the table. His pupils were dilated, almost wild-looking, like a gambler running out of chips in a no-limit game. Jack knew what was coming. However bad the odds against him, he had to push the rest of his chips into the pot as a bluff.

"You obviously don't have her notes or any recording, so shut up." He was playing out the clock, counting on Gorton to cut it off so he could get back to the White House.

"I obviously don't," she mocked his words. "I must have left them in my other pajamas. So instead, we'll visit the website where I uploaded her digital recording and scanned copies of her notes. You really should keep up with technology, Mr. Sinclair." She looked at Gorton. "Mr. President, can one of the agents bring in a laptop?"

Jack glanced at Gano, who looked relieved. Events had moved so fast since Debra had joined them at the Aerolitoral Airlines hangar, he knew nothing about what she'd been doing.

Gorton summoned an agent who arrived in seconds with a laptop and left.

Debra brought up her website and turned the sound up.

"You realize," a woman's voice said, "that shutting down this operation sticks me with expensive trucks and equipment that D-TECH can't use."

Debra stopped the playback. "That's Dr. Klein speaking. We'll have no trouble finding her voice recorded elsewhere so experts can verify that." She clicked PLAY and the woman spoke again.

"I can't just go on the Internet and offer nuclear waste haulers for sale. I demand—"

"You can't demand anything. This whole operation was my idea. You're nothing but a slut running a truck stop." The brutally sarcastic voice was familiar to everyone in the room.

"Let's call it severance pay," Dr. Klein said smoothly. "Five million. Don't you think that's fair . . . Justin?"

Zinger. Jack smiled. The woman had used the name on purpose to tag Sinclair.

"I don't have time to fuck with you," the man's voice said. "I'll get the money to you the usual way. Just don't screw this up, bitch." A click followed. Debra closed the laptop.

Sinclair's face was reddish-purple as he pushed away from the table and rose.

Gorton stood, followed by Jack, Debra and Gano, and poked Sinclair's chest with his finger, "Don't say one word. You are a goddamn disgrace to every lawyer, every politician, every, every—" Apparently he was so mad he struggled to come up with an image bad enough to describe what he was thinking. "—every decent American. You make me sick."

Gorton looked out the window for a few moments, gathering his thoughts, and then looked at Jack. "I've known Sinclair for thirty years, or thought I knew him. As I listened to that recording, I tried to tell myself it was a hoax, but it's not. And the other allegations you've made, including murder, are also true, aren't they?"

Jack nodded.

"But why did he do it? It can't be just the money."

"When evidence first pointed at him, I didn't believe it either," Jack said. He looked at Sinclair. "You had everything. I couldn't figure out why you would risk it all. Then I realized you gave me the answer on the day you interviewed me. You *didn't* have everything. You no longer sat at the head of the table on the world stage. You were desperate to prove you could still pull off something big, something no one else had thought of."

"Don't you dare psychoanalyze *me.*" Sinclair's face was flushed.

Jack crossed his arms. He was in the groove. "That's exactly what I did. For the evidence to make sense, I had to understand what was driving you.

I got an important clue from your Mexico City law partner. He said many Mexican leaders detest you for something you did while you were Secretary of State. That surprised me, so I did some research."

Sinclair had stumbled away from Gorton, clearly shaken. "That means nothing. Making some people angry comes with the job," Sinclair said, "but you wouldn't know about that. You've never played in the big leagues."

Jack ignored the jibe. "I found out what they were angry about. When Mexico had an economic crisis, you tried to stop the U.S. from supporting the peso. You failed, but you were able to impose conditions that forced Mexico into a recession. Here's the clincher. A *Wall Street Journal* article reported that the President of Mexico, in retaliation, intervened with the Nobel committee to prevent you from receiving the Peace Prize. You also told me how much you resented not getting the Nobel. That's why you hate everything Mexican. You didn't give a damn that filling that cave with nuclear material was dangerous to Mexicans. And if the Juarez aquifer got poisoned, even better for you. You knew that *maquilas* would move away as soon as they saw how vulnerable the water supply was. That would break the back of the Mexican economy, unemployment would skyrocket, and the peso would crash. You'd have your revenge. Fact is, you have not a shred of conscience. You, sir, are a classic sociopath."

"Good God." Gorton breathed as he took it all in.

Sinclair looked dazed, as though Jack had blindsided him by drilling into a part of his psyche he'd repressed. His stunned silence confirmed the truth.

Finally, Gorton said, "Here's my problem. If I bring a former Secretary of State to court on these charges, they'll investigate every decision I made when he was involved. The UN will crucify me. Mexico might cut us off and sell its oil to China. I can't let any of that happen."

"Mr. President. Jason." The features of Sinclair's Charlton Heston-like face sagged. His voice was weary. He'd become old in the solarium. "You have no right to talk about me like that. I'm a former—"

"I don't care if you think you were formerly Winston Churchill," Gorton said angrily. "What you *are* is a traitor." Gorton took a deep breath to reset. "You claimed the threat of dirty bombs was terrorism. Well, I say *you* are a terrorist, and that's how I'm going to treat you."

"Terrorist?" Sinclair said in a suddenly shrill voice. He seemed not to believe the word "terrorist" could possibly apply to him. "I'll fight you in court. You'll regret this."

"You're missing my point. I said 'terrorist.' There won't be any court. I'll have you held incommunicado while charges are 'pending.' You'll be in isolation 24/7. No more seats on corporate boards, no yacht club, no Cuban cigars, no 25-year-old single malt scotch. You'll be transferred through so many security screens even I won't know where you are, except you won't be in this country. That's the same procedure you praised in your speeches on fighting terrorism."

Very shrewd, Jack thought. Gorton was going to make Sinclair disappear, a punishment that would also let Gorton escape without a scratch. It was obvious now that when Gorton walked into the solarium, he intended to let Sinclair go free. When the facts forced him to admit Sinclair's guilt, he had altered course pragmatically. Had he come up with that solution on the spot? Not likely. Odds were good he had used "disappearance" as a solution in the past. That was a chilling thought.

"You won't get away with this," Sinclair blustered. "The partners in my law firm will raise hell if I don't return."

"No, they won't. I'll get word to your partner, Simms, that if he wants his firm to survive he'll devise a plausible explanation for your absence. You people at State play at diplomacy. In the White House, we play hardball. So long as I or people like me are in power, you'll be a nonperson. If we go out of power, the Attorney General at that time will receive a sealed indictment charging you with treason and murder."

Sinclair's head fell forward. His broad shoulders slumped. Without looking up he said, "Jack, please . . . tell the President there's some other way to handle this." Then he looked at Jack, eyes pleading.

Jack kept his face impassive, giving Sinclair nothing.

"Tell me what you want, Jack. For God's sake, man, you owe me." The final words came out in a whisper.

In a way he did owe Sinclair for sending him to Juarez and the beginning of his new life, but that was a debt Sinclair would never understand.

Sinclair shifted his gaze to Gorton, "Jason, don't throw away America's future. We need nuclear power, but power plants are shutting down because we can't get rid of nuclear waste. I solved that problem. I'm a patriot. I don't deserve—" He broke off when Gorton walked out of the room and closed the door.

Jack was silent as he looked from the closed door back at Sinclair. The man was like a corrupt king whose obsessions had brought him down, not in his castle but in a shabby solarium. After the way Gorton vacillated aboard Air Force One, this show of muscle was amazing.

Gano high-fived Jack. "Home run, Babe." He fist-bumped Debra.

Sinclair straightened to his full height. Deep-set eyes burning, he glared at Jack. "Whatever happens, wherever I am, I swear I'll make you pay for this."

"Well you better be good at mental telepathy," Gano scoffed, "because they're gonna put you where the sun don't shine."

Gorton returned, followed by a bald man in a single-breasted suit who walked straight to Sinclair.

"Sir, please empty your pockets."

Sinclair held both hands up in front of him like a shield. "Jason, we're friends. Don't do this. I beg you."

Gorton nodded to the Secret Service agent who got a firm grip on Sinclair's upper arm. Sinclair tried to jerk away and was immediately immobilized in a hammerlock. The agent emptied Sinclair's pockets with one hand and then handcuffed him. Having looked at no one else in the room, the agent asked, "Is there anything else, Mr. President?"

"Report to me when he reaches Stage Three. You're dismissed." As they left, Gorton wandered to the far end of the solarium, as if numbed by the drama, maybe shocked by what he'd just done.

Sinclair's fall was complete. Jack had won his case and his freedom. But he had more to do. "Mr. President, that brings us to Samuel Butler, Dean Emeritus at Stanford Law School. I believe he acted as Sinclair's chief operating officer. All he had to do was supervise a small staff who recruited businesses to send their nuclear waste to D-TECH."

Gorton looked at him, his expression baffled. "Why would he help Sinclair with this . . . terrorism?"

"Butler has lined his office walls with expensive reproductions of Paul Gauguin originals. Recently, he replaced one of those reproductions with an original worth millions. He denied it to prevent me from wondering how he could afford an original. If he reported all his income, the IRS will be able to trace a very large amount to Sinclair. Or else Sinclair obtained the original Gauguin and gave it to him. For Butler, that would be a powerful incentive to do anything Sinclair told him to do."

Another father-figure bites the dust, Jack thought sadly. Early in his life, he had pictured lawyers as committed to having a positive impact on society. That image had given way to ugly reality.

"Could be tough to prove if Butler denies it," Gorton said.

"He won't. He's at the end of his career and would hate being humiliated in public on the way out. You could require him to resign from the law school, donate his art collection to the Smithsonian, and pay a big fine."

"As I recall," Gorton said, "Gaugin died alone and penniless. That seems fitting for Butler. I'll have someone approach him. Now what about Dr. Klein? Sinclair couldn't have done what he did without her."

Jack nodded. "She gave us information against Sinclair because she wanted revenge, not justice. All she asked in return was that she be given time to slip out of the U.S. Debra couldn't agree to that, of course, but I imagine she's already disappeared from D-TECH."

Gorton's slight smile showed he understood that Jack had given him a way out. "I'll have Klein's passport revoked in a few days. Any request to return to the U.S. will be denied. Now I have to get back. Someone will drive you over to the White House later. Civilian clothes will be waiting for you. Remember, Mr. Strider, you owe me an answer to my offer."

Jack just nodded. At the moment, he felt vindicated but not ready to celebrate. There were still a lot of loose ends and people who would be much safer with him out of the way.

Chapter 56

July 14
7:00 p.m.

PRESIDENT GORTON rose and came from behind the historic Resolute desk in the Oval Office, hand extended, smiling broadly. Early evening summer sunlight drifted through south-facing windows.

Gorton was a flawed president, but the Oval Office was still the center of the political universe. It was impressive.

Gorton pumped Jack's hand. Waving his right arm to include Debra and Gano, he said, "Make yourselves comfortable on the couch." He settled into a wing chair with his back to the fireplace on the north wall.

"Sorry I couldn't see you until now," Gorton said. "It's been a madhouse here."

"I can imagine," Jack said. "We haven't gotten any news the last couple of days, so we're eager to find out about Albuquerque and the other dirty bombs."

"As far as Albuquerque," Gorton said, "we now know that the driver abandoned the truck in a four-story parking garage outside the Kirkland Air Force Base gate. The garage and a dozen buildings on the Base were blown to hell, but a lot of the radiation was contained. There was no wind, so the airborne contamination settled straight down on Kirkland. I slapped a top-secret quarantine on the affected area. The worst news is that Sandia National Labs, located on the Base, housed one of the biggest supercomputers on earth. That area is so radioactive that the computer complex will be out of commission forever. That's a killer for one of our nuclear programs just when we . . . well, it's a big problem."

"What's the public reaction?" Debra asked.

"The media vultures were all over it for a twenty-four hour cycle. But we had the Air Force spokeswoman report to the media that a truck transporting mildly radioactive waste exploded as it left the base. After about twenty interviews in which she emphasized that it had been a one-in-a-million accident and not terrorism—with no deaths, no blood—they lost interest. The local folks know what kind of work goes on at Sandia, or they think they do, so they weren't surprised. The public is never going to know what really happened. Of course," he paused, looking steadily at the three of them, "if someone offered a different version of what happened we'd produce plenty of evidence to support what we put out. Anyone have a problem with that?"

Jack thought about it. Since it hadn't been terrorism, nothing would be gained by contradicting Gorton's spin. Trouble was, the number of things Jack wasn't disclosing was too large. He didn't like that. No one would know Mac had been assassinated, let alone why. Sinclair's whereabouts would remain a mystery. The public would never learn that Montana had damn near devastated four cities, or how close El Paso and Juarez had come to having their water supply poisoned. Keeping it all under wraps let Arthur Palmer and Samuel Butler off too easy, but going public would do more damage than it was worth.

Gano and Debra were watching him. When he remained silent, they followed his lead.

Gorton, apparently uncomfortable with the silence, walked to his desk and took a cigar from a top drawer. He distractedly pawed around for a lighter, then gave up and walked back.

"As for the other bombs," Gorton went on, "our undercover CIA teams searched the cities you suggested in places where a dirty bomb would have the most impact. Within hours, they found trucks in El Paso, Chihuahua City, and Mexico City. Even though it was the middle of the night, deactivating the booby-traps drew attention. In fact, the team in Chihuahua City had to get rough when some street thugs tried to take the truck away from them. We still have teams sniffing around to be sure there aren't any more trucks."

"How are you handling D-TECH?" Debra asked.

"I sent troops from Fort Bliss to lock the place down. The D-TECH Board members are very savvy, so they won't get out of line. And I sent people from the Army Corps of Engineers, all in civvies, into Juarez to dismantle the pipeline, cement the wells, drain the tanks, and treat the toxic waste properly."

"They also need to shut down the incinerator until it's refitted to scrub all dangerous chemicals from the exhaust," Jack said. "And I suggest that the EPA unofficially keep inspectors on the Palmer site until all violations are remedied."

"I'll make that happen," Gorton said. "Look, Jack, you and your friends know a lot more about the facts on the ground at Palmer Industries than I do. Any other suggestions?"

"Arthur Palmer instigated or defended Montana's illegal actions in Juarez. With Montana dead that would be hard to prove, but you should require the Board to fire him immediately. Edward Palmer, Arthur's brother, is a decent man, and you should get him down there to take over. The plant is still open and hazardous waste is pouring in from the U.S.

Gorton nodded. "If the Palmer Industries Board fights me on that, I'll make sure the company lives in regulatory hell until they change their minds."

Jack waited a moment, then said, "That still leaves a much bigger problem, Mr. President."

"Let's see," Gorton said, "Kirkland Air Force Base shut down. Three other cities almost got bombed. And if the public finds out about all this, my approval ratings will drop below freezing. What's the 'bigger problem' . . . an alien invasion?"

"It's those containers crammed into the cave near Batopilas. They contain hundreds of truckloads of nuclear waste, some of it high level. You can't leave it in that cave."

Gorton rubbed his eyes. "I haven't forgotten, but there's nowhere to put it. Even if we could figure out where it all came from, it makes no sense to send it back. I assume you know about the Yucca Mountain fiasco. Hoping Congress will solve this problem is like expecting elephants to jump." He stared at the Great Seal of the United States woven into the dark blue carpet.

"No scientist would sign off on the cave site as a secure repository," Jack informed him, "and it's very likely to be in an earthquake zone. And when decrepit shipping containers degrade, the contents can contaminate the underground water system. The radioactive material can also get hot enough to explode. One way or another, that cave will become a disaster. You should have the contents trucked to D-TECH where security is already in place."

"For temporary storage," Gorton said. "After that, I could expand a site in Skull Valley, Utah and use one of our bases in the New Mexico desert. Either way, I'll have to force Yucca Mountain or some other permanent storage facility onto a fast track."

"The time pressure is greater than you may be aware of," Jack said quietly. "Imagine you're a worker at that cave when the trucks stop showing up. No paycheck. What will you do? Maybe you'll contact a drug cartel and offer to sell radioactive material. The leader of the cartel can use a dirty bomb to blackmail a city it wants to take over. Or use a dirty bomb to destroy a town controlled by a competitor. Or the workers sell to real terrorists, who then smuggle dirty bombs into American cities. Even securing that cave temporarily means having a sufficient force on site to fight off a cartel." He sensed Gorton's political brain realizing that all of this could happen on his watch.

"I can fly in Special Forces and run trucks 24/7 until the cave is clean."

"That couldn't be kept secret down there for even twenty-four hours. Don't you have to tell the Mexican president about the cave?"

Gorton shook his head in disgust, in resignation. "I guess I do. After he stops shouting at me, he'll list every concession Mexico has ever wanted and ram them all down my throat." Gorton's bleak expression showed he finally understood the gravity of the crisis.

"Pardon me, Mr. President," Gano said into the silence. "I'm curious about that $100 million Montana tried to scam."

Gorton's grimace showed that the $100 million might be the last thing he wanted to talk about. "I made the transfer. If I'd known you were about to kill Montana, I could have saved the taxpayers a lot of money."

"But you got the money back?"

"No, damn it," he admitted wearily. "Montana's automatic bank-to-bank forwarding network operated in seconds. My Treasury people will try to trace every step, but he probably chose banks in countries where we have no jurisdiction. We can threaten, but if even one refuses . . ." He shrugged.

"So," Gano kept after it like a terrier, "$100 million of taxpayers' money is sitting—"

Gorton's venomous glance shut him up, but only for a couple of seconds.

"Yes, sir, nothing else you could do," Gano said bobbing his head in fake deference, "but I was also wondering, sir, about the cash we took away from Montana. No big deal, just a million or so. We left it in his Land Rover. I was thinking maybe that little bit of money might be considered a reward for us, you know, like salvage rights at sea." His face was deadpan.

Jack smiled to himself. No matter what the situation, Gano was Gano.

Gorton's questioning expression showed he had no idea whether Gano was serious. "Salvage rights? I don't know. I'll have to talk with someone about that."

"Mr. President," Jack said, deciding it was time to change the subject, "earlier today you offered to nominate me to fill a seat on the 9th Circuit bench." He gave Gorton a few seconds to wonder whether he was going to have to come through with the bribe Sinclair had put him up to. "I have to decline that offer, but I have a proposal of my own. Your White House Counsel has just resigned to run for governor of Texas. I respectfully request that you offer me the Counsel's job and hold a press conference to praise your nominee."

Gorton didn't answer right away. "No offense," he said warily, "but I'm not sure we're politically, um, compatible."

That had to be the understatement of the year.

"I understand, so I'll think about your offer for a few days and then regretfully decline. The offer is important to me. As Sinclair made clear aboard Air Force One, my reputation has suffered because of what my father did. Offering me the White House Counsel's job will be a big help in getting my own good reputation back."

Gorton smiled, relieved. "I'll make the announcement."

"And there's one final thing."

Now they'd dealt with all the bad guys, except for one. Judge H. Peckford Strider had left more destruction behind than a hurricane—the young girls he'd stolen from Mexican families and turned into prostitutes, the deaths aboard *Pacific Dawn,* the scourge of HIV he'd spread, even infecting his lady friend Anita. No matter how much time passed, he'd never forget what Peck had done, but that wasn't nearly enough. He needed to pay down the debt his father owed to Mexico.

"There's a place some people call the Borderlands," Jack said. "It runs along both sides of the 2,000 miles of border from San Diego to Brownsville, Texas. It's in terrible shape."

"I know about the Borderlands," Gorton said. "But most of the problems are on the Mexican side. Homeland Security briefs me that drug cartels kill policemen and politicians there every day. And they've slaughtered more than 35,000 civilians in the past five years. But that's out of my hands," Gorton said defensively, as if bracing to be blamed for the violence of the cartels.

"What I'm talking about is the fact that NAFTA led to a huge increase in assembly and manufacturing plants along the Mexican side of the border. Those jobs drew millions of Mexicans from all over the country. Populations in border cities exploded. Mexican governments can't deal with the poverty and violence in those places."

"Hold on," Gorton stated, frowning. "I supported NAFTA. Are you blaming it for those conditions?"

"Blame gets us nowhere. I'm talking about reality. I'd like to see America help out."

"I'm sure you understand that most of those problems are beyond American jurisdiction."

"There are four things you *can* do. First, provide technical assistance and technology to improve water quality, access to potable water, and water conservation in the Borderlands, starting with Juarez. Second, many of the companies that operate *maquilas* are based in the U.S. You can strongly encourage them to have their *maquilas* offer more social services and training and to use their clout to force the police to crack down on local crime. *Maquilas* should be good corporate citizens, not geese that fly away to another country with any change in the wind."

Gorton's chin went up and he pursed his lips, pondering the

proposals. "Those are reasonable. What else?"

"American gun dealers have sold more than 60,000 high-powered weapons across the border in the past few years, mostly to the cartels. That greatly increased violence in Mexico, and now some of those guns are being used in U.S. border cities. You need to stop those sales."

"That could be tricky. I'll think about it."

Meaning he wasn't going to touch the gun issue unless he could maneuver someone else into taking the heat.

"And fourth, you've seen how easy it is to smuggle nuclear waste into Mexico and dirty bombs into the U.S. It's time to pay more attention to what really matters in border security."

"Homeland Security keeps telling me they're on top of it. Obviously, they're not. I'll crank them up before something else happens. And I'll get some Mexican experts up here to meet with our people. They'll figure out how to get this stuff done."

Gorton wasn't going to apologize for siding with Sinclair, or locking up the three of them in the safe house, but he had agreed to most of Jack's wish list. It was time to walk away.

Gorton stood, and so did Jack, Debra and Gano. "Things will work out better for all of us if we keep all of this strictly among ourselves." He looked at Gano, then Debra, then Jack. "I know I can count on you." He hauled out the classic politician's ear-to-ear smile, and said, "We're done here."

Jack shook Gorton's hand when it was offered, but he was keenly aware that Gorton's self-serving blunders had permitted Albuquerque to be bombed—and it could have been much worse.

He looked into Gorton's eyes and saw what Debra and Gano did not. The President of the United States of America still wasn't sure whether Jack Strider was a potential friend or potential enemy. Gorton owed him a lot, and maybe that's the way he saw it. Or maybe Gorton saw him as a threat, and Jack would have to guard his back.

Chapter 57

July 30
9:30 p.m.

SHE'S GORGEOUS, Jack thought.

Debra sat across from him, sipping champagne, black hair shining, eyes sparkling. He winced as he glanced down at the fading abrasions left by the tape Montana had used to bind her wrists.

"I'm glad to be back in San Francisco," she said, "but I miss having Gano around. He was the perfect counterpart for you."

"That's because he operates on the basis of what he called 'ground truth.'"

"Meaning?"

"Geologists use the term to describe reaching conclusions from hands-on contact with soil and rocks in the field, contact with reality. It means getting dust on your boots instead of sitting in an ivory tower reading books."

"Well, my friend, you have a lot of dust on your own boots now, and it suits you." She smiled. "Where is Gano anyway?"

"Probably hanging out on the deck of the Hotel Divisadero Barrancas which, by the way, I found out he owns. He's looking across Copper Canyon, with a Tecate in one hand, waiting for whatever turns up. We'll see him again."

"What about Montana's getaway million he was after?"

"Montana probably skimmed it from Palmer Industries, but no one knows. If the government tried to give it back, there'd be a paper trail. It would leak that it had come from a dead man's Land Rover in Juarez. No way Uncle Sam will open that Pandora's Box. That's why I brought it up to Gorton. He said he'd arrange a deposit in Gano's bank, no paperwork."

"If Gano has a conscience," she said, "he'll transfer most of it into your account."

"That's not how Gano thinks. Here's to the future, starting right here at Boulevard." They clinked glasses. "That's the reason for the champagne."

"So what's next?" she asked, studying him with an expression he couldn't decipher. "Are you going to become a white-water river guide or maybe hang out on that deck with Gano?"

"I'm going to practice law."

She raised an eyebrow. "Then why, since we flew back here from D.C. last week, have you spent most of your time sailing?"

"When I saw *Simba* again, I couldn't resist taking her for a run up the coast. But I've been doing a lot besides sailing. For one thing, I had a call from the DA, Rick Calder, to congratulate me on President Gorton's announcement that he had offered me the post of White House Counsel. Calder acted like we were best friends. It's interesting what a dash of fear can prompt an ambitious DA to do. I reminded him that not long ago he'd been determined to prove I profited from Peck's crimes. He immediately offered to hold a press conference to announce that there are no ongoing investigations and that the case is closed. I let him off with that, because most of the reason he was so mad at me was because the girls Peck exploited were Mexican, and he couldn't punish Peck. That's understandable. Even after I turn down that Counsel's job, he won't forget my White House connection. I can count on his cooperation any time I need it.

"I also arranged for Ana-Maria's body to be transported home to her village. As soon as I get settled, I'll set up a trust fund that will send her sisters through college and help her parents until the girls are self-sufficient and can pitch in." He took another sip of champagne.

"Well done, and I want to compliment you for something else. During this entire dinner, you haven't said one word about caves or nuclear waste." She speared the last morsel on her plate. "There must be a new chef here. This Lobster Martinique is much better than the first time we came here."

"Last time, you walked out on me."

She reached across the table and squeezed his hand. "That was then. This is now."

The server poured more champagne. After some small talk, he said, "I'm ready to leave if you are. I thought we'd take a short drive."

As they walked to the valet parking stand, he put his arm around her shoulders and drew her close. He'd definitely never had feelings as strong as these before.

She slid into his BMW. "Where are we going?"

"There's something I want to show you." He turned onto Broadway and headed east. A few blocks later, he squeezed into an unofficial parking space on The Embarcadero, got out, and opened Debra's door. "It's not far."

They strolled in silence past the historic piers that run from the Ferry Building to Fishermen's Wharf. He turned onto Pier 9, and they walked out toward the end, water to their right, solid mass of old buildings on their left. He loved these old piers where immigrants had poured in and gold had flowed out. He felt at home at water's edge with a panoramic view across the Bay.

"Listen to the seals bark," she said, "and the water lapping against the pilings. It's perfect."

He pointed ahead to the left. "That's where we're going."

"You mean where the sign reads 'Bay and River Pilotage since 1830?' You're still finding weird places to take a woman on a date."

"Look at the sign past that one."

Her eyes went to the elegant, hand-painted sign. He watched her face as she read the words.

Strider & Vanderberg
Attorneys

She threw her arms around him, laughing. "I can't believe it."

He grinned down at her. "Do you accept my offer?"

She stepped back and studied his face. "Well, I'm used to making big bucks as a rising star at a powerhouse firm. Exactly what terms are you offering at your little start-up outfit, Mr. Strider?"

"It's not the terms you should consider, it's the working conditions. Besides, in those powerhouse firms, sometimes the captain falls overboard and is never seen again."

She nodded. "Which can cause some of the crew to jump ship."

"So a hot new firm on Pier 9 should sound pretty good. To pay the bills, we'll build a practice in international business, corporate law, and a couple of other specialties. The buildup Gorton gave me at that press conference was worth millions in PR. When I turn him down next week, I'll make it clear that our new firm will be open for business within a month. Clients will line up."

She frowned. "But if it would be like a baby Sinclair & Simms, what's the point?"

"That revenue pays for our public interest law practice. Water problems, pollution, alternative energy start-ups—that sort of thing."

She looked at the sign, then at him. "I accept your offer." She kissed him. "Can we go inside?"

"Nothing in there. Finding the right place and negotiating the lease took a lot of time. The sign wasn't finished until a couple of hours ago."

"Then let's walk out to the end of the pier and look at the stars."

They settled into a couple of worn lawn chairs, probably someone's lunch spot. To their right stood the sweeping arch of the Bay Bridge; ahead, the low profile of the former Treasure Island navy base. Far across the Bay to the northeast, Berkeley and the lights of the UC campus rose up the hillside.

She broke the stillness. "I was surprised that you turned down Gorton's offer to appoint you to the 9th Circuit bench. Now I understand."

"I made that decision before I got to the Oval Office. When my father realized he would never be appointed to the Supreme Court, I think he decided to set that goal for me. Or maybe he thought my appointment would make him look good. Either way, it was my father's dream, not mine. It took me a while to understand that."

"It still must have been hard to give up."

"Not after I recognized the truth. Being Chairman of the International Law Department would have trapped me in the academic rat race. S & S would have been just another kind of trap. The time I spent in Mexico helped me realize that a judge gets into the process long after the damage has been done. For example, after a plant has contaminated drinking water and given half the town cancer. As a public advocate, I can help prevent the damage. Being a judge, even moving up to the Supreme Court, isn't what I want to do with my life."

"I'm with you, partner," she said. "So let's talk about it over a nightcap at Auberge du Soleil."

"That's in the Napa Valley, more than an hour from here. We wouldn't get back to the city until two a.m."

"Right. So what would you think about sealing our partnership in one of their lovely cottages?"

He grinned and nodded. "But I have one question."

She gave him a quizzical look, and he knew she held back what was bound to be a flippant comment.

"If a fellow knew what he wanted in life and was strongly motivated and fearless—" He let several seconds pass. "—do you think that someday he might make a good governor?"

Acknowledgments

My sincere thanks to Linda Kichline for her insightful editing and TLC as publisher.

My gratitude also to those who read the manuscript in its varying stages of disarray and offered input as professionals and/or avid readers: Marq de Villiers, Maria S. Lowry, Debra Dixon and Pat Van Wie, Chris Hagler, Jr., Anne Holmes, Dr. Ann Livingstone, Sammie Morris, Bob Sehlinger, Don Sedgwick and Shaun Bradley, and Frank Williams.